THE SON OF
JOHN DEVLIN

THE SON OF JOHN DEVLIN

CHARLES KENNEY

WITHDRAWN

BALLANTINE BOOKS · NEW YORK

A Ballantine Book
Published by The Ballantine Publishing Group

Copyright © 1999 by Charles Kenney

www.randomhouse.com/BB/

Library of Congress Cataloging-in-Publication Data

Kenney, Charles.
The son of John Devlin / Charles Kenney.—1st ed.
p.   cm.
ISBN 0-345-43294-0 (alk. paper)
I. Title.
PS3561.E435S6   1999
813'.54—dc21   98-6695
CIP

Manufactured in the United States of America

First Edition: January 1999
10   9   8   7   6   5   4   3   2   1

For Charles Frederick Kenney and
Elizabeth Smith Kenney—
who help me make sense of it all.

"So we beat on, boats against the current,
borne back ceaselessly into the past."
The Great Gatsby
F. Scott Fitzgerald

"How do you leave the past behind when
it keeps finding ways to get to your heart?"
Rent
Jonathan Larson

THE SON OF
JOHN DEVLIN

CHAPTER 1

"THE DIRTY COP will inevitably reveal himself," Del Rio said. "He'll always give off a sign, an indication."

Del Rio buffed a crisp, red apple on the chest of his jacket, regarded the apple, then bit into it.

"Why do I say this?" Del Rio asked. He sat back in the passenger seat of a black Jeep Cherokee and stared at Detective Jack Devlin, positioned behind the wheel. "Why do I say that the dirty cop will inevitably reveal himself? With Moloney here," he went on, motioning vaguely toward the street as cars rode by, headlights shining, "With Moloney, there's just always been something about him. He's shrewd, it's true. Clever guy, by no means stupid. But he's a pig. He could have been a player within the department. But he's one of those who gave in to the anger and bitterness. It's a fucking way of life in Boston, isn't it, Jack?"

Devlin nodded slowly as he stretched his head back, his arms to the sides. "It was ever thus," he said, preferring not to delve into a topic where the shoals and eddies held more danger than one might imagine.

"Anyway, he's a fat asshole," Del Rio said, a look of disgust crossing his face. He waved dismissively, as though banishing thoughts of Moloney from his mind.

Devlin looked at Del Rio with a half smile. "You hide it well," Devlin said.

Del Rio appeared puzzled. "What?"

"Your dislike for Moloney," Devlin said. "You camouflage it nicely."

Del Rio laughed. "Fuck him," he said. "My point is simple: The dirty cop will always show himself. Eventually. There'll be a sign. Know why?"

"Tell me," Devlin said.

"Because the dirty cop is arrogant, by definition. Otherwise he is not capable of doing what he's doing. He's incapable. To go bad, a cop has to believe he's higher than the law, or not so much higher as exempt from it. He has to believe it doesn't so much apply to him."

Del Rio, the deputy superintendent of the Boston Police Department, chief of all detectives, munched on the apple as he thought about this topic. He glanced out the window, then looked at Devlin.

"You know what the character flaw is with these guys?" Del Rio asked.

Devlin shook his head.

"Hubris," Del Rio said. "They're all guilty of it. Hubris." He paused. "You familiar with this concept?" Del Rio asked.

Devlin nodded. "Arrogant pride," he said. "It's—"

"Exactly," Del Rio interrupted. "Arrogant pride. Overreaching. Most of those who go bad have something in their record, some achievement, sometimes amazing things. They think, you know, they're above it all. Not accountable. Derived from the Greeks. Aristides the Just was the classic case. He ruled, what was it, Athens? A city-state. Ruled with such a level of purity, self-conscious purity always on display, that they drove him from office. But it wasn't long before corruption had taken root in the city and they were clamoring for his return."

Suddenly, Del Rio caught himself. "You know this," he said. "You're familiar with this. Not new territory to you." He paused. "Somebody said you're the only Harvard man on the force. That true?"

"Evans went to the Kennedy School," Devlin said.

Del Rio squinted and shook his head. "Some mid-career bull-shit," he said derisively. "Doesn't count. You're the only one was an undergrad. Plus law school."

Del Rio took a breath and was about to speak again but then caught himself, as though he wanted to avoid saying something impolitic. But he appeared to change his mind just as quickly and he cocked his head and regarded Devlin.

"Sometimes, the well-schooled aren't particularly well-educated," Del Rio said. "I'm an autodidact. I take a certain pride in that."

Del Rio had rough edges, but though he lacked a certain polish, Devlin could see he was very smart.

"I was diagnosed as dyslexic when I was fifteen," Del Rio said. He shrugged. "Attention deficit, too." He grimaced. "Charles Schwab, the investment guy. He's dyslexic." Del Rio nodded. "It was a struggle. They always said in school I was stupid. They told my parents. I never believed it. I was the only one. I would hang back, quiet—"

Devlin reacted with surprise, and Del Rio saw the look.

"Well, quiet for me," Del Rio said. "I'd hang back, sullen. I was a sullen kid. I'm thinking the whole time, 'Fuck them, they don't know shit about me, about what's inside my head. I'm smarter than all of them.' And I was. Shrewder. I'm not bragging, I'm just telling you what it was like.

"So I stumble along, dogshit grades all the way, and then I learn about the dyslexia and attention deficit and I get a tutor and three years later I'm in community college. Straight A's. Then Northeastern. It's not Harvard, but—"

"Great criminal justice," Devlin said.

"And I went straight through nights. By this time I'm in the academy days and school nights and I'm acing every fucking course and I don't think I've ever been happier. I loved it. I fuckin' loved school. You?"

Devlin nodded. "I did," he said. He unscrewed the thermos of decaf and offered some to Del Rio, who declined.

Devlin poured more into his plastic travel cup and screwed the top back onto the thermos. He nodded, still thinking about Del Rio's question. He had loved the solitary nature of study, loved the exploration as an undergraduate, the feeling that there was this massive amount of knowledge sitting there waiting to be absorbed. Perhaps most of all he had loved law school and the remarkable clarity and order of the law. In a world where there were too many shadows and shades of gray, the law laid it out clearly and definitively for anyone who cared to read and understand. The weighty codes of criminal and civil laws defined what the society was; defined what man's responsibilities were; defined the boundaries.

"I thought about going to law school," Del Rio said. "I actually applied to Northeastern and got in. But by then I was on the force and moving up. I think I'd just made lieutenant, and the two kids and OT and . . . Jesus, it just seemed like too much. Four years, nights. A backbreaking workload. And for what? I knew I'd never practice. And I was already moving up the ranks as quickly as could be expected. It wasn't as though it was going to give me any real edge. So I said fuck it, and I didn't go. Every now and then I regret not having done it. You know?"

"I'm the only person I know who actually enjoyed law school," Devlin said. "It was so well-ordered and what was required was so plain and direct. It wasn't as though you had to be some sort of analytical genius. It's not like math or the sciences, where breakthroughs are what matter. There really isn't anything new to learn. It's all there, collected in one place, all the rules are there. I like the tidiness of it. The clarity."

"You like I.A.?" Del Rio asked abruptly.

Devlin considered this. "I'm not in I.A.," he replied.

"For all practical purposes," Del Rio said. "I mean—"

"I'm not technically in I.A.," Devlin said.

The assignment had come to Devlin during a private meeting with the police commissioner. He'd received a call from the commissioner one night, at home, asking whether he could stop by to discuss a confidential matter. Twenty minutes later Commissioner Nicholas Sullivan had knocked on his back door.

"We need to talk," Sullivan had said. And talk they had, for more than two hours. Jack Devlin had listened carefully as the commissioner expressed his frustration with corruption and his apparent inability to do anything about it. He was embarrassed, Sullivan had said, that the United States Justice Department in Washington was beginning to focus on Boston as a dirty department.

"Going through the normal channels hasn't worked," he told Devlin. "So I want to try something different."

The something different was Devlin. He would be detached from his regular duties and given free rein to investigate corruption within the ranks. He would report directly to the commissioner. It was the surest way to become the least popular member of the Boston Police Department, but that was all right. They agreed that the nature of Devlin's assignment would be conveyed to very few people. Over time, they believed that as Jack became more active, word would get out about his activities.

Devlin did not believe most Boston cops were on the take. He did believe, however, that there was a stubborn, deeply rooted culture of corruption, a virulent strain that would be difficult to defeat.

Del Rio shrugged. "If it walks like a duck . . ."

"It's okay," Devlin said as he turned away and looked into the street. The Cherokee was tucked behind a small commercial building at the corner of Centre and Arborway, an ideal position from which to monitor activity in front of 322 Arborway. At that location, Luis Espado Alvarez, a native of Puerto Rico and convicted drug dealer, waited, bait in a trap.

"Let's get some air," Del Rio said. He opened the passenger door of the Cherokee and got out. Devlin followed suit, and the two men stretched and stood by the Jeep, windows down so they could hear their bug and radio.

Del Rio was a compactly built man, five-nine, 160 pounds. He was trim and fit from regular workouts and bounced on his feet with nervous energy. He wore black jeans, a brown leather jacket, and construction boots.

Jack Devlin was a much bigger man, six feet two inches tall, an even 190 pounds. Devlin had the physique of an athlete, a build he had assiduously maintained since his days as a college hockey player. In blue jeans, Nikes, and a black wool sweater, Devlin was ruggedly good looking. His jaw was firm and prominent, his longish black hair thick and wavy, down over his shirt collar. His deep-set eyes at times gave him a look of menace in marked contrast to the warmth of his smile, which showed off his (mostly) straight white teeth, all of which he'd managed to keep, even through years of hockey. But there were two reminders of his hockey days on his face. One scar ran from his right eyebrow about an inch toward his temple. Devlin had been cut by the blade of an opposing player's stick during a summer league in Canada. The other was on the upper left side of his mouth, a scar no more than a quarter inch long. It had come when an opposing player, in the same summer league, had cross-checked him in the mouth with his stick. The force of the upward blow had been so great that it drove one of Devlin's teeth through the skin of his lip, opening a deep gash. He'd bled all over his uniform jersey and the ice. Seven stitches had closed the wound, and eventually, the soreness had gone away, but the scar and a slight puffiness had remained. From a certain angle, he appeared to have a permanent fat lip on the left side.

"I heard the new fitness instructor ask someone about you," Del Rio said. He glanced at Devlin out of the corner of his eye. "You've seen her. Runs the gym at headquarters. Aerobics, weights, whatnot. The black spandex." Del Rio raised his eyes.

"Oh," Devlin said. "I've seen . . ."

"Yeah. You've seen, I've seen, we've *all* seen. Are you kidding me, or what. Jesus."

Devlin laughed.

"What?" Del Rio demanded. "You mean to tell me you don't get a woody in that gym with her snappin' that bottom around?"

"She seems a little young," Devlin said.

"Twenty-six. Conboy filled me in. She's a paramedic, wants to get on the job, figures working the gym will help her get to know people."

"She's something," Devlin said.

"Something?" Del Rio repeated with mock indignance. "Something? She's one of the greatest physiques anyone's ever been blessed with. I see her, I want to weep. Why weep? Because she'll always go for the young bucks. She wouldn't give me the time of day."

Devlin smiled. "Some young women prefer a distinguished older man," he said.

"I told you she asked Conboy about you," Del Rio said. "You were in there one day working out and she asked him, 'Who's the tall guy?' "

Devlin frowned. "You're bullshitting me."

"I shit you not!" Del Rio said, his voice going up several octaves in pitch. "I'm serious. No shit. She did. I think you've got some potential there. In fact, if I was you, let me tell you what I'd do . . ."

THE CRISP NOVEMBER air was a relief after sitting in the car for over two hours of a stakeout. Devlin turned and studied Del Rio, who was now gazing off down the Arborway. He'd known Del Rio only in passing prior to this assignment, had been aware of Del Rio's rapid and steady rise through the ranks, but had little contact with him. Devlin knew from his reputation that Del Rio was as savvy as they came. Blustery, coarse, a cowboy, contemptuous of authority, mocking of bureaucracy, constantly bending the rules. Yet effective. The uniformed officers loved him and believed in him.

Where they generally disliked and were suspicious of the civilian-appointed department brass, they liked Del Rio's grit and straightforward nature. He did not mince words, did not speak in the language of the politically correct. He was outrageous in his comments and sometimes in his approach, but he was as hard a worker as there was on the force, and he was more connected with the rank and file than anyone else on the command staff. Del Rio understood his populist appeal and he played it to the hilt. At every opportunity he sought to tweak the department brass.

Del Rio reached into the Jeep and pulled out a bag of popcorn. He offered some to Devlin, who declined.

"It's ironic, isn't it?" he said as he chewed the popcorn. Devlin had his arms folded across his chest as he leaned back against the Cherokee and gazed down the Arborway to the entrance at 322.

"About you and your current gig," Del Rio said.

Devlin looked at Del Rio coolly and said nothing.

"You have to admit, it is ironic, no disrespect intended, I hope you know that," he said, a look of plaintive concern suddenly crossing his face.

"I understand," Devlin said.

"Please don't take offense," Del Rio said, leaning forward, eyes wide, brow knitted in an earnest look.

"I don't," Devlin said quickly.

Del Rio nodded. "I mean, you know . . ." He shrugged again.

"It is, yeah," Devlin said. And surely it was. The son of the infamous Jock Devlin taking on the assignment to clean up the department.

"YOU EVER BEEN married?" Del Rio asked, anxious now to change the subject.

"Never," Devlin replied.

"Guy like you must do well with the senoritas, eh?" Del Rio's smile was conspiratorial. "I mean, Jesus, you're a big strong guy, good-looking, smart. You got it all." Del Rio made a face and shrugged. "Except money. But, hey, the young ones, most of them, they don't care about money. They want love. They see past money. It's only when they get older and don't care about getting laid anymore that they turn their attention to the dough. They get older, it's the size of your bank account rather than your dick that really matters."

Devlin laughed out loud.

"Come on, hey, it's true," Del Rio said. "But I'm telling you, you're lucky you've never been married. I'm no good at being married. I'm terrible at it, is the truth. And I know it now. Never again." He shook his head and gazed out the window.

"I make a good buck, you know, but when all is said and done, I end up with the doughnut. Child support, alimony. The child support I don't mind, of course. They're my kids. But the fucking alimony. She's got a boyfriend. Loaded. The fuckin' guy is loaded. But she won't marry him, to spite me. 'Cause if she marries him, then I pay no more."

"Come on," Devlin said.

Del Rio's eyes widened. "I shit you not. She told me herself. She told me. To my face. And she laughed." Del Rio, in spite of himself, laughed out loud at the recollection. "She's a hot ticket, I have to admit that. My ex. Jeannie. A beautiful girl in her prime."

He thought for a moment. "It was my fault. She tried as best she could. But I couldn't keep my pecker in my pants. I mean, it's not easy. This guy said to me once, and it's true, 'If you're not thinkin' about pussy about ninety-five percent of the time, you're just daydreamin'.'"

DEL RIO BALLED up the popcorn bag and tossed it into the backseat of the Cherokee. "I'm chilly," he said, and got back into the Jeep. Devlin followed suit.

"So how'd you get this guy to cooperate?" Del Rio asked.

Devlin hesitated, then shrugged: "We came to an agreement."

Del Rio nodded understandingly. "What's his story?"

"Junkie," Devlin said. "Dealer. What can you say?"

"So gimme a preview."

"They'll serve the warrant, frisk him—ostensibly for a weapon, but as much for a wire. They're very careful about wires."

"So where'd you put it?" Del Rio asked.

"Radio speaker on the kitchen table," Devlin said. "They'll never detect it."

"So they frisk him . . ."

"And look for the dope, but while they're looking for the dope, they look for cash," Devlin said. "They'll find both. A decent stash of coke and about twelve thousand dollars in cash. They'll talk to Luis and try and come across as reasonable. Then maybe they'll scare him. Luis is a nice target because he's got two felony convictions for trafficking. One federal. They could put him away a long, long time."

"Which is why he's being a good boy for you," Del Rio said.

Devlin nodded, then straightened in the car seat as he saw the dark blue Crown Victoria pull up in front of 322 Arborway. "Here we go," he said.

They sat silently, watching the two detectives get out of the sedan and start toward the entry to the red brick apartment building. Moloney led the way. He was six feet three inches tall, 240 pounds, a beefy man with thick fingers and thinning hair. The fat of his neck prevented him from buttoning the top button of his dress shirt, leaving his necktie askew.

Bobby Curran, Moloney's partner, was a short, stocky man with blow-dried, light reddish hair. While Moloney wore a light gray Dacron suit, Curran wore his customary uniform of black slacks and a brown leather jacket.

Del Rio and Devlin watched as Moloney and Curran glanced up and down the street while making their way to the entrance to number 322. Before they entered, Moloney flicked a lit cigarette butt to the pavement.

"Okay, Luis," Del Rio muttered, "prepare to meet two charming gentlemen."

Devlin took a deep breath and sat forward in the seat. He reached down to the console where the receiver from the bug had been placed. He switched it to the On position and they instantly heard Latin music through the static. The receiver would allow them to hear whatever was said in the apartment and also tape-record the conversation. They heard loud banging on the apartment door.

"Jesus, man!" they heard Luis say. The Latin music was shut off and they heard Luis saying something, but the banging continued. Seconds later it stopped and they heard the detectives as Luis's high-pitched voice protested vehemently. They heard footsteps echoing, and quickly Luis and the two detectives were in the kitchen.

"Sweetie, come on, where's the shit?" they heard Moloney ask.

"There's no shit, man," Luis said, trying to sound indignant. "Where's your warrant?"

"Here, sweetheart," Moloney said, and then they heard Luis grunt.

"Fuck you, man," he said.

"Moloney whacked him," Del Rio said.

"Yeah, fuck me," Moloney said. "I bet you'd like that, wouldn't you, darling?"

"Jesus," Del Rio muttered.

"You got nothing on me," Luis said.

"We'll see, sweetie," Moloney said. They heard the two men moving and surmised that Moloney was frisking him.

"See?" Luis said. "I'm clean."

"Bingo," Curran said from an adjacent room. He entered the kitchen, holding his find.

"Ahhh," Moloney said triumphantly. "This is clean, sweetheart? I'm afraid you'll have to be placed under arrest and brought downtown and, my oh my, will they enjoy you in the lockup. You'll be the tastiest little morsel they've had in a while."

"Man, I don't know how that shit got there, I swear to God," Luis said desperately.

"By the time those boys are through with you, your asshole will—"

"I'm tellin' you, man," Luis screamed, suddenly hysterical. "That's not my shit, man. I'm straight. I'm clean. That must be that chick's man, that chick wears black and the cape—"

There was a crack then, the sound of an open-handed slap as Moloney sent Luis to the floor.

"Jesus Christ, man, I didn't—"

"Okay, pussy," Moloney said. "Where's the dough?"

"There's no money, mister," Luis said. "I got no money. I'm just—"

They heard the crack again.

"Mister, Jesus!" Luis screamed. "Leave me alone."

They could hear Moloney breathing heavily, and when he spoke, he sounded very angry indeed.

"Where's the money, you little faggot?" he demanded.

"I don't got—"

"Bingo, again," they heard Curran say. "Bingo, again, my friends."

Curran had entered the kitchen with two fat wads of cash wrapped in a brown paper bag. It had been stashed in a tile above the drop ceiling.

"Oh, Little Bo Peep," Moloney said. "Little Bo Peep, you're back. You little sweetheart, you. Okay, honey, we're going downtown to let the savages have their way with you. How about it?"

They could hear a muffled sound, and did not know what it was at first, but then Devlin realized Luis was crying.

"Fuckin' kid is good," Del Rio said. "We're talking Oscar nominee."

"I'll do anything," Luis said through his sobs. "Don't put me in jail, man."

This was precisely the type of situation that Moloney and Curran fed off. They held all the cards. The solution to Luis's problem was so neat, so easy.

"Hey, we'd like to help," Moloney said, "but there are rules. There's—" He caught himself. "Maybe, though, maybe there's a way to work things out. . . ."

"I'll do anything, mister," Luis said.

And so they quickly arrived at a mutually beneficial agreement. Luis would keep the dope. Luis would remain free. Luis would not be arrested or charged or jailed or sodomized by the most brutal of men. And the detectives, the servants of the people, the men with the gold shields, Moloney and Curran, two fine Irish Catholic lads who'd sworn to uphold the law, would take the cash, twelve thousand U.S.

DEVLIN PULLED THE Cherokee out of the alleyway and onto the street, accelerating quickly down to the front of 322, pulling in directly behind Moloney and Curran's Crown Vic.

Devlin and Del Rio were out of the Cherokee, moving swiftly toward the entrance to the building, when Moloney and Curran stepped outside. Just as they did, Curran, seeing the two men, turned and started back inside the building. Del Rio was suddenly at his side, just inside the door, holding it open with his back as he grabbed for Curran's jacket and yanked him back out onto the sidewalk.

"What are you goin' back inside the building for?" Del Rio asked. "What's in there? What, you forgot your hat? What?"

"I was gonna . . ."

"You were gonna what?" Del Rio asked. "You were gonna do what? It looked like you were duckin' me, Bobby, huh?"

"No, I—"

"What's your problem?" Moloney asked Devlin. "What's this fuckin' attitude?"

He regarded Devlin suspiciously, then turned to Del Rio. "What's the fuckin'—"

"How'd the bust go?" Del Rio asked, jerking his head, motioning toward the building.

Moloney hesitated. "Dry hole," he said. He shrugged.

"Dry hole," Del Rio repeated, nodding.

"It happens," Moloney said.

"Nothin'," Del Rio said. "No dope?"

Moloney shook his head.

"No cash?" Del Rio asked.

Moloney paused, staring at Del Rio. "Dry hole," he said as he took half a step back, eyeing Del Rio, then Devlin. Moloney's hands were in his raincoat pockets, and as he took them out, Devlin watched him carefully. Devlin held his right hand behind his back, gripping his service revolver.

"Whaddaya got in the pocket?" Del Rio asked Moloney.

"Look," Curran said, his voice trembling with fear, "is this some kind of a . . . what the fuck is this?" he asked, turning to Devlin. "Jackie, we've worked together. What's up here?" Devlin could see that Curran was on the verge of panic, heard it in Curran's voice as he implored him to intervene.

"What happened up there?" Devlin asked, his voice calm, even subdued.

"Jesus," Curran said, "routine. The kid's clean. Big deal. It happens, huh? Jackie, you know."

"Empty your pockets," Devlin said, turning to Moloney.

Moloney appeared stunned by this. A look of disbelief came over his face. He feigned amusement. "Who the fuck do you think—"

"Now," Devlin said. "Empty them now."

Moloney froze. He reached into his pocket and took out the cash, holding it in his fist.

Devlin and Del Rio stared at it.

"So I gamble," Moloney said. "Big deal. Violation of department rules, so sue me."

"Gamble?" Del Rio said. "What the—"

"I won this in a card game," Moloney said. "In Southie. Over on the—"

"We have it all on tape," Devlin said quietly. "We taped the whole thing."

There was a moment of silence, a shattering moment when reality struck home and Moloney and Curran could think of nothing to say.

"Dear God," Curran whispered.

When Moloney spoke, his voice had lost its arrogance. "Let's talk about this," he said. "We know each other. We go back," he said to Del Rio. "Nobody's perfect. There's—"

Devlin stepped behind Moloney and reached around to remove his service revolver. Moloney did not resist. Del Rio did the same with Curran, who stood speechless.

"We'll go downtown now," Devlin said. "We'll all go in the Cherokee." But nobody moved.

Moloney stood frozen for a moment, then squinted at Del Rio. He held his hands out by his sides, palms up. "What . . . can't we talk?"

"What's to talk about?" Del Rio asked. "You guys—"

"We go back," Moloney said, looking pleadingly at Del Rio. "We go back. Let's show some respect. . . ."

Del Rio shook his head. "We'll talk downtown," he said. "Let's go."

Suddenly, the gravity of it all seemed to strike Moloney a thunderous blow. He turned to Devlin, fury evident in his eyes. "What is this?" he said. "The sins of the father. You avenging—"

But Moloney did not finish his sentence. For, suddenly, Jack Devlin had grasped Moloney's left shoulder in his left hand while he took the fabric of his raincoat in the back—as though Moloney were a human ramrod—and rammed Moloney into the wall, banging the side of the big man's face into the bricks, scraping away layers of skin from his forehead and down across his cheekbone on the right side of his face, sending blood down to his shirt collar.

Devlin, teeth jammed together, jaw clenched, put his face up so close against Moloney's he could smell the beer on Moloney's breath. Bringing his mouth close to Moloney's ear, he whispered so that Del Rio and Curran could not hear: "Don't ever say that again. Don't ever say it again as long as you live."

CHAPTER 2

JACK DEVLIN FANTASIZED that the most alluring woman he had
ever met was secretly in love with him. When Emily Lawrence
walked into the room, Devlin did not focus on the smoothness of
her skin or the silkiness of her jet-black hair, cut short high on the
back of her neck, or the prominent cheekbones or the full lips or the
narrowed waist or the shapely calf muscle. When she walked into
the room, his gaze was instead fixed upon her blue eyes, on their
bright awareness. She moved easily toward her seat at the head of the
conference table, and as she did so she greeted those in attendance
with brief hellos. He followed her closely as she moved, expecting
her to say something to someone else before turning to him. But she
looked in his direction abruptly, and he was caught staring and felt
his face flush as he quickly looked down and then back up, smiling
at her. She watched him for a moment as though amused by his reaction. She stepped in his direction, and the beat of his heart quick-
ened. She reached out to shake his hand, and held it a moment
longer than she'd grasped the others'. Or had he imagined it?

Emily Lawrence was Assistant United States Attorney for the
criminal division in Boston. She was thirty-three years old, five
feet seven inches tall, with the physique of an athlete. In college,
she'd been a champion squash player, and still played at a top ama-
teur level. In her dark blue wool suit and beige silk shirt, she looked
serious and businesslike. Yet beautiful. She had an open face, high

cheekbones, a delicate jawline, and a generous, infectious smile when she let it be seen.

She began the meeting, but Jack was not paying attention to what she was saying. He thought instead about the two occasions when they had discussed the possibility of going out, only to have circumstances intervene. He'd met her at a law enforcement conference and later called to invite her to a movie. She'd had plans, however. A month later she invited him to dinner. He had had plans. That was three months ago, and nothing had happened in the meantime.

Emily Lawrence took her place at the head of the conference table. Seated around the table were Luke Downey, director of the State Attorney General's Criminal Division; Kevin Duffy, chief of investigations for the FBI in Boston; Anita Rogan, Assistant District Attorney for Suffolk County; and, from the Boston Police Department, Devlin and Del Rio.

Emily looked around the table to make sure everyone was in place. She glanced down at her notes and began speaking.

"We have some information that a major deal is in the works," she said, her voice quiet but firm. "The information comes from a source who has proven reliable in the past. One Mr. Jones."

"From the Suarez case?" Anita Rogan asked.

"The very same."

Those around the table nodded, for Mr. Jones had established himself as a knowledgeable and reliable witness. In the Suarez case he had traded his testimony for a substantial reduction in his sentence.

"So he's talking again," said Downey, the man from the State Attorney General's office.

"I thought he was tapped out?" said the FBI's Duffy.

"He was," said Emily Lawrence. "But he's still connected, and he has fresh information."

"Out of the blue?" Duffy asked.

"His lawyer came to us, told us he had something he wanted to talk about," said Emily. "Something new."

"Any good?" Duffy asked.

Emily Lawrence shifted in her chair and leaned forward. "Very good," she said. "Potentially very good. Mr. Jones says there is a very significant deal about to happen. When exactly, he cannot say. But soon. What's significant about it is that it involves new people. Who, he will not say, at the moment. But he said there's a new cast, and a new product."

There were looks of surprise around the table.

"Not coke or smack?" Anita Rogan asked.

"Morphine," said Emily Lawrence. "Pure, medical-grade morphine."

"Wow," Downey said. "That's different."

"Very," nodded Emily Lawrence.

"Morphine?" Del Rio said, clearly surprised.

Emily nodded again. "And the highest grade of morphine," she said. "A grade so high, of such purity, that we speculate it comes directly from one of the pharmaceutical companies."

"A theft, hijacking?" Duffy asked.

"In all likelihood," said Emily Lawrence.

"They're very sensitive about that," Duffy said. "They rarely report to us when a shipment has disappeared. It's a bigger problem than people realize, shipments of controlled substances not reaching their destinations."

"Mr. Jones says the idea is to target the suburban and college markets in Greater Boston," said Emily Lawrence. "We know independently that there has been a reduction in drug use among college students in the past few years. Ditto for the suburbs. Mr. Jones says the dealers have been searching for a product that will prove popular. Most of these things scare people, but they've done some test-marketing and Mr. Jones says the response to morphine has been very strong."

"Test-marketing?" Downey said with disbelief.

Emily Lawrence nodded. "They think that with the economy so strong, they can build the business very substantially among these two target groups."

Anita Rogan nodded. "Makes perfect sense."

"That's what's scary about it," said Emily Lawrence. "It's so plausible. So levelheaded. So perfectly sensible from a business standpoint. They believe that morphine is right for a number of reasons. It's safe. In part because it's so high-grade. It's taken orally, so there isn't an HIV issue. It's priced within reason. And it's one of the greatest highs ever. Obviously, whoever is behind this knows what they're doing. There are more than a half-million students in the Greater Boston area. Another million yuppies in the suburbs making good money. Think of the implications."

And to these law enforcement professionals experienced in the drug wars, the implications were immediately clear. Such a product could have enormous appeal, and if sold and distributed by a new broker, would attract that traditional source of narcotics—organized crime—and quite likely result in a vicious and deadly territorial war.

These men and women knew that the suburban cocaine scourge of the 1980s had been defeated not only by the collapse of the economy, but by the diligence of law enforcement officials. It had been very difficult, nasty work, however, and fighting again in the leafy suburbs was not something they wished to do.

"I don't want to sound preachy, but I say this because I believe it: Those of us in this room can stop this," said Emily Lawrence. "It will require the same diligence and persistence we all displayed fighting cocaine. And it will not be easy, but it will be vastly easier if we're able to cut it off before it begins. And that means doing whatever we have to do to prevent the shipment that's coming from reaching its distribution channels. Ideally, obviously, our goal is to figure out who's behind this, grab them and the morphine before the deal is consummated. And I think we can do that. But it will take some cooperation."

She glanced around the table at the men and the woman from the various law enforcement agencies. Everyone nodded in agreement, with the exception of Del Rio. He sat stonily silent.

"Do we have any idea when this is coming down?" Duffy asked.

"Mr. Jones wants to talk about the terms of a deal before he says anything more," said Emily.

"Have you pressed?" Del Rio asked. He set down a Dunkin' Donuts coffee container and sat back in his seat.

Emily shrugged. "As much as we're able. Mr. Jones is rather theatrical. He goes at the pace he wants to go at. In the Suarez case it took him a year before he was ready to give us everything."

"But it sounds like there's a sense of urgency here," Anita Rogan said.

"How much leverage do we have?" Downey asked. "I mean, I wonder how far a judge will let us go in cutting his sentence."

"We've already reduced his sentence about as far as it can go," she said. "But there's still some wiggle room."

"He's in for?"

"A somewhat unattractive homicide," said Emily Lawrence, a sense of irony in her voice.

Del Rio's eyes widened in mock horror. "'Justice Department Springs Killer!'" he said, smiling. "I can see the headline already." He sat at the end of the table wearing blue jeans, black lizard cowboy boots, and a brown leather jacket. He sipped his coffee and peered over the top of the container.

A couple of people at the table laughed, but Emily Lawrence looked coolly at Del Rio. U.S. Attorney Norman Kearney, her superior, was an able man, though he was prone to considering the political calculations of various prosecutorial options.

"The other factor," Emily proceeded smoothly, "is that Mr. Jones's theatrical nature is such that he likes to draw things out over two or three acts. He likes to keep us in suspense. He enjoys that. So we can only push him so far."

Emily held a pencil between two fingers of her right hand and tapped it in a barely audible drumming motion on a pad of paper. She appeared quite intense. Her brow was knit, her eyes narrowed. She took pride in her reputation as a skilled narcotics prosecutor. Assistant United States Attorneys from around the nation had visited Boston to study her investigations and prosecutions, and she'd given presentations at a dozen or more seminars for state and federal prosecutors. Her two biggest scores had involved prosecutions of a heroin ring and a crack cocaine organization. Altogether, in the two cases, she had prosecuted and sent to prison eleven dealers for an average of nine years.

For some time her energies—all of her energies, it seemed—had gone into her work. She remained single, despite her best efforts. She was childless. And, at the moment, there were no prospects in her life.

Now, as Emily Lawrence gazed at those seated at the table and contemplated the case at hand, she felt a sense of fear. She feared that the deal would be completed before she could stop it. She feared, as well, that the information about the deal would find its way back through the Boston Police Department to those distributing the narcotics, for she and others had been burned badly by the BPD before.

There was no question that there were leaks within the department. The only question was the source.

Emily Lawrence thought back to when she'd developed an informant within an Asian-run heroin ring, a year earlier. For nine and a half months they had plotted and waited, and waited and plotted. Her target had been Raymond Chan, the overseer of the Chinese gangs in Boston, a thin, laconic man who smoked Gauloises with a gold cigarette holder and was rumored to have two wives at two different residences: one in suburban Lincoln, and another, not yet seventeen, somewhere in Chinatown. There were numerous deals about which the informant had provided information, deals the FBI was eager to act upon. But Emily Lawrence had been insistent that they wait until a situation presented itself that allowed them to catch Raymond Chan. Such deals, only the largest, were rare. And they were exceptionally well-concealed, for above all else, Raymond Chan valued his freedom.

Her conflicts with the FBI throughout the process had been widely known. She had refused to relent when the FBI insisted on raiding one particular deal for fear that Raymond Chan would not show. And he had not shown. And the bust had been held back.

Finally, the time had come. The informant told of a deal involving three-quarters of a million dollars' worth of heroin to be delivered to a Chinatown social club. The plans were well laid: Raymond Chan and his men would be involved in a poker game, and the heroin would be brought in by two men from New York in boxes designed to carry poker chips.

Two days before the deal was set to happen, Emily Lawrence went to the Boston Police Department. The club at which the buy would take place was known for its gambling. Every now and then it was raided by the BPD, and she wanted an assurance that there would be no raids on the night in question, for a raid would lead to cancellation of the deal.

She met with the commissioner and explained the significance of the raid. At the time, she'd had no reason to feel guarded in her dealings with the Boston police. And so she had freely described the federal plan.

Two nights later everything was in place. But when the FBI showed up at the club, they found Raymond Chan playing poker with a few associates. No heroin, no drugs of any kind. Emily Lawrence had been at the scene, and what she remembered most clearly—the detail that would stay with her always—was the expression on Raymond Chan's face. His smile told her all she needed to know. It said, "I outsmarted you. You thought you had me, but you have been fooled."

There had been seven important cases over a four-year period where the DEA or FBI drug raids in Boston had been anticipated by their targets.

"So what sort of facility is he in?" Duffy asked. "Minimum, I suppose."

"Medium," said Emily. "Danbury. And that's our leverage. He's dying to go to a federal country club."

"So present him with an alternative," Duffy said. "He pitches in or goes to maximum." Duffy shrugged as though to say, What could be simpler? An arrogant scowl crept onto his face.

Kevin Duffy was a heavyset man in his late thirties with soft pink skin and wisps of thinning reddish hair. He was chubby through the middle and had developed an extra layer of fat around his neck. Duffy possessed a weak chin, which he attempted to disguise with a goatee, but it was a scraggly, ill-trimmed patch of orange on his chin. He was a dutiful agent who took his work seriously, but often appeared to think of himself more as a tough, urban detective than as an agent of the FBI. It seemed he decided too late in life that he'd chosen the wrong career path, and so now took on the affectations of a detective who'd seen all of the hardscrabble life of big-city crime. That he was, in other words, Del Rio.

But Del Rio hated Duffy, as Del Rio hated all FBI agents. Del Rio believed the FBI was incompetent and arrogant. One of his men, Detective Steve Burke, had been shot by a drug dealer in a raid that Del Rio believed had been botched by the FBI, a blunder Del Rio would never forgive. He struggled to mask his contempt for the FBI in general and Duffy in particular.

"We actually used that a couple cases ago on him and it had the opposite impact," said Emily Lawrence. "He shut up for months."

Duffy sat forward in his seat, folding his hands on the conference table. He was clearly annoyed. "Look, let's talk real-world here," he said. "Let's sit Mr. Jones down and give him a choice between his continued incarcerated comfort or some genuine discomfort." He startled the others by banging the palm of his hand down on the table. "Let's try this. Let's move him. Why don't we just move him. Roust him. Couple marshals escort him at three A.M. to a bus for a ride to Illinois and then maybe down to Texas. See if that doesn't strengthen his vocal cords."

"Strengthen his vocal cords?" Del Rio repeated with a laugh.

"Look, if we do that, we could lose him completely," said Emily Lawrence. "That works with certain types of characters, but it's too big a risk with Mr. Jones."

"What do we have to lose?" Duffy asked.

Emily frowned. "We could lose him completely," she replied, as though the point was obvious.

"But it might open him up, too," Duffy said, warming to the idea. "Nice long bus ride," he added with a smirk, "has a way of changing behavior."

"No," said Emily, clearly annoyed that Duffy continued to pursue his notion. "It's too risky, Kevin. We can't afford to have him go into a shell. He's too valuable."

Duffy shook his head regretfully. "I don't know. Little castor oil works wonders."

Del Rio laughed out loud again. "Castor oil?" he repeated. "Thanks for the analysis, Sam Spade," he said in a mocking tone.

The situation reminded Jack Devlin of a fight between two hockey players with a long-standing mutual grudge. They needed no excuse, no cheap hit, no cross-check. All that was required was for one to look at the other and recall his hatred.

Duffy glared back at Del Rio. "This is a federal matter," he said. "We'll deal with it."

Del Rio's expression indicated grave confusion. "May I make a query here, Madam Chairwoman," he said in a mocking tone. "Here is the sum and substance of my query. Upon hearing my colleague from the Federal Bureau of Investigation, I ask this simple question: Are agents in the employ of the Federal Bureau of Investigation currently involved in an experiment that includes the smoking of marijuana or the use otherwise of hallucinogenic substances?"

Duffy glared across the table at Del Rio, who could not help but smile.

"Del Rio," said Emily Lawrence. "I don't think—"

"I'm not going to sink to his level," Duffy said angrily. "I have a strong conviction a long bus ride would work."

"And you base that on what, Kevin?" Emily Lawrence asked calmly.

"Astrology," Del Rio said, deadpan.

Emily Lawrence was suddenly red-faced. "Superintendent Del Rio," she said sharply as she turned to face him. "Our purpose here is to compare notes and see whether this tip we have has any shape yet in the real world. And if you can be instructive in that vein, by all means speak up. Otherwise, I would ask that you refrain from succumbing to your juvenile instincts."

The room fell silent. No one spoke to Del Rio that way. The silence seemed prolonged, growing more awkward with each moment.

Del Rio nodded very slowly. "You're right, Emily," he said. He turned to Duffy. "To the gentleman from the Federal Bureau of Investigation," he said, sounding contrite, "I would like to apologize for my mocking comments and tone, and I will do so as soon as he admits that because of his incompetence one of my men—"

"Jesus Christ!" Duffy shouted, banging the table.

Emily Lawrence sat forward in her seat, clearly angry. Her meeting was being destroyed. "I think the Boston Police Department would do well to avoid throwing stones," she said, "at least perhaps until it is a place where one can readily tell the difference between the cops and the crooks." As she uttered these words, her gaze shifted to Jack Devlin and fixed on him. The sentence hit Devlin with remarkable force, like an unseen punch to the gut.

Where one can readily tell the difference between the cops and the crooks.

Though Devlin was aware of Duffy saying something about Del Rio, and then other voices joining in the fray, he did not hear what they said. He sat silent, stung by Emily's words, for she'd been looking right at him—not as though to say the department was crooked, but as if to say, "You, yes you. You know whereof I speak. You know what I'm saying is the truth."

Suddenly, the meeting was breaking up, everyone rising from the table; accusations were traded, voices raised. Devlin rose, too, and followed Del Rio out of the conference room and down the hallway.

As Devlin left, Emily Lawrence watched him, and realizing that he'd taken her words personally, she felt instant regret for she had not meant to hold his gaze as long as she had; had not meant, at least not consciously, to imbue her words with such meaning.

"So?" Del Rio said as he and Devlin walked quickly toward the bank of elevators.

"So, what?" Devlin asked.

"So tell me I was wrong," Del Rio said. "Tell me I went too far. Tell me I'm an asshole."

"It was uncalled for," Devlin replied.

"I can't help it," Del Rio said, turning away, fidgeting, clearly struggling inside.

"You have to help it," Devlin said. "We have to work with these people."

Del Rio abruptly turned to face Devlin. He looked furious. Del Rio was a full half foot shorter than Devlin and not nearly as broad-shouldered, but he exuded a sense of energy and power.

"You fuckin' listen to me, Detective Devlin," he said, poking his forefinger into Devlin's chest. "That guy's not just an asshole, he's a dangerous asshole. And I can't look at his ugly fucking face without thinking of Stevie Burke being undercover and almost getting whacked by some Jamaican fucking posse because the Federal Bureau of Investi-fucking-gation in the person of that asshole Duffy is an incompetent dick. And so when I go into those meetings, I have the very best intentions, but when I look at him I think of Stevie and I think, 'Fuck it!' 'Cause the truth is the truth is the truth, Jack, and don't forget it."

Spittle had come flying from Del Rio's mouth and he was breathing hard now, his fury only barely under control. And before Jack Devlin could say anything, Del Rio turned, ignored the elevator, and took the stairs, twelve flights down to the street.

CHAPTER 3

JACK DEVLIN RODE the elevator to the ground floor of the John W. McCormack Federal Courthouse in Post Office Square, stung from the rebuke. He could not get her look out of his mind, that steady, determined, insistent gaze when she had said it to him.

Where one can readily tell the difference between the cops and the crooks.

Jack walked through the lobby of the building, past the metal detector, and took the staircase that led to the parking garage. He got into his Cherokee and sat back in the seat, rubbing his forehead with his fingers. Wonderful, he thought. He had managed, in a single meeting, to incur the wrath of both Emily Lawrence and Del Rio. He glanced at his watch and saw that he had an hour to get out to Holy Name. He could drive the long way, take his time, and still be early.

He started the Cherokee and began to ease it out of the parking space. He was headed toward the exit at the rear of the building when a stairway door flew open and Emily Lawrence burst forth directly into the path of his vehicle.

"Stop!" she shouted, her face flushed, thrusting out her hand as though she were a school crossing guard blocking a speeding driver.

She moved quickly around to the driver's side as Jack rolled down his window. Her brow was knitted and her lips pursed. She was clearly troubled. "Can we talk?" she blurted. "Do you have a minute?"

She had just insulted him in the most pointed way possible, he

31

thought, and now she wanted to chat. His jaw clenched and his eyes narrowed. He cocked his head and said to her: "You and I have nothing to discuss, counselor."

As he said this, he pressed a button and the window on the Jeep slid up and closed in her face.

She frowned and grew red-faced. "Goddamnit, give me a chance," she shouted at him. She was so loud that the garage attendant turned, startled.

She pounded on the glass so hard that he thought she might break it. "Just give me a chance to explain!" she shouted as he rolled his window down again. "At least give me that."

She was breathing hard and there was a vein bulging in the side of her neck. She came quickly around the Cherokee, got in the passenger side, and slammed the door. "Just get off your high horse for a minute and let me explain, will you?" she asked, glaring at him.

But her anger only served to incite Jack. He looked at her in disbelief. "You insult me up there and now you come down here and bark at me because I don't want to talk to you?" he said. "I have to tell you, I don't deal well with brats."

Her eyes widened. "Brats?" she said in astonishment. "That's lovely," she added sarcastically. "Very impressive. I come racing all the way down here to apologize to you, and you get all huffy and call me a brat. Very mature."

There was a loud honking behind them. She looked back and saw U.S. District Court Judge Henry Weedon looking at her as though to say, What gives?

"Jesus, you're blocking Judge Weedon," she said. "You better move."

Jack waited for her to get out of the vehicle, but she didn't move. "Go!" she ordered. "Come on!"

"You better get out," he said curtly.

But she did not budge.

"Just go, will you, please, before he gets really angry?"

Reluctantly, Jack Devlin put the Cherokee into gear and eased it forward through the garage exit and out onto Congress Street. He drove a block and pulled over, waiting for her to get out. Again she did not move. They sat in a prolonged silence until finally he said, "I need to get moving. I have to be somewhere."

His tone was cool.

She took a deep breath and exhaled slowly. When she spoke, her tone was calm, her voice much quieter than it had been. "If you would let me ride with you, I would appreciate it," she said. "There's something I want to say."

He considered this, shifted the car into drive, and pulled back out onto Congress Street.

"Just go wherever you're going and I'll catch a cab back," she said.

He drove in silence along Congress Street over to Cambridge Street, then to Storrow Drive. Finally, she spoke.

"I want to say that I am sorry for what I said," she said, her tone measured, careful. "It was an overheated atmosphere and I was angry that the meeting was destroyed . . . angry at BPD, and I blurted something that I shouldn't have said, and I certainly should not have been staring at you when I said it because I realize you probably took it personally, and it was not intended that way. So I am sorry and I hope you'll accept my apology."

He glanced across at her as he drove and could see by her expression that she was deadly serious. Her face was flushed still, and strands of hair were out of place and had fallen into her face. She brushed them away as she looked at him. There was no artifice about her.

"Of course I will," he said softly, graciously. She looked over at him and held his gaze, and he drifted into the passing lane, a cabdriver honking furiously.

He shifted his eyes back to the road, and she looked out to her right across the Charles River toward Cambridge.

"Where are we headed?" she asked.

"Roslindale," he said.

"Whereabouts?"

He hesitated. He was not sure whether he wanted her to know, but could think of no other response, so he told the truth: "Holy Name Church. Out on the parkway."

She knitted her brow. "What's happening there?"

"Mass," he said, without shifting his eyes from the road ahead.

"Mass?" she repeated, clearly surprised.

He nodded.

"In the middle of the week?"

"Right," he said.

All right, he thought. She'll make some wiseass anti-Catholic comment, and when she does I'll pull over and kick her ass out of here.

But there was no comment. Merely a brief nod.

Jack turned off Storrow Drive at the Kenmore Square exit and followed the ramp up to Boylston Street behind Fenway Park.

"Pull over here," she said. "I'll run in and get us some coffee. Go ahead, pull over."

He did as instructed, and she disappeared into Dunkin' Donuts, reappearing minutes later with two cups of coffee.

"You know, I don't have any money with me," she said, not the least bit sheepishly. "My bag's back at the office. Can I borrow a couple of bucks?"

He wanted to laugh out loud but instead reached into his wallet and handed her a five. She ran back inside and paid for the coffee. When she was back in the Jeep, she sipped her coffee and spoke in a much brighter, more cheerful voice than before. "You know, it occurs to me that to get a cab—"

He couldn't help but smile. "Here," he said, handing her a ten-dollar bill.

"Great," she said. "Thanks."

She sipped more coffee and stared at him. "So?" she said.

"So, what?" he replied, pulling into the traffic headed out Boylston to the Riverway.

"So I'm very glad that you accept my apology," she said. "I can't stand ungracious people. Speaking of ungracious," she continued, "I must tell you that I do not think your pal Del Rio was very constructive in that meeting."

Jack was mildly taken aback. They had just settled an unpleasant conflict and she was jumping back in.

"I really don't," she added.

"I believe you," he said.

"I mean, why be so sophomoric?"

"He has a visceral hatred for Kevin," Devlin said. "He looks at him and he sees only the FBI putting Steve Burke's life in jeopardy. He can't get past that."

"It's very counterproductive," she said. "It doesn't help."

"And it would help what, exactly, if we were to work with the FBI?" Jack asked.

"You're kidding, right?"

"I'm not," he replied, sipping his coffee.

"Well, obviously—"

"Nothing's obvious," he said.

"Okay, Counselor," she said, sitting up straighter in her seat. "It is asserted that the sum of the law enforcement parts could be— could be—greater than the whole. That there is a synergy that could be achieved by having all the parts working together."

"If there was mutual trust and confidence, I'd agree," he said. "But look at it from Del Rio's point of view. Does he want to send detectives, including those under cover, into an operation in which the FBI has had a hand, given Kevin's track record? Would that be responsible? Why risk it? Why put your people into situations that someone else controls?"

"He could try and handle it another way so that Kevin isn't completely humiliated and the meeting ruined," she said.

"But he *wants* the meeting ruined."

"Oh, that's wonderfully mature. So professional. And you like this guy?" She made a face indicating her distaste.

"He thinks the Fibees are classroom criminologists who don't really grasp that there are posses out there with big handguns who wouldn't think twice before blowing a hole in a Boston police detective."

"But that's—"

"Entirely rational," Devlin said. "He wants a bad relationship so we don't have to work with them."

"It's so Machiavellian," she said as they curved around the Holy Name rotary and pulled into the church parking lot.

"There's a cab stand across the street," he said.

"Listen," she said. "I meant what I said. I am sorry for my stupid comment. I really am."

AS SHE WAITED for a cab, the skies opened and a cold, sleeting rain poured down on the city. Emily raced across the street, toward the church, seeking refuge from the storm. She would wait until it passed and then catch a cab.

She quietly entered the back of the church and took a seat in the very last row. It was a cavernous place, with huge stone columns and seats for what must have been a thousand people. She looked up toward the front and saw Jack toward the altar. The crowd was sparse, no more than a few dozen. She noticed that most of them were older men, at or past retirement age.

As the Mass began, a couple of elderly men were finishing their work of going row to row to place booklets at the end of each bench. Emily picked one up and examined it. It was small and printed on cheap white paper. Her curiosity was aroused when she saw the seal of the police department of the city of Boston on the front of the booklet. She opened it and found that this was a memorial Mass to pray for the departed souls of members of the department "who had served honorably." The booklet was a listing of all deceased members of the Boston Police Department who had "served honorably." There must be thousands of names, she thought, as she thumbed through and saw them in column after column, jammed onto the pages.

The booklet was organized into decades—men who had died in the 1990s, for example, were listed alphabetically together. She began thumbing through the various decades, looking, in each section, for the name of Devlin, and she found several Devlins, two of them from the 1950s and another in the 1930s, but none more recent.

She forgot about her cab and sat watching the Mass. Soon it came time for the sermon, and the priest moved to a small podium set at the front of the altar, facing the worshipers.

"We gather here this afternoon as we do every month at this time to pause for just a moment from our daily lives to recall the good works of so many of our brothers and fathers and grandfathers and beyond who served as police officers in our city," the priest said. "This month, as we do each and every month of the year, we add two names to our roll of honor. Patrolman James Manning and Sergeant Warren Gustavson were taken by God this past month, and so we pay special notice to them today and ask God to place them in a special place near him in Heaven for all of eternity. And we pray for all of the others listed in your booklets, available to you in the pews or in the back of the church."

As the Mass proceeded, she sat stunned at what she'd just witnessed. Jack had come here to this Mass whose express purpose was to memorialize the dead among the police force who had "served honorably," as the booklet said, as the priest himself had said. And yet Jack's father's name was not among those who had rendered such service. As the Mass drew to a conclusion, Emily slipped out the back door and returned to her office.

AS WAS HIS custom, Jack Devlin lingered inside the church after Mass. He sat in the pew while the others departed and, soon,
he was alone. He looked around and felt comforted by this setting
that was so familiar to him. The gray stone walls of the church,
the heavy steel light fixtures hanging down from the forty-foot ceiling, the dozens of stubby white candles, flames sending shadows
shimmering up the walls, the stained-glass windows, the drafty
creakiness of the place. He very much liked that the new style of
Mass—post–Vatican II—was said in a setting that evoked the old
church of the Latin Mass. Now the altar had been turned around so
the priest faced the congregation, embraced the congregation, invited the people to participate in this sacrament.

In the empty church, Jack slid off the bench and knelt down,
propping his elbows on the bench in front of him. He made the Sign
of the Cross and began to pray. He prayed for the repose of his father's soul. He believed in the afterlife, in the concept of Heaven, and
he believed that his father's spirit existed in that place. And though
his father's body was long dead, his spirit existed, somewhere in the
universe, and would for all of eternity. This he believed.

And so he prayed for his father, whom he had loved so dearly.

Then hated so desperately.

Then loved so dearly, yet again.

CHAPTER 4

THE LIVING ROOM was not particularly large, but its southern exposure had sunlight streaming in on this frigid December Sunday. It was shortly after ten A.M., and already Jack Devlin had been to an early Mass and taken an eight-mile run through the streets of West Roxbury. He'd showered, changed, and lit a fire in the fireplace. The pale, milky light of December filled the room as he brought a storage box of photographs and files out of his basement and set them down in front of the sofa.

Jack was comfortable in his modest home, a Cape Cod–style two-bedroom on a side street off the VFW Parkway. He set a mug of coffee on the side table and leaned forward on the sofa, reaching into the box.

Jack removed a large manila envelope thick with photographs, undid the clasp, and slid the pictures carefully out of the envelope. He set the stack down on the coffee table and picked them up one by one, studying each for a moment or two. Though he hadn't touched the contents of this box in several years, these were photos with which he was intimately familiar. The instant he looked at one, he would immediately be flooded with recollections of that time or even of that moment. Most of the photos were of himself or of him and his father. There were a few with his mother, all in black and white. There were a few of just his father or of his father with some friend from the department.

Jack had been nagged by the thought that it was time to organize this material, to pull it out, look through it all, and somehow make sense of it. But how did one organize the remnants of a life? Here were the official papers of his father's existence: bank and insurance records, pension and Social Security information, letters from lawyers for the city, the police department, the detectives' union.

As he sifted through it, Jack was struck by how little information was here. He'd read all the documents before, reviewed them with his lawyer's eye, studied them, processed them. They held little meaning for him now.

It was the photographs that captured him. There was a black and white shot of him and his mother standing on the seawall at Nantasket, the water to their backs, looking across at Paragon Park. Her face was freckled, her hair pushed to one side by the wind. Both of them wore bathing suits, hers a one-piece that flattered her, his a droopy one with the drawstring hanging down the front. She was holding his arms, for he was not yet a year old and was unable to stand on his own. It was odd looking at pictures of his mother, for Jack had no recollection of her at all, no memories that evoked her presence, no remembrance of her voice or how she moved or even her smile.

He flipped to the next picture, this one of him and his father at his grade-school graduation. With his father he remembered everything. He could close his eyes at any time—in fact he'd done so hundreds, no thousands, of times—and imagine his father, recalling with ease the sight of him, the sound, the smell, everything about him. He recalled the precise timbre of his dad's voice, remembered how he walked, the exact gait. He remembered so very much and was pained by it.

And in remembering, Jack felt the stab of his most painful memory.

HE HAD BEEN awakened in the early morning and gone from his bedroom to the kitchen, where he would have a bowl of cereal each morning with his father. But at the kitchen table on that morning he'd found his aunt Sheila, a fat policeman who seemed unable to look him in the eye, and Father Hogan. Aunt Sheila sat with a vacant look, clutching rosary beads in her arthritic fingers.

Father Hogan was an older man, heavyset, his black suit dotted with cigarette ashes. The priest was smoking when Jack walked into the kitchen, and Jack watched as he cupped the butt in his hand.

"A sad thing, Jackie," the priest had said. "Sit up here now and listen to me, boy."

The police officer scooped him up and sat him on a chair facing the priest.

"Jackie, the Good Lord works in ways we don't always understand, and last night God called your father to Heaven. You see, Jackie—"

"To Heaven?" Jack said, a look of bewilderment on his face. His dark hair was pressed down on one side, sticking up on the other. The soft, warm cheeks of his face were creased with sleep.

Jack did not understand, but instinctively he knew that something very bad had happened. He could tell by the tension in the air, by the looks on the faces of the adults, by the very fact of their being there. He looked from the priest to his aunt and back to the priest.

Father Hogan spoke very softly. "Your dad died, Jackie," he said, his Roman collar pressed against the reddish flesh of his neck. "God took him to Heaven last night."

"What happened to him?" Jack asked reflexively, not yet absorbing the awful truth.

"He took a heart attack, Jackie," the priest said. It had been the story the adults had settled upon before he'd awakened.

Sometimes, when he was very young, not yet eight years old, Jack would wake in the middle of the night and think that he was alone; that his father, like his mother, was gone. He would get out of his bed and rush into his father's bedroom, where Jock Devlin would quickly wake up at the sound of his feet on the hall floor.

"Bad dream again, pal?" his father would say.

And sometimes the nightmare was so powerful that Jack could not calm his racing heart. And he would lie there clutching his father, squeezing him as though his very life depended upon it.

One night Jack had experienced the nightmare and raced to his father's room, and the child's worst fears were realized. His father was not there. Jack called out, but there was no answer. He called out louder and louder, running to the kitchen, but there was no response, and Jack knew then that he'd been abandoned, that his father was gone. And he began to cry and shake, and he felt fear and dread swell in his chest.

He sobbed and sobbed, and though it was barely ten minutes before his father—who had had insomnia and gone outside to enjoy a cigar—returned, it was as though his life had been shattered. When his father came back into the apartment and found Jack balled up on the floor, shaking, tears streaming down his face, he'd taken him in his arms and struggled to calm him.

"I thought you were gone," the child said, gasping for air between sobs.

"Dear God," the father said, "you don't think Dad would ever leave you. I would never, ever leave you for any reason ever. Ever."

He squeezed his child so tightly, Jock Devlin feared he would hurt the boy. He took him by the arms and pushed him away, holding him at arm's length so he could see that he was all right.

"I will always be here for you, Jackie," the father said. "Always. I will always be here. Do you understand me?"

And the boy had nodded and wrapped his arms around his father's neck and head and held on tight.

"I will always be here for you, son," the father had said. "I will never, ever leave you."

And Jackie had believed him.

On that fateful morning, nine-year-old Jack Devlin looked at the face of the policeman, at his aunt Sheila, at Father Hogan, and suddenly burst into tears, for his worst nightmare had come true.

THE LINE OF blue-suited policemen wound from the casket, across the funeral home parlor, out the front door, down the stairs, and around the building into the parking lot. And it was there, inside the funeral home, that Jack had heard one policeman talking to another, two men just around the corner from where he stood, obscured by a mound of coats. They said his father had killed himself.

This could not possibly be true, he thought. It was the very last thing his father would do. They were mistaken; they had to be. For Jack knew that his father would fight to the last to remain alive. For him.

But then, the next day, he saw the newspaper front page: COP KILLS SELF.

His aunt Sheila snatched the newspaper away from him when she discovered him reading it. She was a high-strung woman and she immediately panicked because Jack had seen the paper. She sought to convince him to put it out of his mind, but the news was all that Jack thought about. The realization was like a massive weight that suddenly fell upon him, crushing him in the most brutal fashion. It was this news that caused his life to spin out of control. For Jack Devlin felt the worst possible feeling, worse even than the blinding grief caused by the loss of his father—he felt betrayed. For surely his father must have known that the worst thing he could do was what he'd done; the most terrible, brutal thing he could do was to end his own life, to take himself away from his son, to deprive the boy of what mattered most in his life.

Why? Jack wondered that day and countless days thereafter. Why? How could you do it, Dad? he wondered hour after hour, day after day. It was not as though he raised this question in his mind consciously, not as though he would pose it to himself. Rather, it was there, fixed in his mind, an uncovered, glaring white light causing one to turn away and cover one's eyes.

To characterize the hurt as massive or traumatic was to understate it, for the truth was that it consumed him. His suffering invaded his cells, leaving him with a sense of loss that was like an illness.

It had very nearly destroyed him.

Somehow, though, it hadn't. Somehow, he had survived. And for a reason. He had survived, he believed, at least in part, so that he would be able one day to go back and look around in that part of history; to go back and understand more fully what had happened.

This was what his life was about now, understanding. Discovering. Learning. He had reached a point where he was in a position to find out the truth. And so that had become his mission. His passion. His obsession.

His plan had been formulated. If it worked, he would soon know the truth. If it didn't, he would soon be destroyed.

CHAPTER 5

COAKLEY, THE LAWYER, rode the elevator down from his fourth-floor office at 16 Beacon Street, just down the hill from the State House. Coakley, the lawyer, wore a brown suit, slightly bagged in the knees, shiny in the seat and elbows. The collar of his pale blue oxford-cloth shirt was worn, and his necktie, wrapped in a fat, Windsor knot, was tugged down from his bulging Adam's apple. Coakley felt the pressure of his belt buckle against his ever-expanding stomach, and vowed that upon his return to the office he would take the stairs back up. In fact, he thought as he walked along Tremont Street past the Granary Burial Grounds, from now on he would use the stairs exclusively. That would be, what? he wondered. Anywhere from four to six trips a day. That would make a dent in his weight problem, get his heart going, blood pumping.

It was cool, a gray day, but Coakley wore his trench coat open as he made his way along Tremont to the Park Street MBTA station. He descended the long flight of stairs and felt the wave of heat from under the streets of the city. The screech of subway cars entering and exiting the station filled the air. Since it was late morning, the crowds were sparse. He walked to the end of the outbound platform and caught a Green Line D car, which traveled west under Boston Common and out Boylston Street.

Coakley sat facing the opposite side of the train, and in the darkness of the tunnel he caught sight of his reflection in the window. He looked pale and drawn, his round face fleshy and pleasant in its way, though hardly distinctive. When he was a younger man, in his twenties, Coakley had been considered somewhat handsome. But now, at fifty-eight, he was a sorry sight, and he knew it. His hairline had receded and there were but wisps of grayish straw across the top of his bald pate. His nose was thick and reddish, capillaries broken beneath the skin leaving spiderwebbed veins of red and purple. Coakley stared at the pale, fleshy image in the darkened window but had to turn away. He did not wish to see what he'd become.

He rode out past Kenmore Square into Brookline. Getting off at the Brookline Hills stop, he walked across the parking lot to the athletic fields in front of Brookline High School. On the far side, past the playground and basketball courts, were several sturdy wooden benches. Coakley took a seat and picked up a *Boston Herald* someone had left behind. He flipped the paper over and read an article about the Bruins' new cast of characters, led by one of his favorite players, winger Rick Tocchet. Coakley admired Tocchet's grit and determination. He was a man of character, he thought. He set the paper down and thought that if he were to do it all over again, he would seek to emulate Tocchet—to have backbone; to be willing to stand up and face down the demons. To have honor.

He sighed.

"Sounds like the weight of the world," said Jack Devlin, who approached and took a seat next to Coakley on the bench.

Coakley looked at Devlin. "Feels it sometimes," he said.

"Here." Devlin handed Coakley a brown bag. "Thought you'd be hungry."

"Jeez, I'm trying to cut down," Coakley said as he opened the bag and discovered a turkey sandwich and Diet Coke. "Thanks," he said. "That's very thoughtful."

He spread out the *Herald* and placed his sandwich on it. As he did so he saw the back-page photograph of Tocchet.

"You ever run into Rick Tocchet when you played?" he asked.

Devlin nodded. "After school, the summer after school, I played in a league up in Quebec. Tocchet and some other guys from Philadelphia—back when he was with the Flyers—played, too, to stay in shape. Nothing too serious, except everything is serious with those guys."

"Good guy?" Coakley asked.

"The best," Devlin said.

Coakley nodded. "So you regret you didn't sign the contract?"

Devlin shook his head. "Not really. It would have been fun, but, you know, I had other stuff to do."

The contract to which Coakley referred was an offer from the Montreal Canadiens. As an all-American in college, Jack had been drafted by the Canadiens, who sent no less a personage than Serge Savard himself to convince Devlin to sign. And as much as he loved the game of hockey, the truth was that he wanted to get on with his life.

Devlin pulled a sandwich of his own out of another bag and began eating. "So how's your man?"

Coakley nodded. "Not bad," the lawyer said. "Making progress." Coakley hesitated a moment, then added, "I think."

"You think?"

"He's antsy," Coakley said. "It's a medium facility and not so pleasant. There are guys who, you know, would do unpleasant things to him if given the opportunity. So this stalling, he's not too keen on it."

"He did it before on his own," Devlin said.

"Felt he had no choice," Coakley said. "He had to wait for some people to pass on before he could cough up that stuff. Jesus."

Devlin nodded his understanding.

"Anyway, he wants to move," Coakley said. "He wants to get going. The feds will never be more eager than they are now. They know him, they trust him, and they're ready to act based on his say-so. But they need something more. They're hounding his ass, to tell you the truth."

"When are you going to see him next?" Devlin asked.

"Whenever you say."

"I think it would be good to get to him as soon as possible."

"I can drive down today. I'd just as soon. It's relaxing, the drive."

"So you can tell him that the delivery is about to be made," Devlin said. "Within a matter of a few days."

Coakley raised his eyes. "A few days?"

Devlin nodded.

"Where?" Coakley asked.

Devlin shook his head. "That's enough," he said. "That will get the feds' attention."

"They'll want a location," Coakley said. "Something more than that it's happening soon somewhere. Somewhere's a big place."

"That's okay," Devlin said.

Coakley shrugged. What choice did he have? He was receiving information from Devlin that was relayed through Mr. Jones to the federal authorities in Boston. The information could only help his client get favorable treatment and possibly get moved to a minimum-security facility.

Coakley chewed on his sandwich, then took a long sip of Coke. Jack Devlin finished his sandwich, rolled the paper into a ball, and stuffed it into the bag. He finished his Coke and placed the can in the bag, as well. He got up from the bench and walked a few dozen yards to a trash can and dropped the bag in, walked back to the bench, and stood with his foot on one end, gazing out across the fields at a group of schoolchildren playing soccer.

Coakley put his sandwich down and sat back. He folded his arms across his chest. He'd been providing information to Devlin for nearly two years and was, by far, Devlin's best informant. Over many late-night conversations Devlin had learned that Coakley was cooperative because he felt the need to atone for past sins.

Coakley had once been a young state representative with a promising future, when a scandal broke involving two prominent state senators who took payoffs in return for a favorable oversight report for a construction company building the UMass Boston Harbor campus. While Coakley was never formally charged, he was named by the grand jury as an unindicted coconspirator. That information, naturally, had been leaked to the press by prosecutors, and Coakley was defeated for reelection. Because of the scandal, his law practice crumbled. He then turned to representing anyone who would have him, which meant dealers and low-level wiseguys. Through the years, he had established a profitable practice representing dealers of various sizes and shapes.

But Coakley had tired of his clientele. His Catholic-size conscience weighed on him. He had never represented an innocent man, and that took its toll—even on a lawyer. He also felt a debt to the Devlins.

"Young's okay?" Devlin asked.

Coakley shot him a quick sideways glance. "Okay?" he asked as though it was a foolish idea. "What's your definition of okay, Jack? Is someone who does dope at breakfast okay? Jesus." He shook his head and took a deep breath. "He's ready."

Coakley bundled his trash together and shuffled over to the rubbish barrel. He shuffled back to the bench, running a hand through his hair. The two men watched in silence as a child who had skinned his knee in the playground went crying to his mother.

"To me, it's got a bad feel to it," Coakley said. "It's a business best left to those who know it." He shook his head. "I don't know . . ."

"So if you were me . . ." Devlin began.

"If I were you, I would have signed the contract," Coakley said. "You'd have been a big star in Montreal. No better city in the world to play in. Endorsements, whatever you wanted. I would have signed, to be honest with you."

Coakley turned to Devlin and looked him squarely in the eye. "I mean, what kind of life is this, you snoop around talking with people like me. Chasing crazy kids around bad neighborhoods." He looked away and waved his hand as though dismissing the entire idea. "Fuck that."

Abruptly, he turned back to Devlin. "You went to law school to do *this?*" he said, as though the notion was obviously preposterous, and shook his head again.

Jack Devlin had grown accustomed to Coakley's outbursts. The lawyer had a propensity to tell him how he should or should not live his life. Devlin didn't mind. He liked Coakley.

The two men rose from the bench, as if on cue, and began walking slowly toward the subway stop across the way. At the edge of the park they came to a stop.

"Thanks," Devlin said. "I appreciate it."

Coakley nodded, but then he could not help himself, could not stop himself from blurting what he felt. "I don't have a good feeling about this, Jack," he said. "Something's not right here. Really not right."

CHAPTER 6

JACKIE DEVLIN STOOD in the schoolyard on a chilly fall day glaring at the two eighth graders taunting him. Their insults had come after a group of eighth graders had beaten Jack and other seventh graders in a game of schoolyard basketball. Recess was over and time had come to return to class.

Dozens of children were moving from their activities—basketball, kickball, tag—to form lines leading back into school. The two nuns on schoolyard duty were back inside the school, at the head of the lines. Jack and the two boys were all the way across the yard, near the basketball hoop, two hundred feet from the school.

The taunting from the other boys triggered something within Jack Devlin and he reacted suddenly, instinctively. He flashed a right hand that caught the first boy, the bigger one, by surprise. The bony knuckles of Jack's small, hard fist landed on the bridge of the boy's nose and then there was blood pouring down over the boy's mouth and chin. He crumpled to the ground.

"You little asshole," the other boy, McKay, said.

McKay was the toughest kid in the eighth grade, a boy who never let a week go by without an after-school fight along the railroad tracks. He quickly put up his fists and moved toward Jack in a crouch.

The bigger boy, Dillon, was still on the ground, blood staining his white dress shirt.

McKay pounded Jack with a right hand that landed on Jack's left cheekbone, but, oddly, it did not bother him. Jack was extremely calm and in a crouch, his fists high. McKay threw the same punch several more times, landing it on Jack's cheekbone again. Jack kept moving forward until he quickly threw his own right hand, which landed just above McKay's left eye and made him wince in pain.

Though Jack Devlin was smaller than the two eighth graders, he was thick and powerful, far stronger than either one. Instinctively, Jack maneuvered himself into position so he could grasp the shoulder of McKay's shirt. He clutched the material with his left hand, clamping it down so McKay could not throw a punch with his right hand. McKay was left unprotected as Jack threw a series of rights at his face and head, vicious blows delivered in rapid-fire fashion.

Dillon got to his feet and watched in horror as his friend was beaten up by a younger, smaller boy.

One of the nuns charged across the pavement, screaming at Jack to stop. But he did not stop, for he now had McKay helpless, defenseless. McKay had turned away, trying to hide and protect his face, and Jack shifted position so he could continue to pound away.

"Stop this minute!" the nun shouted as she charged at Jack, reaching out to grab his arm.

He slipped her grasp and threw yet another punch, this one landing squarely on McKay's nose. McKay cried out in pain and slumped to the ground, facedown. Blood from his nose formed a small pool on the pavement.

The nun, stunned by the ferocity of what she had witnessed, involuntarily made a rapid Sign of the Cross.

"John Devlin, go into the school right now!" she ordered furiously, and without a word Devlin obeyed. The nun helped McKay to his feet and walked with him and Dillon into the school and down to the basement nurse's office.

The school principal, Sister Marguerite, trembled with rage when she saw the faces of McKay and Dillon and the blood soaking their shirts. She trembled with anger as she sat Jack Devlin down in a chair in her office, the door closed.

"I want an apology this instant, young man," she said, her voice struggling to control her anger.

"Sorry," Jack said without a bit of sincerity.

"You don't sound very sorry," she said.

"I'm not," he shot back.

She was stunned by his insolence. Was this the boy who had proven to be the brightest in his class? The boy who had been so introverted since the death of his father that the school had summoned a priest from the archdiocese specializing in psychology to come and talk with him every month?

"Do not speak with disrespect to me, mister," she said harshly.

Jack looked down at his shoes. His white shirt was torn, one of the buttons ripped off in the fight.

"Look up at me, Mr. Devlin," she said angrily.

Jack did, and it frightened her. His eyes were vacant. He seemed so very cool and calm. She had seen many boys through the years after schoolyard fights, some rather nasty. And in every case, without exception, the boys were trembling, shaking from the trauma of the violence. And here was Jack Devlin sitting calmly, not breathing heavily, looking as though he had just come from the library. She looked into his eyes, and he seemed untroubled. He seemed, she would later recall, to be a boy without a conscience, without a hint of remorse for what he had done.

"What happened?" she asked.

"They were picking on me," Jack said.

"Why?"

"We had a basketball game and they beat us and they were ranking on me," Jack said.

"And?" she asked.

"And I didn't like it," he said.

"We are going to go down to the nurse's office right now, John Devlin, and you are going to apologize to those boys and then you are going to your classroom and stand up front and tell the class you are sorry for bringing discredit upon the seventh grade, and then you are going across the street to Father Graham to say your confession and beg for—and I do mean beg for—God's forgiveness."

Sister Marguerite walked him along the silent hallways of the school, down a flight of stairs to the basement to the nurse's office. McKay and Dillon were sitting side by side, chunks of cotton up their noses. The nurse had wiped the blood from their faces and she was tending to a scrape on the side of McKay's face, sustained when he hit the pavement.

"John Devlin has something to say to the both of you," Sister Marguerite said.

"Sorry," Jack mumbled as he averted his eyes.

Sister Marguerite was about to ask for something more sincere but decided she had gotten the minimum required.

"He attacked us," Dillon said weakly. "For no reason. He—"

Sister Marguerite silenced him. "We will sort it out later, William," she said, turning and leading Devlin from the nurse's office.

"Mrs. Creedon, could you please bring the boys to their classroom now," Sister Marguerite said. "I want them present for John Devlin's comments."

Sister Marguerite and Jack went to his classroom, where the principal interrupted class and had Jack stand up and apologize for bringing discredit upon the seventh grade. He did as he was told, again without any hint of remorse.

And then Sister Marguerite walked Jack Devlin out into the hallway. There, they stood silently as Dillon and McKay walked into the eighth-grade classroom. When they were settled, Sister Marguerite entered the room with Jack. The room fell silent. Sister Marguerite, and the nun who taught the eighth grade, walked to the rear of the classroom. Jack stood in front. He looked out over the class and his eyes came to rest on McKay, who had a look of malice. He mouthed words for Devlin: *After school. After school.* He mouthed them again. And again. He was taunting Devlin again.

"John Devlin, do you have something to say?" Sister Marguerite asked.

"Ah . . ." Devlin said, hesitating, fumbling for words.

He paused. There was a long, awkward silence.

Sister Marguerite was exasperated. "John Devlin, do you have an apology to make?" she asked.

"I'm sorry," Jack said in a rapid monotone.

Sister Marguerite had had it. "John Devlin, this class requires a sincere apology."

Jack glanced again at McKay. *After school,* McKay mouthed again. *After school.*

"Sorry," he said, this time with a hint of mockery in his voice. Sister Marguerite's nostrils flared.

"John Devlin," she said crossly, "you—"

"I'm sorry I beat their fucking heads in," Jack Devlin said as the nuns and other children gasped. "And after school I'm going to do it again."

And he had.

CHAPTER 7

EMILY LAWRENCE RAN along Beacon Street in Waban and turned off on the side street leading to her house. She checked her watch and saw that she'd been running for fifty-three minutes, about six miles. She walked the few hundred yards down her street to begin the process of cooling down. At home she checked her answering machine and found she had several calls, including one from Jack Devlin. They were talking every day and sometimes several times a day. She thought about Jack and how different he was from the other men with whom she'd been involved.

She had been serious about three men in her life. Steven Tucker had been a law school classmate, a personable, hardworking man with a passion for the law. They had lived together in New York the summer between their second and third years in law school, when Steven was working for an urban antipoverty agency in the Bedford-Stuyvesant section of Brooklyn while she worked on the legal staff at the EPA. Emily had been very much in love. She'd believed that after graduation they would continue to live together and, at some point, get married.

That changed one late summer weekend. Emily had gone to visit her parents, while Steven stayed in the city to prepare for a trial. But when she returned late Saturday afternoon—long before her scheduled return on Sunday—she'd opened the door to their studio apartment to find Steven in the act with a girl who looked barely sixteen.

She'd been so stunned that she merely stood there as her beloved Steven—so engrossed in his new friend that he had not heard her enter the apartment—continued on his energetic way.

So that's what it looks like to a third party, she thought. My God! So much more elemental than she would have imagined.

"Steven . . ." she'd said, with more annoyance than outrage. The girl lay there, on her back, frozen in horror, staring at her. Steven whipped around and his eyes bulged in cartoonlike fashion. He literally jumped to his feet and turned toward her, which only made matters worse. Much worse. Emily burst into tears then, turned, and ran from the apartment building, never to return. She and Steven had two subsequent conversations, via telephone, both ending with him begging her to forgive him. In fact, she wanted to forgive him, and would have, she thought, if she hadn't seen him in the act. The image was fixed in her mind and she could not erase it.

James had been older and more mature. He was ten years her senior, which did not bother her. She was attracted to him for his innate kindness. He was a gentle soul, an enormously decent man. He worked as the executive director of a foundation that provided medical assistance to the emerging world. He was well-traveled, spoke four languages fluently and two others passably. She found herself so very comfortable with James. He was the easiest man to be with she had ever met, unfailingly pleasant. They never once had an argument.

And that, it had turned out, had been the problem. James would not be engaged, could not be engaged, in any sort of discussion of an intensely personal nature. A discourse on the travails of the economies of sub-Saharan Africa? James was your man. Details about relief programs in former Soviet satellites? James had them. But talk about the future? About life together? About one's most intensely personal hopes and dreams? James might just as well try and propel himself to the moon by flapping his arms. James, Emily discovered, was the poster boy for modern man's inability to commit, or discuss anything related to commitment.

It ended not in anger, but frustration. Emily had had a hard time getting over James.

Ian had helped. A native of Glasgow, he was a graduate of the London School of Economics and fancied himself an entrepreneur. He and a partner started a small software firm that had been quite successful. But that had been some years earlier, and Ian had more bluster than energy, it turned out. He loved life, travel, and learning about other cultures, knew wine and poetry and had actually read Proust! But Ian's ideas, charmingly dashed out on cocktail napkins, proved more fanciful than real. And in the end Emily had quietly withdrawn from the entanglement.

That had been a year ago. Since then she'd been unattached, and had made a point of dating no one. She'd avoided social settings, feeling instead the need to recharge her batteries and think about what she wanted from life. And it was so very simple: She wanted love. Children. A family. A chance to do work that meant something. She wanted a good man who was strong and stable, someone who would be as good a father as he was a husband. She wanted two or three kids and an opportunity to provide them with a good life. She wanted to be a loving mother. She wanted all those things that she thought of as the components of happiness.

Emily Lawrence was a very bright woman, and she knew there would be hard moments. She knew that even the happiest and most fulfilled life was not without struggle or pain.

Now, she took off her windbreaker and black running tights, sat down in her kitchen, and took a long drink from a bottle of water. She dialed into her voice mail and listened to Jack Devlin's message for a second time.

"Hi, it's Jack, and I just wanted to say hello and see how you're doing, so give me a call when you get a chance. I hope all is well so, ah . . . take care, okay, Em?"

She smiled and saved the message.

So take care, okay, Em?

He said it with sincerity, with an earnestness that she liked. In some ways he seemed like such a simple man, so straightforward. He worked, he played ice hockey with his friends, he went to church. Was it because of his simplicity that she was drawn to him? she wondered. She loved that there was no artifice about him. She thought he was perhaps the least pretentious man she'd ever met. There was a genuine sense of humility about Jack Devlin, and she loved that. She believed in being humble, in recognizing the natural and spiritual forces that dwarfed individual human beings. And Jack Devlin struck her as a genuinely humble man.

She also found him terribly attractive. He was tall and strong, and there was a handsome kindness to his face that was appealing. She was even intrigued by the scars, one by his left eye and the other over the right side of his lip. The one by his eye gave his face character, she thought. The one by his lip, from certain angles, was all but invisible. But from the side, particularly from the left, it appeared he'd just gotten a fat lip. When she was close to him the other day, she'd caught herself staring at it. The truth was, she thought Jack a very sexy man.

Of all his characteristics, however, Emily was most taken with his perseverance. She was deeply impressed that he'd been able to do what he had, in light of his upbringing. To go on to achieve so much success both athletically and academically, after the traumatic nature of his childhood, was quite extraordinary.

As she cooled down, Emily felt a chill. She went to her room and got into a hot shower. Afterward, she dressed in corduroy slacks, a cotton shirt, and a dark green wool sweater. She returned to the kitchen, drank more water, and peeled an orange, separating the sections on a paper towel spread on the kitchen table.

She thought about Jack as she ate, and wondered whether she was capable of opening up to him. A certain level of efficiency in her social life was important to her now. She had no interest in developing casual dating relationships for the sake of having something to do on a Saturday night. For the sake of companionship. She wasn't uncomfortable alone. Sometimes she actually had to try and push herself out of those comfortable weekend nights when she would sit at home by the fire with a glass of wine and a good book. The sheer indulgent pleasure of it was alluring, and the time alone relaxed her as nothing else could. If she was going to go out with a man, she'd by now decided, she had to see the reason for it beforehand. Was that cold-eyed realism? She supposed it was, but what was wrong with that? What was wrong with not wanting to waste her time and energy? If a relationship didn't have the potential to go anywhere, why pursue it?

She chewed an orange slice and wondered whether there was potential with Jack. Instinctively, she thought there was. They were clearly attracted to each other. And so they would take the first step in trying to get to know each other, and see where it went.

She finished the orange, took another long drink of water, and dialed his number. He answered on the first ring.

"Hey," she said cheerfully. "Thanks for the message."

"Emily," he said, clearly pleased. "How are you? I'm glad you called."

"You are?" she said. "How come?"

"I just am."

"Come on," she said. "It's okay to tell me you like me." She laughed.

"I'll have to work up to it," he said.

"Listen," she said. "I have a great idea. Want to hear it?"

"I do."

"The idea is that I make this pasta dish I saw in a magazine, with scallops and mussels—it really sounds great—and I make that and you come over for dinner. Say, Saturday night?"

Her manner was light and breezy, but she was nervous. She very much wanted him to come, yet feared that he might have other plans.

Jack, meanwhile, felt a sudden sense of excitement. He'd been thinking about asking her to go out Saturday night but hadn't yet done it.

"Did you have plans?" she asked.

"I did have plans," he said. "My plans were to ask you to go out to dinner with me."

"Really?" she said, clearly pleased.

"Really."

"Well, sorry," she said. "Can't make it. I'm having dinner here with you."

CHAPTER 8

JACK FELT A sense of anticipation as he drove through the streets of Newton, following Beacon Street out to the Waban section, an affluent residential neighborhood. Emily lived in a modest-size brick Tudor-style home on a quiet street. He was unexpectedly nervous as he approached her front door.

Emily looked quite beautiful, he thought when he saw her. She wore black linen pants and a simple black wool sweater, and was clearly delighted to see him. She ushered him into the kitchen and poured him a glass of red wine. Then when he was seated comfortably by a living room fire, she quizzed him about his days as a hockey player.

"I actually saw you play in college several times," she said. "My boyfriend at the time—a guy named Jerry Wilkins, did you know him?"

"I knew who he was," Jack said. "He was a senior when I was a freshman."

"He was a real hockey nut, and he'd take me to games. I remember watching you because he would talk about how fabulous you were. He said you had the hardest shot in the league."

"I knew I liked Jerry," Jack said, smiling.

"I don't mean to be too personal—if I am crossing some imaginary line, let me know," she said as she refilled their wineglasses. "But isn't it something of an odd choice, after going through Harvard, to join the Boston Police Department? I mean, the opportunities available to you . . ."

Jack shrugged. "It seemed a logical choice to me. I liked the law and wanted to learn it, and I thought I'd practice but then decided I wanted to become a cop."

"I think you are a very complex man, Mr. Devlin," she said.

DURING THE COURSE of dinner, he managed to turn the conversation away from himself and on to Emily. She talked about her upbringing in New York, her school years at Wellesley, how she got into the law. Her father had been a partner at a major New York firm, and when she passed the bar exam, he hoped she would join his firm.

"I told him, 'Dad, you shouldn't have taken the Justice Department job and exposed me to the public sector.' He still thinks I might go and join the firm. He still has hope."

Jack sipped his wine. "You think you might at some point?"

She shook her head dismissively. "Never say never, but I can't imagine it, to be honest with you. It just doesn't appeal to me. I find some of the work interesting in a theoretical kind of way, but I can't imagine doing it day in and day out. What the precise terms of a contract are concerning an offshore offering of stock is not an issue that enthralls me."

Jack nodded. "I'm the same way," he said. "I find all the tort and financial issues interesting as kind of intellectual exercises, but the practicality never appealed to me. When I was done with contracts in school, I was done with contracts. It's not that I can't see the appeal of it. I can. I think there's an intricacy and a sense of vision and anticipation that you need to be a great corporate or contracts lawyer. But it's not for me."

"Yeah," Emily said as she went into the kitchen. Pouring rice into boiling water, she looked back at him through the open doorway. "So what is for you?" she asked.

Jack shrugged. "What I do," he replied.

She appeared surprised. "Forever?"

"Maybe not forever, but at least for now. For a while."

Emily returned, popped the cork, and poured more wine into both their glasses. She put the wine down on the coffee table and sat back on the sofa. Jack sat opposite her on an easy chair.

"So let me ask you about business," she said. "I've heard through the grapevine that you busted Moloney. That's pretty big."

Jack was surprised, though he knew he shouldn't have been. "Jeez, I thought that was pretty tightly held," he said.

"It is," she replied. "But the commissioner briefed us. He wanted to be on the record as letting us know so there couldn't ever be an accusation of a cover-up within the department, though he explained that you're going to try and deal with it internally for the moment."

"But?" Jack said.

"What do you mean?"

"Sounds like there's a but coming."

"Well, I mean, if he's committed a crime, I don't see how . . ." She hesitated, catching herself. "Look, I don't want to be judgmental, because I understand that it's important to avoid tainting the department, but if someone's committed a felony and you have evidence to that effect, then the best way to clean the place out is to make an example of him."

Her face flushed with color as she realized that Jack could take her comment quite personally. He chose not to, however.

"But that's another subject," she said. "More to the point, how'd you do it?"

"There'd been talk about him for a while, and some of it involved dealers. I had known a fair number of dealers myself from having been at Narcotics, so it was really a matter of finding someone who would be willing to work with me, and I had this one guy in a tough position."

She shook her head in admiration, then raised her glass in a toast. "Nice work," she said seriously.

"Thank you," he said. "I appreciate that."

She paused for a moment and studied him. "So what do you hear about the morphine deal?"

He appeared surprised. "Is that why I was invited here tonight?" he asked, a half smile on his face.

"Of course not," she said. "You were invited here because you are an interesting, attractive, somewhat mysterious man."

She stood up and reached her hand out to him. "Come on," she said, smiling. "Here." She handed him his glass. "Have some wine. I'm sorry. I can't help myself sometimes. This stuff is important to me. And this idea of not working together drives me absolutely nuts. It is just so . . . so absurd. The possibility that you would have information that could be useful, but it isn't shared with us just—"

She shut her eyes and shook her head.

"But look," she said, "I invited you here with no professional ulterior motives. I mean, being with you the other day and getting a glimpse into . . . into I don't know what. Into your life! I was touched by it, in a way. I think you are a fascinating man." She smiled.

"So who's your source?"

She laughed. "Just kidding, just kidding," she said.

He laughed as well.

She went to the window and leaned out so she had a view of the sky. "Oh, look," she said. "Full moon. Come on." She walked into the kitchen and he followed. In the back hallway she got a black fleece pullover and put it on.

"Put your jacket on and follow me," she said, and he complied.

They went out the back door and down a stairway, following a flagstone path to the back lawn and across to a cedar fence.

"Here's the tricky part," she said, turning sideways and sliding through a narrow opening in the fence. "This is the way I screen men," she said as he made his way through. "I bring them here, and if they can't squeeze through, it means they're too fat and I dump them."

They stood on a golf course, on the edge of a hole that was wide and long, a ribbon of fairway that wound up a slight hill, then down a gentle slope along a meandering stream. The moon painted a wide yellow pathway across the water, across the fairway to where they stood. In the cold night air the pale yellow light was crisp and bright enough so they could have hit shots and seen the ball land a hundred yards away. They sauntered side by side along the fairway.

"May I tell you something?" she said.

"Sure," he replied.

"The other day, at the church, I went to the cabstand, but then it began to pour so I ran inside the church to wait for it to let up. I sat down in the last row."

She glanced at him to see whether she was crossing some invisible line.

"And I looked at the booklet and saw that your father's name was not listed. And I wanted to tell you I happened to see that because I think, for you in a way, that's the heart of the matter, isn't it?"

He walked a few more steps without reacting, then nodded.

"And I thought about it when I was back at my office, and a very powerful sadness kind of overcame me. I thought about you back all those years ago, and tried to imagine this little boy, nine years old, and his entire universe centers on his parents and his family, and one day the father is at the heart of the biggest scandal in the city and then he's dead. And someone had told me that your mother had died when you were very young, is that right?"

"My mother died soon after I was born," Jack said.

"Oh, God."

"It's okay," he said. "I was so young that I'm not really sure it's made much difference in my life. It's not as though I had her for so many years and then lost her and felt her absence. I never had her, really, so I've never felt any real sense of loss in that way. Does that make sense?"

Emily nodded. "Unlike with your father," she said.

"My father was everything. He filled both parental roles, and I had him until I was nine years old, so that loss . . ."

She shook her head in sorrow. "And the idea that you were alone in this world," she said. "I hope you don't mind my inveterate candor, but I wanted to tell you that. How affected I was by that experience."

He smiled at her and looked into her eyes for a moment longer than he'd meant to.

"I kind of like your inveterate candor," he said, "so I'm not offended at all." He was pleased, in fact, that she held such an interest in him.

Emily shut her eyes for a long moment. When she opened them, they were wet with tears. "Do you miss him often?" she asked.

"Every day," he said without hesitation. "I feel no sense of closure with my dad at all. Just the opposite. He was there one day and gone the next, and I was stunned by it and didn't at all get it. And I have a retrospective sense that he was a profoundly unhappy man when he died, and that, for a son, is very painful to think about. It's very hard to think someone you loved that much suffered so terribly."

"What do you remember about your dad?" she asked. "Your most vivid memories?"

"That's easy," Jack said, smiling broadly. "Hour after hour after hour of him playing catch with me in the yard when he would come home from work. I remember him first in uniform, those dark blue, heavy, coarse wool uniforms. He wouldn't change, he'd just walk through the door and I'd race to hug him and beg him to play catch, and he'd grab his glove and we'd be out the door. And then, later, I remember him as a detective coming home in a baggy old suit, his necktie half undone, shirt wrinkled, and the same thing: He wouldn't change, he'd just head right outside and we'd throw the ball back and forth for forty-five minutes or an hour, sometimes longer. And he'd throw me pop-ups or grounders. And he never got tired of that, never complained. He smiled throughout and joked with me and would tell me when I made a nice catch or a strong throw and when I didn't.

"I can recall very vividly him standing there with his suit pants on, his shirt, his tie sort of hanging to one side, his jacket laid out on the grass nearby. I remember the fence to Mrs. Dacco's yard where the ball would go if I made a high throw. I remember my dad would have a cigarette, a Camel, usually, dangling from his lips while we played.

"And, finally, when we were done, we would walk slowly to the door and he'd put his arm around my shoulder, and what I remember about that is just being completely happy. Just really happy."

Happier, Jack thought, than he'd ever been.

THE NIGHT WAS cold as they made their way back to the house, then huddled before the radiant warmth of the fireplace.

"So how do you think it happened that he got in with that crowd?" she asked.

"I wouldn't—"

"If you're not comfortable," she said quickly, "then I don't want you to feel as though, you know . . ."

"No, I'm comfortable," he said. "It's just not something I talk about very often."

"But you think about him all the time," she said.

"I do. Yes."

"Because you loved him so, so much, and that shows through," she said.

He was surprised. "I wasn't aware that—"

"Are you kidding?" she said. "You guys had something special. I think that's so wonderful. I'm just sorry that, you know, he was involved in all that. It's just a goddamned shame."

She seemed angry all of a sudden, angry, perhaps, that this father had done that to his son. She was not the first person in his life to express a feeling of anger toward Jock Devlin. Nor, he suspected, would she be the last.

But Emily could see she had gone too far, and she retreated to the kitchen.

"So what happened after your father was gone?" she asked, upon returning from the kitchen.

He was momentarily confused.

"To you," she said.

"Oh, well, I went to live with my aunt, my mother's sister." He looked into the fireplace for a moment but said nothing more.

"And how was that?" she asked.

He shrugged. "That was fine. She was a nice person, but life kind of overwhelmed her. She was widowed. Her husband had worked for the MBTA and died of a heart attack on the job, so she got an annuity plus a Social Security survivor's benefit, so she had enough money to get by, but she was a fragile woman. She had three kids of her own. They weren't too thrilled when I moved in."

"You were lucky to have her," Emily said.

"I guess," Jack said, "though I never felt that way. She was reluctant to have me, but there was no alternative. There were no other surviving relatives, nowhere for me to go. I mean, a foster home, but she couldn't live with that on her conscience. The best thing was that they lived in Roslindale, and so my entire routine—school, sports teams, friends—all remained the same. None of that changed."

She frowned and cocked her head to the side. "So who were the adults who mattered in your life?" she asked. "It doesn't sound like you were close to your aunt."

"Not at all," he said. "It was a very reserved relationship. Very arm's length. But I had several people who were important to me. One was a hockey coach I had, Mr. Edwards. He was an older guy, his own kids were grown, but he loved to coach and he really kept an eye out for me. He always made sure I had a ride to games.

"And there was Tom Kennedy, of course," he continued. "He very quietly made sure I had whatever I needed in the way of equipment or money for travel to tournaments, that kind of thing."

"Tom Kennedy the deputy superintendent at BPD?" she asked.

He nodded. "He'd been my father's partner way back. And he really was more of a mentor to me than anyone else. As a matter of fact, when I was I think ten or eleven, he took the initiative to go and sign me up for the Dexter Hockey Camp in Brookline, and I spent the summer there. That's what turned me around in hockey, helped me turn it up a notch. I was a much better player at the end of that summer, and the following winter I was recruited for Catholic Memorial. In fact, he paid for that camp, which was not cheap. He paid for the whole thing. And I remember when one of the coaches there said my skates were too small and that it was time I had a really good pair, Tom drove me out to Needham Sporting Goods and bought me my first pair of Tacks."

"Tacks?"

"Made by CCM," Jack said. "The Cadillac of hockey skates then. He was very supportive of me. He knew people at Catholic Memorial and helped me get in there."

"So you lived with your aunt through high school?"

"Yes," he said. "But I was never there. I'd leave for school early in the morning, and then I'd have practice after school and I wouldn't get back to my aunt's until maybe six o'clock or later, and then I'd do my homework and go to bed."

"Was she a good cook?" she asked.

Jack shook his head. "She was a funny woman, Emily," he said. "I can't answer that because she never cooked."

Emily reacted with surprise. "What do you mean?"

"I mean she never cooked. She'd heat up frozen things like vegetables or macaroni and cheese or TV dinners. But I don't ever remember her actually cooking anything, like making a meat loaf or cooking pasta or anything like that. She never did it. A lot of the times I'd eat at school before going home. The Irish Christian Brothers would have their supper at five-thirty, and a lot of nights I'd get something there. Or I'd get pizza or a sub on the way to my aunt's."

"You're kidding," she said.

He shook his head. "No, I'm not kidding at all. Mr. Edwards gave me money, and Tom Kennedy, too. Both of them had a sense that my aunt wasn't exactly with it. And they knew I couldn't get a weekday afternoon job because of sports, so they made sure I had money for lunch and pizzas and stuff. To go to school dances. They were both very generous to me."

"And you stay in touch with both of them?" she asked.

"Tom and I have lunch every few months, yeah," Jack said. "Mr. Edwards is quite elderly now. He's in a nursing home in West Roxbury and I see him at holidays mostly."

"Amazing that now you work with Tom," she said.

"It's ironic," he replied, "because when I was in college he and I would get together regularly for lunch or whatever, and when I was beginning my senior year I told him I was thinking of joining the force and he told me I was nuts. He all but made me apply to law school. His whole argument was that I was opening doors by going to law school. Increasing opportunities. He was right."

"You know, whenever you mention where you lived you say 'my aunt's,' you never say 'home,' " Emily said. "I guess it didn't feel much like home."

"It was just a place to be, a place to stay," he said. "I knew I was there because I had no place else to go. It never felt like home to me in any way. I remember what feeling that was, the feeling of being with my dad, and staying at my aunt's was—I mean, Jesus, it was never anything like that.

"If you want to know what my relationship with my aunt was, on the day of her wake, when we were all at the funeral home, after the wake everybody went back to her apartment because her three kids were all there. This was my senior year in high school. The middle of winter. And after the wake I went to practice. My life went on. It was not that big a deal. We never connected in any way, so it was never a loss for me. I mean I was sad for her kids, but it had no real meaning for me."

"That's too bad," Emily said.

"I guess," Jack said. "It's okay, though."

"So life just sort of went along for you in high school? Smooth sailing."

Jack hesitated. "I wouldn't say that."

"Oh?"

He shifted his position. "I had some . . . ah . . . some difficult times."

She waited, but he said nothing more.

When he did not reply, she said gently: "I'd like to hear."

He looked away, then back at her. Why did she want to know? he wondered, but he knew as soon as he'd asked himself the question that he was being defensive. She wanted to know because she was interested in him. Because she cared about him.

"I got into some trouble," he said evenly. "When I was in school. I had a kind of violent temper, and every now and then I'd fly off the handle and get into a fight." He paused and looked down at the floor. "I was a very angry young man."

She nodded sympathetically. "Understandably," she said.

"And every once in a while my anger would get the better of me."

"Isn't that part of being a boy?" she asked.

"These were nasty."

She hesitated. "Nasty?"

Jack took a long, slow breath. "There was a kid named Hills," he said, "who played defense for Matignon High School. They were our main rivals. We'd win the state championship almost every year, but when we didn't win it, they did. Anyway, the games between us and Matignon were always very intense. Hills was a big kid, six-five, something like two twenty-five. Great skater and he hit very hard. So we were playing them this one night and he was really on me all through the game. Lot of trash-talk, taunting me. He wanted me to do something stupid so I'd get a penalty. You can't score from the penalty box. So I ignored him, but then in the third period we get caught up ice behind the play. Ref is down the other end following the play, nobody's looking, so he gives me a couple of slashes in the back of the knees. No padding. It hurts, but it can also do some damage. I ignore it, though, because the ref usually sees the person retaliating and I don't want to get a penalty.

"But on the next shift, there's this kid we have, a little guy, a freshman, very fast, who's on our fourth line. A great kid, very talented, extremely enthusiastic. But small. And he's out there and he's along the boards, his head down, and Hills comes in from behind and levels him. Totally illegal check with no purpose other than to hurt the kid. Which he did. The kid's knee buckled, went the wrong way, and bang, he was out for the rest of the season. Hills gets a two-minute penalty and skates to the box with a big smile on his face.

"Fortunately, we go on to win and the game ends, and we go into our locker room and they go into theirs and we shower and change and kind of hang around. So after a while I leave the locker room and I'm walking down this long hallway under the stands, and suddenly I come to the end of the hallway and there's this waiting area near the rear entrance to the rink. And there are a couple dozen people milling around. I don't pay any attention and I'm walking out, and all of a sudden I hear this low voice, kind of whispering, saying: 'Going to the hospital?'

"And I turned and there's Hills, standing right behind me. 'Going to the hospital to see your pal?' he says. And he's got this smile on his face as though he's happy this little kid has been hurt. And he's talking very quietly because he doesn't want any of the parents or other people around to hear him.

"I'm carrying my equipment bag and a couple of sticks, and I put them down and look up at him and say, also very quietly, 'Let's go right now.' And he starts to step back, but I don't let him. I throw a punch that just catches him on the edge of the jaw and kind of stuns him."

As Jack said this, Emily turned away and winced.

"And it got worse from there," Jack said. He did not tell her all of the details—did not tell her that he had caught Hills with eleven unanswered punches to the head, eleven exactly, for one of the parents there had counted and later provided testimony in court. The whole incident lasted no more than twenty or so seconds. Eleven punches in under twenty seconds, with Hills, staggered by the first blow, attempting in vain to cover up.

At the hearing in juvenile court, one of the parents testified that Jack Devlin had seemed as though he was "insane. We screamed at him to stop, but he wouldn't. And we saw him reposition himself so he could get his punches in at the boy's mouth."

By the time three of the fathers were able to drag Jack off, Hills was bleeding from the nose and mouth, with three of his front teeth shattered and his nose broken.

The last punch, one of the parents testified, sent Hills against the wall, falling heavily in an awkward position, the back of his head crashing into the cement. He'd slumped to the floor, unconscious.

"I thought the boy was dead," one of the parents said in court.

"How much worse?" Emily asked.

"He hit his head," Devlin said. "He fell unconscious and they took him to the hospital. In the fall, his skull was fractured."

Jack frowned and looked away when he saw the horror on Emily's face.

"My God," she whispered, putting her hand to her mouth. "You must have been terrified."

He considered that. "I wish I could say I had been," he said. "I wasn't."

She was surprised.

"I didn't care," he said.

Emily was shocked. "At all?"

He shook his head. "No," he said, regretfully.

"I don't get it."

"I just didn't care," he said. "About anything."

She shook her head slowly in amazement.

"They took me into juvenile court and had a hearing, and I was found guilty of criminal assault. They put me on probation and required that I go through a program of counseling with a therapist at a state clinic in Boston. Which I did."

"And what happened there?" she asked.

"I'd talk with the psychologist, and he would ask me questions and we'd discuss anger and I would say, 'Yes, I feel betrayed,' and 'Yes, I despise my father for abandoning me,' and 'No, I wouldn't hate him if he had had a heart attack and died or been struck by lightning, but he wasn't, he took his own life, and that's more than I can handle.' And on and on and around and around, never getting anywhere."

"And did it help?" she asked.

He hesitated. "Did it help really or did I pretend that it helped?"

"Which was it?" she asked.

"I pretended," he said. "I was kicked off the hockey team, of course, which at the time was the worst thing about it. And they said that if I went to every counseling session and stayed out of trouble, they would consider taking me back onto the team the following year. Fortunately, I was able to skate with some guys on a club team three times a week, and so I stayed in shape. And since the only thing that mattered to me was playing hockey, I did what I had to do. Every Wednesday I rode the subway to the Hurley Building and had a session with a therapist, and I stayed out of trouble. And in the fall they let me back on the team."

They stared at each other throughout a long pause in the conversation.

"But you hadn't changed?" she finally asked.

Jack shook his head no. "I was exactly the same angry young man. I couldn't fight anymore because I knew that would get me kicked off the team. So I looked for other ways to be defiant. And when my aunt told me one day that we would all be going to my father's grave on the anniversary of his death, I had one. We had gone every year since his death, me and Aunt Sheila. And I had just always gone along because she said I should. But this year—my senior year in high school—I said no. I said I'd had it with remembering him and he had done what he'd done and that was it.

"And so on the day of the anniversary she ordered me to go with her, and I refused, and she threatened to call the probation officer and the school principal."

He stopped talking and shrugged.

"And?"

"And I said that if she did that I would take off and no one would ever hear from me again. And my aunt Sheila knew I was capable of it and so she let it go."

Emily studied him carefully. "And you would have, wouldn't you?"

He squinted as though the light were too harsh, then slowly nodded.

SHE COULD NOT sleep. After they had talked until two, she had cleaned up the kitchen and gone to bed, but once there, she had tossed and turned and eventually, she lay on her back, hands folded behind her head, staring at the shadows on the ceiling. After a while she got out of bed, put on her robe and slippers, and went downstairs. There were embers in the fireplace, a bright red illumination from within the charcoal-gray ash.

She flicked on a reading lamp and picked up a magazine, but her mind was racing and she was unable to concentrate. She paced the room and walked to the sliding glass doors that led outside to the deck. Putting on her down parka, she unlocked the door and went outside. She stood on the deck, arms folded across her chest, gazing out over the golf course. The moon seemed huge, and it cast a wide swath of gold light on the fairway. She looked up, and as her eyes adjusted she was able to see the stars.

She could not understand her agitation, and then was struck with the thought that her agitation was excitement, because of Jack.

That's it! she realized. She felt a sense of possibility, of potential. She'd been mesmerized as Jack spoke about his upbringing. Her heart had ached when he'd told her about his father and mother, and she'd been stunned at his tale of violence.

I can help him! Emily thought. I can help him! And she felt a surge of triumph at the thought. She was exultant that she might be able to help ease the suffering to which he'd been subjected. She thought of the fullness of her own childhood, the opportunities that had been open to her as an adolescent and a young woman, in contrast to what Jack had struggled through, and she was humbled by the difference. Would she have been able to do what he had done under those circumstances?

She stood shivering against the cold, and yet she smiled, thinking that there was something here, something that could grow and develop. And part of the nurturing of it could be that she would help him. Because she had learned a great deal about Jack Devlin during the course of this evening: that he'd suffered, but more than that, he suffered still.

CHAPTER 9

JACK REMEMBERED THE day years earlier when his life had changed. He had walked along Batterymarch Street, checking the numbers on the buildings as he went. The noontime crush of office workers crowded the narrow sidewalk. People moved briskly in the chill of the gray November day, the dense, leaden clouds preventing the sun from warming the cold heart of Boston.

He had been a third-year law student at the time, a week shy of his twenty-fifth birthday. As he walked, Jack thought about the telephone call he'd gotten the previous week. The caller had identified himself as Thomas Fallon, a Boston lawyer.

"My father, Thomas Fallon, Sr., was a lawyer for many years as well," Fallon had said. "And when he died I took over the practice. There were many files accumulated by my father over the years, Mr. Devlin, and one of them involves you."

"In what way?" Jack had asked.

"I won't go into it over the phone, Mr. Devlin," the lawyer said, "except to say that the document has remained in the trust of this law firm and it is intended for you. If you come by, I will explain further."

"Can't you just tell me now?" Jack had asked, irritated.

"It must be done in person, Mr. Devlin," Fallon replied. "It is a document I have to pass along to you, for one thing. I would much prefer to do it in person."

Jack was annoyed. "At least tell me who the document is from," Jack asked.

Thomas Fallon paused for a moment before responding. "The document, Mr. Devlin, is from your father."

THOMAS FALLON, JR., was a small man with pale skin and thin lips. He was in his mid-forties, but appeared much older. His wispy, dark reddish hair had been carefully combed. He wore a starched white shirt with a navy-blue necktie with minute white polka dots. Fallon sat with excellent posture across a conference table in a glass-walled room of his law firm. A man with a precise, formal manner, he set a single file folder on the table in front of him.

"I had been in practice with my father and another associate for a number of years, Mr. Devlin," he said, "until my father died over a year ago. After he passed, I decided to hire an additional lawyer and to move our offices. We had been in cramped quarters on School Street, and I selected this space. When we moved, I undertook to review the contents of a safe that had been my father's. It was quite a large safe, a Mosler, which he had used for many, many years for filing and storage of various documents. I had never had occasion to look in it before because files common to firm business were contained in other file cabinets to which I had access.

"But after my father passed, and in concert with our move, I took it upon myself to review and organize the contents of the safe. As you might imagine, many of the documents it contained were quite old and out of date. Many were of little if any value to anyone. Some of the material was of a personal or financial nature. But most were things that could easily have been disposed of long, long ago.

"Among the items was an envelope," Fallon said. He opened the file folder and removed a large manila envelope with a string that affixed a wide flap.

"Here is how it was labeled," Fallon said, turning the envelope around and holding it so Jack could read it. There was a plain white label in the center of the envelope on which had been typed: *Re: John Devlin Sr. Correspondence to John Devlin Jr.: Transmit Nov. 3, 1984.*

"As you can see, Mr. Devlin, this was to have been transmitted to you on your twenty-first birthday," the lawyer said. "Unfortunately, that did not occur. I understand any distress you may feel as a result of this delay and I apologize. But I have undertaken to present it to you as soon as the error was discovered."

Jack began to reach for the envelope, but the lawyer drew it back. "When I found this, it meant nothing to me," Fallon said. "Opening it, I found a memorandum dictated by my father to the file."

Fallon unwound the string from around a round clasp on the body of the envelope. He opened the flap, reached inside, and withdrew a single sheet of yellowed paper.

"This is rather fragile, Mr. Devlin, so you won't mind if I handle it myself," Fallon said. "Permit me to read it to you. It is on the letterhead of the law firm. It reads:

"In the matter of John Devlin, Sr.—Mr. Devlin was referred to this office by Attorney John Burke, who is representing Mr. Devlin in a criminal matter. Mr. Devlin is a detective on the Boston Police Department and he has been charged with extortion. Mr. Devlin was referred here by Attorney Burke for a noncriminal matter. Mr. Devlin brought with him a handwritten letter, seven pages in length, that he asked me to place in safekeeping. He asked that the letter be given to his son, John Devlin, Jr., on his twenty-first birthday. John Devlin, Jr., is nine years old and will turn twenty-one on 3 November 1984.

"I asked Mr. Devlin why he wished to convey a letter to his son in this manner, and he said he wanted to make absolutely sure the letter reached him in the event that he were to be deceased prior to Devlin Jr.'s reaching the age of majority. I explained that it was not normally the type of professional service for which I was retained. He said he had chosen me on Attorney Burke's assurance that I was trustworthy.

"It was my impression that Mr. Devlin was under great stress, as could be expected of someone facing trial in federal court. In view of the circumstances, I have agreed to provide custody for the letter until 3 November 1984, at which time it is my intention to turn it over to John Devlin, Jr. (Social Security number 010-42-0391, current address: 17 Gurnsey Street, Roslindale, Mass.). The letter has been placed—unread by me—in the accompanying envelope and sealed."

Fallon set aside his father's memorandum. He was about to speak, then hesitated.

"What's the date on your father's memo to the file?" Jack asked.

"Yes, Mr. Devlin," Fallon said. "I was coming to that. The date my father wrote this—the date your father came to see him—was November eleventh, 1972."

Jack thought of his father, and for some reason remembered his father's hands. They were very large and thick, exceptionally powerful. He'd been a physically strong man, and he had inherited his father's physical characteristics. Jack thought of his father taking a pen in hand, sitting down with a sheet of paper and writing out a letter to his son, a letter intended for delivery twelve years later. His Dad had written this letter, brought it to the lawyer, gone home, and a mere three weeks later he was dead.

"As you can see," Fallon said, his voice soft, respectful, "this envelope remains sealed."

The lawyer removed an eight-and- a-half-by-eleven-inch envelope on which was written by hand: *To my son Jack on his twenty-first birthday.*

Fallon was saying something about the paper, lack of moisture in the safe, and the passage of years, but Jack did not hear him. He was aware, instead, that he held in his hands an envelope with his father's handwriting, a message to him. He was twenty-five years old and had been through a great deal in his life. But nothing had prepared him for this moment.

He felt a sudden surge of anxiety as his chest tightened, and he struggled to take a deep breath. He felt angry that he was being confronted with this after so many years. He'd struggled to deal with his father's death, and had somehow come to an accommodation with it. He had by no means fully accepted it, but he'd put it in the back of his mind, a terrible thing that happened so very long ago to a child.

"I'm sorry," Jack said, looking up, hearing the lawyer once more. "I didn't . . ."

Fallon rose from the table. "I assumed you would want some privacy," he said.

Jack sat very still and thought about this. "I'll take it with me," he finally said in a whisper.

"Fine," Fallon said. "I'm sorry, obviously, that this did not reach you—"

Jack waved away his apology. "I understand," he said. "Things get lost through the years and—"

"If you would be kind enough to sign this form acknowledging receipt of the document," Fallon said. He slid a single sheet of paper in front of Jack and handed him a pen. Jack scrawled his name, thanked Fallon, and, grasping the envelope in his right hand, left the office.

He walked down Batterymarch to Franklin and cut over to Arch Street. He entered the Arch Street chapel through the main door and walked all the way down to the left, to the far corner of the church.

There were only a half-dozen people in the place, no one any closer than fifty feet away from where Jack seated himself, in a wooden pew two rows from the front. Dozens of small votive candles on the edge of the altar sent shadows dancing up the cool stone walls.

Jack sat for a moment and gathered his thoughts. He took a deep breath, knelt down on the cushioned kneeler, made the Sign of the Cross, and bowed his head. Then he prayed, as he did every day, for his father and mother. He prayed for their souls to be blessed with grace and that they find comfort in eternity. And he prayed now for wisdom and understanding and for strength.

He sat back in the pew, holding the envelope in both hands, looking down at what was written on the label. *To my son Jack on his twenty-first birthday.*

The writing, in blue ink, was in a somewhat undisciplined, looping style. The letters were too large, lacking in sophistication. Jack peeled away a small piece of the envelope flap from the corner. It was easier than he'd expected, since the glue had dried over the years and lost its strength. Making a small hole, he slipped a finger in and carefully ran it along the envelope, tearing open one end, then bowed the envelope so he could see inside. There was a surprisingly thick width of paper, which he removed. The paper was white, with thin blue lines. It was dry, and some of the sheets flaked at the bottom.

He set the sheets on his lap and began reading.

My dear son, Jack,

Let me begin by saying to you on your twenty-first birthday that I love you very much, far more than probably you can imagine as a young man.

It is my hope, and I certainly expect, that you will never read this letter, because I expect to live a nice long life. But if anything does happen, I want you to know, in my own words, what went on. That's important to me, especially now.

As I sit here very, very early in the morning, a few minutes before four A.M., I have just come back from your bedroom where I pushed the hair off your forehead and felt your sweaty neck under the covers. I leaned over and kissed your forehead and then I sat down on the edge of your bed and gathered you into my arms and I felt so much love for you.

And now I am at the kitchen table and I made a pot of coffee and I am gathering my thoughts as best as I can so that you will know the truth, because to me at this point that is more important than anything, and I include in that the trial, which is all anybody talks about to me anymore.

The honor that I once had is now gone.

To me, this is the worst part about the whole thing because we have our honor and what else do we have? Money does not matter in the end except as it relates to being able to take care of the basics for your family. Money does not matter, believe me when I tell you this. Don't do anything for money alone. If you do something you love to do and there is money, fine. But otherwise, no.

So how did it come to this? is what you probably most want to know. What was really going on. But it is important to me that you know everything.

When I first went on the job, it was very different from the way it is now. It was a much simpler time. That's all changed. Now things are filled with angles. But when I started out, I went on the job because it appealed to me and I thought I would be good at it and it was a place where you could get some security and be sure there would be a job there until retirement.

I started out pounding a beat in Roslindale Square, as you know, and I enjoyed that very much, with the people there, from Henry Goon, the Chinaman, to the colored woman at Lodgen's, to Sam the Jewish butcher, to all of them. If you had gone up and down Corinth or Wash or Centre or Belgrade, whatever, to Boschetto's, anyplace, and asked, they would have told you the same thing: Jock plays it straight. Jock watches out for you whether you're a Jew or colored or Italian or whatever you are or may be. Jock watches out, keeps an eye out. And it's true.

From the very beginning there were gifts at Christmastime. Considerations from the merchants. They appreciated what you did and so there may have been a bottle from Henry Goon or two pies from Mrs. Cunningham and whatnot. There were gifts that came my way, and to not accept them from people who were truly grateful to have a cop who did the right thing for them would have been the height of what was rude and wrong.

Everyone did this. It was the rule, not the exception. I have had many discussions with my lawyer preparing for trial and he has talked incessantly about the police culture, and one of the points he will try to make to the jury is that this has been a way of life for many, many years, and it has. Under the federal law, when you receive something from someone it is called a gratuity. As though it was a tip of some kind. But to me these have always been an expression of gratitude and I have never ever had any trouble with my conscience or otherwise accepting these things. Would anyone? I don't think so, not anyone reasonable.

The problem started when I made detective, not right away but soon after. When you make detective it is an entirely different ball game, obviously, from having a beat, a defined small area. As a detective you have a sector of the city, and mine included, as you know by now, the Fenway and a piece of the Back Bay. Not starting out, because I started in East Boston, but that only lasted a couple of years and soon enough I was in the Fenway and Back Bay, and those areas are filled with bars *and nightclubs and the lion's share of the work involves those places.*

These were places where all of the worst things about a city can be seen, which includes prostitution, dope, weapons, etc. Wiseguys tend to hang at certain places, planning their jobs, be they housebreaks, jewelry, hijackings of trucks with goods, whatever. Also, there are prostitutes run out of certain joints or queers concentrated in a place or dope peddled under a certain bar, whether it be pot or whatever it is.

And so as a detective you are in constant contact with the proprietors of these places, keeping an eye out for whatever it is, and in many cases, I would say most cases, the owner is doing a decent job at running a clean place. Some will have prostitution or whatever but in most joints if there is something going on, it is under the owner's nose but not the owner actually doing it. It may just be a handful of wiseguys hang at a particular place and do their business there but have no connection with the owner other than that they know him.

A good detective knows what's happening where. A good detective will protect a bar owner from the bad apples. Should a guy have his place shut down because you have some punks selling five dollar bags out of the back, by the pinball machines? Or should a guy be closed because some guy gets ten dollars of action in the booth? Or lose a license because someone divides up the loot from a hotel job at the Copley Plaza? No.

And so, many of these men who own such establishments are grateful to detectives, and as with a beat, they offer presents at Christmas. But these presents aren't pies or a fifth. These presents are cash. It started out around twenty-five, fifty bucks, but then over time it would become a hundred and then more.

Why did I accept this money? Because everyone else did it. All the detectives in my area. Can you understand this: To not take it would have been a much, much bigger deal than taking it. It would have meant you were an outcast, disliked by all. And these club owners were genuinely grateful for what we had done for them. They would call, and whenever necessary we would weed out a bad element.

But as time went by I began to feel uneasy about this. There would be money handed to me in an envelope by another detective from a bar owner who I had never met in my life, never mind helped out in any way. It got to a point where it was almost as though there was a billing system and each owner would be told to pay so much at Christmas, and they would do that and the money would be distributed to each man in the area. And then someone came up with the idea of doing the same thing in summer for summer vacation. It all became clear to me one night when I'm down on Boylston out behind Fenway Park and there's a ball game and the owner of a joint maybe had a couple of belts in him and he starts screamin' at me about the theavin' cops and whatnot and I calm him down and it's very clear that he has no desire to pay this money whatsoever and is doing it because he believes if he doesn't do it he's got problems with the BPD.

That caused me to do some thinking about the situation, really to think it through, for the first time ever. Until then I had just gone along like everyone else and it had started small and built and it was just the way things were done.

And by this point it was no longer personal, no longer Boschetto himself handing me a fifth two days before Christmas. It was you collect an envelope from this guy on Landsdowne and this guy on Boylston and you distribute the contents to the other detectives and it was a system. And it was all of a sudden real money—two hundred, three hundred per man from each of a half dozen or more bar owners—and all of *a sudden you're getting twelve hundred, fifteen hundred bucks at Christmas and then maybe another eight hundred in the summer.*

I'm sorry to say, this went on for years. But then one day I woke up and wanted out. I just decided one day that it wasn't right and I couldn't do it anymore. And I went to a couple of guys and told them, "Cut me out from now on," and they were very concerned and not at all comfortable with that. But they knew me and they knew there was no agenda here, that my mouth was closed, and so I took myself out of it. That was eight months before the FBI showed up.

Probably you know the whole story by now, from reading the newspaper files or hearing from people. I'm sure someone told you that that was the day when I happened to be going to this joint to interview the owner, Fahey, about a stabbing the Saturday night before. It was the Monday before Christmas, and one of the guys grabs me before I go over and asks if I'll bring an envelope back. The snow was coming down and the driving was lousy and he didn't want to have to go out and I was going anyway. And I was not at all comfortable but I thought, what the hell, it's not a big deal.

And so I interview the guy and he gives me the envelope and I stuff it in the pocket of my raincoat, a London Fog, and I walk outside and there's three FBI agents and they grab me and search me and cuff me and take me to their office and begin questioning me and that was the beginning of the end. From that day until this, and it's been eleven months now, it hasn't let up. Hardly a day goes by that I'm not in the newspaper. For months my picture was on TV every night.

The newspapers talked about the systemic corruption and the massive FBI investigation and there were rumors that the entire command staff would be indicted, brought down, but none of that came true of course, for one simple reason: I wouldn't open my mouth. I couldn't do it. Too many of these guys, the detectives and patrolmen, were my friends. What was I going to do, sit down and tell some little asshole from Harvard Law School that "yeah, they're all crooked 'cause they took a turkey at Christmas"? They were insufferable, relentless. It was as though there was evil incarnate on the force and I was the symbol of it. And they offered me every conceivable deal in the book, all amounting to "rat on your friends and you walk."

Son, I cannot do it. These were my friends. These were people I grew up with, had worked with, been in jams with. Good men who had gone along with the system. And I was going to be the one to ruin them? Cause them to be indicted and put on trial and disgraced?

I can't do it. I just cannot.

And so I won't.

But that is not to say that these are all good men, because they are not. I don't know about anyone beyond my small group of nine detectives, nine men I know for certain have been receiving money. And I would put seven of them in the same category as myself.

And I would not blame you if you were skeptical of your dad saying, "Well, yeah, I used to take the envelopes but I don't anymore, son, because I've seen the light." I don't blame you a bit. That's why I'm giving you two names of guys who you can go and talk with privately. Ask them about me. Ask them whether I stopped taking the dough. They know. The two men are: Ray Murphy, who lives on Joyce Kilmer Road in West Roxbury, a brown house on the left toward the end; and Eddie Quinlan, who also lives in West Roxbury, up on Oriole Street.

I don't know what you'll end up doing, and maybe you'll run as far from the BPD as you can go, and probably you'll go to medical school because you've been so goddamned smart since you were a little kid, reading at age four and whatnot.

But I have a funny feeling that possibly you might end up a cop. Maybe it's in the blood, I don't know. And if you are, I know you'll be a good one.

But I'm off track here.

All that matters now to me is you and your future. My lawyer figures I'll get three years and have to serve one. Being a cop in prison, a nasty federal place, will not be pleasant. But I can handle it. I can handle anything because I know that my ultimate responsibility is to be there for you, and I will. I will serve my time and then that will be that and I'll get some kind of job and we'll have a grand life together.

The worst thing about this to me is that you will now grow up known by some as not just Jackie Devlin, but as Jackie Devlin son of Jock Devlin, the crooked cop, the cop who went to prison. I am sorry for that. But I will make it up to you.

If you are reading this, then that means I am gone. How strange this is to write this. If you ever read this I want you to know that your father is out there somewhere and that he loves you with all his heart.

Dad

Jack sat in the stillness of the Arch Street chapel. He held the letter in both his hands, staring down at the pages yet not seeing anything, not seeing the paper or the writing, but focusing instead on an image in his head of his father's face, a beefy, smiling face. A joyful face.

He did not move for several moments. While he felt a profound sense of sadness, Jack also felt a sense of confusion, for the tone of the letter was not that of a man who expected that his life would soon end.

Jack Devlin sat back in the pew and tried to relax his shoulders, hunched and tense from reading the letter. He closed his eyes and sought to absorb what he'd read, sought to order it in his mind. He leaned forward in the pew and placed his forehead on the bench in front of him. He began quietly to cry, for at that moment he felt as acute a sense of abandonment as he had ever felt in his life. He cried and cried and did not care about the other churchgoers who looked his way. He cried and he cried, for although he had come to hate his father, he also loved him and he missed him still.

And he fell to his knees and prayed, asking God to help him gain the strength to stop hating this man who had left him alone so very long ago.

CHAPTER 10

JACK THOUGHT BACK to his final year of law school and could recall with a remarkable sense of clarity how acutely he had needed to
find the truth. Eight years had passed since then, but he remembered
it as though it had been eight days ago. All through the spring of that
year he'd thought about what to do. He did little school work and
found himself instead sitting alone with his father's letter, reading it
over and over again. He read it to understand, to hear the rhythm of
his father's voice.

One night he woke shortly before four A.M., panicked that something had happened to the letter. He scrambled from his bed and
opened the top drawer of his dresser. It was there, right where he always kept it. But the fear of losing it spurred him to action. He
quickly dressed in jeans and sneakers, put the letter in a thick manila
envelope, and left his apartment building. At the time, he lived in
graduate student housing, subsidized by the university. His apartment was in a building on the edge of the law school campus, a few
blocks from Harvard Square. He hurried out of the building and followed Mass Ave. down into the square to an all-night copy place. He
did not want anyone else handling the letter, so he asked the clerk if
he could make a copy himself, and the clerk was happy to oblige. He
made a copy and placed both the original and the copy in the manila
envelope. He carried it down the block with him to a diner, where
he got a cup of coffee to go. He walked down Boylston Street, out
of the square, down to the Charles River, crossing over the bridge

toward the stadium and the Business School. He walked through the chilly early morning darkness, following a bend in the river for about a mile, and sat down on a park bench facing eastward. Soon enough the sky in the east went from black to deep purple. Then, very quickly, it seemed to Jack, there were streaks of fiery orange light, and then the unmistakable yellowish hues that announced the rising of the sun over the Atlantic Ocean. Jack sat back on the bench, holding the letters on his lap, watching as the light brightened the sky and bounced off the tall glass buildings of downtown Boston.

He smiled. The sky was clear, and he could see it was going to be a beautiful spring day. A day of renewal.

After the sun had risen, he crossed the river and walked slowly back toward Harvard Square, on the Cambridge side. Back in the square, he bought the *New York Times* and read it over coffee and a muffin.

At nine A.M. he was standing at the front door of the Cambridge Trust Company. At nine-fifteen, after filling out several forms, he placed the copy of the letter in a safe-deposit box. He considered putting the original into the box, but he wanted it nearby, so he could touch the pages his father had touched.

In the days ahead he thought very carefully about his future path. The federal court clerkship that had once seemed so alluring held little appeal for him now. Joining a major firm was out of the question, and the thought of becoming a prosecutor held only marginal appeal.

Initially, the notion of becoming a police officer seemed absurd. It was not what graduates of the Harvard Law School did. For it would invite the view that one was an oddball, bring accusations that one had wasted one's legal training.

Jack found himself in the school chapel praying for guidance. He was at first wildly uncomfortable with the idea. It seemed crazy, yet he kept coming back to it. He would go for long runs—sometimes late at night, sometimes early in the morning. He would loop down around the river, deep into Boston, and then back around to Harvard Square. Or he would go off into North Cambridge, out toward Arlington. He enjoyed these jaunts, believed the vigorous runs, his arms pumping, legs going, helped clear his mind.

It was a singular time in the life of a man who did not socialize much, who preferred to be by himself; to think, to reflect.

It was not a sudden thing, but a gradual change, an evolution that by graduation day brought him to the point where he knew he had to embark upon a search for the truth. Who had his father been? What sort of man had he really been? As he came to this understanding of himself—for it was a recognition of the needs within him—he realized that it would take time. It would require great patience. But he accepted that. As the Chinese said, if it took one, ten, or a thousand years, that was okay. He saw it not as a permanent thing, but as something he would do for a portion of his career. The only course could be a patient search for the truth. A search to understand. And if he was really to understand his father, to know who his father was and what he was about, then Jack Devlin knew that, in certain respects, he had to become his father.

And so it was, on the day after he received his J.D. degree from Harvard, that Jack arrived at the headquarters of the Boston Police Department and filled out an application to join the class entering the academy later that month.

THE RECORDS OF the Boston Police Department indicated that Edward Quinlan had retired as a patrolman in 1989 and died in 1990. Raymond Murphy had retired in 1992 and, according to department records, still lived on Joyce Kilmer Road.

Jack drove out to West Roxbury as a chilly November mist fell over Boston. He rode out the VFW Parkway to West Roxbury and followed Baker Street to Joyce Kilmer Road. Murphy's house was down toward the end, a small, brown clapboard structure with a well-kept yard.

When Jack arrived, it was late afternoon, not long before the rapid November descent of darkness on the city. He pulled up to the house and saw a man working on a picket fence in the side yard.

"I'm looking for Ray Murphy," he said as he approached the man.

The man stopped his work and looked Jack up and down. "You a cop?" he asked.

Jack nodded.

"I always believed I could spot a plainclothes man anywhere," he said.

Jack smiled. "You've got a good eye," he said. "I'm Jack Devlin. Jock's son."

"Jesus Christ," Ray Murphy said softly as he received this news. He stood motionless and stared at Jack. His eyes blinked several times as though he was trying to refocus. He looked hard at Jack, studying him, not shifting his eyes, not looking away. Jack stood unmoving.

Ray Murphy nodded slightly. "You look like him in a certain way," he said. "There's a resemblance."

With that pronouncement, Ray Murphy abruptly took a couple of steps toward his house, away from Jack. He turned to the side, glancing back over his shoulder at Jack.

"I've got to get inside now," he said.

"I'd like to talk with you if you have a minute," Jack said.

Murphy glanced down at his watch. "Jesus," he said, "I'm running behind. Another time." He moved toward the back door of the house, and Jack quickly followed.

"When?" Jack asked.

"Give me a call sometime," Murphy said. "Maybe, I don't know . . ."

Jack followed him up the back steps. "Look, you're not behind, you're not going anywhere, and I don't want to have to bother you again," he said. "Why don't we spend a few minutes talking now, and then it's over with and you don't have to do it again."

Ray Murphy was now visibly agitated. "Who the fuck are you to tell me I'm not behind schedule when I say I am?" he demanded. "Who are you to tell me what to do?"

"We need to talk," Jack said. "It's important."

Ray Murphy shook his head.

When he spoke, Jack's voice was filled with passion and intensity. "Look, you know why I want to talk to you. You know how important this is to me. He was my father. I need to know some things. Please."

Ray Murphy was not an inherently compassionate man. He knew that he should not speak with Jack Devlin, yet he could not help himself. In a way, he'd been wanting to talk with him for many, many years. He felt it was his duty.

Murphy said nothing. He went inside, and Jack followed.

The house was stuffy. The smell of stale cigarette smoke hung in the air. Ray Murphy went to the kitchen sink and washed his hands. He poured a shot of V.O. and drank it. He poured another shot of V.O. and set it down on the kitchen table, next to an ashtray with a picture of one of the Boston Bruins.

Ray Murphy sat down at the table. His eyes were heavy and sad. He was fleshy around the jaw and neck, and there was two or three days' stubble on his face.

"My wife's dead two years now," he said, shrugging. "I get by."

Jack looked at him carefully. Ray Murphy had the look of a bitter man. His face was set in a permanent scowl. He picked up the shot of V.O., killed it, then lit an unfiltered Pall Mall. He exhaled slowly, letting the smoke drift into the air so it formed a bluish cloud over the kitchen table. There were many faces to the city of Boston, Jack thought. And this was one of the classics: a bitter, angry man alone with his drink.

"You?" Murphy asked, holding the shot glass.

"No, thanks," Jack said.

"So?" Murphy asked.

"So, I was hoping you could tell me some things," Jack said. "Help clear some things up for me."

Murphy shrugged dismissively. He flicked an ash onto the face of the Bruin.

"What's to clear up?" he said. "You must know the story. How could you not? He walks out of that place on Boylston, what was it called? I don't remember. Anyways, he walks out of the joint and the feds are there and they grab him and he's got the cash on him and the owner says, 'Yeah, he was holding me up.' And that was that. Airtight. They had him. Do you follow? They had him. That was it."

"And the money was for him?" Jack asked. "Him alone?"

"Ahh, you know, Jesus, there was speculation. The papers day after day, I mean the speculation was endless, but that's what happens in those situations. The feds have a thing about us. Probably to this day. They think we're all a bunch of thievin' micks. So here they had a guy and he's got the cash and so they say, 'Hey, he's carryin' for so-and-so and so-and-so and so-and-so.' They would have jammed the whole force if they could. That's how they are."

Jack watched as Ray Murphy went to the counter and poured another shot of V.O. He took it all down at once and banged the shot glass on the counter.

"Shit burns," he muttered.

"But was it his?" Jack asked again.

"What does it matter now?" Ray Murphy asked.

"It doesn't," Jack said. "Not to anyone but me. To me it matters a lot." To me, he thought, it's everything.

Ray Murphy scowled and looked away, shaking his head. "I've watched you over the years," he said. "I've been aware of you but I don't really get you. What are you up to? You a plant or legit or what's up with you?"

"What does that matter?" Jack asked.

Ray Murphy took this in. "I suppose," he said.

"So," Jack said, "was it his?"

Ray Murphy shook his head. "No. It was not his. It was everybody else's but."

Jack shut his eyes for a moment as he processed this information. "Are you sure?" he asked.

This was clearly offensive to Ray Murphy. His face and neck reddened. "Am I *sure*?" he asked, barking out the word *sure*. "Am I sure? I knew what was happening, if you follow me. I knew what was going on. I'm sure, yeah."

Ray Murphy paced across the kitchen, upset now, agitated. "You want to know about your old man? Okay, I'll tell you about him. Jock Devlin. I'll tell you about Jock.

"Was Jock bad? No. Was Jock weak? Jock was weak. I was weak. We all were. We went along because we went along and because they treated us like shit anyway. And what was a few bucks here or there? They were grateful, most of them. We did the work and we did it well.

"See, we started out small. You get a nice Christmas gift from a guy maybe you did a favor for or kept an eye on his place or whatnot. And then time goes by and you get more of these, and in time it becomes a part of the thing. It's expected. It's how it works. And then all of a sudden you're a detective and you're in with guys who know what's going on in the town. I mean they know. They know everything. And they're smart and they're careful and all of a sudden you have a chance to have a piece of the action, and they take you into their confidence and build you up and you feel good because you belong.

"That's what the job's about, in a way. Belonging. You belong to something big, something important." Murphy lit a Pall Mall. "So you belong and you feel good and it's not a problem because you're in with good guys who have experience and they're fucking good detectives and everything's okay.

"And then some time passes. And then some more time passes. And what happens? You begin to feel the grind, feel the wear. It's fuckin' stressful. All the time wondering, being careful. You pick up this, and I'll get that and deliver it, and you're always carrying an envelope. It's the most fucking dangerous thing in the world for a cop. An envelope."

Ray Murphy was slurring a word now and again.

"So we would go along and every now and then someone would maybe say something about getting out," Murphy continued. "Every now and then it would come up, but it was not a common thing and no one ever did it or came close. It was a closed circle. Very tight."

Ray Murphy poured himself another shot and threw it back hard.

"And then he went and fucked it all up. Your father said he wanted out. And it ruined everything."

Ray Murphy hung his head and rubbed his eyes with his right hand. When he finally looked up, Jack could see there were tears in his eyes.

"He fucked it up and nothing was ever the same again," he said. He turned his head and stared off toward the window that overlooked the side yard. Darkness had fallen. A cold wind rattled the storm door.

A long time passed, a minute or more, before anyone spoke again.

"I'm sorry," Jack said quietly. "I don't understand."

"He was not a bad man, but he was a weak man, like the rest of us," Ray Murphy said. "Or so we thought. But once he decided he wanted out, that was that. Everyone talked to him, see, because to have a defector was like having a traitor. It was like one of us saying you're wrong and bad, and there was always the thought out there that, hey, what the fuck, is he talkin' about us to anyone or what?"

Murphy stared at Jack. "You follow me?" he asked.

Jack nodded. "So other guys went to him and tried to persuade him to keep at it. But he wouldn't."

Murphy shook his head emphatically. "He wouldn't. Wouldn't budge." Murphy shrugged. "And that was his undoing."

Abruptly, Murphy went to the door and flung it open. "That's it," he said. "I've done my part. I've paid my debt. Don't come back."

Jack was surprised. "I don't understand," he said. "I wanted to—"

"No more," Murphy said. "I've said enough. Too much. Years ago we decided . . ."

But he did not finish the sentence.

"Who's we?" Jack asked.

But Ray Murphy did not answer.

CHAPTER 11

JACK AND DEL RIO walked up to the third-floor corner office of Thomas M. Sheehy, the deputy commissioner of the Boston Police Department. Sheehy was a huge man, six feet five inches tall, over 260 pounds. He greeted the two detectives in a businesslike manner and sat down behind his desk.

"Did you assault Detective Moloney?" Sheehy asked Jack. Devlin's hair had fallen forward over the right side of his face. He slowly brushed it back, running his right hand through it, back over his ear and down to the back of his neck. Jack was dressed in khaki pants and an old black turtleneck sweater. His face turned pink and his jaw tightened. The scar by his right eye grew purplish. He frowned, and when he did, the darkness of his deeply set eyes made him appear angry.

When Jack did not answer right away, Sheehy grew impatient. "Did you?" he demanded.

"I had to deal with him," Jack replied.

"Did you assault him?" Sheehy asked. "It's a simple enough question. Yes or no, did you assault Detective Moloney?"

"Moloney's an asshole, Tom, you know that," Del Rio said.

Sheehy turned to Del Rio. "Whether Moloney is an asshole is not the issue. The issue is whether one officer on the Boston Police Department assaulted another."

"I assaulted Moloney, yes," Jack said.

"Very professional," Sheehy said sarcastically. "Very professional, indeed. Because now Moloney's lawyer can say, 'Hey, they had a per-sonal beef and one guy went after another and there was a plant and whatnot.' And if the tape is not admissible—you listening carefully, counselor?—if the tape is not admissible, then Moloney says, 'Hey, I took some dough off the kid because that's all we found. Of course I had cash in my pocket, because we were headed downtown to do a report and turn in the money, as we always do when we hit some-body like that.' And that leaves us in a funny position. No tape ad-missible, then no case, and no case, we got egg all over our kissers, don't we?"

"It was deliberate provocation by Moloney," Del Rio said. "No question."

"Look, Detective Devlin, let me be as clear as I can be," Sheehy said. "I find the whole matter distasteful. If Moloney and Curran did what is alleged, then I am disappointed in them. But I am also dis-turbed that one officer assaults another; that a sting of two officers is mounted by another officer and the brass is not made aware of it—"

Jack cut in. "That's why I asked Del Rio to come. So the brass would not only be informed, but present, as well."

"Well, this brass wasn't informed, and neither was anybody else," Sheehy said, his huge face turning red with anger. "And I don't like it when somebody fucks with my department. I know the mayor likes this idea; I know the commissioner likes this idea. But I don't. Noth-ing personal, I just don't like certain of my men snooping around trying to catch others of my men with their dicks in their zippers.

"Because morale is everything," Sheehy continued. "And you have someone snooping around from within the ranks, that's bad news. Sends the wrong signal. 'Go out and risk your life for us tonight, but, oh, by the way, empty your pockets and up against the wall, motherfucker.'"

Sheehy glared at Devlin, who said nothing.

Sheehy rose from his chair, hauling his huge frame to its full height and walking to the window of his office. He took a deep breath and exhaled as he shook his head.

"Moloney was a moron," he said. "Demented. Insane." He glanced across the room at the two detectives. "But the problem is, if you think you know him from that incident, then you don't know him, because as is the case in many situations, things are a little more complex than they might originally appear to be. Look, did he fuck up?" Sheehy laughed in a mocking way. "Oh, he fucked up. No question. But you know, here's a guy, last year laid down on a table and let them slice him open to take out one of his kidneys and put it in his sister. His baby sister, okay? I mean, let's get fucking real here, guys."

Sheehy stalked across the room toward his desk. His face had reddened again. "And now she's in bad shape," Sheehy said. "Looks like she won't make it."

Sheehy stood behind his desk, hands on his hips, looking down at the floor. Suddenly, he looked up.

"What's served by going to the mat on this?" he asked. "What do we accomplish? Okay, let's look at it. We get Moloney and Curran out the door. Forced retirement. Maybe they lose their pension, maybe not, but probably they do. So they're gone, right? And if they go, maybe they sue us, probably they do, and the whole thing gets in the papers and the fucking scum at the papers couldn't be happier, and so they'll have the articles every day for about a year. By the time they're through with us, there won't be any reason to believe there is now or ever has been an honest cop in the city. You know that to be true. It's indisputable. And so the question I'm raising—asking you to consider—is whether it's worth it?"

Sheehy walked to the window and stared outside for a long time. Neither Devlin nor Del Rio spoke.

"You perfect, Jack?" Sheehy finally asked. Devlin did not respond. "I'm asking you, Jack, you perfect?"

Devlin shook his head no.

Sheehy nodded. "You ever make any mistakes? You ever fuck up? Ask to be forgiven?"

Sheehy was clearly agitated. He stalked back to the window, folding his arms across his chest. There was silence in the room for a minute, perhaps longer. When Sheehy spoke again, his voice had lost its edge. He spoke softly, almost plaintively.

"People make mistakes, Jack," he said. "I would think you would understand that. People make mistakes, and then they get another chance and sometimes they do something with that second chance. Sometimes they blow it. But the ones who don't, now, that's something good. So you tell me, Jack, do we give Moloney a second chance? What do we do? You tell me. Give him a chance or ruin his life?"

"SO YOU GETTING on with the commish okay?" Deputy Superintendent Thomas Kennedy asked.

"No problems when I see him," Jack replied, "though that's rare. It's funny, I'm really off doing what I'm doing, and there isn't all that much supervision. He's really given me a free hand."

Jack sipped his Coke and regarded Kennedy. "I get the sense you're not all that high on him these days," he said.

Kennedy frowned. He put his fork down and took up his napkin, wiping his mouth. He paused to reflect for a moment.

"It's not him, per se," Kennedy said thoughtfully. "It's the structure. I'm not comfortable with a civilian running the show. I think it works better when someone other than a political appointee is in charge of a force of two thousand uniformed personnel. And don't give me the military analogy. That's war, and you don't want generals running the Pentagon because then they're making policy, deciding whether to bomb Bosnia.

"Fighting urban crime is an ongoing operation. It's not a question of whether to take it on but how to take it on, and it's just so obvious to me, Johnny, that the people best qualified to run that are the people who know it from the street level up. The people who've worked their way up through the ranks."

Jack smiled. This was a familiar refrain from Kennedy.

Kennedy laughed. "I know, I know," he said. "You've heard it before."

Jack and Kennedy tried to meet for lunch every other month or so, a ritual that had begun when Jack entered the academy. Kennedy had been his father's partner when the men were detectives, and now he'd risen through the ranks to become the second highest uniformed officer on the force.

"It's a reasonable point of view," Jack said. "Entirely reasonable. But I've found the commissioner to be very smart and a good listener. That's a good combination, where he sits."

"No question he's intelligent, but it is frustrating to be talking to someone about some sort of community policing plan and know you're talking to someone who has never felt what it's like to do this work at the most basic level. Who's never responded to a domestic dispute call."

Kennedy's eyes widened. "Imagine that, Jackie," he said, the astonishment clear on his face. "Never once had to go into an apartment in some shitty area and sort it out, figure out who's doing what to whom and how to try and stop it, or at least tone it down."

Kennedy shook his head, part amazement and part disapproval. "That makes no sense to me. None. The idea that the most basic elements of police work are things he's only heard or read about but never done. Never once! It's lunacy.

"Anyway, that's my only frustration," Kennedy continued. "On a day-to-day basis I have no real difficulty with him. But what I think about him, you've heard before, too many damn times, anyway. I'm more interested in how you're doing. Things okay so far?"

"Actually, there's something I wanted to ask you," Jack said. "I know you've wanted to leave it to the commissioner, but I have a judgment question here and I'm not sure someone who's a civilian can answer it adequately."

"Don't sell him short, Jackie. Cop or no, he's sharp, as you yourself just pointed out."

"I'm not selling him short, I just want your opinion," Jack said. "You're aware of the sting on Moloney and Curran, and you're aware that we have a disciplinary hearing coming up in a few days. The issue in my mind is how hard to push on this. Curran doesn't bother me. I think he's harmless, basically. I think he's influenced by the strongest-willed person around.

"For me," he continued, "Moloney's the issue. Basically, it's a very straightforward case. Moloney and Curran find a dealer who's particularly vulnerable in terms of the amount of time he'll do if he's brought in, and they hit him for cash. It's not the first time they've done it, but I can't honestly say it's the hundredth, either. I don't know."

"Dealers, Jackie, Jesus," Kennedy said, an edge to his voice. Jack had heard the lecture a number of times through the years—dealers of narcotics had forfeited their basic rights, in Kennedy's view. "I mean, come on."

"The point is, though, Tom, what Moloney and Curran did was a felony. It's ugly stuff."

"Hey, no question," Kennedy said. "They should not have done it. I'm not going to defend them. I'm only making a distinction that it's not as though they went after someone you would have sympathy for, that's all. But as for what they did, you get no defense here, Jack."

"But the question now is, what to do," Jack said. "The hearing's coming up and I sense there's a kind of vacuum, and I think they're going to look to me to a certain extent, and Del Rio, to see how hard we're going to push on this. How much of a stink."

"How much of a stink relative to what do they do with it, you mean," Kennedy said.

"Right, I mean—"

"It's a hot potato, no question," Kennedy said. "And what you're asking is, do we make a federal case out of this, in which case a lot of dirty laundry gets aired; and the question is, does the airing of that dirty laundry serve a purpose within the department."

"So?" Jack asked.

Kennedy considered this, gave vent to a deep, weary sigh. "So it's your call, Jackie," he said. "I'm not going to tell you what to do. You have good judgment. Use it. Just make sure that, either way, you feel comfortable inside with it, that's all."

Kennedy shook his head. "I have to say I was personally disappointed, bitterly disappointed, about Moloney. He and I have known each other, Christ, thirty-plus years. And to do this . . ." He shook his head distastefully.

"But you're right. It showed this is serious, and that has gotten guys' attention. And I have to tell you I looked at the report you wrote, and all I can say is that I'm not sure I've ever seen a tighter, more professionally written presentation in my entire career. You handled every detail of that superbly. I mean that sincerely. You should feel proud."

Jack was deeply flattered by Kennedy's comment. He stirred his coffee and nodded. "Thanks, Tom," he said. "That means a lot to me, as I'm sure you can imagine."

"You know I mean it," Kennedy said softly, smiling. "To see what you've done with yourself, your career . . . you're such a credit to yourself." Kennedy paused and looked down at the table. "To your dad."

There was a prolonged, awkward silence. Through the years, whenever the subject came up, Kennedy had a tendency to become morose, to blame himself.

"If only I had been there," he would say. "If only I had been there."

But they had covered that ground.

"Any advice?" Jack asked, for toward the end of their lunches, Kennedy would often offer some bit of advice or wisdom about life in the Boston Police Department.

"Be careful," the older man said. "There are elements within the force who have no use for this. To some guys, the thought that a cop is chasing other cops . . ." Kennedy had a grave look on his face and shook his head.

"I've heard some grumbling," he continued. "Nothing too bad, but there are people who are unhappy about it, and the sooner it ends, the better, as far as they're concerned. So just be careful. You're under a microscope. And if you screw up, they'll know it and they'll exploit it to high heaven and use it against you."

"Like who?" Jack asked.

"Some are obvious, and I would have mentioned Moloney before the events of this week, to tell you the truth. But that's just it, Jackie. That's the problem."

Kennedy glanced around the restaurant, which was two blocks from police headquarters, then leaned forward, his elbows on the table. "That's the problem," he repeated, his voice low. "I don't know who, exactly, you know what I mean? But there are certain elements who have something to lose here, obviously. Everything to lose. And they won't like that. So be careful. Very careful."

JACK DEVLIN SWUNG the net, took a pass from the defenseman and headed up the left boards with the puck. Through center ice he picked up speed and saw the center on his line twenty feet to his right gaining speed. He could see that in a second or two the center would be open for a pass. But Devlin also saw, thirty-five feet away on the far right, that his right wing was streaking through center. The defense would expect Devlin to pass to the center. But he kept the puck until, out of the corner of his eye, he saw the right wing approaching the blue line at top speed. It was then that he sent a hard pass all the way across the ice. It hit the tape on the right wing's stick just soon enough to keep him onside, and suddenly he was in behind the defense, all alone. He faked the goalie to his left, then went to the other side and slid it easily under the goaltender's pads.

It was an informal pickup game of guys Jack had known in high school and college, an easygoing affair. Toward the end of the game, he spotted Coakley standing over by the warming hut, and at game's end, he came off the ice and toward Coakley.

"You're early," he said.

"I wanted to see if you still had any moves," Coakley replied.

"And?" Jack said, smiling.

"Not bad. A little rust, but not bad."

In the warming hut, Jack removed his skates and they went back outside and up a few steps by the rink. On a terrace, there was a commanding view of downtown Boston, lights glittering from Brookline all the way to the waterfront. The night was frigid and clear, a huge pale moon high in the jet-black sky over Boston.

Jack loved it up here, especially on a clear winter night. There was something about the panoramic nature of the view, something about seeing so much terrain at once, that deeply satisfied him. So often he could see but one small piece of the puzzle, one piece that seemed at times to bear no relation to any other. The contrast was sharp and satisfying.

"So he says he's got four guys breathing down his neck," Coakley said. "He's desperate for the delivery. Says he's got to have it."

"How did he seem to you?" Jack asked.

"On the verge," Coakley said. "Not panicking but not far from panicking."

Jack did not want that. He wanted nothing sudden or foolish. "Okay," he said with a sigh.

"Okay, what?" Coakley asked.

"Tell him it's on its way. Tell him it'll be here any day."

Coakley nodded. He would do as instructed. He sat back with his hands folded on his ample lap and thought for a long moment.

"I heard something . . . ," he began, but did not continue because he was not certain what words to use.

Jack turned his head, studying Coakley closely.

"What?" he asked.

Coakley frowned, and as he did so, brought his chin down toward his chest. In this position he seemed particularly heavy, the flesh of his face running uninterrupted down to the top of his chest. He pursed his mouth and his eyes narrowed as though he was concentrating on a puzzling bit of mental gymnastics.

"I'm not sure whether it's anything, but I heard from a guy I know what sounded like general rumblings," he said.

Jack waited, but Coakley did not continue. He seemed stuck, for some reason.

"Rumblings," he said.

Coakley nodded.

"About?"

"You," Coakley said.

"Me."

Coakley shifted his weight and crossed his arms. "Moloney has friends," he said. "Bobby Curran, too."

Jack nodded. He was not surprised. Ever since taking on the assignment he'd known that the possibility of trouble existed. To be on an assignment resembling Internal Affairs was not the way to endear oneself to fellow officers. Jack knew that through the years various I.A. officers had been harassed and some had been threatened; threats that had been taken seriously. One I.A. detective some years back was beaten up twice, but that had been as much because he was an offensive asshole as anything else.

Jack was careful, for he knew that the type of man who joined a police department was far more comfortable than most with the idea of violence, the use of force. When all else failed, force was, after all, the way cops imposed their will.

"Keep your head up," Coakley said.

Jack smiled. It was an old hockey expression. Those who skated with their eyes on the ice got blindsided.

"I do," he said.

"I mean, these people . . ." Coakley's was an expression of concern.

Jack nodded. "I know," he said.

CHAPTER 12

HE THOUGHT ABOUT her much of the time now, thought about her as he was getting up and getting ready for work, thought about her as he was driving downtown to police headquarters; thought about her often as he went about his business during the day, when he attended boring meetings about various topics, gave depositions in the matter of Detectives Moloney and Curran; before he went to bed at night.

And when she called him at his office, he was glad. "How are you?" he asked.

"I'm great," she said. "And I'm even better because a trial we had scheduled to start this week has been postponed. So, guess what?"

"What?"

"I have an invitation for you," she said.

"Yes," he said. "I accept."

"You accept what?" she asked.

"I accept whatever invitation you have."

She laughed. "No, listen to what it is."

"I don't have to," he said. "The answer is yes. Tell me where to be and when."

"But you don't know what *it* is!"

"I told you," he said, laughing, "it doesn't matter. The answer is yes."

"Great!" she said. "Pick me up at seven o'clock tomorrow morning. And pack a bag."

"A bag?"

"Shorts, bathing suit, tennis racket, whatever," she said.

He was taken aback. "Where are we going?"

"I thought it didn't matter," she challenged. "I thought you accepted?"

"I have accepted," he said. "I am going. *We* are going. I'd just like to have some idea where we're going."

"Florida," she said.

"You're kidding?"

"Would I kid you?" she said. "We fly into Palm Beach and drive up to a place called Jupiter. I have friends who have a house there, and they're loaning it to me for a few days. The weather forecast is perfect, I checked. And I'm desperate for a break."

Jack considered it. Certainly he could take some time off from work. He had five weeks vacation coming to him, two still unused from the prior year. In a way, it was an ideal time to get away.

"I'll pick you up at seven," he said, and hung up.

Then he sat alone in his dingy office the size of a broom closet and contemplated a trip with Emily. But as he thought about Florida, his mind turned to someone else—to Alden Farmer, who had retired to Vero Beach.

Jack went down to the police department's resource room and dug out an atlas. He found a map of Florida and saw that Vero Beach was only about fifty miles from Jupiter. This trip was fated, he thought. This was his opportunity to do something he'd considered doing for several years, his opportunity to try and track down Alden Farmer, to meet with him face-to-face, to talk with the former agent for the Federal Bureau of Investigation who had arrested his father.

THE BOEING 737 lifted off the Logan runway at 8:34 A.M. and climbed into a sullen, gray November morning. The jet bounced through a dense layer of clouds and broke into a clear, sunny sky as it settled into a smooth ride south.

"Wow," Emily said, "I didn't know how good it would feel to get out of town. But there are times when that place can just choke you."

Jack understood. Boston sometimes felt like the smallest, most claustrophobic place on earth; a place where everyone had an angle, where it was sometimes difficult—even with a scorecard—to tell the good guys from the bad. It was a place, as someone once said, where the prevailing disease was Irish Alzheimer's: You forget everything except the grudges.

Jack had always had an intuitive feel for the politics of the city; politics that penetrated all manner of business done, especially in law enforcement. This was, after all, a city where the mayor's son worked as an assistant in the D.A.'s office; where a judge's brother was a lead defense lawyer in town; where cops and lawyers were sisters and brothers and husbands and wives and cousins and neighbors and blood enemies. This was a place where love and hate coexisted easily, and where they sometimes even blended into one.

Jack Devlin felt a pleasant sense of relief as the plane climbed higher in the sky and moved away from Boston. He and Emily settled in over coffee and corn muffins.

"I just think sometimes it's too much," she said. "I feel as though there are times when I'm working on a case and I pull a single thread and I pull it and tug at it and pull it some more and I follow it and it winds throughout the whole city from City Hall to the State House to God-knows-where.

"Don't get me wrong, I love living here, but sometimes it's all a little too cute and cozy and too inbred, and you get to a point—or at least I do—where I feel like I can't even breathe."

"That's true on the BPD," he said. "It's very much that way. And while there's a positive side to that, there's that claustrophobic downside, too. Where everything's just a little too cozy, and when a nod and a wink can either make or undo a deal."

She turned in her seat and smiled at him. "I'm really glad you could come," she said. "This is great."

She looked to him like the most beautiful woman in the world; her shiny black hair neatly brushed back, her gorgeous smile; her pretty slender neck; her bright, blue eyes.

"I'm really glad you invited me," he said. "I really am."

THE HOUSE WAS set on a bluff by the ocean, a pink cottage with white shutters and Italian tile floors. The kitchen led out to a large deck that overlooked a private beach. The sun was high in a clear blue sky, the temperature pushing 80 degrees. They changed into bathing suits and went down to the water. He had never before seen her like this. In a black two-piece suit, he could see her slim, athletic build. She was trim and firm from regular workouts. And very sexy.

The water was cold, and she pulled back when a wave washed up over their feet, but Jack kept walking at a steady pace and soon was chest-deep. He dove in and took a leisurely swim out and then back. He felt reinvigorated.

Emily, too, dove in, but was quickly out. They went back to the house, where they lay down on chaise lounges and allowed the warm sun to dry their bodies.

She lay there, eyes closed. "Have you noticed I'm a little on the chatty side?" she said.

"Not really," he replied.

"Well, I am," she said. "I often say what's on my mind."

"That's okay."

"May I say something to you?" she asked.

"Of course," he said, half sitting up and looking over at her.

"I think you're a very attractive man." She said it without opening her eyes or moving from her supine position. "Do you think I'm too forward?"

He laughed. "No, I do not. I happen to think you're a very attractive woman."

She waited a beat. "That's it?" she said. "Just very attractive?"

"Beautiful," he said.

"Ah, much better. Thank you."

"You're welcome," he said.

"Good night," she said.

"It's noon."

"I know," she said, and with that, fell asleep.

He read for a while, then quietly opened a large deck umbrella to keep the sun off her. And he dared for the moment to indulge in the pleasure of watching her sleep.

AS THE SUN went down, the sky on the horizon turned orange, then purple. At dusk they sat out on the deck and gazed across the water at some distant ship inching its way south, already lit for the night. The house was close enough to the ocean so the sound of the waves washing up on shore at high tide had a mesmerizing syncopation.

They sipped cold white wine and looked at the sky and the water, and, to Jack Devlin, Boston and the reality of his life seemed very far away. But he could not shake it from his mind. Nor did he wish to.

She made a salad and he grilled fish, and they ate in the dark on the deck and strolled on the beach after dinner, holding hands. As they walked he kept shifting the position of their fingers. He was surprised at how small and delicate her hands were; surprised as well at how tightly she squeezed his hand.

When they returned to the house, they stood on the deck and embraced. He could hardly believe it, standing there under the warm, moonlit sky, embracing the most beautiful woman in the world.

"WHAT A WAY to live," he remarked the following morning, as they sat on the deck, the warm sun rising in a cloudless eastern sky. The sunlight twinkled on the water as it rolled to shore. Over a breakfast of juice, bagels, cereal, and coffee, they looked out over the sparkling blue ocean.

"It's amazing, isn't it?" Emily said.

"Very calming," he replied.

"Although for me it's amazing because it's so different from my real life. I wouldn't want this to be normalcy." She hesitated a moment and regarded him. "Would you?"

He laughed. "I don't know. Pretty tempting."

"Come on, Jack," she said.

"What's wrong with living a life where you have the ocean and the sun and you don't have to deal with frigid mornings and cars that won't start and slush and ice and snow and all of those problems that come with a place where it's gray and sullen for three or four months of the year?" He smiled and cocked his head to the side. "What would be so bad about walking on the beach in the early morning and fishing and living life outdoors much of the time?"

She feigned amazement. "You sound like such an old fogy, Jack," she said.

He laughed. "Really," he said, "what would be so bad about a laid-back life down here in the sun?"

She frowned. "I know you're kidding because I know that you understand completely what would be wrong with it."

"Such as?"

"Such as no work," she said emphatically.

"No work," he repeated.

She nodded as though she'd just delivered the decisive blow. "No work."

"And that is a problem?" he asked.

She sipped her coffee and smiled at him over the rim of the cup. "I know you're pulling my leg," she said, "because it's obvious how important work is to you. It defines you. What you do defines who you are. Gives you a reason to put one foot in front of the other each day. It sustains you, energizes you, makes you interesting, makes everything else in your life possible."

Suddenly the joking tone was gone, her gaze was steady and level, and he listened intently.

"It's who you are," she said.

He hesitated a moment. "And how can this be discerned?" he asked.

She watched him carefully, pursing her lips as though considering whether to say what was on her mind. But for Emily Lawrence, that was not a difficult call, for she was a woman accustomed to saying what was on her mind.

"Because there's nothing else in your life," she said in a soft voice.

Jack was taken aback. She had said it not as a rebuke, but as a statement of fact, a simple observation of what was so obvious, so clear. And he was jarred by the starkness of it, by how apparent it was to the world that this was his life—his work. That he had no other dimension.

"Of course, it so happens that your work coincides with your mission," she added. "So there's a lot that's intertwined."

He sat in silence, not sure what to say, thinking he would make some kind of joke, but nothing came to mind, and he felt not at all humorous or flip. What could he say? Yes, Em, you are correct. Correct that there is nothing in my life but my work. Correct that I love what I do, define myself by what I do, derive what self-esteem I have from what I do. And yes, you have also seen the essential truth: that layered in with my work is my mission. It is true. You see it all so clearly.

She cocked her head to one side and wrinkled her brow with concern. Leaning forward, she stretched her arms across the table, reaching for his hand.

"I've hurt your feelings," she said in barely a whisper, grasping his hand in hers. "I didn't mean to."

"No, no," he said.

"I'm sorry. I hope that—"

"It's okay," he said. "Really. I like it that you see who I am. I don't want any false advertising here. You're very perceptive."

She smiled. "More coffee?" she asked.

"Let me get it," he said. He poured refills for them both and returned to his seat. There was a freshening breeze off the water as the sun rose higher in the sky.

"So tell me," she said, "if you could create the perfect sort of balance in your life, what would it be? I mean let's say anything is possible and that you can come to a place like this when you want, work or not work, travel, whatever."

"So money's not an object?"

"Within reason," she said.

"That's easy. I'd continue to work, of course, but I'd have control of my schedule, and whenever the cold and gray of Boston got to me, I'd hop a plane down here and hang out. Fish, whatever. I might even commit to learn golf."

"Ah," she said. "See, I told you you'd come around one day." Emily was an avid golfer and had tried to explain the bliss of the game to him, but he insisted it was a pursuit best left to the old and sedentary.

"What about you?" he asked. "If you could create the ideal kind of setup."

Her eyes widened at the prospect. "Well . . . let's see. I would continue to work, of course, although I'd want the same thing. Control of my schedule. Maybe I'd work four days a week. Take Fridays off. And I'd live probably where I live now, somewhere with an easy commute. And I'd of course be married and have the most supportive husband in the world. And I'd have two kids, a boy and a girl, and they'd be three years apart so they wouldn't fight too much. And I'd bring them all down here for vacations, and one weekend every month we'd come down for a long weekend, and once a year we'd

jump in the car and drive to Disney World and the kids would go insane and we'd fish together and play tennis and golf and go to
church together and take walks on the beach and—" And suddenly
she stopped as she gazed out over the water. Slowly, her eyes shifted
back from the horizon and settled on Jack. And she looked at him
very directly for a long moment. And then, very softly, she said: "Life
would be great."

EMILY WAS DESPERATE to play a round of golf, and he encouraged her to do so. For the four hours she would be out on the course,
he said he'd take a drive and explore the area. The phone book listed
Alden Farmer at 2971 Pelican Drive in Vero Beach, a condominium
development.

The drive up the coast went quickly, and Jack found the place
easily. It was like so many other Florida developments, attractive
enough, with clustered homes built around a golf course and a man-
made lake.

On a hunch, he tried the golf shop first, and learned that Alden
Farmer had teed off three and a half hours earlier. He was due in
any time.

Jack found his way to the eighteenth green, a short walk from
the golf shop. Behind the green a few seats and benches were scat-
tered for spectators, and Jack settled in on one of the benches. He
wore a polo shirt and khaki Bermuda shorts and had lathered up
with sunscreen. Even with sunglasses the glare was strong, yet he
enjoyed the warmth of the sun as he sat and watched golfers make
their way along the hole. Most of the players appeared to be in their
sixties or seventies. There was about an even mixture of men and
women, and many of them were proficient players.

Jack studied each foursome as it came over a hill perhaps three
hundred yards from where he sat. He had been watching for thirty-
five minutes when he thought he spotted Farmer. He knew from

reading old press clips that Farmer was quite tall, nearly six-five, and very thin. He'd been described in some of the newspaper articles as "storklike."

Farmer was in a foursome with three other men. They all walked and pulled handcarts bearing their golf bags. Farmer walked down the left side of the fairway and stopped at his ball, just in the rough. He selected a club and struck the ball, sending it high into the air to land with a thud in the bottom of a yawning sand bunker adjacent to the green. The others hit their second shots in the vicinity of the green, then pitched onto the putting surface.

Alden Farmer selected his sand wedge and went down into the bunker. Farmer set his feet, and then Jack saw the cocked club and the smooth, deliberate swing. The club slid easily through the sand and lifted the ball high up over the lip of the bunker and landed it on the green, where it rolled slowly along a ridge, broke right a few feet, and trickled down into the cup.

Alden Farmer held his hands aloft and smiled, acknowledging the shouted kudos of his playing partners. After the others putted out, the four men came off the green and headed toward the golf shop.

"Nice shot," Jack said, approaching Farmer.

"Better to be lucky than good," Farmer replied. "Never birdied that hole before."

"I wonder if I might have a word with you for a moment?" Jack asked.

Farmer squinted. "Do I know you?" he asked.

"You're Alden Farmer?"

"I am," he said. "And you are?"

"Mr. Farmer, my name is Jack Devlin. I'm the son of Jock Devlin."

Farmer drew back, cocked his head to one side, and looked closely at Jack's face. He pursed his lips and squinted tightly.

"Yes," he said, nodding. "Yes, I can see that you are." He shook his head in sorrow, looking away. "It was all very sad," he said. "Very sad."

There was a long moment during which neither man spoke.

"I'd like to sit down and talk a little bit," Jack said.

"Talk about . . ."

Jack shrugged. "I'm trying to come to grips with it all." He forced a smile. "In my own way. You can probably understand that."

Farmer nodded. "Of course," he said. "But it's been a long time. A very long time."

"I know," Jack acknowledged. "But if we could just talk awhile . . ."

Farmer stared down at the ground, frowning. He seemed suddenly angry. He shook his head. "He shouldn't have done it," he blurted. "He shouldn't have done it. It was wrong. Not just for himself. For you. I've thought about you now and then through the years. My wife and I have talked about it. It was—" Farmer caught himself. He'd just met this young man who, he was sure, had suffered greatly because of his father. Farmer decided he didn't need to make matters worse.

Jack stood silently, glancing off toward the fairway, then looking back at Farmer.

"Go ahead up on the terrace there," the retired FBI man said, his voice warmer. "I'll just put my clubs away and be right up."

Farmer went off toward the golf shop with his clubs, and Jack took a table on the terrace. From there, he looked out over the course and the homes tucked into the woods off the fairways. They were relatively small houses, most for retirees, Jack supposed, three-bedroom Cape Cod–style structures with well-kept yards and decks with gas grills. The houses were pink and white and a light bluish color, all pastels, most of them stucco. They were the homes of people who had worked for many years, Jack knew. People who were now reaping their rewards. They had come to Florida to find comfort and to enjoy their lives. His father would have liked this, he thought. He would have liked being able to get up early and go fishing. He would have liked schmoozing with his friends and neighbors. Jock Devlin had been able to talk with anyone, make friends with anyone.

Jesus, Jack thought. His father had missed so much. So much. He'd missed Jack's hockey games through high school and college. Missed his graduations. Missed his passing the bar. Missed his proms and his trips and all the experiences that meant something.

Jack looked toward the practice green and saw an old man bent over, teaching a child how to hold a putter. Christ almighty, he thought. His father had missed so much.

Farmer emerged with a towel draped around his neck and a glass of iced tea in each hand. The old man looked at Jack and squinted. "You okay?" he asked.

Jack nodded.

"You look kind of pale," Farmer said.

Jack forced a laugh. "Not much sun in Boston this time of year."

"I don't miss that," Farmer said. "Not a bit." He smiled, a friendly smile. He was a nice-looking old man, his skin brown and weathered, his hair white and wispy. He appeared fit and very alert. It was clear Farmer had taken care of himself in retirement.

"So," Farmer said, regarding him. "Why now? Why twenty-five years after the fact?"

"Well, Mr. Farmer, I'm trying to close the loop on it in a way. I'm a detective now myself and—"

Farmer was astonished. "You're kidding."

"No. I've been on the force seven years, a detective for four."

Farmer half smiled and slowly shook his head in amazement. "I'm sorry," he said, "it's just that it strikes me, I don't know, it seems so ironic in a way."

Jack smiled. "It is that," he said affably. "It certainly is that."

"Well," Farmer said. "A belated welcome to the fraternity. Now we can really talk. Although I'm not sure how much I can say that you don't already know. I mean, the way the newspapers covered it, good God, it was a frenzy."

Farmer sipped his iced tea and gazed off out over the practice green. "So," he said, "where do we begin?"

"Well, I suppose the best place is at the beginning," Jack said. "I've read about how it was supposed to have started, but I'd like to hear from you how it was really initiated."

Alden Farmer sipped his tea again and nodded. He looked out over the golf course and for a moment was lost in his own thoughts. "Jeez," he said. "It was a long, long time ago."

He shook his head again as though he found it hard to believe how much time had passed. "You have only a personal interest in this, then?" he asked.

Jack nodded.

"Because if you're here in an official capacity in any way, I mean I don't see what it would be exactly, but if you were . . ." He laughed at himself. "We're trained to be cautious, and cautious I am."

"It's personal," Jack said.

Farmer was silent as he closely studied Jack. "A personal situation such as yours would be one where we could have an informal conversation, but it's not the sort of thing that would be appropriate to view in any way other than an informal discussion. For personal purposes. Because if it were in any way—"

Jack shook his head gently, reassuring Farmer.

The retired FBI agent took a breath. "It's been a long time and I see no harm in discussing it with you," he said. "You seem like an earnest young man. Would you believe it all began as a result of a divorce proceeding? No one ever really discovered this, but it's true. There was a guy in Brighton who owned a couple of clubs and he and his wife had split up. In the course of going through the divorce proceedings, she asked for a certain amount of money in child support and a certain amount in alimony. When the husband's lawyer counters with much, much lower numbers, the mediator says he wants to look at a net worth and income statement from the husband. These club owners hide a lot of their income, and this guy was probably no different. He comes back with numbers that are surprisingly low. The woman got very angry and says to her lawyer that he'd have more money if he didn't have so many cops on the payroll. Her lawyer questioned her about this, and she insisted it was true. She said he had told her many times about paying various cops, some of them substantial amounts. The attorney took this seriously and called one of our people. And thus it began."

"And that's when you got involved?" Jack asked.

"In fact, no. I had been working in the Kansas City field office for several years, and one day I got word I was needed in Boston. It's common that whenever there's a major investigation either undercover or politically sensitive, that people from out of town will be brought in. And so that happened here. There was another fellow, Clive Miller, who came in from Atlanta, although he wasn't around for very long. I came in and took over and, soon after that, we were underway."

"But it took a while?" Jack asked.

"We got nothing at all for a while," Farmer said. "Or, I should say, nothing that mattered. Cops getting free meals or special treatment in some places—that sort of thing goes on everywhere. People feel safer having a cop around, so they treat them in a different way. That never bothered me, although I'll tell you some of the purists were put off by that.

"But, no, we had nothing really for quite a while. There was no shortage in the rumor mill, though. And there was plenty to chase down. We heard lots of rumors about cops on the take, but for months and months we came up empty.

"So we turned up the heat," Farmer continued. "We started setting up a target list of people within the department for audits, people we were suspicious of. We thought that kind of an approach would coax a little cooperation out of them. Because up until this point—and this is key—we had had no cooperation whatsoever from the BPD. I mean none. Lip service from the top and nothing but obstruction from underneath. Nothing.

"So we established this list and the subpoenas were served, the first dozen or so, and they screamed bloody murder. I mean to tell you they howled. Civil liberties, intrusive, harassment, all that."

Farmer took a long drink of tea and wiped his forehead with the towel.

"As obnoxious a tactic as it was—and we knew it was—the fact is, it worked. Pretty soon we were having some reasonable discussions. And around that same time we had a couple of club owners loosen up on us. Two guys, in particular, the Fahey brothers. We immunized them at the start. They were bit players but they did have some firsthand information, and I'm sorry to say it was about your father."

"Oh?"

"They had made Christmas payments to him for some number of years, I forget, three or four years. And they detailed this."

"How many others?" Jack asked.

"Did they pay?" Farmer asked.

Jack nodded.

"None they admitted to," Farmer said.

"And you found that credible?" Jack asked.

"No," Farmer said. "I didn't. But we felt very fortunate to have them talking with us at all. Because remember, up until then it had felt like a dry hole. And when you've put your time and resources in and come up empty . . ." Farmer did not have to tell a fellow investigator that that was the worst possible fate.

"No, I did not find it credible, but it was a strong point, and I was convinced we could squeeze the Faheys," he went on. "And at the same time that we were hearing this from the Fahey brothers, we began to have more candid discussions with people within the department, and the same message was coming back from all of them: There is corruption, but it is very limited and isolated. There were four guys within the department, at various levels, who we talked to in a candid way, and it was from them that we began to believe that maybe it was actually possible that it was limited and contained."

"Did you believe that then?" Jack asked.

Farmer appeared troubled. "I didn't have much of a choice, whether I believed it or not. I had to accept it. It was the reality we were dealing with. At least it was something. We had committed resources to this matter on the basis that indications initially indicated that something was going on here, something systemic. Because that's what we were interested in, let's put our cards on the table. The idea that a few cops here and there were off freelancing wasn't of great interest to us, not initially, anyway. But the possibility of systemic rot was something that got everyone excited. And there's a progression you go through in these things that I think is pretty typical.

"You begin with indications of something large, something with tentacles that reaches into many of the levels and corners of an organization. There are extravagant claims made by certain people early on, but they seem credible, or more likely, you want to believe; you want to think that you are on to the case of your life. And so you go along for the ride convinced that you are about to untangle a spectacular mess.

"And then reality strikes," Farmer said, pausing for a moment and taking a breath, frowning as he looked out over the eighteenth hole.

"Reality strikes," he repeated softly. "And reality is that you can't get anything meaningful. Reality is that time passes, weeks, months, in some cases years, but time passes and you begin to believe that you may have been delusional up front or that there is the most massive and effective cover-up ever. Conspiracy of silence.

"And you become desperate."

Farmer tightened his lips and ran the towel over his forehead, leaning his elbow on the table. His tone was confessional.

"And reality is that after a certain amount of time there is an impatience within the system," he continued. "It's never stated overtly, at least it wasn't in this case. But the pressure is there. The attorneys you're working with evince it in certain subtle and not so subtle ways. Your bosses, locally, show it, although they were probably the most supportive. And you feel it from Washington, where there are people whose jobs were to watch field agents and hound them, dog them.

"And, naturally, you feel it from yourself. And because of all this pressure there comes a day which is a defining moment when you have shifted from looking for the big score to deciding you will settle for just about anything."

Farmer raised his eyebrows in a look of resignation and sighed heavily. "And that's what happened," he said. "That's what happened." His tone was wistful, and he turned from Jack and looked back out toward the eighteenth hole.

Farmer fell silent for a minute or more, and Jack waited out the silence.

"It's strange, you know, after all the years, to think about these things, because I don't much think of them anymore," Farmer finally said. "I don't like the memory of this thing because I was convinced at the time that corruption in the BPD was systemic. I believed—there were so many indications to my mind's eye—I believed that there were many, many guys of various ranks who had their fingers in the pie. But everybody did his job to batten down the hatches and squeeze everything tight so we would get minimal information.

"There were good people who tried to be helpful from the beginning. I remember that. Is Tom Kennedy still on the force?"

"He's deputy commissioner," Jack replied.

"Tom was a young lieutenant back then," Farmer said. "Bright as hell and ambitious. He helped. Quite a bit."

"How so?" Jack asked.

"The thing with the department was that most were overtly hostile to us. Wouldn't say hello, or acknowledge us in any way. Literally. There were guys I'd walk by in the hallway, and they'd tell me to go fuck myself. Then there were guys who would keep away from us, never say anything. And then there were a few who would sit down and have coffee and talk about the department and about the rules and customs. Kennedy was one of the few, and he was very smart. Insightful. He's a good man."

Jack nodded his agreement. "So how did you know my father was making the pickup that day?" he asked.

"I probably shouldn't tell you this, but, what the hell, I'm an old man now and it's been so many years, what does it matter?

"I got a tip," he said. "Out of the blue one day I got a phone call. A patrolman. He'd had nothing to do with anything, and all of a sudden he calls out of the blue."

"Who was that?" Jack asked quietly.

Farmer regarded him. Jack could tell the old man felt for him. "I remember him," Farmer said. "His name was Moloney."

CHAPTER 13

AT DAWN, SHAFTS of light slanted through the kitchen skylight, illuminating the wooden table. Christopher Young, M.D., sat with a mug of instant coffee, working his way rapidly through a stack of papers. He had a massive amount of work to do, and though he knew he wouldn't be able to do all of it that day, he needed to do enough to get by. He had been doing just enough to get by now for close to a year. Had he sat back and taken a careful look at his life, he would have been astonished at the precipitous nature of his decline. But taking the long view, sitting back and engaging in thoughtful introspection, was not something in which he had much interest.

Young sipped the coffee and rose from the table. He crammed the stack of papers into his worn leather briefcase—a gift from his parents when he'd graduated from UCLA Medical School—and put on his overcoat. He moved quietly, for he knew that his wife and three-year-old daughter would sleep at least another hour. He went from the kitchen into a passageway that led to the garage, got into his Saab 9000, and backed out onto the quiet suburban street. At this early hour his commute to his office at Brigham & Women's Hospital took fifteen minutes.

Young parked in the part of the garage reserved for physicians and was walking rapidly toward the hospital when the garage attendant called out to him. "Hey, Doc! Lights."

Dr. Christopher Young turned back and saw that his headlights were on. He waved his thanks to the attendant, went back and shut off his lights, then hurried into the hospital. He rode the elevator to the fifth floor, where the Pharmacology Department was located. His office was down the far end of the hallway, on the corner. All the other offices were still dark. Pharmacology was not like the surgical units or Anesthesiology, where everyone arrived early. At this time of day, Young's department was deserted. He knew this, since it was the time he arrived each morning. This was the time when he could do what he needed to do without being discovered.

Young entered his office, switched on the light, and locked the door. It was a good-size space, tastefully furnished with a dark Oriental carpet, a burgundy leather sofa, maple coffee table and desk, and bookshelves built into the walls. On the wall behind his desk were his degrees—a B.S. from UCLA (summa cum laude) and an M.D. from UCLA. On the far wall was an Audubon print. He'd sold off the original for $11,000 a few months earlier, though that had hardly made a dent in his financial situation.

Dr. Young pulled the blinds shut and hung up his overcoat. He was sweating moderately now and his breathing was shallow.

Behind his desk there was a small alcove containing a sturdy lead file cabinet, fireproof, theftproof, intended for the most precious research and other documents. Young spun the dial on the combination lock and opened the second drawer. He reached inside and removed a small plastic container. He opened the container with great care and used a very small spoon to remove a small amount of white crystalline alkaloid: morphine. With water from the bathroom off his office, Dr. Christopher Young diluted the alkaloid and absorbed it into a syringe. Undoing his belt buckle, he pulled down his pants and, sitting on the edge of a chair, picked a spot just below his boxer shorts. He pointed the needle up into the air, drew back the plunger, held the needle just above his thigh, and slowly slid it into a clear spot, several inches from other needle marks. He pressed the plunger forward slowly, feeding the narcotic into his bloodstream. The impact was nearly instantaneous. Then he placed the syringe and box of morphine back in the file safe and shut the drawer, went across his office, and shut off the light. Stretching out on the sofa, he soon fell deep within the seductive grasp of Morpheus, the son of Hypnos and the most important mythological god—the god of dreams.

AT MIDDAY, CHRISTOPHER Young walked through the lobby of Brigham and Women's Hospital, his white physician's coat crisply starched. Young was tall and lean, six feet three inches, 180 pounds. His dirty-blond hair was on the long side, stylishly cut and swept back in waves. He was an attractive man, thirty-four years old. On the outside, it seemed Young had it all: He was adjunct professor of Pharmacology at Harvard Medical School and heir apparent to become chief of Pharmacology at the Brigham, one of the most prestigious hospitals in the world. He had a beautiful wife and daughter, and it appeared that his life could not be more perfect.

But ever since he'd broken his leg in a painful mountain biking accident, Young's life had been sliding out of control. Initially, the morphine had been administered when he was in the hospital having his leg set. Once out of the hospital, he'd continued to take it. When his prescription ran out, he took some from the Pharmacology Department's own supplies. Before he was aware of what was happening, Young had raided the department stock to the point where he was forced to doctor the books—books governed by state and federal law, available for inspection by FDA officials at any time, and reviewed carefully by the hospital's auditors every year.

State and federal narcotic statutes are extremely precise, and major medical centers are rigorous in their enforcement of those rules. Young was an extremely bright and resourceful young man, and he managed to create a bookkeeping system that masked the truth of his morphine consumption. But ultimately it was a Ponzi scheme, and Young knew it was only a matter of time before hospital auditors would discover that he'd embezzled funds from the hospital to pay for additional shipments of morphine, all for his own use.

By now, he'd stolen nearly $114,000 from the department over a ten-month period. Young knew that unless he was able to come up with that money and return it to the hospital accounts, he would inevitably be discovered, and discovery would mean the ruination of his career. If he were caught, he would be prosecuted and no doubt convicted, and a felony conviction would surely mean the loss of his license to practice medicine, and that would destroy his life.

And so he had done what people through the ages had done to cover their crimes: He'd committed other crimes.

The two sales that had been made by Young—through channels Coakley had identified—involved the sale of amphetamines, but yielded only a modest amount of money. When Young had gone to Coakley seeking a much bigger deal, Coakley and Devlin had found their man.

The agreement had been simple: Young provided Coakley with detailed information about where large supplies of morphine were held; Coakley would arrange for their theft; Young would meanwhile seek to sell the drug through distributors identified by Coakley. It was a very neat package in which everyone was a winner. Young had provided the relevant information, Coakley had arranged for the theft and storage of the drug. And Young had successfully made contact with the distributors Coakley identified. All was set. When the deal was done, Young would use his share of the proceeds to pay back the hospital accounts and he'd be a free man once more.

YOUNG TOOK A cab down to the fish pier, on time for his meeting with Coakley. The pier was wide and long, and dozens of boats were tied up at the dock, scores more out to sea. Men with weathered faces moved easily back and forth from boats to storage facilities, wheeling huge bins packed with fish. Young stood nervously, feeling wildly out of place, waiting. He paced for a time and then, after half an hour, sat down on a bench looking out at the harbor. Herring and black-backed gulls, their high-pitched wails filling the air, swept in low over the pier, scavenging bits of fish and bait.

After ten more minutes, growing increasingly anxious, Young got up and again began to pace. Coakley watched from behind a shed on the edge of the parking lot across from the pier. He felt a tinge of regret, but knew that Devlin was right: Young had to be in a state of great anxiety or else their leverage over him would be minimized.

Finally, Coakley slipped out from behind the shed and made his way toward the pier. Young spotted him and began walking in Coakley's direction.

"Sorry I'm late, Doc," the lawyer said. "I was detained by a client."

"Where do we stand?" Young asked abruptly. He was agitated, trembling slightly, Coakley could see. And sweating.

Coakley took a deep breath as a pained expression crossed his face. He appeared reluctant to speak, and he turned and looked down the fish pier. Dozens of men in heavy boots and slickers moved deliberately about the business of unloading huge stocks of fish from grimy-looking sixty-foot vessels. The low rumble of diesel engines could be heard on the water.

"We've hit a couple of bumps in the road," Coakley said as he gazed out across the water, his eyes following a fishing boat lumbering in toward the pier. It was a trawler, perhaps 130 feet long, sitting low in the water, desperate for a paint job.

Young shut his eyes for a few seconds, as though trying to block out of his mind whatever bad news he was about to hear. He drew a deep breath and exhaled slowly. Coakley's silence distressed him.

"What bumps?" he asked.

Coakley finally turned back from the water and looked at Young, then looked down at his shoes, as though embarrassed, then looked back at Young.

"The delivery's being delayed," he said.

Young shut his eyes again and his nostrils flared. "You promised me," he said. He moved away from Coakley and half turned, then turned back, hands thrust forward, palms up, as though pleading. His jaw was clenched, eyes narrowed.

"You assured me . . . ," Young said, too angry to complete the sentence.

Coakley was unshaken. "This is a different kind of business," the lawyer said. "Not everything runs on a precise schedule. This ain't Mass General."

Young nodded. "I understand that," he said. "But—"

"Do you?" Coakley asked, a quizzical look on his face. "Do you really? You did a couple of deals, upscale cokeheads, and all went well, and so you want to step up, which is fine, and I provide you with an opportunity to step up, but I'm not sure you understand that this is a business where things go wrong all the time. I've had clients who thought they had all their ducks in a row, and by all appearances they did, and then the next thing you know they're in Leavenworth."

Young was suddenly quiet. For the moment, his anger was overshadowed by the stab of fear that came whenever he considered the possibility of getting caught.

Coakley could see that Young was momentarily chastened.

"Look," he said, "I know this puts you in a bind—"

"I made commitments to people," Young said. "They're expecting it. The timing is important."

Coakley nodded. "They'll wait," he said, and he knew they would, for he'd dealt with them before. "But we may have something else to deal with in the meantime." Coakley looked away from Young and watched as the big trawler docked.

"Such as?" Young asked.

"The cops," Coakley said.

Young seemed puzzled. "How so?" he asked.

"They like a piece of whatever action they know about," Coakley said. "They don't like people doing business without paying them for protection. If they know about someone's deal, then they either get paid to let it happen or they work quite diligently to destroy it. You have entered into something where people pay a great deal of money for the privilege to do business. You've paid nothing. If they detect this deal, you'll either pay to participate or you won't be in business."

Young hesitated. "How would they know about this deal?"

"I'm not sure how much they know," Coakley said. "I had a guy sniffing around it. But it wouldn't surprise me if they had the basics down."

Young was clearly alarmed. "But how would they know?" he asked, incredulous.

Good question, Coakley thought. How would they know? They would know if I told them. They would know if I discreetly passed along the information to someone I know within the department, to a man to whom I have occasionally provided information through the years. They would know if I offered that tip to this man—a lieutenant in Narcotics—a man who spent his nights seeking opportunities for shakedowns; a man who sought out deals so he could find a way to take a piece of the action. That's how they would know. And Coakley had been certain—as certain as that he had fucked up everything he'd touched in his life—that his tip would get passed along and that the information would find its way to the people in charge of these operations; the people behind it all, who made it all work. And they would find the deal no less than irresistible.

Coakley shrugged. "People hear things, pick things up, and things get passed around," the lawyer said.

"So what did they say?" Young asked.

"General questions around the edge. You hear about a new thing, new deal, new people? Around the edges."

Young considered this. "You think we'll be okay?" he asked.

Coakley shrugged. "There's no way of knowing. For all we know, they're watching us right now." Young looked down the pier at the fishermen unloading the trawler. He looked back out toward the street, at the parking lot next door.

"How do we know they're not over there," Coakley said, nodding down the length of the pier. "They could be watching us this very minute. There could be a photographer somewhere with a zoom lens. There are microphones, you know, that could pick up every word of our conversation from as far away as—see that van over there, Mulligan Brothers Oil Heat—from as far away as that. Pick up every word."

There was a long moment of silence. Had he been naive? Young wondered. He'd planned all along to keep his hands clean, to stay as far from the product itself as possible. He would organize, plan, and run the operation, but it was his intention never to be in possession of any illicit substance.

"What could they do to us for talking?" Young asked.

Coakley looked sharply at him. "For talking?" he said. "You should learn to be more precise in your choice of verbs. For conspiring? For planning? For what the federal people like to call racketeering? What could they do to you, a young man with a future? They could ruin your life. They could take away everything you own, strip you of your dignity. They could deprive you not only of your freedom, but of your hopes."

Coakley regarded Young. "They could make your life so miserable you'd want to die."

Young stood motionless, his heart pounding in his chest.

"That is why, if they learn more about this operation and if they approach us, we will do whatever it is they want done. Because to do otherwise would invite them to destroy you."

Young waited a moment.

"What about you?" Young asked.

"Me?" Coakley said. "There's nothing left to destroy."

CHAPTER 14

"LISTEN, I'VE GOT some bad news," Del Rio said, speaking on the phone from Boston. "Ray Murphy is dead. Shot in the head."

Jack Devlin stood in the kitchen of the pretty pink house on the bluff overlooking the ocean and sought to steady himself.

He did not know what to say.

"You there?" Del Rio asked.

There was more silence before Jack replied: "I'm here."

"So we have a problem at the moment, which is that Murphy's daughter says that the other day he was very upset after talking with you. You evidently paid him a visit of some kind?"

"Yeah," Jack said.

"What about?" Del Rio asked.

Jack hesitated. "My father."

"And he was reluctant?" Del Rio said. "The daughter says he was reluctant."

"He wasn't overjoyed."

"He told her you bullied him," Del Rio said. "So this word gets around with the brass and they want to sit with you. I'm telling you this so you're prepared. You understand?"

"I appreciate it," Jack said. "I'm headed back in the morning."

"I think it'd be better this afternoon," Del Rio said. "They're kinda looking for you."

"What do you mean?" Jack asked.

"Let me put it to you straight here, Jack. Murphy, let's be perfectly candid about it, he was an asshole. I make no bones. But the thing is that he's a former cop and doesn't really do anyone any harm, and one day he's fine, according to his daughter who visited with him daily—lived up the street—and the next day he's all discombobulated and all upset and fucked up. And why? Well, seems he's been paid a visit by the cop, this dick. Big kid, strong, kind of pushes his way in the door. Maybe has a threatening manner. And shit from years ago gets dredged up, and the guy is upset and then doesn't calm down but gets more upset and maybe he shouldn't have told the guy what he told him and maybe he should call him back and tell him to forget the whole thing, and then wham, he's dead.

"And the problem is that the M.E. is positive he was taken out by a Glock nine, and there's been a quick check run, and your weapon isn't in your locker."

"That's where I left it," Jack said. He did not mention that he had another Glock nine tucked away at home.

"Well, it ain't there now," Del Rio said. "So you hop a plane and come on back and we'll figure out how to deal with this."

"Wait a minute," Jack said. "Are you saying that I'm suspected of—"

"I am merely conveying to you what I know, which is: that, one, Murphy was found dead by his daughter Maureen; that, two, the M.E. says he was shot early Sunday afternoon with a Glock nine; that, three, when asked if anything unusual had occurred of late to her father, the daughter responded by saying he had been quite upset after a visit from the son of Jock Devlin; that, four, someone in the brass got the bright idea to check out your weapon, and it is reported missing; that, five, someone around here—and I don't yet know who—has a hard-on for you.

" 'Cause get this one: Moloney's lawyer went to the commissioner. This is what I hear. His lawyer went to the commissioner and says Moloney wants to fess up to certain indiscretions. He's willing to admit that he crossed the line, took some dough, whatever. But he insists the incidents were rare and the amounts minor."

"It's a fucking joke," Jack said.

"The brass are not laughing, however," Del Rio said. "No laughter. No peals of laughter, as one might say. No yukking. No guffaws. No smiles. No grins. Many, many the pursed lip. *Comprende?*"

Jack looked out the glass doors leading to the deck. He saw a sailboat riding on the horizon.

"I'll get a plane early this afternoon," he said. "There's something at one or one-thirty. Let's assume I can get on that. I'll come straight to your office at, say, four. I'd like to talk this through with you before I see anyone else."

JACK DEVLIN REACHED Deputy Superintendent Tom Kennedy at his office at police headquarters.

"Jackie, where are you?" Kennedy asked, concern evident in his voice.

"Florida," Jack said. "Del Rio called me about Murphy. I'm on my way back now."

"Jesus, Jackie, your name is flying all over this place," Kennedy said. "What's this about you going to Murphy's house and pushing him around?"

"I didn't push him around, Tom. We had a conversation. I was there less than an hour."

"About what?" Kennedy asked.

"About my dad."

"Jackie, listen to me now," Kennedy said. "There's word going around from Murph's daughter, evidently, that you went over there and muscled him and scared the shit out of him for some reason."

"I was persistent with him," Jack said. "I wasn't threatening."

"But Jack, what the hell are you doing going over to a guy like Murphy anyway? I don't get that."

"Jesus, Tom, I just wanted to talk with him about my father, that's all."

"But I don't get why you'd want anything to do with that kind of a guy, a bitter old man, a hater, a poisonous guy, Jack."

Devlin was jarred by Kennedy's reproachful tone. For a moment he considered telling Kennedy about his father's letter, but he had never told anyone about it, and he quickly dismissed the idea.

"I mean why Murphy, Jack, can you tell me that?" Kennedy asked.

"I just thought, maybe . . ." Devlin said, stumbling along. "I don't know, Tom. I just had an instinct is all."

"Well, you've got yourself in an uncomfortable situation and we've got to get you out of it," Kennedy said. "There's going to be a greeting party for you, a couple of guys who'll question you. When I heard about it, I screamed bloody murder, but it's a necessity based on what the daughter is saying."

"That I was somehow—"

"That you bullied him and pushed him around and that he was very much shaken up when you left."

"Jesus," Jack muttered.

"So listen to me, Jackie. When you sit down with these guys—I think it'll be Buckley and Lopez—stay very, very cool. Whatever you do, stay cool. Buckley can be a little crude, as you know. Just do me a favor, whatever you do, stay cool."

"THEY FEEL THEY have to be scrupulous in a case like this," Emily said as the plane to Boston rose above the West Palm Beach airport. "I'm trying to think about what I would do if the same thing happened in my office. Let's say an ex–Assistant U.S. Attorney turns up murdered. And the day before, he had a visit from a current member of the staff. And the dead person's daughter says he was distressed by the visit. I would definitely feel the need to sit down and talk with the person. Immediately."

Jack sat back in the seat. "Rationally, I agree," he said. "But I don't have a good feeling about this."

She reached over and took his hand, squeezing it. "It'll be fine," she said, smiling. "I'm absolutely sure of it. They'll ask a series of questions, which we could predict right now. And they'll put the conversation on the record, and that'll be that."

He hesitated, and she caught his look of concern.

"What should I do?" he asked.

"Precisely what you are doing," she said. "Go back, go through the interview. Answer every question." She hesitated. "Assuming the tenor is one of goodwill."

He gave her a quizzical look.

"If it's a collegial tone, then cooperate fully," she explained. "If it's clearly something they feel is required, something they must do, have no choice, that sort of thing. If, however," she said, turning in her seat to face him, "there is any indication of hostility, if it at all feels adversarial, then walk out of that room and retain counsel."

He was surprised. "Really?" he said.

She nodded emphatically. "If the temperature is high in that room and there's any indication they might be coming after you, then absolutely."

He leaned his head back against the airplane seat.

"Jack, I'm sorry if that surprises you," she said. "But my interest here is protecting you. And these people are your friends unless they are not. And when they are not, they are not neutral, they are your adversaries. Look, I'm assuming that this will be a breeze. I don't want to blow it out of proportion. I don't want you going in feeling all sorts of anxiety. I really believe you'll go in, have a perfunctory chat, and that's it. But if not, if it feels like something more than that, then don't be foolish. Get out. Exercise your rights."

He watched her as she spoke, and saw the intensity in her eyes. She was so clearheaded, so smart. And she clearly cared about him.

He smiled at her. "I feel very lucky at this moment," he said softly.

She cocked her head, puzzled. "Lucky how?"

"Lucky to be with you."

"Oh," she said. "Jack . . ." She smiled and took his hand. "I feel lucky, too," she said. "Very."

WHEN JACK DEVLIN walked through the front door of Boston police headquarters, he was greeted by a young uniformed officer. "Detective Buckley asked me to meet you here," the young man said, "and bring you to Conference Room 2B right away."

Jack hesitated. He wanted to speak with Del Rio first.

"He asked that it be right away," the young officer said insistently.

"Okay," Jack replied, and they headed up the stairs to the second floor. Conference Room 2B was long and narrow, with windows on one side facing out over Berkeley Street. On the opposite wall there was a white board. There were three large ashtrays arranged on the table.

When Jack walked in, two homicide detectives were seated at one end of the table. Walter Buckley was the big one, six-two, well over 200 pounds. He wore charcoal-gray slacks and a light gray sweater vest over a shirt and tie. Buckley was in his early sixties, twenty years older than Alberto Lopez, his partner. Lopez was of medium height and build, with coffee-colored skin and a well-trimmed mustache and beard. Lopez wore a black Armani sport jacket and tight blue jeans.

The three men exchanged stiff greetings.

"So we, ah, are looking into this matter of Ray's death," Buckley said. He glanced at his El Producto panatella, at the growing, crooked ash, and reached over and flicked it into the ashtray. "So, ahh, what can you tell us?" Buckley asked.

Jack looked at him. Buckley's face was broad and fleshy, his eyes rheumy, veins cracked and red on his nose. His hair was black and gray, thick and disheveled. His shirt collar was open, his necktie askew. Jack saw that the gray sleeveless sweater vest had several small burn holes on the front.

"Nothing," he replied.

Buckley raised his eyes and glanced toward Lopez. Buckley stuck the El Producto into the side of his mouth and spread his arms out to the side. "Then I guess we're all done, Detective," he said sarcastically. Buckley looked at Lopez and nodded. "We all done? 'Cause he knows nothin'. We must be done, huh?"

Lopez smiled at his partner's theatrics. "If you could just walk through with us, Jack, maybe pitch in a little here," Lopez said. "Just walk through."

"The daughter doesn't say 'nothing,' " Buckley said. "She did not say that. She says you pushed Ray around pretty good, is what she says."

"That's bullshit," Jack said.

"Oh, bullshit, huh?" Buckley said. "So, what, the daughter did it? She shoot Ray, you think? Pro'ly, huh?"

"Walter, let's back up here for a minute," Jack said. "You have a problem with me for some reason. What the reason is, I'm not sure exactly, but whatever it is, you obviously have a problem. I want to make clear to you that I don't have a problem. You do. If you want to know what I know about the murder of Ray Murphy, I've told you. I don't know anything. If you want to ask me directly whether I killed Ray, if you think that's a possibility, then ask me directly and I'll tell you I did not kill him. But don't play some juvenile fucking game with me."

Buckley's face turned red. He glared at Devlin. "You think you're a tough guy, huh?" he said.

Jack frowned and turned to Lopez. "You want to ask me anything, because if not, then I'm going to go do some work."

Lopez nodded. "I do, Jack, yeah, have some questions," Lopez said. "If you could just walk through with us, Jack. Just walk through. You go to Ray's house when? Sunday is it?"

"I drove out there Saturday, late afternoon, around four-thirty or so," Jack replied. "He was outside working in the yard. I introduced myself and said I wanted to talk with him. We went inside and talked."

Lopez nodded and shrugged his shoulders. "So you show up, Jack, and Ray's outside working, like what, on the shrubs, what?"

"Cleaning up the yard, leaves, that kind of thing."

"And you go up to him and say, what?"

"I asked if he was Ray Murphy, and he said yes, and I told him who I was."

"And what did he say?" Lopez asked.

"He said, 'Jesus Christ.'"

"'Jesus Christ'?"

Jack nodded.

"So he was surprised?" Lopez said.

"Yes."

"Did he say anything else?"

"He said I looked like my father," Jack said.

"You looked like your father?"

Jack nodded.

"Anything else?"

Jack shook his head.

"So where'd you talk, outside, inside?" Lopez asked.

"Inside," Jack said.

"He invited you in," Lopez said.

"He wasn't eager to talk to me," Jack said.

Lopez drew back and squinted. "What do you mean, Jack? How did that manifest?"

"He said he was busy, had other things to do. I all but pleaded with him. And he let me inside and we talked."

Lopez seemed puzzled. "All but pleaded with him, Jack? I don't get that. Help me with that part."

"I was very eager to speak with him and I thought this was my chance and I didn't think coming back another time would work, so I wanted to nudge him and get him to talk to me."

"So this was very important to you, obviously," Lopez said.

Jack nodded.

"What was so important?"

Jack hesitated. "That's a personal matter," he said.

Lopez held up his hands as though to back off. "I respect that, Jack," he said. "I do. But unfortunately, Walter and I are supposed to, you know, gather whatever information we can. We've got a retired cop here murdered in his home in one of the safest neighborhoods of the city. Shot with a police-issue weapon. I mean this is not a pretty picture. So while I'm sure it's personal in a way, I have no choice but to ask about it. You understand this, I know."

"It was about my father," Jack said. "I asked about things that happened years ago when my dad was on the force."

"Like?"

Jack looked away down the conference table. He looked at Buckley sitting sullenly, a scowl on his face, the El Producto between his fingers.

"I'm not going to get into that," Jack said. "It was personal. Private. About my dad."

Lopez seemed sorrowful. "Okay," he said, "if you insist. But Jack, I don't think . . ." He shook his head.

"So how long were you there?" Buckley asked.

"Less than an hour," Jack said.

"And you're not going to tell us about that conversation?"

"Other than that it was a personal conversation about my father, no."

"So when you left Murphy's house he was fine?"

"Absolutely," Jack said.

"What was he doing?" Buckley asked.

"He was just standing there, holding the door, in his kitchen."

"And you left and went where?" Buckley asked.

"Saturday? I went home," Jack said.

"And you were home all evening?"

"No, I went home and showered and changed clothes and went out for the evening."

"So you could give us the name of someone who could attest to your whereabouts Saturday night?" Buckley asked.

"I could."

"So?" Buckley said.

"Is it necessary?" Jack asked, glancing at Lopez.

"Do you have something to hide here, Detective?" Buckley asked angrily.

Jack hesitated. "The person's name is Emily Lawrence," he said.

Lopez and Buckley looked at each other. "With the feds?" Lopez asked.

"Yes."

"My compliments," Lopez said. "Quite the beautiful girl, that one. Quite."

Jack did not know what to say.

"So she could attest to your whereabouts for what period?" Lopez asked.

"Saturday evening from about seven until maybe two or so Sunday morning."

Buckley laughed.

Jack turned and regarded him. Buckley drew on the El Producto and exhaled slowly, laughing again.

Jack tried to ignore him.

"You didn't go to F.L.A. with her?" Buckley asked.

"Is that relevant?" Jack asked Lopez.

"Look, I know it's kind of obnoxious," Lopez said, "but you've done this kind of thing enough to know that if you were in my shoes you'd ask these questions. Am I wrong, Jack?"

"Yeah, I went to Florida with Emily," he said.

"And the trip had been planned for a while?" Lopez asked.

"It was a spur-of-the-moment thing," Jack replied. "Very spur-of-the-moment. We both decided we needed to get away for a few days and we just went."

Lopez nodded and made a note on his pad. "So let's just go back for a second," Lopez said. "You did not have any sort of confrontation with Ray Murphy, is that correct?"

"Not a confrontation," Jack said. "He didn't really want to talk with me and I pushed it."

"Pushed it how?"

"Rhetorically," Jack said. "I pleaded. I think in a way he wanted to talk. He was relieved to talk."

"Relieved?" Buckley said. "Why would he be relieved?"

Jack thought about it. "I think in a way he had long expected me to come talk with him, and I think he was glad to get it over with."

Lopez got up and walked to the window. He looked out on Berkeley Street, hands in his pockets, the Armani jacket hanging in elegant folds.

"You're throwing me off a bit here, Jack," Lopez said. " 'Glad to get it over with.' Get what over with? Why would he be glad?" Lopez shrugged. "Walk me through, Jack."

"Ray Murphy knew what was going on back there," Jack said. "He knew a lot. It was not a conversation he wanted to have."

"Knew a lot about?" Lopez asked.

"What was going on."

"How would he know?" Lopez asked.

"Because he was involved," Jack said.

"Ray Murphy?" Lopez asked.

Jack nodded.

"Bullshit!" Buckley said. "That's bullshit. I knew Ray Murphy." Buckley leaned forward across the table. "What the fuck, the poor fucker is dead and you want to smear him in death. Jesus Christ!"

Lopez shook his head. "That's rough stuff, Jack," he said.

"You asked me why he was reluctant to talk," Jack said. "I answered your question."

"You fuckin' guys," Buckley said, shaking his head. "The educated man. Holy Christ! What a bunch of baloney." Buckley laughed a harsh, mocking laugh. "I heard this woman once on the TV when they asked her what did women most want in a man, and she said an educated man. She'd studied this, see. And she said women want an educated man. What do you think of that, Devlin?"

Jack ignored Buckley. He rose from the table, ready to leave. "You all set?" Jack asked Lopez.

Lopez shrugged. "I got nothing else," he said.

"Have you found that because you're an educated man you get more pussy?"

Jack started toward the door.

Buckley laughed the harsh, mocking laugh again. This time there was a guttural tone to his voice.

"How about the federal woman, Devlin," Buckley began. "How about her—"

Jack turned quickly and faced Buckley. "Don't go there, Walter," he warned in a calm voice. "Don't go there."

Buckley reddened. "I bet she gets a wet pussy, huh?" Buckley said, leering.

Jack knew that he should walk out of the room, knew what

Buckley wanted him to do, knew he was being set up; but he could not help it. Something inside him flashed when he heard what Buckley said, and he responded with a hard right hand that caught Buckley on the side of his head, just above eye level, and sent him crashing to the floor. Buckley lay there with both hands covering the spot where he'd been punched.

"That was very foolish, Jack," Lopez said. "Very foolish."

CHAPTER 15

HE KNEW MOLONEY was a bad man, and he thought it possible that Moloney was an evil man. Jack had heard the rumors, the whispers that the owner of the Blackthorn had been making payments to cops. Had those payments gone to Moloney? he wondered.

To build a strong case against one of the most visible veteran detectives on the force would send a message to the rank and file like nothing else possibly could. Moloney was smart, experienced. He'd been through Administration, Vice, Narcotics, Homicide. He'd been detached to work on a joint city-state task force with the Massachusetts State Police. He'd been a speaker at various law enforcement symposia at Northeastern University's School of Criminal Justice. He'd been on special assignment to the office of the Suffolk County District Attorney.

Was it possible that Moloney could be the key to cleaning up the entire department? Possible that he was so emblematic of the corrupt cop that were he to fall, the others would quietly close up their operations? For if Moloney could be brought down—Moloney, who was tougher and smarter and better connected than the rest—then anyone could be brought down.

Was it naive, Jack wondered, to think there might be a domino effect? He knew there were the hard core who would never go straight, but he also suspected that there were a fair number of marginal characters in the department, weak men who did what they did because it was done, it had been done, it could be done. And because it could be justified. Moloney was a big shot and a success, had a drawer full of citations and was respected, and he supplemented his income so they'd say to themselves: Why shouldn't I?

THE BLACKTHORN WAS an Irish pub a few blocks out past the hospital district near the Fens. It drew hospital workers from Beth Israel, Children's, Deaconess, and Brigham & Women's, as well as students from Simmons, Emmanuel, and art schools near the Gardner Museum and the Museum of Fine Arts. It was a small, cramped space set belowground in a run-down building on a block with a Laundromat, a variety store, and a secondhand music shop. The bar attracted a good crowd on weeknights and was packed on weekends. You entered from the street down seven steps to the basement room, long and narrow, no more than twenty feet wide at any point. There was a bar to the left and tables crammed together to the right. The walls were black and dark green with posters and signs evoking Dublin.

The legal capacity was 151 patrons. This number was set by the licensing commission based on a formula that included square footage and available egress. Every public facility in Boston had an assigned capacity, from the Blackthorn to the Ritz ballroom.

Donald Dineen had owned the Blackthorn for five years. For the first year in business, it had been a cowboy bar operated under the name Valley Ranch. But in that incarnation it had attracted a few country music fans and more bikers than Dineen wanted to deal with. When he switched the club to an Irish motif and renamed it the Blackthorn, the patrons began pouring in.

For Donald Dineen there was but one problem: His capacity was too low to make the kind of money he was sure he could make.

Bar owners had a basic rule of thumb: On weeknights, their patrons turned over twice; on weekends, they turned over three times.

In other words, if a hundred people showed up at peak on a week-night, you could project that a total of two hundred would enter the bar during the course of the night. On average, the per-customer expenditure was twelve dollars on weeknights, fifteen on weekends. Thus, on a weekend, defined by bar owners as Thursday, Friday, and Saturday nights, Donald Dineen had four hundred customers per night spending fifteen dollars each. That gave him a nightly take of $6,000 or a total of $18,000 gross for the three nights.

Weeknights were not an issue because he rarely reached capacity. But weekends were a problem because there was always a line outside, always more customers clamoring to get into the cigarette smoke and rollicking jukebox and Guinness on draft.

What it boiled down to for Dineen was simple: If he could add another fifty people at peak—for an additional two hundred per night on weekend nights—he could make an additional $9,000 per week. That translated into an extra $468,000 per year merely by adding a few extra people over his capacity three nights out of the week.

And so, sometime back Donald Dineen had found himself deal-ing with Detective Moloney. They held a series of confidential discus-sions, and the result had been an agreement: Moloney would make sure that the capacity of 151 was not enforced Thursday through Sat-urday nights, and guaranteed Dineen protection from any possible sanction. The agreement had lasted three years, and in that period Donald Dineen had grossed an additional $1.4 million as a result. Dineen had paid Moloney and other officers an average of $4,000 per month over that time for a grand total of $432,000, leaving himself $972,000 to the plus side.

Two people in the world had known of this arrangement, had known the full details and story. But now there was only one, for in a cruelly ironic twist, Donald Dineen had died in a fire in the Blackthorn; a death fire that investigators attributed to "severe overcrowding."

The four buildings that comprised the project were brick, square, five stories. The O'Neil Project was one of the safest and quietest in the city. About a third of the residents were Americans; the rest were immigrants from India, Ireland, Haiti, Belarus, Vietnam, and the Czech Republic. They had joined together over very little, but the death of Jenine O'Connor had affected them all. She'd been just nineteen, a nursing school student who lived in the project with her father, a retired city worker on hundred percent disability.

Jack Devlin climbed the stairs of building number four, the sound of his shoes echoing on the cold cement stairway. He arrived at the landing on the second floor and knocked on the steel door to apartment 49.

Joe O'Connor peered through the peephole in the door and saw Devlin. "What?" he said.

"Mr. O'Connor, please," Jack said.

"What is it?" O'Connor asked.

"I'm Detective Devlin," Jack said. "I'd like to speak with you."

Joe O'Connor unchained the door. He unsnapped a lock, opened the door, and stared at Jack. O'Connor was five feet nine inches tall and weighed under 150 pounds. He wore a V-neck T-shirt and green work pants. He was bent over slightly, leaning to the side, his stability aided by the use of a cane. His on-the-job back injury had cost him the ability to earn a living.

"You're a detective?" O'Connor asked.

Jack nodded.

"Got ID?" O'Connor asked.

Jack showed his badge and picture ID.

After O'Connor had confirmed that Jack Devlin was, in fact, a member of the Boston Police Department, he turned sideways, as though to permit Jack into his apartment. Instead, however, O'Connor took his cane in both hands as though it were a baseball bat and was suddenly swinging it wildly in the direction of Jack's face. Jack reacted instinctively, pulling back and bringing his left hand up to block the blow. But the cane glanced off the knuckles of his left fist and caught him just above the left eye. He went down hard on to the concrete floor of the entryway.

"You fuckin'," Joe O'Connor said, his jaw clenched, spittle coming from his mouth. O'Connor moved forward, but his disability slowed him and Jack recovered quickly enough to block the next blow with his forearm and, with a quick move of his right hand, to seize control of the cane. As he did so, jerking it away with his vastly superior strength, Joe O'Connor lost his balance and went spinning to the floor.

The apartment door across the way opened and an elderly man emerged.

"That you, Joe?" the man asked, surveying the scene. When the man realized what was happening he registered alarm. "What the—"

Jack was on his feet, a gash opened over his left eye, dark fresh blood streaming down his face. The cut was right next to the scar Jack had carried for years, the result of a high stick in hockey. While the new wound bled profusely, the scar puffed up, angry and swollen.

The neighbor across the hallway was confused by the scene. Here was a big man, over six feet, powerful-looking, who'd been beaten to the ground by a crippled old man.

Notwithstanding his condition, Jack spoke calmly. "Everything's okay, sir," he said, turning to the old man. "I'm a police officer. A misunderstanding."

The man froze.

Jack nodded assurance to the man.

"You okay, Joe?" the man asked.

O'Connor was breathing hard. He nodded, out of breath. "All right, Arthur," he said.

Jack reached his hand out to help O'Connor up off the floor. "I'd like to talk privately," Jack told him.

O'Connor watched him carefully, and finally reached up and permitted Jack to pull him off the floor.

They went inside the apartment, and Jack shut the door. The blood from his forehead was in his right eye now, coming down his face. "May I borrow a dish towel?" he asked.

O'Connor went to a drawer and took out a clean towel. Jack dampened one end under the faucet and dabbed the cut clean.

"Ice?"

O'Connor nodded toward the freezer, and Jack helped himself. He wrapped three cubes into the other end of the towel and placed it against the cut.

Then Jack went to the sofa and sat down. He could see that the easy chair, well-worn, placed in front of the TV set, was O'Connor's.

"You're pretty handy with that thing," Jack said, trying to force a smile as he nodded toward the cane. "Play any hockey?"

O'Connor said nothing.

Jack took a deep breath, looked down at his feet, and nodded. "Listen, I'm really not here in any official way. I would like to ask some things, but I also want to say to you—and this is personal— that I am sorry for what happened. And I've heard the rumors just like you have, and if any of our men were in any way involved, I am sorry and ashamed."

Jack paused for a moment. His head throbbed and he was having only modest success holding back the blood from the cut above his left eye. He held the ice in place with one hand while running the other through his hair, front to back, trying to put it in place. But it was more nervous gesture than anything else, for he was deeply humbled in the presence of this man who had suffered the loss of his only child. Jack believed that whatever emotion he felt, whatever words he offered, were woefully inadequate to the moment. But he had to try.

O'Connor was a thin, pale man with a two- or three-day stubble. He stared at Devlin with a mixture of disbelief and confusion.

"If any—" he said, and stopped. He looked off to the side and shut his eyes tightly for a long moment.

There was the smell of something burning, and O'Connor went and flipped open a toaster oven and pulled out a charred English muffin with melted cheese. He plucked it with a fork and held it for a moment as though wondering what to do with it. Suddenly, he flung it hard in the direction of the sink, but it was too high, struck a coffee mug and knocked it against the wall, breaking the handle.

O'Connor turned red with rage and faced Jack.

"God knows what happened," he said. "God knows the truth. But I believe what I believe, and that is that they were on the fuckin' take. I believe it!"

Jack nodded. "I've heard that," he said quietly, earnestly. "And if it's true, I want to know. 'Cause it's my job to prosecute them."

O'Connor looked down at the frayed carpet for a moment, then limped to his chair and fell heavily into it. He thought, as he had countless times before, about her last night. His daughter had come home from nursing school having learned her grades for the term, as proud as she could be with her B-plus average.

"If it wasn't for chemistry," she had said, "it'd be an A-minus."

He had been very proud of her indeed, and reality struck home when he saw the report: She really was going to be a nurse; she really was going to make it. One more semester and she would be out, finished, ready for her training.

They had chatted for a while, sitting right here in this space.

O'Connor recalled sitting precisely where he was now, and Jenine had been sitting exactly where the detective was now. She'd been wearing a turtleneck shirt, red, with navy-blue sweatpants. And on her feet she'd worn those furry slippers she always wore around the apartment.

It had been one of his favorite times, the early evening on a Friday, when she was done with her schoolwork for the week and looked forward to a night out with friends. She socialized primarily with other nursing students and several girls she'd known in high school. She'd had a couple of boyfriends, but those situations hadn't worked out, and O'Connor was just as glad. She was only nineteen, after all, and seemed to him so much younger than that.

That had been the night she'd shocked him. He had been enjoying the conversation, enjoying their private, intimate moment, when he could sense her tensing up. She sat on the sofa with her legs tucked underneath her.

"There's this notice on the board at school," she said. "They're recruiting nurses at the big medical center in Jacksonville."

Jacksonville. He had heard the word, but it had not registered.

"Florida, Dad," she added.

"Florida?" he said, clearly stunned. "Florida, honey," he said again, as though it were off somewhere spinning in orbit around Mars.

"They pay really well, Dad, and one of the girls told me they have beautiful condos not far away, a pool and tennis and anything you could want, plus they subsidize your monthly payments. You get a discount if you're a nurse at the center."

He had sat in his chair, openmouthed, speechless. The thought of her leaving, of picking up and going off to Florida to live there and work there. He would be alone, and the thought of not having her was suddenly terribly painful.

"But what's wrong with . . ."

What's wrong with me? was what he'd been thinking. What's

wrong with me? was what he'd wanted to ask. But he hadn't dared, for he had feared the answer. He had feared she would say, "What's wrong with you is that you've done nothing with your life. What's wrong with you is that you've always been dim-witted and never amounted to anything, and even when you had steady work with the city you fucked it up by getting injured and going out on disability, not when the payments were high, but after there'd been a crackdown and the payments were the lowest they'd ever been. What's wrong with you is you took the life insurance money after my mother died and blew it on that foolish investment your friend talked you into. What's wrong with you is that you're aging too fast and the apartment is too small and it's in a fucking public housing project and I'm sick of this life and I want to go to a better place, a new place where the sun shines and I might meet someone and start a family and have my own life."

He wanted to ask the question, but did not dare.

"It's not something I would jump into," she had said, shaking her head as though the idea was the furthest thing from her mind. "But it's something to consider. I mean there aren't that many good jobs around here. Too many experienced nurses. In Florida and Arizona, there's lots of opportunity, and I've got to take that into consideration."

And after she had gone out for the evening, to the Blackthorn, he sat there in his chair and broke down and cried. For the first time in so many years, he broke down and sobbed, and it had taken a good long while before he was able to get himself under control. He'd cried at the prospect of her moving to Florida.

And then, a few hours later, with more than two hundred patrons jammed into the Blackthorn, a fire broke out, panic ensued, and Jenine was cut off from the exit, knocked by the stampeding crowd to the ground, where she was overcome by smoke. It was there, on the floor of a grimy bar, that Joe O'Connor's baby had died.

JACK WATCHED AS O'Connor sat motionless, staring off into space. His face had a grayish pallor, his eyes were sunken in dark holes. He was a man, Jack could see, who had been broken by the loss of his child. What must it be like, he wondered, to have no family other than a daughter, and then to suddenly lose that child? He could not imagine how terrible it must be.

Jack was numb with shame. For although he did not know the facts, he was sure that Jenine O'Connor was dead because of the corruption within the Boston Police Department. The corruption was not abstract, not some offense against a civil society: It was a profound and savage violation of humanity. He ached for this man.

"I've been over it in my mind a hundred times," O'Connor finally said. "Anyone who knows why it happened knows because they were in on it. Taking money. Nobody in that position will ever admit anything because they'd be admitting to manslaughter. So the story has gone to the grave with Dineen."

Jack, too, had thought about it. He'd gone over the various possibilities. He'd heard the rumors, the intimations, the whispers. But there had been nothing concrete, nothing more than speculation. Nothing more than talk. And that was why he knew that O'Connor was right: Any possibility of revealing the truth had gone to the grave with Dineen, for anyone with knowledge would be culpable in a crime.

"I thought maybe there was a possibility someone had said something to you," Jack said, "maybe that you'd heard a name, something . . . a rumor, anything."

Joe O'Connor looked at him and shook his head no.

JACK PLACED THE file folder from the insurance company's investigation into the fire at the Blackthorn on his desk. He began thumbing through the records, not sure precisely what he was looking for, but believing there had been a corrupt deal between the Blackthorn owner and someone within the BPD.

Jack did not know the extent of corruption in the Boston Police Department. He did not know who, exactly, was involved in whatever scams were being run. But in the months since he'd undertaken to investigate corrupt activity, he had theorized that corruption among uniformed officers was probably about what it had always been. But while there continued to be the sort of corruption he'd caught Moloney and Curran at, there was a new level of corruption, more elusive, more sophisticated, less visible than before. How did they hide the money? he wondered. He knew there were men who stole money from dealers, from bookies, and stuffed wads of cash in their pockets. But he believed there were some who had gotten past that. There had to be another mechanism for payoffs; a way to absorb, conceal, and distribute the proceeds.

The insurance company file included a copy of the Boston Fire Department's report on the fire, in which it had been ruled that the blaze was not a result of arson. The file included a copy of the Blackthorn insurance policy, details on the Blackthorn's owner, a list of employees, major suppliers, a copy of the state-issued liquor license, and various bank records.

Jack pulled the bank records out and began going through the details of the Blackthorn account. Payments had been made, during the prior year, to a long list of suppliers, including distributors for various beer, wine, and hard liquor companies. There were payments to food vendors, to a cleaning company, an exterminator, a painting contractor, the insurance company, the state of Massachusetts, the IRS. There were payments to the telephone, electric, and gas companies.

He was skimming the expenditure summary, about to set it aside, when a number caught his eye. Listed under the charitable contributions—to the Boy Scouts, the local youth soccer and baseball leagues, the YWCA, CYO, and more—he saw an organization called CrimeStoppers. While donations to the other organizations ranged between fifty and a thousand dollars for the year, there were four donations to CrimeStoppers, each for $36,000, for a yearlong total of $144,000. It struck Jack as very odd indeed.

JUST AFTER MIDNIGHT, he left police headquarters and began driving home. He'd gone about a mile when he noticed the Le Sabre tailing him on Boylston Street, behind Fenway Park. When he stopped at a light, he saw the Le Sabre hanging back a couple hundred feet. When the light changed, he accelerated quickly and drove rapidly toward Brookline Avenue, where he hit another red light. In his rearview mirror he could see the Le Sabre speed up to stay with him and then abruptly decelerate when the red light appeared.

Why would they tail him? he wondered. It wasn't as though he'd been hiding out. They knew where he lived, where he worked. His whereabouts were never a secret. He had believed that if they were to act against him, it would come at his home, at night. But he felt secure there. He'd had an advanced detection system installed so it would be impossible for anyone to invade his house while he was asleep without tripping a sensitive alarm.

As he rode out the Riverway, the traffic thinned noticeably. Jack stayed at 40 miles an hour, the precise speed limit, and watched the Le Sabre hanging back several hundred feet. He checked and made sure the doors in his Cherokee were locked. He followed the Jamaicaway out into Jamaica Plain, and as he drove up the hill toward Perkins Street, he wondered whether fatigue hadn't created paranoia within his mind. At Perkins he waited for the red light to turn green, and when it did, he accelerated as though he intended to continue along the Jamaicaway. Instead, at the last possible moment, he jammed his steering wheel all the way around, took a hard right, floored the Jeep, and fishtailed along the street. Within seconds he was going 65 miles an hour in a 35-mile zone, and as he reached the back side of Jamaica Pond, he saw the Le Sabre coming, accelerating hard. There was now no question. Jack slowed down as he proceeded up Goddard Avenue toward West Roxbury, and the Le Sabre slowed, too.

Jack took his Glock nine-millimeter out of its shoulder holster and placed it on the passenger seat and took it off safety. He continued driving at a leisurely pace, the Le Sabre following. He considered calling the Area E station house and asking for a cruiser to meet him at his house, but couldn't bring himself to do it. It would appear that he could not handle himself. When he reached his street, he turned in. The Le Sabre followed. When he got to his house and turned into the driveway, the Le Sabre pulled ahead and idled in front of his house. He hesitated, then got out of the Jeep, dropped to one knee, and aimed the Glock at the Le Sabre, sixty feet away. But the Le Sabre did not move. They knew he would not shoot first. He tried to make out shapes in the car but could not; the windows were heavily tinted.

He noted the license plate number—and would later learn that the vehicle had been stolen earlier in the evening—and remained in a crouch, weapon ready, for a full minute, when the Le Sabre abruptly pulled away.

Jack took a deep breath and put his gun away. He went to the side door of the house and checked the security system. It was armed, just as he'd left it that morning. He disarmed the system, entered the house, and immediately rearmed it so that any entry from the exterior—through any door or window—would set off the alarm. With the doors locked and the system armed, he felt safe.

But then his sense of security was shattered, for when he walked into his kitchen, he was stunned by what he saw. There, sitting on his kitchen table, was a white index card propped against a saltshaker.

Someone had disarmed his security system, entered his house, then rearmed it. He picked up the card and read its three typewritten lines:

Convinced we can do what we want when we want?
Stop the foolishness for everyone's sake.
Yours included.

CHAPTER 16

AT TEN MINUTES before six in the morning the temperature in Roslindale stood at 7 degrees. It was dark as Jack drove toward Holy Name Church, past a Hood's milk truck and a *Herald* newspaper delivery van. He parked in the lot behind the church and entered the side door of the chapel. The early morning weekday Masses were celebrated here in this space barely one-tenth the size of the main church upstairs. Jack went to a pew about halfway back. He knelt, made the Sign of the Cross, and prayed. After a moment he got up off his knees and sat back on the wooden bench.

He felt someone moving close behind him. There were no more than a dozen other people spread throughout the chapel, and Jack thought it odd that someone would sit so close.

He turned and saw an old friend of his father's, Eammon O'Brien, his hands clasped in prayer, his head bowed.

"Don't turn around, Jackie," O'Brien whispered. "Don't pay no attention to me. You don't know who's observing."

"Eammon, you—"

"Let me finish, boy," said Eammon O'Brien. "I come to tell you to watch out for yourself, Jackie. These are bad people, Jackie. They don't hesitate to hurt anybody they want. Nothin' will stop them. Your father would be proud, Jackie. You've made him proud. So enough is enough. Leave it alone. I am telling you as God is my witness and judge to leave it alone and don't go no further. Nuthin' will ever change this. They won't allow it."

"Eammon, I—" But O'Brien had risen and moved quickly away, farther back in the church, shaking his head as if to say, Stay away, stay away.

"THE HEARING'S TODAY," Jack said from his car phone. "And I wanted to see whether you had any advice."

"Do what you think is best," Tom Kennedy replied. "Use your good judgment. That's all."

"We'll go and listen and go through the whole thing today so that we get out on the table how tight our case against them is," Jack said. "Then, once we've done that, my inclination is to back off, give them a break. See if we can get them to pitch in and help us. See if we can rehab them, basically."

"I guess I would have to say I'm a little surprised," Kennedy said.

Jack hesitated. "Surprised good or surprised bad?" he asked.

"Just surprised," Kennedy said. "I know you don't like Moloney."

"I think he's a bad actor, but I also think that if there's a chance these guys can turn it around, I mean . . ." He paused. "Plus, the idea that the department gets subjected to a barrage of negative publicity and speculation is too high a price to pay. Sheehy's right. It would be destructive. I really think it would."

Kennedy said nothing.

"So?" Jack said finally.

"So, what?" Kennedy asked.

"So what do you think?" Jack asked.

"I think you're being very wise," Kennedy said.

JACK STOOD IN disbelief when he heard the clerk's words.

"It's not here," the clerk said. "Someone must have removed it."

"I brought it here myself," Jack said. "I filled out the form. Here's the duplicate. Here's the number. Please check again."

The clerk frowned and disappeared into the back room. He

returned, shaking his head. "You sure you didn't take it out?" the clerk asked.

"Positive," Jack said. The rules of the evidence locker were clear: Only clerks were permitted within. It was a sanctuary of sorts. No uniformed officers or detectives were permitted inside without written permission. But Jack now placed his palms flat on the counter and vaulted it.

"Hey, come *on*, Detective," the clerk said as Jack brushed past him into the evidence room. He went to the numbered bin matching the number on his receipt. It was empty. He stood, staring down at it, growing angrier by the moment. Angry not with Moloney or Curran or any of the other corrupt cops involved in stealing the audiotape, but angry with himself for being foolish enough to trust anyone but himself with it.

Jack returned to the front. He made a fist and pounded it down on the counter. What a fool he'd been. What a fool! How had he underestimated them? After so much thought, after such careful planning, how had he underestimated them?

He took the back stairs and walked up to the third floor. When he arrived at the conference room, everyone else was in place: the clerk magistrate, who would preside over the hearing; Detectives Moloney and Curran and their attorneys; Del Rio, and the police department lawyer, Steven Driscoll.

Jack tapped Driscoll on the shoulder and motioned with his head toward the door. Driscoll rose and went out into the hallway with him.

"The tape is gone," Jack said.

"What!"

"It's not in the evidence locker. They obviously ripped it off."

"That's our case," Driscoll said. "That's it."

The two men stood silently in the hallway. Finally, they entered the conference room and took their seats.

"Let the record show that this is a preliminary hearing held under the rules of disciplinary procedures and practice of the Boston Police Department," said Renolds W. Granby, the clerk magistrate in charge of the hearing. "This is an administrative hearing and its findings do not preclude other action in other jurisdictions."

Granby was a man of fifty, with a gray suit and horn-rimmed glasses. He had an owlish look about him. He sat at one end of the conference room, adjacent to the office of the city's police commissioner. Granby glanced to his right and looked at Detectives Moloney and Curran and their lawyers, then to his left at Detectives Del Rio and Devlin, and Steve Driscoll, counsel for the police department.

"Does everyone understand the rules under which this hearing is being conducted?" Granby asked.

All present nodded.

"Does anyone have any amendment to the written statements submitted to me?"

This was a standard question, part of the procedure at such hearings, and ninety percent of the time the answer was no. Once in a while someone would have some bit of information to add. It was unheard of to withdraw a claim of evidence.

Driscoll glanced at Jack. "We do, actually, Mr. Granby," Driscoll said. "We had represented in our memorandum that we would present an audiotape recording made of the events of the night in question." Driscoll paused and glanced down at the conference table. "I would like to amend our memorandum by withdrawing that representation."

Granby seemed stunned. The lawyers for both Moloney and Curran drew back in surprise. Moloney raised his eyebrows as though to mock Devlin, as though to say, Ah, what a pleasant surprise. Curran looked down at the floor. Moloney and Curran's lawyers conferred in a brief, whispered exchange. Then Moloney's lawyer spoke.

"We move to suspend the hearing," he said eagerly. "The essence of the complaint against our clients has been withdrawn. Without material evidence, this proceeding should be suspended."

Granby seemed troubled. He turned to Driscoll. "Mr. Driscoll, are you certain of this?" he asked.

Driscoll nodded. "Yes," he said.

Moloney's lawyer, his eyes wide, saw his opportunity and moved for the kill.

"In the petition for this hearing," he said, "it was represented that there was an incriminating audiotape. In view of the withdrawal of that representation, I submit that this proceeding must be suspended."

Jack sat frozen at the table. He did not move; he could not. The idea that Moloney would walk out of this room without so much as a reprimand, with nothing on his record, with no change in his status as a sergeant detective on the Boston Police Department, was more than he could handle. Jack would have bet anything that Moloney had been involved in the Blackthorn deal, had exacted payments from the owner to protect him from overcrowding citations. He could not prove that, but believed it. And he also believed, in fact knew, that Moloney was in the business of shaking down drug dealers for cash. He'd had several dealers tell him that, and he had set up his own sting operation, an operation that caught Moloney in the act.

But no audiotape meant no case. For Jack had studied the law before undertaking his assignment, and he knew that hard evidence would be needed if he was to crack the brotherhood. He knew the department rules and procedures, the collective bargaining agreement with the detectives union, and the applicable law would favor an officer in a dispute when it was one person's word against another's.

They could go before the disciplinary board and seek dismissal or suspension of Moloney and Curran based on the direct testimony of Devlin and Del Rio, but that would be the word of two cops against two others.

Granby sat back, contemplating the situation. After a moment's thought, he leaned forward again.

"Mr. Driscoll," he said. "The department is alleging breach of duty. This is a grave charge. It is alleged in your memorandum of complaint that the two detectives violated their oaths of office and should be removed from the force. That they confiscated private property in an improper manner and subsequently committed perjury. Unless you have significant physical evidence to this effect, I see no alternative but to suspend this proceeding."

Driscoll said nothing.

Granby nodded. "I hereby grant the defense motion," he said. "This proceeding is suspended."

SHE HAD NEVER heard him sound so distressed.

"What happened?" Emily asked.

"I'm sorry to bother you," he said. "I really am." He was sweating and breathing heavily. He'd quickly left police headquarters and strode down the sidewalk, past heavily bundled shoppers and office workers.

"What's all that noise in the background?" she asked. "Where are you?"

"Boylston Street," he said. "Pay phone."

"It's freezing," she said. "Why are you outside?"

He sighed heavily. "I had to get out of there," he said. "The hearing was a disaster."

"What!"

"Disaster," he repeated.

"What happened?" she asked.

"Remember I told you about the tape of the bug we had?"

"Of course," she said.

"It's gone. I went to Evidence this morning and it was gone."

There was silence on the other end of the line. Then she said, "What do you mean you went to Evidence?"

"To the evidence room in the basement of headquarters," he said. "Where I'd filed it the night of the bust."

Silence again. "Jack, I don't know what to say. I mean . . ."

Of course, he thought. How could he have been so foolish? How could he have possibly believed that a particular portion of the department would have any integrity? How could he have been so naive, so foolish, as to believe that the tape was safe in the hands of the Boston Police Department? He'd been so careful, so very scrupulous in everything he'd done, in all of his thinking and plotting and planning, and he'd made a mistake a rookie wouldn't make. What could he possibly have been thinking?

"Where are you exactly?" she asked.

"Uh, Boylston and Berkeley," he said.

"Okay," she said. "You know that little hole in the wall on Newbury, right near Clarendon?"

"Yeah."

"I'll meet you there in ten minutes," she said. "I'm on my way."

She raced out of the office, caught a cab, and arrived at the restaurant a minute after him. They took a booth near the back and had coffee.

"You look exhausted," she said. "You desperately need a rest."

He slumped in the booth, looking defeated. "I blew it," he said. "I could have had real leverage, and I lost it." His visage grew dark and angry. "Because I'm a fucking incompetent!"

She gave him a reproachful look. "Hardly," she said. "All this does is prove you're human. You've thrown yourself into your work with a vengeance and focused too intensely for too long and you made a mistake. So you're human. Big deal. Plus you weren't going to prosecute anyway, so the result's the same."

"But it isn't," he said. "Because I would have been the magnanimous one, the reasonable one, and it would have softened the edges of some cops in the middle, some guys who might have come forward and talked. And it would have given me leverage over Moloney for next time, and we both know there will be a next time. I could have used this next time to force his resignation. That was my whole plan."

EMILY LAWRENCE WALKED down the hallway on the twelfth floor of the John W. McCormack Federal Courthouse, the heels of her black pumps clicking loudly on the polished floor. She walked swiftly from her office to the far corner of the floor where two holding rooms, secure facilities, were used for federal prisoners brought in for trial.

Larry Crapo had been arrested a day earlier for violating a restraining order taken out by his ex-girlfriend. Crapo had been charged with going to the woman's Milton apartment and slapping her around. She had reported him, and when he had been arrested, later that night—or, more accurately, at three-thirty in the morning— he was in possession of a substantial cache of cocaine as well as an unregistered handgun.

None of these offenses in and of themselves were particularly grave in nature. Individually and collectively, however, they constituted a violation of Crapo's federal parole. After having served two and a half years for dealing cocaine, he was on a three-year probation, with terms that required him to refrain from any sort of brush with the law.

In cases such as these, prosecutors had broad latitude, and federal judges were in the habit of granting prosecutors' petitions.

So it was that Larry Crapo, facing the prospect of going back to a federal prison to do an additional year or more, had talked with the FBI about his knowledge of a particular crime that had yet to be committed. He insisted upon talking about this face-to-face with one person alone, and that was the Assistant United States

Attorney who had prosecuted him and sent him to prison, one Emily Lawrence.

Emily entered the outer room and walked toward the holding area. She saw Larry Crapo slumped in a chair with handcuffs and leg irons. There was a small conference table, four metal chairs, and a large glass ashtray on the table. Two U.S. marshals stood nearby, chatting.

"Would you mind waiting outside, gentlemen," she said to the marshals. They got up to leave but she stopped them. "Those aren't necessary," she said, indicating the leg irons and cuffs. A marshal removed both.

Larry Crapo smiled as they left. "A pleasure to see you again, Emily," he said.

"It's always a delight to see you, Larry," she said sarcastically. "Beating up girls now, are we?"

His face reddened. "We had a misunderstanding," he said, looking down at the floor.

"The coke was a misunderstanding, too, probably."

"The coke was a plant," he said.

Emily regarded him with contempt. She folded her arms across her chest and glared at him. "If that's the kind of conversation you want to have, then there's no point in having a conversation."

He said nothing for a moment. Then, "So what am I up against?"

"You're going back to prison," she said flatly.

"How long?" he asked.

"I would say a year on the assault, a year on the gun, and two on the coke," she said quickly. "I would say four."

He was stunned. He sat with his mouth open, eyes wide.

"Possibly five," she added.

"Five . . ."

Larry Crapo was speechless, but only for a moment. For the idea of going back to prison was utterly repugnant to him. And he would do anything, literally, to keep from having to go back.

Emily stood with her arms crossed, waiting for him to edge toward the point. But she did not want to seem overeager.

"I've got work to do," she said, turning and moving toward the door, "so if—"

"If I say to you the word morphine, morphine in its purest form, would that mean anything to you?" Larry Crapo asked her.

She turned around quickly, her head cocked to one side, clearly taken by surprise and unable to hide it.

Crapo saw this and was encouraged. There was hope. He sat forward on the chair. "Come on," he said, "sit down."

She did. "What do you have?" she asked.

"So you do know about it?" Crapo said.

"I know of a deal involving very high-grade morphine, yes," she replied. "What can you tell me about it?"

"I need assurances that—" Crapo began, but before he'd finished his sentence she was vigorously shaking her head, dismissing what he had to say.

"No assurances," she said. "Tell me what you have. If it's good, we'll make a deal. If it's no good, we won't."

"I got no protection," he complained.

Emily shook her head with disgust and got up from the chair, moving quickly toward the door.

"All right, all right," he said desperately.

She stopped and turned, but remained standing.

"It's coming in here, into Boston, soon," Crapo said. "This'll be the first market where it gets any distribution. I know guys in on the ground floor."

This, Emily suspected, meant that Larry was in on the ground floor. "Go on," she said.

"It's been tested here. Test sales. Small amounts as samples have gone out, and the reaction's been strong. Very strong."

"Tell me," she said.

"I know a guy got the rights to distribute the South Shore," he said. "I know the guy, and so he takes samples out to customers who he thinks might be potential buyers, and some of these customers are themselves distributors but on a smaller scale, see. And the reaction is excellent."

"So who's in charge?" she asked.

Crapo suddenly grew serious. "That's what it comes down to, then, isn't it, Emily? Who's running the op? Who's the man? Who's breaking new ground here, doing what no one's done in years and years—bringing in a new product for an affluent market. No scuzz-balls. No ghetto shit. No crack crowd." He made a face indicating he found that notion profoundly distasteful.

"Who had samples?" she asked.

Crapo shrugged. "Don't know. I'd guess a handful, maybe two or three, maybe a half-dozen distributors."

"And the reaction was . . ."

"People flipped," Crapo said. "Very smooth. No hangover, minimal hangover."

"So who's behind it?" Emily asked.

Crapo fell silent, watching Emily closely. She waited.

"One very smart man," Crapo said. "One very smart, successful young man."

Emily waited, but Crapo was silent for a long moment. "I need some sign, some indication this will affect my status," he said. He said it quietly, humbly.

"You tell me who's behind it, and it has an impact on my investigation, and I will absolutely go to bat for you," she said.

"Plead everything out?" he asked.

"Except the assault," she said. "You pay a price for that."

He looked shocked.

"Beating women up, Larry," she said. "It offends me."

He reflected upon this, and then finally nodded. "Okay," he said. "Guy's a doctor at Brigham and Women's. Very big."

Emily was incredulous, though in the drug trade, she knew that nothing should ever surprise her.

"His name is Young, Dr. Christopher Young," Crapo said. "He's the brains behind the whole thing."

THE CRIMESTOPPERS BANK records indicated that the organization had revenues during the previous year of $144,000 and expenditures of the same amount. All of the money had gone in a single transaction as a donation to another not-for-profit charitable trust called the Law Enforcement Education Association. Jack Devlin looked at the document before him. He had never heard of the Law Enforcement Education Association, just as he'd never heard of CrimeStoppers before seeing it on the Blackthorn bank records. That it received all of its funds for a year from the owner of the Blackthorn, and that he had then immediately transferred all of those funds to another charitable organization—LEEA—struck Jack as quite peculiar.

He would have some research done into both organizations. But he knew he had to be careful. He didn't want whoever was behind these organizations to know he had an interest in them.

He put in a call to a man who could be trusted in the police department Technology Division, a young fellow who worked part-time while he attended law school nights. And he asked that some research be done carefully and with discretion.

COAKLEY ASCENDED THE stairs from the Copley subway station and paused for a moment to catch his breath. It was a bright sunny day, but the sun's warmth was lost in the arctic wind that swept down out of the north and whipped across the city of Boston. As the wind ripped across the open Copley Square park—a sizable quadrangle bound by the stately beauty of the Boston Public Library, the elegance of the Copley Plaza Hotel, the magnificent glory of Trinity

Church, and the towering glass and steel presence of I. M. Pei's Hancock Tower—Coakley turned his head and hiked his shoulder to protect his face from the sharpness of the cold.

Boston, he thought as he began to walk as briskly as he could across the plaza, was a place of extremes. In six months the temperature in this very place could easily be ninety degrees higher. He glanced up for a moment as he walked awkwardly, his hands thrust deeply into the pockets of his camel's hair overcoat, and looked at Trinity Church, a nineteenth-century work of architectural art, its spires reaching for the sky in the greater glory of God. And there, only feet from where it stood, was the Hancock building, soaring five hundred feet higher, yet the two structures seemed peaceful, even mutually complementary neighbors. In fact, the magnificence of the church was reflected, literally, in the massive glass panels of the skyscraper.

But Boston was a place of extremes in other ways as well, Coakley reflected. It was a city of great beauty and sophistication in some areas, home to great works of art and some of the world's most brilliant minds. But it was a venal place as well, small and ugly, a place where flashes of violence born of hatred and resentment were not uncommon. It was a place where history mattered. Not just history in the broad sense, not merely the recording of notable civic events, but personal history—alliances, entanglements, betrayals—reaching back for generations.

Coakley bent his head lower as a gust moved across the frigid pavement and then ascended so powerfully that it pushed his head back. The cold brought tears to his eyes, reddened his face, and numbed his toes.

"Jesus," he muttered under his breath, quickening his step.

The lobby of the Hancock Tower brought relief, with its warmth. Coakley was able to stand up straight and draw a deep breath. He rolled his shoulders and felt his body unclench. Though he unbuttoned his overcoat, he did not remove it, for he could still feel a chill.

He cursed silently as he boarded an elevator marked OBSERVATION DECK. He hated these things, these flimsy boxes that hurtled straight up into the sky at a frightening speed in a building that had been designed to literally sway in the wind. His ears popped and his chest tightened as the elevator seemed to slow long before they would have reached the top, and the prospect that he would be stuck in this thing rendered him so panic-stricken that for a moment he was unable to catch his breath.

But then the car settled and the doors slid open. He got off and breathed once again, making his way to the observation deck. There were windows on four sides, glass from floor to ceiling offering the most spectacular views of Boston from anything except an aircraft. Coakley preferred to stand back a bit from the windows, and he did so as he sauntered along looking out over the Back Bay. There had been a time, years past, when he'd aspired to live there in one of the nineteenth-century brick mansions with their bow-front windows and old-world charm. He loved the gaslit ambience of the neighborhood, was enamored of the broad, tree-lined walkway up the middle of Commonwealth Avenue. There were benches and impressive statues of historical figures. And the walkway led all the way down Commonwealth to the Public Garden, where a huge statue of Washington astride a steed guarded the entryway.

Coakley looked out over the Back Bay rooftops, over buildings that averaged only four or five stories high, to the Charles River, winding out toward the west, separating Cambridge and Boston. He looked across the river and saw the buildings of MIT and Harvard. He walked slowly toward the northern side of the building and looked up the coast, toward the North Shore, and then moved to the east side and gazed out across the harbor and toward the airport. There were two massive tankers making their way into port as a British Airways 747 glided in for an effortless landing.

Coakley brought his gaze in closer, moving from the distance toward the inner perimeter of the city, and he saw Mass General

Hospital. He thought about Harvard and MIT and Mass General, and it made him feel as though he was in a substantial place, as though this city was a place that mattered, a place where important things happened.

He moved around to the southern side of the building, saw the Boston Medical Center, and suddenly felt a need to account for the medical greatness of the city. He went back to the western side of the building and looked down and saw the Deaconess, Beth Israel, Brigham & Women's, and Children's Hospitals.

Children's Hospital. He tried to count up from the bottom to the seventh floor of Children's, but he was not sure if he was seeing seven or eight, and picked what he thought to be seven. He tried to find the window, and thought he had, in fact, zeroed in on the window of the very room where so many years past his son, at age eleven, had drawn his last breath.

CHAPTER 17

JACK DEVLIN SAT back in his office and looked through the pages once again. The young law student in the police department computer operation had given him the report earlier that afternoon. Jack was captivated by the sequence. He had now established that the late owner of the Blackthorn had made four equal payments, each four months apart, to CrimeStoppers, a charitable organization in name only. It had no other assets and made only one donation—to the Law Enforcement Education Association, another charitable trust. It was clear to Devlin that CrimeStoppers was merely a front. But for what? If there were legitimate contributions being made to charitable organizations, why channel them through a shell?

When he'd been at law school, he learned that the law was often a puzzle and to trust his instincts. As a student of the law, one was often called upon to work one's way through a maze. Jack thought of it as akin to the mazes children are given as place mats in restaurants. You start at the lower left corner and trace your pencil through the maze, avoiding dead ends, trying to get to the finish. He'd learned as a law student to trust what made instinctive sense to him.

And that was precisely what he was doing now.

It was snowing lightly as dusk settled upon the city. In light snow, Boston's traffic became unbearable. Combine light snow and slippery conditions with rush hour, and you had something close to gridlock. Jack, however, did not care. He got into his Cherokee and headed out Columbus Avenue toward the Fenway. The two-mile ride took thirty-two minutes. He pulled into Landsdowne Street, which ran behind Fenway Park's Green Monster. He zipped his parka all the way up, put on a Bruins cap, and walked along Yawkey Way, checking out the names of the bars that lined the street. As he walked he jotted every name in a small notebook. On Yawkey Way alone he listed nine bars. He proceeded up to Brookline Avenue and down into Kenmore Square, continuing to write. Most were relatively small, simple gin mills doing a decent weeknight business but cramming in the crowds on weekends. This area was the heart of the city's middlebrow bar scene. It lacked the glitter of downtown, but the prices were reasonable, and young people, from college students to singles in their thirties, flocked to the area.

He kept walking, enjoying the brisk air, pleased to be moving along at a steady clip while the traffic was at a near standstill. He followed Commonwealth Avenue into the Back Bay and on to upper Newbury Street, then Boylston. He circled back around to Fenway and, after a ninety-minute walk, reached his car.

Jack drove back to his office and reviewed the list of bars, thirty-seven in all. He then did what he'd been assured he had the authority to do when he received his current assignment: He picked up the telephone and called the commissioner.

Nicholas Sullivan took his call right away.

"You said if I needed anything along the way I could call you," Jack said.

"What is it?" Sullivan asked.

"I need someone I can go to at the state Department of Revenue," he said. "I need to be able to go over there and have them do a computer search for me. Can you arrange that?"

Sullivan thought a moment. "Yes," he said, "definitely. Let me make a call. I'll get right back to you."

Six minutes later Sullivan returned his call and gave Jack a name at the Department of Revenue.

"WHAT IS IT about cops?" Jack wondered aloud. "Why are so many cops other than what they pretend to be?"

Del Rio shrugged. "They go sour," he said. "It's not surprising."

"Sour?"

Del Rio nodded. "It's all the fault of the patrol cars and their subconscious impact on the minds of children," he said. "The black and white car."

Jack frowned.

"Why do I make that assertion?" Del Rio asked. "For this reason: Cops start out thinking that the world is painted in black and white. When they're little kids they see the patrol car. Black and white. Symbolizes the job for them. Symbolizes the *world* for them. So they think there's black and there's white and they choose white. They want to be on the side of good. And so they become cops. Why? Because cops stand up for what's right. They do good."

"And then?"

"And then they collide with reality," Del Rio said. "And it is a rude fucking awakening. Rude." Del Rio lowered his gaze and nodded. "Why? Because all of a sudden they're introduced to an alien concept. And that alien concept is ambiguity. Do you understand the nature of this beast, ambiguity?"

Jack nodded.

"Because ambiguity is the source of sourness in cops," Del Rio said. "It is the undoing of cops. Why? Why do I say this?"

Del Rio paused, but Jack did not reply.

"I say this because—think about this for a moment—think about this kid who's thinking all through high school or community college or the service or whatever that he's going to become a cop to do what is right. And he or she goes through the academy and learns the absolute pure bullshit dished out there, and then this person is placed in a uniform, silver shield on chest, and sent out into the world, lance tucked under arm, to tilt with the great churning windmills that dot the landscape.

"Except the problem is that nobody ever told them they were going to be tilting with windmills. Everyone always said they were gonna do what was right, protect what was good and honorable.

"Now, there are some boys and girls who come through here who think that means keeping the boogies out of nice neighborhoods. And in the right situation they work out beautifully because they really do see the world as black and white, purely black and white. Their approach is keep an eye on the brothers, and if a brother breaks into a nice white home, whack him around and throw him in the can with other brothers.

"Most aren't from that rudimentary a level within the animal kingdom," Del Rio continued. "But they are still thrown by the concept of ambiguity. Because in practice—live, real time on the streets—ambiguity in action is a very slippery, difficult thing to deal with. 'Cause it means there's sometimes not a clear right and wrong.

"When you show up at a domestic dispute and she's cryin' and says he had a few and fuckin' belted her, and you go to take him in but she says, 'No, I love him, don't take him away,' and you look at your partner and he looks at you and you say to the lady, 'You sure?' and she's sure, and so you leave and later that night, you get another call, same address, and you go back and she's fuckin' black and blue from head to toe. . . . Or worse.

"Did you do the right thing? And then the newspapers get into the act and the politicians, and they think you're an asshole and you're lazy and have bad judgment and you're callous and you really don't give a fuck about anything except hanging around Dunkin' Donuts . . ."

Del Rio sat back and shrugged.

"But in the first couple years, of course, you're excited and the guys are excited for you and it's a thrill, your first partner, and patrols, and your first few pinches, I mean, Jesus, it's a rush, there's no denying it.

"But then you get into a beef here and there, with some asshole on the street, and they complain, or you work for a fool who thinks it's a federal offense 'cause you whacked some brother during an arrest, and suddenly it's not all so hunky-dory.

"And then a few more years pass and you're doing as many details as you can to make a decent buck and standing in a snowy street in the freezing fucking cold for a few extra bucks and it gets very old very fast.

"And while this is all happening you come to realize that there are rules of procedure and laws that actually constrain you in some respects as much as they do the real bad guys.

"And so what do you do? You rebel. Like any frustrated adolescent who's confused and uncertain. And that's what cops are in some ways, isn't it, frustrated adolescents? They're simpleminded, a lot of them. I mean, hey, let's be truthful, Jack, there are a lot of cops who aren't too fucking bright. What are the requirements? Not so bad. Anybody can be a cop, really. So anybody *is* a cop.

"And so you find over time that they get sour and they turn inward and they're pissed off at the world because they didn't get to do what they were supposed to do, which was make sure the good guys are protected and the bad guys fuckin' whacked around."

Del Rio took a deep breath and slouched in his chair.

"And so they go sour," he said, stretching. "They go sour because what looked for a time like it was black and white turned out to be gray. Because of ambiguity. Because they couldn't become what they wanted to become."

Jack considered this. "And the ones who go bad?" he asked.

"They're justified," Del Rio said, suddenly animated. "They

think it's cool. It's okay. It's okay because they've been screwed over. Because everybody pisses on them. Because their pay is too low. The level of respect accorded them is too low. Their fucking self-esteem is too low. And so they make up for it by saying, 'Fuck it, I'm entitled.' And they take some dough and then some more, and then more, and they're hooked. They can't quit.

"Most of all, though, they do it because they decide in their own minds that they are the law. They don't enforce it. They *are* it. So what they decide goes. And what they decide is, 'Fuck it all, man, I'm taking the dough. Because they can't pay me enough to live in this fucking sewer that this society really is.' "

JACK HAD NEVER met Del Rio's girlfriend, Lisa Storer, and Del Rio insisted that he join them for drinks. Jack was running behind and arrived after Lisa and Del Rio had had a couple of rounds.

Jack saw Lisa at the end of the bar, seated next to Del Rio. She was slender and striking in a form-fitting black dress, her long blond hair piled on her head. When Del Rio introduced Jack to her, she smiled and cocked her head to one side. It appeared to Jack that she'd already had a couple of drinks. Sitting in front of her on the bar was an Absolut on the rocks, nearly drained.

Del Rio, in the midst of working a case, excused himself to make a phone call.

"So you two have become quite the team," Lisa said. "A couple of white knights."

"We've done okay," Jack said.

She looked over the rim of her glass at Jack as though considering whether to share her thought with him. "He's a difficult man, sometimes, don't you think?" she said.

Jack hesitated. "He has his views," he replied. "He knows what he believes."

She smiled. "He has his views," she said. "Knows what he believes." She nodded. "Yes, yes he does, doesn't he?"

She finished the Absolut and signaled the bartender for another.

"So you're going to clean up the place?" she said. Her tone wasn't quite playful. There was a slight mocking edge to it.

"We're trying," Jack said.

"I wonder," she said, "whether it's possible." She said it as though issuing a challenge.

Jack regarded her and saw that she was watching him closely. "I think it is," he said.

She frowned. "I wonder whether it isn't bred into the genetics of the place, sort of the DNA of the BPD." She laughed out loud, pleased with her thought. "Part of the organization's genetic code," she said.

"So what have you two been talking about?" Del Rio asked when he rejoined them.

"We were analyzing the culture of this organization for which you both labor so diligently," Lisa said, sipping her drink. It struck Jack that she seemed intent upon getting drunk.

Del Rio's gaze lingered a beat longer than it might have otherwise. "Oh?" he said.

"I was asking Jack whether he thought you two could gallop through the town on your white steeds and make sure all the women and children were safe, all the scoundrels locked away."

Del Rio smiled. "And he said no frigging way, right?"

"He said absolutely," Lisa replied.

"Never happen, of course, but a worthy goal," Del Rio said. "Never happen because human nature won't permit it. Whenever you're trying to accomplish something, always go with the grain. If you have a choice between being a liquor wholesaler, for example, or a leader of a temperance organization, go with the booze. People are people. Human nature is what it is. When you buck it, you're in for a hard ride."

"And what do people want?" Lisa asked Del Rio.

He shrugged his shoulders and laughed. "Hell if I know," he said, sipping his beer.

"Come on," she said.

Del Rio considered this a moment. "Depends," he said.

"On?"

"Well, Jesus, are we talking someone old or young, male or female, American or what? Lots of factors here, Lees."

She sat up in her chair. She liked this. "Okay. Female. Age seventy-five. What does she want?"

"Easy," Del Rio said. "A few more good years. Enough dough to pay the bills. Not to be a burden on her kids."

"Male, age thirty-five?"

Del Rio laughed. "A good blowjob."

"Of course," she deadpanned. "Female. Thirty-two."

"Marriage," he said without hesitation. "Kids."

She narrowed her eyes. "We're so predictable, aren't we?" she said. "So easy to pigeonhole. How old are you, Jack?"

"Thirty-four," he said.

"Okay," she said. "Let me ask you. Male, thirty-four?"

"Oh, Jeez, I don't think—"

"Don't be a chicken," she said. "Male, thirty-four."

"What does he want?" Jack asked.

"Really want," Lisa said. "More than anything."

He looked at her and saw that the smile had faded. He glanced at Del Rio, looking for help, but he saw that Del Rio was sitting back, an impassive look on his face. Jack suddenly felt an odd sense of responsibility to answer the question seriously. There was something about how Lisa had asked him; something in her look and in the gaze from Del Rio.

"If I were to answer honestly, I guess I would say honor," Jack replied, his voice soft. "Honor would be what I'd want."

Lisa watched him very carefully, searching for some hint of mockery, finding none. "Honor," she said, slowly nodding. Her voice was very quiet.

She sipped more of her drink and nodded ever so slowly, as

though just now beginning to understand. She nodded and a pained smile appeared. She looked at Jack as though she somehow found this quaint.

"You are a noble savage," Del Rio said. "Here's to Jack." He raised his glass.

"To honor," she said, her eyes fixed on Devlin.

Del Rio nodded. "To honor," he said. They raised their glasses and drank.

Del Rio spotted someone nearby and moved down the bar to talk with him.

"So how does an honorable man fit into that place?" Lisa asked Jack. "Do they all despise you, Jack?"

"Not all of them," Jack said.

"Most?"

"I'd never thought of it in those terms."

She cocked her head to the side, her eyes wide in a look of mock drama. She brushed her hair back from her face and leaned forward, her breasts straining against the black silk. She forced a theatrical smile.

"Is your naiveté real, Jack, or part of a marketing package?" she asked. "I must tell you that you are a very appealing man. If all this is real. I mean, there's no sense in pretending. There's a fucking elephant in the room and we're not acknowledging it. Let's not be disingenuous. I hate that. I so hate that. I mean, Jack, is this avenging angel thing, is this real? I need to know."

Jack stared into her eyes and did not blink. He did not answer.

"So what are you trying to prove, Jack?" she asked, quieter, more earnest now. "Because I think they hate you more than you're aware. I do think you are naive, but it's quite honest, isn't it?"

He set his glass down and paused for a moment. He looked at her and smiled. "I'm trying to be a good cop," he said. "That's really it. If it sounds disingenuous, I'm sorry. That's what I'm trying to be."

"And what's the definition of a good cop?" she asked.

"You know," he said. "Effective. Honest." He shrugged.

She stood up, a bit unsteadily, and stared at him. "I think that being an honorable man, being a man who possesses honor—that's why they hate you, Jack. But I think it's also why they fear you."

THE SURVEILLANCE WAS performed by two teams of FBI agents. It was discreet, professional, invisible to all but the most experienced eyes. Christopher Young never saw them, never noticed them when he emerged from his home in the early morning, did not see them in the lobby of the Brigham when he hurried through to work. He did not see them across the room at Au Bon Pain where he had a sandwich for lunch, nor did he see them when he drove to a suburban hospital that night to consult on several cases.

The electronic telephone surveillance yielded nothing, for Young had an instinctive sense of caution on the phone, an instinct that served him well.

Emily Lawrence had a difficult time accepting the notion that the force behind the deal was one Christopher Young. He was simply too inexperienced. An excellent choice as a distribution and sales point, no question. A perfect marketing man for the task. But she didn't think Young was *the* organizer. She believed, however, that if she was patient, Young would lead her to him.

YOUNG ARRIVED AT Starbucks in Coolidge Corner in midmorning. The agents hung back, letting him go inside. Then one of the agents followed him. Young took his coffee to a table in the far corner, no one nearby. He fidgeted nervously and waited. Twenty-five minutes later Coakley arrived. He bought a small cup of decaffeinated coffee and went to the table. There were no preliminaries.

"So?" Young said.

"Within three days," Coakley replied.

Young hunched forward over the table. "You sure?"

"Positive," Coakley said. "It's coming. It's all set."

"How will it be delivered?" Young asked.

"I'll have to let you know that," Coakley said. "No earlier than the night before."

"I need to know," Young said.

"You will, Doc, you will," Coakley assured him. "When you need to know, you'll know."

Young looked down into his coffee cup and frowned. He disliked being treated in this fashion. "So who's making the delivery?" he asked.

Coakley regarded him a moment, then shook his head. Abruptly, Coakley got up from the table. "Soon enough it will all be done," he said. "Soon enough. You'll have your product, your new business. Very soon."

When Coakley, the lawyer, emerged from Starbucks, the agent across Harvard Street, a veteran who had been assigned to the Boston office for over ten years, was taken aback. He knew the face though he could not immediately place the man. He knew that this man had been involved somehow in a case on which he'd worked. But he was not sure how. Then it came to him, the name Coakley.

When he learned from his partner that Coakley was the man with whom Young had met, he went back to the office and dug out the file on Coakley. It was that file, along with a memo on the day's surveillance, that landed on the desk of Emily Lawrence that evening.

THE SKATING RINK in Larz Anderson Park sat atop a hill in South Brookline. Anderson's mansion once was at the peak of the hill and held a commanding view of downtown Boston. But after Anderson's property had been deeded to the town, and after his death, town officials had his mansion torn down. And the gardens adjacent to it—considered to be one of the finest examples in the world of Italianate landscape architecture—had been destroyed. Scores of carved wooden Doric columns were used by the town as curbside markers. And the former site of the Italianate gardens was turned into a skating rink.

Whatever aesthetic offenses had been committed by town fathers were now in the past. What remained was the ice rink, the most beautiful in the land. The dark winter sky was its roof, and from its edges the city of Boston could be seen, from the medical centers only a mile or so east, through the Back Bay and Beacon Hill to the Financial District and the waterfront. The airport, on this clear cold night, seemed part of a Hollywood set: its lights and runways well marked, giant planes floating smoothly, seemingly in slow motion, down for a landing, up for a takeoff.

After meeting with Young in Coolidge Corner, Coakley had taken a Green Line car to Cleveland Circle and then caught a bus that crossed Route 9 on Chestnut Hill Avenue. The bus dropped him on Newton Street, at the edge of the sprawling Larz Anderson Park. Coakley followed a pathway that cut through gardens, the ground frozen hard. A small pond with an arched footbridge sat at the base of a long hill that sloped up to the crest of the property, where the rink sat.

The walk up the hill was perhaps six or seven hundred yards, and halfway up Coakley was sweating profusely. His heart was beating so hard that he was momentarily frightened. He sat down on the hard ground and tried to catch his breath, waiting for his heart to calm down. No one was around. Coakley could see, off in the distance, cars heading up a driveway that circled around up to the rink.

After a few minutes he struggled to his feet and resumed his trek. He walked slowly, conscious of the pounding of his heart. A hundred or so yards later he again felt the need to pause, to wait for his heart to settle, to calm his breathing. Coakley felt foolish, but he decided to traverse the hill, going up in the way a cautious novice might come down a ski slope: back and forth, back and forth. It took much longer, but it also mitigated the steepness of the slope.

At last Coakley reached the rink. He saw the Zamboni making its final swing before pulling off and dumping its shavings in a pile of snow. Coakley went into the warming hut and found it was empty. He looked out the window and saw Jack Devlin in his street clothes sitting on a stone fence with a view of the city lights.

Coakley went outside and walked over to Devlin. "Sorry I missed your scrimmage," the older man said. "I was hoping to catch some of it."

Jack saw the sweat on Coakley's face, saw that he was flushed. "You okay?" he asked.

"I walked up the hill," Coakley said. "I'm not in great shape."

Jack smiled. "But you made it," he said.

"Yeah, I did."

There was a long moment of silence as the two men gazed out over the skyline.

"Listen," Jack said. "I've been thinking, and I want you to know something." He glanced at Coakley and looked back out over the city as he spoke. "I want you to know, whatever the outcome here, whatever happens, I want you to know I am very grateful for what you've done. It means a lot to me."

Coakley sat very still. So surprised was he by the sincerity of Devlin's tone, so touched was he by Jack's words, that he sat speechless.

Jack glanced again at Coakley, and the older man nodded.

"I appreciate what you say," Coakley finally said. "I, ah . . . you know, I hope this all works out for you. I don't know where it's going exactly, but I really do hope it works out. I have to say I admire what you're up to. I admire what you're up to and it feels good to be part of it."

They sat for a long time, neither saying a word. They were soothed by the peace of looking out over the city, by the silence of a city just far enough away so nothing could be heard.

Finally they got up and began walking down toward Jack's car.

"I'll drop you at the subway," Jack said. "So it went all right today?"

Coakley nodded. "Fine," he said.

"The feds saw you together?" Jack asked.

Coakley nodded vigorously. "No question. I'm sure of it."

Jack nodded with satisfaction. "So you'll be picked up soon enough."

Coakley nodded. "Another day or two, I'd guess."

CHAPTER 18

IF CERTAIN OF his clients were to discover what he'd been doing, they would kill him. This was understood.

Coakley, the lawyer, shuffled through his kitchen to the back pantry, reached up into the cabinet, and took down his favorite tumbler, a weighty cut-glass design from Waterford. He had purchased a set of six during his one and only trip to Ireland twenty years earlier. They were intended as a gift for his wife, but upon his return he discovered that she had left him. He had failed in one too many attempts at quitting. She'd had it.

And when she returned to their house to move her things, she discovered him drunk, in front of the television set, and she went into a rage, and in her rage had taken the Waterford tumblers and smashed them against the walls, shattering the five she was able to find. Fortunately for Coakley, he'd been drinking out of one of them when she arrived, and he hid it just as she'd come through the door. A small victory.

Coakley reached up into the cabinet and took down a bottle of his sustenance, Bushmills 100 percent blended Irish whiskey. He poured it slowly until the tumbler was half full. He picked up the glass, short and stout, fitting his hand as though it had been designed for him alone. He had a great fondness for this glass, but, in truth, had the circumstances dictated, he would have drunk his Bushmills from a paper cup.

Standing in the pantry, Coakley sipped the blended Irish whiskey that had been his preference for as long as he could remember. It always warmed his heart. Sometimes it even eased his mind.

He shuffled into his den and sat heavily in his hunter-green leather armchair, the chair he'd been sitting in every evening for so many years. He sipped his whiskey. It was very good.

Coakley held the tumbler in his right hand and set it on his stomach. He thought about Jack Devlin and the scheme Devlin had drawn him into. It unnerved him. Over the past couple of years, he'd helped Devlin out, provided him with a fair amount of good inside information. All of it constituted a betrayal of one or another of his clients. He had provided some information to others within the Boston Police Department as well. He'd embarked on a course that anticipated the day when he would be arrested and charged with money laundering or tax evasion or mail fraud or one of the other crimes federal authorities used to prosecute lawyers who represented the worst people in the world. He had tried to be helpful to a number of law enforcement officials on the theory that the time would come when testimonials from people with badges could shave months, even years, off a prison sentence. For a man who now routinely betrayed his clients, Coakley's conscience was amazingly clear. After all, he reasoned, all of his clients were corrupt and deceitful, and some were quite evil. He did not wish to go too far, however, for as wretched as his life had become, he preferred it to the alternative. In death, after all, there was no Bushmills.

He took the risk willingly, though, for his collaboration with Devlin was no longer a personal protection strategy so much as re-payment of a debt. A matter—dare he say it?—of honor.

Coakley sighed and sipped his drink. He thought about Jack Devlin and realized that he'd grown quite fond of the young man.

The boy was much like the father in some ways—his affability and open manner—but much sharper. Jesus, Coakley thought, the father has been dead for twenty-five years! He could hardly believe it. It seemed to Coakley as though it had been just a few years since he'd been a state representative asked by a constituent to intervene in a dispute the constituent had with the state's Alcoholic Beverage Control Commission. Coakley had looked into the matter and discovered that his constituent, Henry Sullivan, owner of Sullivan's Bar and Grill on D Street in South Boston, had been found to have served liquor to minors, a third offense, which meant an automatic one-week license suspension.

"It'll kill me, put me outta business altogether," Sullivan had said.

Coakley could not let that happen. Thus did Coakley the lawyer, then state representative, propose to a commissioner of the ABCC that the ruling be reversed for a payment of two thousand dollars. Ordinarily, such matters were handled with discretion and grace. But this commissioner fell into the grip of a sudden shudder of conscience and, rather than consummating the deal right away, he informed his friend, Boston police detective Jock Devlin.

Proceed with the deal, Jock had said, and so it was that Jock Devlin had watched the deal take place, seen the envelope change hands, had the commissioner as a solid witness. And on that very afternoon, Jock Devlin went about the task of arresting Coakley. He wanted to do so in a discreet way. It was not Jock Devlin's style to barge through traffic, sirens blaring, to force Coakley to the side of Brookline Avenue, drag him from his Olds and cuff him. Jock followed at a discreet distance, patiently waiting for Coakley to arrive at his destination. It soon became a puzzling ride, for once they reached the hospital district, Jock found that Coakley was circling the area repeatedly. He would follow

Longwood Avenue past Children's Hospital, turn left on Brookline past Deaconess, then left on Francis, and left again on Hun-
tington, past Brigham & Women's, then back around the loop.
These were heavily traveled streets with stoplights on nearly
every block, and each circumnavigation took nearly fifteen minutes. After the fourth lap Jock Devlin's patience was wearing thin.
But he was more curious than annoyed, and continued to follow
Coakley.

After eleven laps over a period of nearly three hours, Coakley
pulled the Olds to the side of Longwood Avenue and got out of the
car. He stood there, looking around, as though trying to get his bear-
ings. Jock watched as the lawyer staggered to one side, fighting to
keep his balance.

Jesus, thought Jock, he's shit-faced. Jock Devlin pulled his
Crown Vic over behind the Olds and got out. It was dark now, and
the streetlights cast a sickly greenish light over Coakley.

"How're we doin'?" Jock asked as he approached the lawyer. The
door to the Olds was wide open, the engine running. Jock could
see the half-pint bottle of Bushmills on the front seat. It looked
empty.

"Representative Coakley, I'm Detective Devlin, BPD," Jock said.

Coakley nodded. "How do you do, Detective," he said, ever
the politician. He showed no sense of alarm, but instead turned
and began walking away, leaving the car door open, the engine
running.

"Hey," Jock said. "What's with this?" He motioned toward
the car.

"I gotta go up here and visit . . . ," Coakley said, gesturing
toward a hospital building.

"Look, Representative, you and I have some business," Jock said,
"but you can't leave the car here. You want me to have it towed
away?"

Coakley thought about this for a moment. "Okay," he said.

How pathetic, Jock had thought. How truly pathetic.

He removed the keys, shut the door of the Olds, and followed Coakley into the lobby of Children's Hospital. Then he pulled Coakley aside into a private alcove and told him he was under arrest for extortion. Coakley seemed puzzled, then suddenly, inexplicably, he leaned forward, placed his head in his hands, and wept.

THAT NIGHT, JOCK Devlin learned that Coakley's tears were not for himself, but for his boy, his only child, who lay gravely ill with leukemia.

Jock Devlin quietly buried the matter of extortion, the payment of two thousand dollars. He went back and talked with his friend at the ABCC, and the deal was never mentioned again. Coakley had tried to thank Jock for his humanity, went to Devlin's home and thanked him profusely. Jock had been embarrassed by it and sent him on his way, saying only: "Take care of your kid."

But Coakley had been unable to do so. Now he sighed heavily at the recollection and looked down at his empty Waterford tumbler. He struggled to his feet and shuffled back out through the kitchen to the pantry. He set the glass down and filled it halfway with 100 percent blended Irish whiskey, shuffled back along through the kitchen, and sat down in his chair.

So often during his life, Coakley had despised himself, loathed what he'd become. He drank himself into incoherence many a night as a way to retreat from his life, to get away from himself. With his second hefty tumbler, he was on a course he knew well. But on this night he did not despise himself. Because although he could not think of a single honorable deed he'd committed during his adult life, he felt like he was moving toward doing something worthy. And he wanted so desperately to do something good! To do something that mattered, something noble.

DEPUTY SUPERINTENDENT THOMAS Kennedy was waiting just inside the front door of his West Roxbury home when Jack Devlin arrived. It was a cold night and Kennedy had built a fire in the fireplace of his book-lined den. His home was tucked away on a quiet side street, and there was not a sound to be heard as Kennedy and Devlin sat down in front of the fire.

Kennedy frowned as he looked down into the fire and then back up at Jack. Kennedy's brow was furrowed and he seemed perplexed.

"I'm sorry to drag you over here at this time of night," Kennedy said, "but I think it's important that we hash some things out here."

"No problem," Jack said.

"Look, Jackie, I'm not going to beat around the bush here. I want to be straight with you. There is a concern, is the best way I can put it, among some senior people in the department about your connection to Ray Murphy."

"But Tom, I—"

Kennedy held up his hand, signaling Jack to stop. "Just let me finish," he said. "So I think you and I had better talk through what's going on. Now, as I said to you on the phone, I honestly do not understand why you would want anything to do with a guy like Murphy." Kennedy suddenly had a look of distaste, and shook his head. "This was a guy—not to speak ill of the dead—but this was a guy who was known to be a bitter, resentful guy. He was full of poison, Jack, a hater."

Kennedy looked closely at Devlin. "What's going on, Jack?"

Jack's gaze seemed fixed for the moment on the fire. He shifted his look to Kennedy and shrugged. "I needed to talk with him, to just close the loop, kind of," he said.

Kennedy frowned. "Was there a history there that you know of?" he asked.

"Between my father and Murphy?"

Kennedy nodded.

"I don't—"

"Because that's the word that's getting around," Kennedy said. "That there was a history there. That you were aware of the history and were carrying out some mission." Kennedy seemed acutely uncomfortable. "This is what's being said."

"Jeez, Tom, there's no great mystery. . . ."

"But you created the mystery, Jackie," Kennedy said, red-faced now and leaning forward, clearly agitated. "You wouldn't tell Lopez and Buckley why you went to see Murphy in the first place. You said personal, private. They came away with more questions than answers. You yourself said to them you asked Murphy about things that happened years ago. I have to tell you, Jackie, you didn't do yourself any good with that interview. I have to tell you. And going after Buckley . . ." Kennedy frowned and shook his head with disgust.

Jack didn't know what to say, so he said nothing. Kennedy sat back in his chair.

"I'm just puzzled, Jack, that's all. Others are as well. Let me say this delicately. There are others who do not have the history with you I have. Others who aren't fond of you, as I am, who—let me put it this way—who harbor suspicions."

Kennedy paused briefly as though considering whether to say anything more. It seemed he could not stop himself.

"And I've got to say, Jack, though it's none of anybody's business, I know, but Jesus, the word is around of your involvement with Emily Lawrence, and I know your business is your business, but Christ almighty, she hates everything we stand for. Looks at us with contempt. It doesn't play well, Jack."

Kennedy shook his head and took a deep breath. He got up from his chair and stood, hands in his pockets, before the fire. There was a long moment of silence.

"I shouldn't tell you this, Jack, but I feel like I owe it to you," he said. "The FBI is interested in this, too. And the talk is that you were settling some score with Murphy, an avenging angel for your dad . . . I mean, I have to tell you, Jack, I think people are beginning to believe it."

CHAPTER 19

ON THE FOURTEENTH floor of the John W. McCormack Federal Courthouse in Post Office Square, a room had been constructed in which law enforcement officials could meet without the slightest fear that any method of eavesdropping, however sophisticated, could be used. This soundproof room had been constructed to foil any electronic or digital efforts to record any aspect of the sound of any voice. The room contained three windows that looked out over Post Office Square, yet the windows were coated with a material that prevented sound waves from penetrating.

Use of the room by federal law enforcement officials was regulated by the United States Attorney's office. Prior to any meeting within the room, it was scanned to ensure that no internal listening devices had been planted.

Kevin Duffy of the Federal Bureau of Investigation entered the room through a detection mechanism that screened for listening devices. Emily Lawrence followed him inside.

Agent Duffy removed a page of notes from a folder and set it on the conference table in front of where he sat. Emily closed the door and took a seat opposite him.

"I'm giving you a heads-up," Duffy said. "There's concern, here and in D.C., that we might collide at some point on this. We'd like to avoid that if possible."

"As would we," Emily said.

Duffy nodded. "As you know, we've been looking carefully at the BPD, but trying to do so from enough of a remove so that we were not detected."

Emily nodded.

"What, exactly, you all have been doing is another matter, although I must tell you candidly that I think we'd all be better off if we spoke the same language here."

"It's not the deal," she said. "It's not what Justice wants. You know that. Let's move on."

"I'm giving you a heads-up," Duffy said again. "I want you to have a sense of what else. There's another layer here. I have to be careful because I'm constrained, but there's another layer here. We think we've broken through in a way. Not fully, but to a certain extent. We think we've punched through some barrier that hasn't been penetrated before.

"We've been able to develop a source of information inside," Duffy continued. "It amounts to an informal cooperation. The information is coming to us. And the picture taking shape—it is by no means fully formed. By no means. But what's taking shape in a kind of rough image is that there's a problem here that's broader and deeper than anticipated. That the problem penetrates. We think systemic. We had believed episodic. We now think systemic."

Duffy paused and looked at Emily Lawrence. "Does this square?" he asked.

"Keep going," she said.

Duffy hesitated. "I was wondering whether this squares, though. Whether we're on the same train here?"

"Keep going," she repeated.

Duffy frowned. "We think systemic," he said. "We think centrally controlled. We do not, I repeat, do not believe these are freelance operations run out of different districts."

"Uniformed or detectives?" she asked.

"Detectives," he said. "Definitely. We think systemic, we think central, we think the normal stuff, club owners, regular payments, violations overlooked. The traditional things. But . . ."

Duffy drew a deep breath and hunched over his notes, and when he resumed speaking, his voice had dropped several decibels, as though he did not wish to be overheard.

"But we believe there are relationships with dealers doing protection money. Possibly, I emphasize possibly, a situation where detectives have an equity stake in some of the deals."

Emily studied Duffy carefully. He was deadly serious.

"Are you saying that these are deals where detectives are, in effect, partners with dealers?" she asked.

Slowly, theatrically, Duffy nodded yes.

"And you're getting this from inside?" she asked.

"Inside," he agreed.

"Someone good?" she asked.

"Someone good," he said. "Unimpeachable."

"Command staff?"

"I can't say."

"If it's someone good, someone who really knows, then it's someone on the command staff," Emily said. "I'm not asking who it is, but I need to know whether to take this seriously, Kevin. Is it someone on the command staff, yes or no?"

Duffy didn't respond for a long moment, then nodded.

Emily was surprised. And impressed. Cracking the BPD command was no easy task. "Congratulations," she said, nodding respectfully.

Duffy smiled, clearly pleased by the praise, then frowned and shifted position.

"There's something else you should know about that's come up," he said. "Nothing official, but some talk out of BPD, and you know how talk is."

He looked down at the table and back up at Emily.

"What is it?" she asked.

"Devlin's name's come up," Duffy said hurriedly, nervously. "It's been mentioned. . . ."

There was a puzzled look on Emily's face. "Come up how?" she asked.

"It's not me," Duffy said defensively. "It's from our sources. People have mentioned his name. As possibly being mixed up somehow in . . ."

Emily cocked her head, the puzzled look deepening. "Mixed up with what, exactly?" she demanded in an angry voice.

"Murphy," Duffy said. "He saw Murphy a day or two before Murphy was found. The daughter said the old guy was scared to death by Devlin. And there's some talk that he's possibly mixed up in it."

Emily sat back and folded her arms across her chest.

"They said he's got a dark side," Duffy said. "They say he's tended to violence over the years." Duffy was calm now. "I don't know whether any of it is true, but I wanted to let you know. I'm aware that you have a connection to him."

"So you've heard from your source on the command staff that Jack Devlin may have been involved somehow in Murphy's murder."

"Correct."

"Who is your source?" she demanded.

Duffy was offended. "That's not something—"

"Who is it?" she asked again.

"Someone reliable," he replied. "Someone very good." Duffy hesitated. "They're watching him very closely," he continued. "He's out of control. Twice lately he's assaulted fellow officers."

"Assaulted?" she asked, incredulous.

"Physically assaulted," Duffy said. He hesitated and looked aside, then back at Emily. "They say he definitely has a dark side. They think he's out of control on some vengeance trip, out to get anybody who was associated with his father back years ago. They think he's lost his grip. Evidently he thought Murphy was somehow an adversary of his father's, somehow hurtful to him. Murphy's daughter told them her father was scared to death of Devlin Jr. Thought he was nuts. Capable of anything."

THE LAW OFFICES of McMahon and McCloskey were located on Washington Street in Roslindale in the space wedged between D'Angelo's Pizza and a coffee shop. Leo McMahon was in his late sixties, and he was the only person who worked in the office. His partner, McCloskey, had long since died, and Leo had let the secretary go some years back. Leo McMahon had once had a busy practice tending to the legal needs of small business people—owners of retail shops, small restaurants, bars—people who tended to have tax troubles with the IRS and the Commonwealth of Massachusetts. The majority of Leo's clients faced liens or other attachments for failure to pay property, income, or withholding taxes.

McMahon's name was in the old newspaper clips as having been counsel to Walter Fahey, the owner of the Oasis. For some years, Jack Devlin had sought to persuade Fahey to sit down and talk with him. Fahey had always flatly refused. In response to letters he'd written to Fahey, Jack would receive terse notes of rejection. Two years earlier, when Fahey had been sent away to a federal prison farm for an eighteen-month sentence for yet another violation of the tax codes, Jack had written to Fahey and received a response that was somewhat encouraging. Fahey had instructed Jack to contact Leo McMahon and discuss the matter with him. Jack had done so, and McMahon said he suspected his client would consider talking on the eve of his release from custody if Jack was willing to keep the information confidential and if he would pay Fahey a fee.

Jack had contacted McMahon and readily agreed to the terms. A fee of three thousand dollars was settled upon. Jack pushed for

Fahey to talk then, but Fahey insisted upon waiting for his release. As soon as he was out of prison, Fahey planned to move to San Diego, where he would go to work for a cousin who owned a club. He would make a new start and put Boston far behind.

Jack arrived precisely on time for the meeting. He went into the law office and found a vacant, open space in the reception area. He walked toward the back and saw an office door open.

"Oh, Mr. Devlin," Leo McMahon said. He was a heavyset man with a nervous manner. "Come in. This is Mr. Fahey." Fahey was smallish, bald, wore a pressed white shirt and smelled strongly of lime-scented cologne. He appeared to be in his late sixties.

Jack and Fahey shook hands. "Sit down," Fahey said, indicating one of the office's two metal folding chairs. There was no desk, only a folding table with a portable electric typewriter on top.

As Jack moved to sit down, McMahon said, "Mr. Devlin, concerning the matter of payment . . ."

Jack reached into his shirt pocket and took out a check, already made out, which he handed to McMahon.

"Oh, a personal check," McMahon said, clearly deflated. "I thought—"

"Forget it, Leo," Fahey said. "Forget it. Just go cash it, then come back later."

McMahon seemed embarrassed by his client.

"Go 'head," Fahey said, frowning.

"I'll return," McMahon said.

"Sit down, hey," Fahey said. "Take a seat. You want anything? Coffee? We can get coffee next door, huh?"

"I'm all set, thanks," Jack said.

"Whatever," Fahey said. "So your old man, huh? You look like him. Definitely there's a resemblance."

"How did you first meet my dad?" Jack asked.

"Oh, Jesus," Fahey said. "You know, I knew all the detectives in my area, and I'd been involved with joints for a while. Started at the

Jungle when I was fifteen, unloading trucks, keeping the bar supplied. So I've worked at a dozen places, maybe more, then me and my brother got a stake in a place and it was off to the races. We got the Oasis and built up a pretty decent business. See, people will come, but only if you're constantly on your toes, running specials. We had a decent location, not the best, by any means, but there are your hospitals and a few offices not too far down from us. Closing the Sears building hurt us very, very bad. They ran a catalogue operation out of there. You know, people mail in what they want out of a catalogue and they'd have guys in there filling the orders. Hundreds of guys, and they'd come in, quite a few of them, after work. We were handy for them. When that shut we was hurt.

"But we pushed it with the hospitals, and the secretaries and the maintenance staff would come in, sometimes a few nurses. And we'd have the free mini-franks and nachos and whatnot. And we put in the video games when that was big. Got a satellite dish, big-screen TV. We worked like a bastard to stay current and even ahead of the game. But in that business you're inviting trouble.

"What do you do when a group of wiseguys comes in? You know who they are, know they're wiseguys, but their money's as good as anyone's. Next thing you know, though, someone rats that this job got planned at the Oasis or this hit or whatever.

"We tried to be careful, but it's not easy. And a simple thing like the taxes, the withholding, that'll kill you every time. You keep the percentage out of the take for the state, and then you get squeezed by this vendor or that vendor or whatever and pretty soon the money that was supposed to go to the Revenue Department ends up going to the Anheuser-Busch distributor in Brockton, otherwise no product. See what I'm saying?"

Jack nodded. He knew the pattern all too well.

"So, listen, what was the idea, here? The idea was to stay out of trouble, because trouble put a drag on business. Trouble cost money. You got the tax people on you, it costs money. You got the cops on you 'cause some guy's running a couple hookers out of your place, some dope, whatnot, it cost money. It cost time. Court appearances. Licensing Board hearings. You been to one of those? Fucking nightmare. Nightmare. Licensing Board." He shook his head. "Fucking guys, half on the take and the other half want to be sainted. Pricks."

Fahey reached into the pocket of his brown leather jacket, which was hung over the back of his chair, and removed a box of Tiparillos. He tapped one out of the box and lit it. He inhaled and let the smoke sit in his lungs for a moment. Then he turned and exhaled away from Jack Devlin.

"So your father was one of these guys I knew, came to know, over time. Tell you the truth, I didn't know him very well, not as well as a lot of other guys. 'Cause we would make up envelopes for individual guys at first, and then it got too much and we would do one for the group, and who exactly was in the group was made clear to me only by comments like, you know, 'You got a beef with this or that, call so-and-so. Don't call this guy or that, call so-and-so.' It wasn't like they gave me a roster," Fahey said, smiling. "You follow? I knew who to call because, you know, I'd feel my way through.

"I called your old man, I don't know, maybe once at the most on some minor thing. Very minor, I don't even recall. Overcrowding notice or something. Maybe parking, I don't know. At any rate it was like maybe once and on some dogshit thing. I can't even recall.

"But then time goes by and I'm talking to one of my contacts and your old man's name comes up and my guy says, 'No, don't call him, call so-and-so.' And I remember I was surprised by that because I must have just dealt with your old man, which is why his name probably come up right then, and my guy shakes his head no, like forget him 'cause he's not in no more."

"So that meant to you—"

"That he was out," Fahey said through the haze of smoke. "Not involved no more. Period."

"Are you sure?" Jack asked, too eagerly.

"That's what it meant, believe me, I know. This was a language I spoke. I understood."

"How can you be sure?" Jack asked.

Fahey straightened in the chair and regarded Jack. "How can I be sure?" he asked, sounding offended. "I'm sure. 'Cause I'll tell you something else—"

Here, Fahey caught himself as though he'd been about to say something he wasn't supposed to say.

"Let's just say I know and leave it at that," he said, tamping out his Tiparillo in an ashtray. "I know," he added, looked at Jack, and nodded.

Jack folded his arms across his chest. He was slightly slouched in his metal folding chair. "Mr. Fahey," he said. "I'm thirty-four years old. My father has been dead for twenty-five years . . ."

"Jesus Christ, has it been that long?"

". . . and I want to figure out what happened back there. I'm trying very hard to piece it all together. And now we come to this point, and you're just out of prison and you're going off to San Diego to start a new life, and before you go you agree, finally, to talk to me. And I fucking pay for that, a lot of money, because it's worth something to me to know the truth."

Jack sat up and leaned forward, his elbows resting on his knees. "It's worth more than anything to me. And now you're saying to me, 'Let's just say I know and leave it at that'?"

Jack's jaw was clenched. His eyes had narrowed and he stared at Fahey. "I've begged you to talk to me. I've promised confidentiality. I've paid you. Tell me what happened. Please, tell me."

Fahey was not a bad man, not an uncompassionate man. He made a face and nervously rubbed his hand over the top of his head. He grabbed the Tiparillo box and tapped another one out, placing it between his teeth and lighting it. He rose from his chair and paced slowly across the room. As he walked by, there was a strong smell of cheap cigar smoke and lime cologne. Fahey paced to the wall and back, twice.

"This conversation we're having," he said. "This goes nowhere, right?"

"Nowhere," Jack replied.

"It's for you, for inside your head, right?"

Jack nodded in agreement.

There was something about the young detective's raw intensity, about his honesty, that captured Fahey.

"I'm an old fuck, now, truth be told," he said, sitting down again. "And I have a fucking conscience, believe it or not, although some people would say or not. And I also have a word from the doc that there's this fucking spot on the X ray, the chestal X ray, and, well . . .

"Look, I'm leaving town and I'm gonna do it with a clear conscience. And you can call me a coward or an asshole or whatever you want, but this is it.

"It's the weekend before Christmas, right, one of the biggest weekends of the whole year. People are pouring in, spending money like it's water. There's like a frenzy, people pulling wads of cash out of their pockets, buying rounds for their friends, for the house, whatever. Tips to the bartender like you wouldn't believe. So it's late, I don't know, like, twelve-thirty or whatever, and all of a sudden in the back a beef breaks out. Okay, so no big deal, right, except some asshole has a knife and all of a sudden it's in another guy's stomach and there's fuckin' pandemonia. Pandemonia. And the cops come and the ambulance and whatnot and the guy is hurt pretty bad but he's gonna be okay. Thank God, right, because a murder in the place is nasty for business.

"The next day, Sunday, I get a call at home from a guy I know in the department. This is a guy I've been dealing with on some Licensing Board matters, very important because they're threatening to suspend my license for a week, and if they do that, I go under. So this

guy, I'm kind of like on probation and if there are any more problems during a certain period of time—overcrowding, prostitutes,
gambling, whatever—then I'm screwed. License heaved and I sink, I
drown. So this guy on the department is helping me. He's looking
the other way on one thing after another. In other words—see if you
can understand my point of view here—this guy is keeping me
open. He's allowing me to stay in business, to stay alive, for Chris-
sakes. Without him I'm dead!

"So Sunday this guy calls me and he says, 'Look, the feds are
swarming still,' which I know because they had come to talk to me
and I'm Mickey the fucking dunce like you wouldn't believe. And he
says, 'Look, the heat is unbearable. We've got to do something.' And
I says, 'Like what?' and he says, 'Here's what you gotta do.' And you
know what he says? He says I've got to go into the tank with the feds.
I've got to tell them I'm paying off the fuzz. And I laugh out loud
and say you're fucking crazy and hang up. And an hour later this
guy, he's at my house. And he walks in and sits down and he says to
me, 'Here's the choice. You don't do business with the feds and your
place is closed next week. You're through. You talk to them, make a
couple admissions, and I guarantee you stay open.' "

Fahey drew back in his chair, his arms out to his sides. "So is this
a hard call?" he asked. "So this guy says what I have to tell the feds is
that there's a guy coming by the next day to make a pickup. A BPD
detective. And so I tell them that, and the next afternoon your old
man walks into my joint to take a report on the stabbing. Routine.
Goes through a series of questions, which I answer in full. And then
I hand him the envelope and he frowns. Your old man. He frowns.
He doesn't like this at all. But he's been told to bring it back. He's
been told to bring it back to the station house. And so I guess he figures he's made enough of a stink over this and what the fuck, it's not
his anyway, so he'll just drive it back and drop it off, and so he takes
the envelope and he walks outside and bang. The feds surround him.
And that was it."

Suddenly, Fahey hung his head. He looked down at the floor, his shame evident. He shook his head at the memory. There was a long period of silence while the two men sat absorbing this, thinking it through. Fahey took another puff of his Tiparillo but still did not speak.

Finally, in a voice softer than any he'd used so far, Fahey said, "I'm sorry, hey. I feel bad for what I did. I feel very, very bad for it. But I wanted to try and do the right thing here . . ."

He shrugged.

Jack nodded, a signal that he appreciated what Fahey had done.

He felt a mix of triumph and anxiety, tremendous, building anxiety. He swallowed hard and then sought to catch his breath but could not. He was on the verge of hyperventilating. He worked to steady himself, his breathing.

"Who, ah, was it?" he asked. "Who set him up?"

Fahey muttered under his breath. "Jesus, mother of God," he said. "You don't know, do you?"

CHAPTER 20

HOW HAD THEY discovered that he'd been to see Fahey? How had they known?

Jack opened his eyes and saw the morning light slanting through the windows of his bedroom. He rolled over and felt a shooting pain in his back. He shifted his weight and felt his knee throbbing. He worked himself so he was flat on his back, staring up at the ceiling. He was fully clothed lying on top of the bedspread. He remembered coming in and collapsing on the bed, his Glock nine-millimeter on the bedside table. He'd considered going to the station house or to a hotel for the night, but had been too disoriented to get anywhere except home.

As he blinked his eyes, he could feel a tightness on the left side of his face. He reached up with his right hand and touched it, and though he pressed only lightly on his left cheekbone, there was a sudden shooting pain. He moved his fingers slowly, gently, and could feel the swelling around his left eye.

Jack checked his watch and saw that it was seven-ten A.M. He'd been asleep about four hours. As he lay still on the bed he thought that if he continued like this it would get progressively more difficult to get up. So he took a deep breath and rolled onto his right side, positioning his elbow directly beneath his body. He pushed off his elbow, raising himself sufficiently so he was able to slowly swing his legs off the edge of the bed and place his feet on the floor. As he did so, he pulled his torso into a sitting position. He then placed his hands on the bed and, steadying himself, rose to his feet. When he rose to his full height, he felt a sudden surge of dizziness, reached out with his right hand, and steadied himself on the bedside table. He shuffled into the bathroom and felt a powerful wave of nausea. His head throbbed. He leaned over the toilet and vomited. He soaked a washcloth under the cold water and placed it against his face. It was then that he saw, in the mirror, the purple swelling around his left eye and cheekbone. His left eye was all but closed. The right side of his face was unmarked. But the left side was swollen badly.

He made his way into the kitchen and wrapped ice in a dish towel. He went into the bedroom, got his Glock and took it into the living room, sat down in an easy chair, and put the gun on the end table next to it. He held the ice to his face and thought about the night before. He'd been at his office until very late, thinking, analyzing, planning. When he left police headquarters, he walked down Stanhope Street to where his Jeep was parked. To get to the lot he had to cut through a short, narrow alleyway off Stanhope, and as he turned the corner they attacked from the shadows.

One moment he was walking toward his car, the next he was on the cobblestones. He thought there had been two, but it was possible there were three. Or more. All he saw for sure were two men, both wearing ski masks and tight leather gloves. The blows rained down on him and he was on the cobblestones and there were more blows, punches, kicks, dozens and dozens of blows, and then, as quickly as it had begun, it was over. He thought it had lasted for no more than twenty seconds. Twenty-five at the outside.

The oddest thing of all was that none of them had made a sound. Not a single word had been spoken. He was all but positive they were not cops. They were young, in their twenties. They were agile and exceptionally powerful, and in their work they had been calm and precise. They moved with certainty, as though doing something to which they were accustomed.

This unnerved him. To contract out was serious business. To contract out meant connections between those in the department who despised him and people involved in some sort of organized crime activity.

To contract out meant they were doing business with these people. And if they could be assigned to follow him in a car, to demonstrate their presence, to get past his security system, to beat him into unconsciousness, they could be assigned to do anything.

There was a progression at work here, he thought. This latest, like the earlier incidents, was a warning. This one louder, more eloquent in its wordless way.

It raised the inevitable question: What next? What could they next logically do, short of killing him?

He arranged for a detective friend whom he trusted to come to his house and sit, armed, in his living room watching sports on television. With the friend settled in, Jack went into his bedroom and pulled off his clothes. He got into bed and, as the swelling in his body throbbed, fell asleep for thirteen hours.

IT WAS A cold, clear night and Christmas shoppers hurried along Tremont Street, cutting down School, headed toward Jordan Marsh and Filene's. Emily Lawrence arrived first and took a seat at the end of the bar. She ordered soda water and settled in to wait for Jack. There was madness on the Boston Police Department, and she needed to see him. To sit with him and enjoy a glass of wine and look directly into his eyes as she asked him some questions.

Did she believe what Duffy had said? She thought it preposterous because, of course, she needed to think of it as preposterous.

Needed to. For she'd reached a point with Jack where she thought of them as being together, where she could envision them remaining together.

Was she delusional? Was she intentionally ignoring clues that lay strewn around her? She thought of Duffy's comments, the crazed rumors he heard from inside the Boston Police Department, and she'd been dismissing it all in her mind until Duffy said that he had heard that Devlin had a dark side; that he was prone to anger and could be violent. She had been shaken by that because she had heard that characterization from Jack himself.

Emily realized that her anxiety was mounting because the stakes were suddenly so high. This man meant so much to her now, and she could not stand the thought that it would not work out.

Jack Devlin, having forgotten his overcoat, limped through the doors of the Parker House, shivering. Inside, the lobby was warm and festively decorated with Christmas lights. A huge tree, laden with ornaments, stood near the far end of the lobby. The chairs and sofas that were set around the lobby were all taken.

Jack moved to the back bar and found Emily standing just inside the door. Though they had spoken earlier and he'd told her about the night before—minimizing the seriousness and the effects of the assault—she was startled by his appearance. The swelling around his eye, the discoloration, were worse than she'd anticipated.

She embraced him quickly when he arrived and looked carefully at his eye. "Jesus, Jack," she said, surprise evident in her voice. "Have you had that looked at?"

He looked away, nodding vaguely.

"Meaning no," she said. "Well, you have to. An eye isn't something to fool with."

She was very cool on the outside because she felt she needed to be. But then, as they moved toward a table in a quiet corner of the lounge, she saw that Jack was limping, and she was utterly stunned by it, rendered momentarily speechless. She stopped and watched as he shifted his weight unnaturally from his wounded leg back to his stronger leg, a pronounced limp that suddenly filled her with the image of Jack as an old man; Jack in his advancing years.

When they sat down at the table, she cocked her head to one side, fighting the burning sensation behind her eyes.

"What is it?" he asked.

To his astonishment, she started to cry. Her chin quivered and her eyes narrowed and she began, quite softly, to sob.

"Em . . ." he said, shocked by seeing what he'd never before seen. Quickly, he got up from his chair and went around to her side of the table. He knelt on one knee beside her and put an arm around her shoulder, holding her close. "Em," he said, "what . . ."

Embarrassed, she fought back the tears and dug a tissue out of her purse. She wiped her cheeks dry, apologizing for her outburst and asking him to take his seat. He obliged because he would have done anything she asked at that moment. That look, the depth of her vulnerability, had sliced through him. She needed him, he realized! Needed his support and protection, just as he needed her, needed her support and protection.

"Em, I don't know what—"

"I'm frightened, Jack," she said, composing herself. "I'm afraid. I don't really understand all that's going on and I'm afraid there are very bad people and look at you, my God, Jack. These people could have killed you."

And she started to cry again, but this time pulled herself back and stifled the sobs. "I'm sorry but I'm very worried about you."

"Come on," he said, rising, "let's get out of here."

He helped her with her coat and they left the hotel, walking slowly down the block to where his Jeep was parked. They got in and Jack drove the few blocks to the federal courthouse, where her car was parked. They sat in silence for a long moment in his car.

Finally, Jack forced a smile. "Everything's going to work out," he said. "I'll be fine."

She did not accept this. She frowned at his attempt to brush past it all. "Is there something you want to tell me?" she asked.

He thought about this for a moment, considered telling her everything right then and there; thought about confiding his plan to her, bringing her into it and making her his ally. But he knew he couldn't do it. He'd come this far through careful thought and planning and discipline, and he felt it was all so very close, within his grasp, and he did not want to lose his focus now.

"Yes," he said. "There is something I want to tell you. I want to tell you that you mean so much to me, that you are very beautiful and quite wonderful."

She did not smile. "I'm serious," she said.

"So am I," he replied.

She frowned and leaned forward in her seat. "Is there something going on, Jack? With you?"

"I'm lost," he said.

"Something I should know about," she said. "Are you involved in something in some way that I should know about?"

He pulled back. "I'm not sure I know what you mean," he said.

She looked down at the dashboard for a long moment. "There are disturbing things going on," she said. "There's some suspicion of you at the moment."

He knitted his forehead, clearly puzzled. "What you're asking, I think, is whether I'm engaged in something I should not be engaged in. Right?"

"Yes," she said.

"But the point is that your question is very broad, amounts to a fishing expedition, and I am therefore going to say no, Emily, I'm not."

She folded her arms across her chest. "Don't be such a frigging lawyer, Jack," she said.

"I am a frigging lawyer, Emily," he replied.

They stared at each other through a prolonged silence.

"Are you in trouble?" she asked him.

He started to respond no, then thought better of it. He considered the question for a moment, then said, "I'm not sure."

"You're not sure?"

"There are people who would like me to be in trouble."

"Who?" she asked.

"I'm not exactly sure," he said.

"You're not being straight with me, Jack." She glared at him.

He said nothing.

"I care about you," she said. "You know that."

He took a breath and looked down at his lap. He nodded appreciatively. He was glad she was concerned, wanted her to be concerned.

Emily grasped herself by the shoulders as though she had a powerful, sudden chill. "I'm frightened of where this is all going," she said. "Goddamnit, Jack, you know how seriously I take all this. This matters to me. It really matters. It's my job to find out who's behind this and to go after them as aggressively as I possibly can and to prosecute."

She leaned forward, glaring. "I intend to prosecute anyone involved in the consummation of this deal. If I can work my way up from the foot soldiers to the general, I will do that. It's what I do, Jack, you know that. Anybody who has a private agenda better understand that that's secondary to enforcing the law."

Jack sat still, listening carefully. But he did not speak.

She gazed into his eyes, a look of pain spreading over her face. She leaned forward and spoke in a low, passionate voice.

"You should get out, Jack," she said. "This is a terrible business for you to be in. These people around you, so many of them are bad people. You know that."

"Why do you say that?" he asked.

"Because it's true," she said. "You know it's true. I know it's true. The pattern . . ." She shook her head. "A lot of people are going to get hurt in there, Jack. Let's make sure you're not one of them."

"I won't be," he said reflexively.

"Don't be cocky, Jack," she said. "They're very smart people. They know how to do this. Better than you and me."

He was momentarily chastened.

"You've done all you can do," she said. "Get out now. Go to Ropes and Gray. Practice law. Make money. Have a nice life for yourself."

He scowled, regarding her as though she were mad. "I can't do that," he said. "You know that."

"Why not?" she challenged. "What are you trying to prove?"

"I want to be a good cop," he said evenly.

She shook her head. "No. You're trying to rehabilitate him, but you can't do it. It can't be done. He's gone, Jack. He's been dead a long, long time."

Jack felt a wave of dizziness. He felt momentarily disoriented. He clenched his jaw.

"Jack, I care very much for you," she whispered. "Do you know that?"

He nodded yes and felt a swelling in his chest. "I care very much for you, too, Em," he said.

Their eyes were fixed on each other. He reached over, took her hands in his, and squeezed them.

She spoke in a very soft voice. "I love you, Jack," she said tenderly. And he felt exhilarated.

She smiled.

"I love you, too, Em," he said, and she shut her eyes for a brief moment and they leaned forward in the front seat of the Jeep and embraced.

She pulled back and watched him carefully. "Because I love you, Jack, I have to be honest with you," she said. Her brow was knitted, her face intense. "You're obsessed with the past. You're stuck in it. It's not healthy, it's no way to live. Let go of it, Jack. Think about all the possibilities that lie ahead in your life. Think of all that you could do, that you could experience."

She placed a hand on his forearm. "Think of what love could do for your life, Jack," she said tenderly. "What the experience could be like. Let yourself go, why don't you? I have great admiration for your devotion to your father's memory, but, Jack, so much of the love inside you—of your focus and attention—is tied up with a man who has been dead for a quarter of a century. Let it go, Jack. Let him rest."

Jack sat motionless for a long moment. When he finally spoke, he did so barely above a whisper. "Once, when I was in the third grade, a nun accused me of cheating on a test," he said. "Her name was Sister Mary Cornelius, and she was a very large woman with a squarish face, very pale, with these cold, narrow eyes. In the midst of the test she grasped the lobe of my right ear and kind of hoisted me up out of my seat and led me out of the classroom and into the hallway.

" 'You cheated, didn't you?' she said. She was furious. And I said, 'No, Sister, I did not cheat.' And she said, 'I saw you look over at David Gustin's paper. I saw it!' But I said, 'I did not look at his paper,' and it was the truth. I hadn't.

"That enraged her. She bent over and held her face close to mine, so close I could smell the starch from her habit. She wore this black, pleated top with a white starched bib, and a skirt that hung to her shoes. Her beads were wrapped around her and a crucifix hung from her throat. It was a very medieval look, and the nuns were treated as though they were kind of mythic figures. They were shown great deference.

"She was so angry her face was tomato-red, and she grabbed my ear and led me down the hallway to the office of the school principal. She had me wait outside while she went in and spoke privately with the principal, Sister Maruna. When they came out, their expressions were very grave, as though there'd been a death.

" 'This is a very serious matter, John,' Sister Maruna said. 'This is a sin and God is angry with you.'

"I said nothing. What do you say to that? And Sister Cornelius said, 'Do you understand what Sister Maruna has said to you?' and I said, 'Yes.' And she said, 'If you admit what you did, it would show you are truly sorry.' And I said, 'I didn't cheat.'

"The principal called my father at work. She told him what happened and asked if he could come meet with her that night. He said he would come right away, and half an hour later he arrived.

"When he got there, he greeted the nuns very warmly. He liked the nuns, thought they were great teachers. He asked, in the most respectful possible way, whether he could speak with me alone for a moment. They left the office. He sat down opposite me and kind of leaned forward in his seat. His brow was knitted and he tried to force a smile, but he couldn't manage it.

" 'You know that I love you more than anything, Jackie, don't you?' he said. And I said that I did. And he said, 'And do you know that whatever happened today, I will still love you just as much. If you cheated, I will be upset, because it's wrong. But I will still love you as much as I always have. You know that, right?' And I said I did. And he said, 'So, tell me, Jackie, did you cheat on the test?'

"And I looked him in the eye and I told him the truth. I always told him the truth, and he knew that. It was a great feeling knowing I could always tell him the truth and he would handle it well. And so I said, 'No, Dad, I'm telling you the truth. I did not cheat.'

"And suddenly this huge smile spread across his face and he nodded and he knew—he *knew*—I was telling the truth.

"And he went and got the nuns and they came in and sat down and Sister Maruna went through this whole thing about how I had to confess to my sin.

"My father listened very respectfully and then he said, 'Well, Sister, sometimes there are misunderstandings, and I think maybe that's what we have here, because Jack is a very honest boy and he told me that he did not cheat. So perhaps we could chalk it up to a misunderstanding and let it go at that.'

"The nuns were speechless. They were so used to getting their way with parents that they didn't know how to handle this.

" 'Mr. Devlin,' Sister Cornelius said, 'I am sorry to say your son lied to you. He cheated on the test. He looked at David Gustin's paper.' She said this with a real edge to her voice. She was very angry.

"My father said, 'Sister, you know, sometimes light and distance and vision play tricks.' He was smiling. Very calm. Very respectful. 'I know from my line of work that that frequently happens. I really believe we have a misunderstanding, and I think it would be good for all of us to leave it at that and move ahead.'

"The nun glared at him. 'I saw him with my God-given eyes,' she said.

"My father looked at her for a long time, then he said, 'Sister, I believe you are mistaken.' He sounded almost regretful.

"She leaped to her feet and shouted at him, 'I am not mistaken, sir! Your son cheated and then lied about it. Your son is a liar!'

"She said it so loudly that it reverberated down the hallway.

"All of a sudden everything was very quiet. There was no sound at all. For a long time. And then, finally, my father spoke. His voice was deep and very comforting to me. He spoke very deliberately.

" 'My son, Sister, may be many things,' he said. 'He is not a perfect child, though he is, as you know, an excellent student and, in general, a very good boy. But he is, more than anything, an honest boy, Sister. He is a person of honor. I am very, very proud of my son, Sister. Jackie does not lie to me. I wish the same could be said for you.' "

Jack shut his eyes and then reopened them, looking into Emily's eyes.

"Em, he believed in me," Jack said. "He believed in me. And you know what, Em? I believe in him."

CHAPTER 21

THE NAVY-BLUE CHEVY Suburban pulled up to the curb as Coakley walked home from the MBTA stop. There were two agents, both in their late twenties, both fit and well-groomed. The shorter, more muscular one flashed his badge as he stepped up to Coakley and took hold of the lawyer's elbow, the better to guide him into the back of the Suburban.

"If you would come with us, please, Mr. Coakley," the agent said.

They whisked him off the darkened street and into the back of the vehicle in a matter of seconds. The driver pulled smoothly away from the curb and headed downtown. One of the agents sat in the third row while Coakley was in the middle row with an agent by his side.

"I do not wish to go with you people," he said. "It is my wish as an American citizen to be set free immediately. Either charge me with a crime or set me free."

The young man raised his eyebrows as he regarded Coakley. "We're not able to do that at the moment, Mr. Coakley."

"What did you say your name was?" Coakley asked.

"Agent Jeeter, and behind you is Agent Hammond, and agent Stanley is driving."

"You mind telling me where we're going?" Coakley asked.

"To the Department of Justice of the United States of America," Jeeter said. Coakley regarded the young man. He wore his hair short, in a crew cut, reminiscent of the days long ago, when Coakley was growing up.

"Why have I been abducted in this fashion?" Coakley asked.

There was no reply.

"Could someone answer my question, please?" Coakley demanded.

"You are being brought to the Justice Department, sir," Jeeter said. "We have been instructed to bring you there posthaste."

"Who am I seeing?" Coakley asked.

No reply.

Coakley turned and looked out the window as the Suburban moved swiftly along Storrow Drive, headed downtown.

"You come at night, you abduct a man off the street," he said. "It's like, it's like . . ." He was going to say it was like the Gestapo, but of course it was not. He wasn't going to be taken to a railroad station, shipped to a camp, slaughtered along with his loved ones. Loved ones? Coakley thought. He had no loved ones.

Jeeter glanced at him again, this time with distaste. "Like what?" he asked quietly.

Coakley shook his head. "Nothing," he muttered.

EMILY LAWRENCE SAT in her office reviewing Coakley's file yet again. She'd read what was available and then done some independent research of her own. She learned that Coakley had grown up in South Boston, gone to Boston College High School and on to Boston College and Boston College Law School. A Triple Eagle. After graduation, he had gone to work for a law firm and run for the Massachusetts legislature and lost. Two years later he ran again and won.

Coakley had had a bright political future. He was extremely popular in his South Boston district and was well-liked by the press. His name was mentioned as a possible candidate for Congress or state Attorney General. Down the road he was considered gubernatorial material.

But then came the investigation into payoffs involving the construction of the UMass Boston Harbor campus. A construction management company hired to oversee the massive project had come under legislative scrutiny. A legislative committee had done a study of the company's work and issued a report. Investigators would prove in court that the original report issued a harsh judgment against the company. Then, later, after company officials were given a secret viewing of the document, they made payments to two state senators and the text of the document was then changed so it was less critical of the company. Two state senators had been indicted, convicted, and imprisoned for their role in the scandal.

Coakley had been named an unindicted coconspirator, extremely fortunate not to have been indicted. He was in the thick of the payoff scheme but his tracks were so well camouflaged that there was not enough evidence to convict him, and so he had not been charged. Nonetheless, the fact that he'd been named an unindicted coconspirator had made it into the press and been widely reported.

The scandal had a devastating impact on his law practice. Respectable clients steered clear of him. As a result, he had gone out on his own and developed a criminal law practice specializing in representing organized crime figures from South Boston.

Through the years, he'd had a number of close calls with law enforcement agencies. At various times, he had been accused, though never charged, with laundering the proceeds from drug profits (true); accused of, though never charged with, aiding criminal clients with income tax evasion (true); and bearing witness to the plotting of the killing of a rival crime figure (false).

A few years earlier he had nearly been named in a RICO prosecution by the federal government. Prosecutors had charged a number of organized crime figures based in South Boston with a variety of crimes under the federal Racketeering Influenced Corrupt Organization statute, which gave them wide latitude in charging individuals with various crimes under the joint venture theory. The

RICO statute was extremely controversial within legal circles. The defense bar argued that it amounted to a suspension of civil rights for the accused, while prosecutors claimed it was the only weapon they could use to destroy organized crime.

The prospect of facing a charge under the RICO law was terrifying, because it provided prosecutors with vast powers.

As the navy-blue Chevy Suburban pulled into the basement garage of the John W. McCormack Federal Courthouse, it occurred to Coakley that a RICO prosecution would ruin what was left of his life.

"MR. COAKLEY, I am Emily Lawrence, Assistant United States Attorney. I have a feeling we've met before. Have we?"

Coakley had just been led into her office by Agent Jeeter. He stood there, still wearing his overcoat, sweating profusely, wondering how soon he would be able to go home, put his feet up, and have a drink. Where Coakley seemed confused, frazzled, Emily was crisp and clear-minded. She wore a charcoal-gray suit, and a white blouse with green pinstripes. He was taken aback by how young and pretty she was.

"A few years ago, a criminal matter involving one of my clients, Jimmy Keegan," he said.

She brightened. "Of course," she said. "I knew we'd met." She turned to Agent Jeeter and smiled. "Thanks," she said, nodding.

"We'll be outside," he said.

She nodded again. "I'm sorry about our method of transport today," she said, turning back to Coakley. "I suppose it seemed a bit abrupt to you?"

"It was illegal," Coakley replied. "You can't merely—"

"Of course, you're absolutely right about it," she said, smiling. "It was entirely illegal. Properly done, there would have been a warrant for your arrest based on some crime you had or were about to commit, and we would have demonstrated probable cause and yadda yadda yadda. You're right. But when one gets warrants in this city, Mr. Coakley, sometimes the target of that warrant will learn of the impending action before its execution. From my standpoint, that is exceptionally inconvenient.

"So I made a decision to keep this as quiet and simple as possible. To include as few people as possible. To make the whole thing . . . how can I put it? Discreet."

She indicated that Coakley should take a seat on her office sofa. "May I take your overcoat?" she asked.

He took it off and handed it to her. She brought it to a closet in the corner of her office and hung it up. Then she went to the easy chair that faced the couch and was about to sit down.

"Can we get you anything, Mr. Coakley?" she asked.

He thought for a moment. "A glass of whiskey," he said.

"Of course," she said. She went to the door of her office and spoke quietly with Agent Jeeter.

"It'll just be a moment," she said, taking a seat in the chair opposite him. "Mr. Coakley, permit me to get a few preliminaries out of the way." She placed a legal pad on her lap. "You are fifty-nine years old, is that correct?"

Coakley hesitated, then nodded. "I'll be sixty in April."

"And you reside at 157 Stratford Street in West Roxbury, is that correct?"

"Yes."

"And with whom do you reside?"

"I live alone," he said.

"You are divorced?"

"Many years ago," he said.

"Children?" she asked.

Coakley seemed annoyed. "That doesn't have anything to do with anything," he said.

There was a quiet tap on the door and Agent Jeeter entered. He carried a highball glass half filled with brown liquid. "Hope scotch is okay," he said. "Sorry we had no ice."

"Thank you," Coakley said, taking the glass in hand. He brought it to his lips and sipped. Jeeter left and Coakley held the glass in his hands, resting on his lap.

The office was very quiet, and softly lit. They had encountered only a few members of the building's cleaning crew when they'd come up from the garage to Emily Lawrence's office. Coakley had been in this building many times before; never under such circumstances, however.

Emily watched Coakley carefully for a long time. She said nothing.

Finally, he spoke: "What do you want of me?"

She nodded as though to say, That's a reasonable question.

"What I want of you is to understand something," she said. "I want you to understand that you need me." She stared intently at him, looking directly into his eyes. "Because if you understand that, if you know the truth, which is that you need me right now, then everything else will fall into place. But we can't do any business, not on a collegial basis, until you acknowledge that."

Coakley sipped his drink and was deeply pleased by the sensation. In a way, he'd already worked this conversation through in his mind, or at least a conversation similar to this one. He'd worked it through in his mind now for years. He was suddenly overwhelmed with a sense of déjà vu.

"And why do I need you, Miss Lawrence?" he asked.

She got up from her chair and went to the office window. She gazed out at Post Office Square, twelve floors below. At this time of night, the city's business district was all but deserted.

"A better way to put it is that we need each other," she said, turning from the window and returning to her seat. She smiled again. "We're codependent."

Coakley was surprised by this twist. "How so?" he asked.

"With your help, I succeed," she said. "I get what I want. Without it, I fail. With my help, you get what you want, or rather, keep what you have. Without my help, you fail, too."

"How do you mean?" he asked.

"You know exactly how I mean," she said. "You know what I'm saying is right. You know it because if you did not know it you would have left here already. Because, of course, you are free to leave at any time. As you correctly pointed out, it violates the Constitution to take a citizen in a car and drive him downtown and keep him without probable cause. It's illegal. And if you're being held against your will right now, then that is illegal. We must charge you or release you—if you're being kept here against your will."

There was a certain force to her voice, a force, he thought, that derived from the simple clarity of her speaking style—direct, unadorned, yet with a certain confidence.

"Shall I tell you what I know and don't know?" she asked.

He nodded.

"I know you are connected somehow to the morphine deal," she said. "I know you are connected because you have met with Christopher Young and because common sense tells one that Dr. Young would need someone such as yourself to provide direction and prudent counsel in such an ambitious undertaking as this. And so I know you are involved. What I do not know is precisely how you are involved. I do not know from whom the drug will be purchased, who manufactures it and where, and, most importantly, to whom it will be distributed. Because my goal here is to prevent the distribution of this substance and arrest those involved. That is my intent. I do not know many things, but I believe that if you recognize our mutual dependence, then I'll have a very good chance of learning the things I need to know."

She sat very still in her chair, her hands on the armrests, her back straight, head slightly cocked to one side.

"And if I tell you that I know Dr. Young because he is a client I advise on tax law, and I walk out of here right now, then what?" Coakley asked.

"Then you will not have finished your drink," she said, nodding toward the nearly empty glass. "And that isn't very hospitable."

She did not want to say it, he suddenly realized. She did not want to behave like a traditional tough guy, making threats. The threat was understood, the sanctions grave. It was in the air, in his own mind, she knew. This she did not have to say. Not unless he pushed her to do so.

"So my choice is to help you or face a RICO prosecution," he said. It was a statement, not a question.

She stared at him for a long moment, then nodded slowly, confirming his statement. A RICO prosecution that would allow the government to seize his property—before a conviction, before trial. He would be left with nothing.

"I need you to help me bring in the man behind this whole thing," she said. She stared at him. "Will you do that, Mr. Coakley? Will you help me and help yourself?"

Coakley gazed into his glass, then took a polite sip of his whiskey. He held the glass in two hands on his lap and nodded. He looked up at her.

"Yes," he said. "I'll need our agreement drawn up in writing. But, yes, I will do that."

She smiled a tight, cold smile. "Good," she said. "Let's jump right in. Why don't you start, Mr. Coakley, by telling me precisely how this all relates to Detective Jack Devlin of the Boston Police Department."

THE REPORT BACK from the Massachusetts Department of Revenue indicated that of the thirty-seven bars on the list he'd submitted, nine had made substantial contributions during the past year to charitable organizations. The pattern was strikingly similar to what he'd discovered with the Blackthorn: quarterly payments in equal amounts to organizations such as StopCrime, KidWatch, and YouthSupport. The donations ranged from a low of $12,000 per quarter to a high of $43,000. The average quarterly payment was $26,000 and the total annual take from these nine bars was $936,000. Nearly a million dollars, from just those nine bars. How many other clubs were involved? Jack wondered.

These contributions, in each instance, were the only donation made to the organizations, and in each case the funds were in turn passed along to the Law Enforcement Education Association.

The LEEA report that he'd requested indicated that the organization, during the previous year, had made donations to community groups totaling $117,000. Jack guessed that amounted to ten percent or less of the LEEA's total revenues for the year. Which meant that the other ninety percent was going somewhere else.

All of these bars, he suspected, made huge amounts of additional money because they were permitted to go way beyond their legal capacity on weekend nights. Thus, these owners must have seen the payments as the cost of doing business, and paid willingly, even eagerly.

JACK SAT AT an IBM computer terminal in the Massachusetts Office of Corporate Records. Within this department's computer was listed every company in the state, as well as every not-for-profit organization of any kind, from world-renowned medical centers to Pop Warner football organizations.

He typed in the words Law Enforcement and found that there were thirty-one entries beginning with the words Law Enforcement. He called the full list to the screen: Law Enforcement Association Pension Fund, Law Enforcement Community Relations Assembly, Law Enforcement Assistance Act offices, and on and on. Halfway down the list he found the Law Enforcement Education Association. He tapped a few keys and called the organization's incorporation records to the screen.

LEEA had been incorporated seven years earlier. It was located in Boston—a post office box—and its listed purpose was "the dissemination of law enforcement education." It was registered as a nonprofit organization and was accorded tax-exempt status by the Commonwealth of Massachusetts. The founder and chairman was listed as Theodore J. Sheehan of West Roxbury. Marion W. Sheehan, of the same address, was listed as the secretary-treasurer.

Devlin printed out a copy of what was on the screen and headed downtown to the headquarters of State Street Bank and Trust Company, one of the world's largest custody banks. It was from within State Street that trillions of dollars in world pension and mutual fund assets were kept track of. Its computer systems were among the most advanced financial systems ever devised.

Jack's classmate from law school, Felix Dexter, headed the bank's technology division. Felix Dexter had been the subject of profiles in the *Wall Street Journal* and other business publications celebrating his genius at financial technology. He'd been surprised to receive a phone call from his old friend Jack Devlin the night before. But, yes, he would be delighted to have Jack drop by.

"So this is the reward of climbing the corporate ladder?" Jack said as he was shown into Dexter's spacious corner office.

"Ah," Dexter replied, "you have more fun, I'm sure. But," he said, turning and looking out toward International Place and, beyond, to the harbor, "I must admit I do like it. I like to come in here, shut my door, get my computers revved, and work the world financial byways as I gaze out over the sailboats."

"So things are going really well for you?" Jack said.

"I'm very lucky," Dexter replied. "And intrigued. When a friend who happens to be a policeman calls you at home at nine o'clock at night and says he has this case, I mean, it's not what I'm accustomed to. So what's up?"

Jack removed the document he'd copied at the Office of Corporate Records and handed it to Dexter. "If I wanted to follow the financial activity of this organization, how would I go about it?" he asked.

Dexter took a moment to look at the document. He shrugged. "To follow a particular transaction?" he asked.

"Yes."

"You'd have to be a party to it," Dexter said. "You'd have to have a stake in the transaction to have access to the information. That or some sort of subpoena."

"Let's say for the moment I had a subpoena," Jack said. "Would it be possible to follow—" He glanced over at the terminals on Dexter's desk. "—from here, for example, what happens to that transaction?"

"You have to be more precise, Jack," Dexter said.

"If a deposit were made into this account, or a series of deposits, and the money was then quickly dispersed in different directions, could it be followed by anyone outside the transaction. Could you follow it, for example?"

Dexter shrugged. "Yeah, well, I mean, it depends on whether I have access to the mainframe at the host institution. If I do, and I can get at the transaction on my machine, then I can mark it and follow it to the ends of the earth. I mean, that's something we're very good at here. There are huge pension funds, at GM for example, that have like fifty money managers throughout the world investing pieces of their pension fund. And somebody has to follow all the transactions all of the time. That's us. So if GM calls me tonight and says, 'Okay, where's my dough?' I have to be able to say, 'Well, you have so much in U.S. equities and so much in Europe and so much in Asia,' and then break it down into the most minute possible detail.

So if you can get me the key to the front door, I can give you a tour of the house. Sure."

Jack considered this. "Would you be willing to do it?" he asked.

"Is this something that—"

"It would mean a great deal to me," Jack said. "A great deal."

Dexter smiled. "Hey, I'm your man."

CHAPTER 22

"IF ONLY I had been there, Johnny," Tom Kennedy had said, hanging his head, shaking it in sorrow. "If only I had been there."

Jack Devlin remembered it well, remembered clearly how shaken Tom Kennedy was at the memory of Jock Devlin's death. Jack recalled the conversation as he drove along Commonwealth Avenue.

"I'd seen him over the weekend," Kennedy had said. "I'd dropped by to say hello, keep him company, try and boost his spirits. He was having an awful time of it. Spirits down in the dumps. Fighting like hell to stay positive and upbeat for you.

"You'd heard about it, of course, from kids in the neighborhood. Some of it was cruel. And you'd asked him questions and he tried the best he could to answer them, and you were okay. You were a tough little kid.

"But he was hurting, obviously. He was hurting very deeply. He was wounded far more than any of us had ever imagined. That's clear now. Wasn't so clear then, although there were signs.

"He and I had a couple beers and talked and watched some goddamn thing on TV, some sports, and I went home. And I planned on dropping by—what was it, Monday night, I guess—but I worked late and wasn't able to, and then the next thing I know I get a call and Jesus Christ almighty."

Tom Kennedy had shaken his head at the memory. He'd sighed and sighed again, and Jack thought of those sighs now as . . . What? Theatrical? But he remembered how they sounded, how they felt,

239

and they felt and sounded as though this man had lost his closest and most trusted friend.

"If only," Tom Kennedy had said, "I had been there."

THE HEELS OF Jack's shoes clicked on the cement floor of the hallway that ran beneath the Mugar Library at Boston University. He followed the hallway to the end and turned into a small, well-lit series of offices. It was nearly eleven P.M., and the library was quiet and all but deserted.

A young man wearing a black T-shirt and an earring sat behind a desk playing a portable video game. He glanced up as Jack walked into the room.

"Hold on just one second," he said, focused on the game. "In the next thirty seconds civilization as we know it will either be destroyed or saved."

"Good luck," Jack said.

The young man's face scrunched as he furiously worked the controls, squinting and blinking as the screen showed some unspeakable mayhem.

"Yes!" he declared a moment later. "Perfect."

"You saved civilization," Jack said, smiling.

The young man looked at Jack as though he were demented. "I destroyed it," he said with a grin. "What can I do for you?"

Jack took a letter out of his jacket pocket and handed it to the young man. The letter, typed on the stationery of the commissioner of the Boston Police Department, requested that Detective John Devlin be permitted to review certain archival records on file at Boston University. The letter cited department regulation F177660, which required that anyone seeking access to archival records was required to have written permission from the commissioner. The letter stated that permission was granted herewith.

The letter, which Jack had composed and typed on a sheet of stationery he'd removed from the commissioner's office, contained the commissioner's signature as forged by Jack Devlin.

The student swiveled around in his chair, facing a computer terminal. He began typing rapidly, and soon, a full-screen graphic appeared: ARCHIVE, BPD.

These files had for some years been stored on paper in a South Boston warehouse, until Boston University president John Silber offered as a public service to scan them onto a mainframe computer at Boston University. It had been a painstaking process scanning each record, but once that was complete, there was a computerized history going back twenty-five years.

The student typed in the date of the report, and a series of options were listed on the screen. "That's everything for that particular day," he said. "So now the question is, which is the file we're looking for. Any ideas?"

"Is it chronological?" Jack asked.

"Sometimes yes, sometimes no," he replied. "You don't want to assume that because you might miss something. But let's try that if you have time."

"Late, like eleven o'clock or so," Jack said.

The student scrolled down toward the bottom of the list and hit the Call File key. A record appeared on the screen, the report of a motor vehicle accident from 9:14 P.M. He stored it, scrolled much farther down the list, and hit the Call File key again. A file appeared marked 11:58 P.M.

"Nope," the student muttered, storing the file. He scrolled back up the list and struck Call File again. A report from 10:58 P.M. Three more tries and an incident report appeared on the screen.

"That's it," Jack said immediately. "May I get in there?"

"Why don't I just print it out?" the student said.

Jack nodded. He quickly turned away from the screen, felt his chest tighten and his hands shake. The printer kicked in, and he looked across the room and saw a sheet of paper moving smoothly out of the machine and settling into a tray. And then there was another. And then a third.

"Can I . . . ?"

"All yours," the young man said.

Jack went to the printer and retrieved the three sheets of paper. He took them to a nearby table and sat down, laying them flat in front of him. The report had been prepared by Patrolman Hank Regan. It recounted a variety of information about the scene. This was not easy for Jack to read. It went through the phone calls made from the Knights of Columbus hall on Park Street in West Roxbury on the night his father had died. As he read, he came across details with which he was already familiar.

The top sheet represented Patrolman Regan's report of that night. His father had arrived at the Knights hall early in the evening. He'd played cards with some of his friends for a while, had a beer, then started home. Soon, though, he returned. There were very few people in the building that night. No one saw him reenter the building. But he had. An hour later, as the custodian had gone to close up, his father had been found dead, a single bullet wound to the head. Ruled self-inflicted.

Perhaps the young officer had been shaken by the events of that evening, as many police officers surely had been. Perhaps that explained why his initial report was not as complete as it might have been. Whether Patrolman Regan had been an ambitious young man or not, Jack did not know. For Regan had died several years earlier. But Regan must have been conscientious, for he'd come back four days later, four days after his father's death, and written a one-and-a-half-page addendum to his report.

The addendum, which Jack held in his hand, recounted much of what Patrolman Regan had reported originally, and then added a random set of facts and details.

He'd noted, for example, that Jock Devlin had won a small

amount of money in the card game. He had noted that, earlier in the evening, another Boston patrolman had been playing cards in the game with Jock Devlin. That man had been Patrolman Daniel Moloney. And Patrolman Moloney had left the Knights hall in the company of Detective John Devlin.

The report noted later that there had been a brief dispute in the bar when someone turned the music up louder than its customary volume. It caused a heated argument involving, in fact, Patrolman Moloney. Patrolman Moloney had insisted the music remain loud for a period of some minutes, the report noted.

What shocked Jack, and yet did not shock him, what caused him to shut his eyes and draw a deep breath, was one small bit of information: Near the end of the report, as though to fill up space, Patrolman Regan had randomly named a half-dozen people who were at the scene. Five of the names meant nothing to Jack. But one meant everything. One name, for Jack, confirmed so much, spoke so many volumes: the name of Lieutenant Thomas Kennedy. Present at the Knights of Columbus hall.

Present on the night that Jock Devlin had died of a single gunshot wound to the head, ruled self-inflicted.

"If only I had been there, Johnny," he had said through the years.

But he had been there.

And year after year after year he had lied about it.

CHAPTER 23

KEVIN DUFFY OF the Federal Bureau of Investigation looked across the table at Deputy Commissioner Thomas Kennedy of the Boston Police Department and felt profoundly grateful. Duffy had often felt the sense of frustration that goes with being in the field of law enforcement. So often in his career he had been close to something big, something that mattered, something that would make a splash. So often he had been close to something for which he would be recognized. But those things had never worked out. The truth was that in law enforcement little was ever clear or clean. Rare were the occasions when you were able to score a decisive victory.

But now as Duffy sat in the FBI office at the O'Neill Federal Building in Boston, he felt a sense of anticipation: Something big was about to happen, and he would be at the center of it.

"We think it's cleaner, better for everyone, if you come in on this now," Kennedy said. He'd spoken slowly, sorrowfully, ever since the meeting had begun. It was clear to Duffy that this pained him. Shocked him.

"Should we bring Moloney in?" Duffy asked.

Kennedy nodded. "Before we do," he said, "understand that we've been watching him for a while, Moloney. I've had my eye on him, but he's very smart. Devlin was supposed to bring him in. And I think the truth is that Devlin had him, in a way."

"And it was in having him that Devlin had the leverage he needed . . ." Duffy said.

"Exactly," Kennedy said, nodding.

Duffy pressed an intercom. "Bring Detective Moloney in now," he said.

There was an awkward silence in the conference room as Duffy and Kennedy waited for Moloney to be escorted from a reception area in the back of the FBI offices. As he was brought in, Moloney's eyes shifted from Kennedy to Duffy and back. He said nothing. His face was pale and beads of sweat covered his forehead and upper lip. His thinning hair was disheveled. He wore a white shirt and tie, loosened at the neck.

When Moloney was seated, Duffy reached over and turned on a tape recorder.

"For the record, I am Special Agent Kevin Duffy of the Federal Bureau of Investigation in Boston, on seventeen December 1997. With me is the deputy superintendent of the Boston Police Department, Thomas Kennedy, and Detective Moloney, also of the Boston Police Department."

Duffy stopped the machine and rewound for a couple of seconds. He hit play and was satisfied that it was functioning properly.

"Detective Moloney," he said, "it is understood that you are here of your own free will, that you have not been compelled to come here, and that you have been informed that if you wish, your attorney may be present here today, is that correct?"

Moloney gave a curt nod.

"Detective Moloney, you have nodded, but would you please give an audible reply."

"Yes," Moloney said tersely.

"Detective Moloney, directing your attention to the night of twenty-six November 1997, when you were apprehended in Jamaica Plain at 322 Arborway at the residence of one Luis Espado Alvarez, would you please explain the circumstances surrounding that event."

Moloney glanced quickly toward Kennedy, who sat impassively. Moloney thought back to the night before, when he'd rehearsed this with Kennedy over and over again, practicing responses to a variety of questions that Kennedy anticipated would be asked.

"Lookit," said Moloney. "Let me get right on the table, to begin with, the fact that I fucked—'scuse me—that I screwed up. There were a couple of occasions where we had dealers and cash on the table and we pocketed a few bucks here and there. Nothing serious. A hundred bucks here, a hundred bucks there.

"Anyway, Devlin came to me and said he knew of this situation at this location and he said there was cash involved here and he indicated that we could make some money."

"And what was your reaction to this, Detective?" Duffy asked.

"I was very surprised," Moloney said.

"Because?"

"Because he was doing an internal investigation and I thought it was kind of brazen," Moloney replied.

"Kind of brazen?" Duffy asked.

Moloney nodded.

"And so how did you respond to Detective Devlin?"

"I told him I already knew about the location, and that we were going to tackle it at some point, my partner and me."

"And you did?"

"Right away," Moloney said. "I thought what he'd said was strange and I wanted to cover it as soon as possible."

"So you went there and what happened?"

"We went there and the kid had some dope and some cash and we collected both," Moloney said.

"But you did not make an arrest," Duffy said. "Why was that?"

"If you made an arrest every time you busted someone for dope, you'd have the courts shut down for months. No, we will frequently try and work out an arrangement whereby we get some leverage with a lower-level dealer like this kid and possibly use that to ladder up in an organization. Otherwise, you make the arrest, and for what? You have some weasel out of operation for a couple nights, but then they've got him replaced before you can turn around. And to get it done we're in with paperwork and processing and it takes forever. The whole thing takes us off the street longer than the dealer. It makes no sense. So we try and scare the shit out of him and see if we can build up some chits, which we call in later."

Duffy was taken aback by what he was hearing. He blushed, for he knew he should not have been surprised. He was struck by the huge gulf between the ways the FBI and the local police operated. He was envious. There was a kind of swashbuckling appeal to the lives of these urban detectives, he thought. Something that was missing in the life of an FBI agent.

"And so you tried to work out an arrangement with this particular person, Mr. Alvarez."

Moloney emitted a harsh laugh. "Well, it was an unstated arrangement. I mean, to be honest, we just try and scare the shit out of him and hope he remembers that next time."

Duffy nodded. "And then you left the apartment building at 322 Arborway?"

"Yes."

"And what happened next?"

"As soon as we got outside we were confronted by Devlin and Del Rio."

"And?"

"They asked what had happened, and we said it was a dry hole."

"Now, Detective Moloney, at some point did Detective Devlin ask whether you had removed cash from the scene?"

"Yes."

"And what was your reply?"

"I wanted to steer clear of that because I didn't know what was up, and I thought maybe he was looking to rip it off or whatever, and so I hesitated and then I made up some bullshit story about having won it in a poker game."

"And why did you do that?"

"Because Del Rio was there and I didn't want to . . . I didn't know what was up."

"And so what happened next?"

"We rode downtown and they interviewed us about this case and a few others and made accusations and whatnot."

"And what is your situation at the moment, Detective?"

"Administrative leave," Moloney said. "They're trying to kick me off the force." He paused for a long moment. "And they'll probably succeed." Moloney said this in a tone of defeat. He suddenly appeared a beaten man.

Duffy was surprised. "Why do you say that, Detective?"

Moloney shrugged. "Because they need a scapegoat. What was it someone said? They need to lance the boil. And once they do that, then all the pressure is off. But they need to do that every now and again, and it's time again. It's time now."

COAKLEY STOOD ON the fish pier, the wind whipping off the water. He spotted Young pulling up in a smart-looking Acura coupe. Young, without an overcoat, came charging along the pier.

"What was so urgent?" he asked.

"Sorry to trouble you, Doc," Coakley said. "But I've got some bad news for you."

Young's eyes widened.

"Or, maybe it's really good news disguised as bad," Coakley said. "Yeah, that's what it is. In truth."

"What is it?" Young asked, clearly concerned.

"You're out of the deal, Doc," Coakley said.

Coakley could see that Young was strung out, his eyes round and dull. He was stunned. "What?" he said, spittle coming from his mouth. "This is my deal."

"This *was* your deal," Coakley said. "Now it's somebody else's deal."

"That's bullshit," Young said. "I developed the distribution channels, I did the sales."

Coakley frowned. "Let's not get carried away, Doc," he said. "You went to distributors whose names I gave you, people who would have a predisposition to become involved. You took a risk and you didn't win. You didn't lose, either. And that's important to recognize. It would have been nice to have the dough. But you'll have to figure something else out."

Coakley knew Young would have little if any recourse. He had screwed up his life and seen a drug deal as the one-time answer to his prayers. He'd been wrong. It wasn't to work out for him. But as Coakley stood on the pier looking out at a Virgin Atlantic jet glide in toward Logan, he felt a sense of comfort that he was doing something useful, something decent. Young had gone bad, and Coakley did not know what would ultimately become of him, whether he would straighten himself out somehow or destroy himself. That would be up to Young. But by driving him from the deal, Coakley believed he was helping to improve Young's chances for rehab. For Coakley believed there was nothing worse than a junkie who believed that dealing was his answer.

"But this deal—" Young said.

"This deal is over for you," Coakley said firmly. He moved closer to Young. "And be glad it is, Doc."

Young straightened up, making an effort to compose himself. "I'm going through with it," he said, a touch too arrogantly.

Coakley laughed out loud. "Good, then tell me, where are you picking up the goods? Who's making the delivery? When and where?"

Young was mute. That information was to have come from Coakley, information controlled by Coakley and Devlin. Young would never know the truth, never know that the deal had been manipulated, information passed, so members of the Boston Police Department had moved into it, taken it over as their own.

"What religion are you?" Coakley suddenly asked Young.

"Episcopalian," Young replied.

"My advice to you is to get in your Acura and drive immediately to the nearest Episcopalian church and get down on your knees and thank God you're out of this deal," Coakley said. "Because if you were to go ahead, you would either be arrested by cops who want you out of the way or killed by someone to whom you are merely an annoyance. So go back and do your job. And thank God you have that. Because I'm telling you that if you try and continue with this deal, you will be apprehended and you will be prosecuted, and I will personally testify against you. You will be convicted, and it will be under RICO, and you'll go away not to a comfortable horse farm in the Pennsylvania countryside but to a nasty federal penitentiary filled with Mexicans who'll slit your throat for a Marlboro."

Young was high, but he was mesmerized now, a look of sheer terror on his face.

"It's somebody else's deal now," Coakley said, more calmly. "Walk away and go have a life. You still have lots of opportunity. Write this off as a foolish experiment. You got lucky. The experiment failed."

"LISTEN, I'VE GOT something that looks like it fits what you want," Coakley said.

"When?" Jack asked.

"Tonight, as a matter of fact," Coakley said.

"Where?"

"New England Medical Center, down on lower Washington Street," Coakley said.

"The hospital?" Jack was surprised.

"They use it frequently," Coakley said. "They meet late. The comings and goings of people of color down there aren't noticed, nothing out of the ordinary. They use the employee entrance, and then there's like a lunchroom inside where they go."

Jesus, Jack thought, dealing in a hospital. "So what is this?" he asked.

"Cocaine," Coakley said. "Modest supply. Some Colombian offshoot selling to Chinese. The Chinese use the hospital. It's a block off Chinatown, so it's good for them."

"What time?"

"Ten," Coakley said. "And because the Chinese are involved, it will happen at ten. They're very punctual. If it gets to be ten past ten, they beat it. Assume something's gone wrong."

"So how sure are you about this?" Jack asked.

"Sure. Very sure. It's definitely on."

"Can I check tonight, around nine, to make sure?"

"I'll be at my office," Coakley said. "They like me standing by, in case . . ."

Jack took a deep breath. "You okay on this?" he asked.

Coakley hesitated. "I think so," he replied. "You can never be sure, but I think so."

"Thanks."

"Hey, I wanted to ask," Coakley said. "Tell me if it's none of my business, but I wonder whether you know yet?"

"Not for certain," Jack said.

"But you're close," Coakley said, finishing the sentence for him.

"Yes. I believe I am."

"Good," Coakley said, nodding to himself. And he meant it, for it all mattered so much to him now.

AT NINE-THIRTY P.M., Jack Devlin pulled into a legal parking space on lower Washington Street a half block down from the employee entrance at New England Medical Center.

He dialed Coakley's office. "On?" he said.

"On," Coakley replied.

Jack clicked off and watched the entrance to the hospital.

At nine-fifty, four Chinese men arrived at the employee entrance on foot. They were dressed casually in leather or suede jackets, as distinctly different from employees of the hospital in dress and manner as they could possibly be. They were tight, cautiously glancing around.

At 9:56 P.M. a dark gray BMW 740 pulled up in front of the employee entrance. Two men got out and looked around. They entered the building. The driver of the car remained behind the wheel.

Jack dialed the number of Del Rio's cellular phone.

"Yeah?" Del Rio answered.

"It's Devlin."

"What's up?" Del Rio asked.

"I was checking up on Carazza," Jack said, mentioning the name of a detective he suspected was crooked. "And I kind of stumbled on something that might be happening, maybe tonight. Very muddled message from a source. Chinatown. Colombians doing coke to the Chinese. Supposedly tonight, but I don't know. If you wanted to get someone on it."

"How good's the source?" Del Rio asked.

"Not great, not terrible," Jack said. "Thinks it's tonight but maybe not. May be too late, too."

There was a pause at Del Rio's end. "Okay," he said, "let me make a call or two." And he hung up.

Jack sat very still in the driver's seat of his Cherokee. He said a brief, silent prayer that it was not true. He had thought Del Rio seemed increasingly on edge. He thought Del Rio seemed a little too inquisitive, more intrusive than he should be. He felt Del Rio's shadow on his back all the time now. And he knew now, because he'd checked, that Lisa had not worked in some time, that she had been in and out of AA and other programs.

Jack calculated within his head the time it would take for Del Rio to dial his cell phone. He would call a contact somewhere who would receive the information with grateful alarm. That contact would then immediately dial the phone connecting him with another cell phone in the pocket of one of the men Jack had just seen enter the building. This would all probably take under a minute.

He held his breath. He very much wanted the six men who had just entered the building to come sauntering out in ten to fifteen minutes. He wanted the deal complete. But he feared what happened now before his eyes. The two men raced out the door and jumped into the BMW, which sped away. The four Chinese men exited the door and dispersed in different directions, racing off into the night, thankful they hadn't been busted, pleased that they had a protector on the Boston Police Department who tipped them to a possible police raid; pleased that they had on their payroll someone as knowledgeable as Del Rio.

CHAPTER 24

"SO WHAT IS it that those guys do exactly?" Del Rio asked. He and Jack stood by a bench in the Boston Public Garden across Arlington Street from the entrance to the Ritz Carlton Hotel. Jack looked over and saw three middle-aged men in dark suits with dark top-coats striding toward the hotel entrance. It was early evening, cocktail time.

"I don't know," Jack replied, uninterested.

"Come on," Del Rio said, "you were on that track once. What are the possibilities?"

Jack shrugged. "Financial services. Banking, insurance, venture capital. Something like that."

"So what do they make, would you say?" Del Rio asked. "Let's say they're moving along pretty good in their careers at their ages, what would you say, like pushing fifty, right? What would they make?"

"Jesus," Jack said. "If they're doing well they could make anywhere from, I don't know, two fifty to . . . if they have a piece of a venture firm they could be making a couple million a year."

"Fuck me!" Del Rio broke into a wide smile. "A couple mil a year? Jesus, we're in the wrong game." He gazed admiringly across Arlington Street. The men had disappeared inside, into the alluring warmth of the bar. "Leave your nice corner office, head over to the Ritz, pick up a cold martini, maybe do it again, head home to a five-bedroom in Wellesley, beautiful-looking wife who works out five days, great body, sweet kids. What the fuck? Nice life, huh?"

Jack nodded.

"That's what you should have done," Del Rio said. "You could be in there now with a nicely shaped martini glass instead of out here in the cold. Instead of running the streets nights and chasing maggots. Snooping around after bad cops."

They looked into each other's eyes, and neither man looked away. A moment of reckoning had arrived and they both knew it. Jack thought he'd grown immune to hurts from others, that he was beyond being disappointed or let down by another human being. He was not angry. He was saddened, deeply so, by this betrayal from Del Rio.

"So I have this theory," Jack said, eyeing Del Rio. It was a cold, raw night, but Jack had insisted they meet. They both wore jackets zipped to the chin, both with hands stuffed inside their jacket pockets. Jack wore a wool fitted baseball cap.

Del Rio, wearing an Irish scalley cap, cocked his head and regarded him. "Everyone has a theory," he replied.

"I have this theory that several forces converged at some point," Jack said. "Three forces, three trends, if you will." He paused. "You familiar with the Turner thesis in American history?"

Del Rio crinkled his eyes and thought for a moment. "Manifest destiny?" he said tentatively.

Jack nodded.

Del Rio smiled. "You impressed?" he said.

"The inevitability of the American push westward. The push across the frontier as far west as the land went."

Jack thrust his hands into his pockets and turned with his back to a sudden gust of wind.

"There's a similar thing at work here, within this department," he said.

"The Devlin thesis," Del Rio said without smiling. He sat down on the bench and looked up at Jack.

"The Devlin thesis holds that there is an inevitable escalation in the level of corruption," Jack said. "That it moves, as though a force of nature, from a free apple or cup of coffee to meals and then to drinks and then some Christmas presents and then cash . . . in return for what? For something. For considerations. For looking the other way mostly. For overcrowded nightclubs or illegal parking or a few blowjobs in the back booths. For considerations."

He stood looking out at the traffic moving down Beacon Street. He glanced down at Del Rio sitting on the bench, his legs crossed.

"So what's the second force?" Del Rio asked.

Jack took a deep breath and exhaled slowly. "The second force is a vacuum. Nature abhors a vacuum. Vacuums are quickly filled. With something. And with the demise of organized crime in the past few years, with all the brains behind O.C. going away or dying, a vacuum was created. All this protection money that had been paid to O.C. guys was now floating, free, available to be paid to someone else willing to render a protective service."

Jack looked at Del Rio. "Make sense so far?"

"Keep going," Del Rio said.

"So those two trends coincide with the third trend," Jack continued. "What I call the growing respectability of the dealers. The move toward the mainstream. The effort to portray themselves as businesspeople rather than criminals. Do they kill people? Not so much anymore, though sometimes. No, the new ones try to keep it clean and simple. Move a product people want for a decent price and make a nice profit. Don't go overboard. But the key is, to make money, you have to be in business, and you can't be in business from prison. So you do whatever you have to do to stay in business, and if that means strategic partnerships, then so be it."

"Strategic partnerships," Del Rio said, repeating the phrase.

"Strategic partnerships are the result of the convergence of the three trends," Jack said. "You have corruption manifest destiny. That is, an ever escalating level of corruption. You add to that the vacuum created by the rapid demise of organized crime plus the growing respectability of dealers, and you have a combustible situation. You have the perfect alignment for a level of corruption the likes of which have never before been seen on the department. Because just as the level escalates—meaning people within the department are looking for new frontiers, new opportunities—just as that happens, it becomes clear that organized crime is all but dead and buried. Not a factor, not happening. Then, voilà, along come the most respectable kind of dealers possible—businessmen in Paul Stewart suits. We'll do a deal, a nice deal, a respectable product. We'll deal to the better classes, we won't have Puerto Ricans knifing Haitians shooting Colombians. We'll stay clean and quiet and everybody makes a tidy profit and goes home happy."

Jack stood staring down at Del Rio, who stared back.

Jack spoke in a quiet voice, a near whisper. "How am I doing?"

Del Rio got up from the bench and looked out over Beacon Street. He stuffed his hands inside the pockets of his black leather jacket and hunched his shoulders. He stared down at the ground as he took a few steps away, then turned back.

"You're not as fucking smart as you think you are, Jackie," he said. "You underestimated just how smart these people are. And how fucking ruthless they are. You don't know."

Del Rio stopped in his tracks and raised his right hand, holding up one finger: "Del Rio's law of crime, numero uno: The only really successful criminals are completely and utterly without conscience. Because conscience is what trips people up. Fucks them up in the head. Produces remorse and the desire—the need—to talk. To talk to someone who talks to someone who talks to someone, and pretty soon someone is sitting on the witness stand in federal court opposite you and you are at the defense table and you are fucked for thirty years because you had a conscience. Not even much of one, just a sliver of conscience.

"While the guy with none is in Boca sitting by the pool, a piña colada in one hand and as much pussy as you'd ever want to have."

Del Rio's face suddenly grew dark and he glared at Jack. "These people have no conscience at all," Del Rio said. "None whatsoever. They have come together through the years and done deal after deal and no one has laid a glove on them and no one will lay a glove on them because they are smart and they don't leave any witnesses."

Del Rio shut his eyes for a moment, his face creased in pain for the briefest flash.

"And the mistake you're making, Jack, is that you think you've got them. You think you're about to put the hammer on them." Del Rio shook his head sadly from side to side. "Sorry, bucko, but it ain't gonna be. 'Cause they got you a lot better than you got them."

Jack seemed puzzled.

"You wired, Jack?" Del Rio asked.

Jack shook his head. He extended his arms to the sides as though about to be frisked. "Go ahead," he said to Del Rio.

Del Rio shook his head and turned away, ashamed. "No, Jesus, Jack, I trust you. Fuck." He looked off into the distance, across the frog pond. Men and women in wool overcoats and down parkas hurried through. Del Rio saw the Christmas lights come on in the Common.

"They've got to lance the boil," Del Rio said. "They know there's pressure from the feds. They know the heat is on, and they know something has to happen. They let you have Moloney. They could have headed that off but they didn't. They wanted to show progress. They saw you coming a long time ago, Jack. And they've waited and waited and been patient because they knew that you'd try and set them up. And now they've turned the tables.

"It's just like years ago, Jack. They needed a scapegoat then and they need one now. They set your old man up to take the fall, and he took it, and now they're doing the same thing to you."

Del Rio shut his eyes again, ever so briefly. "What happened to the father happens to the son," he said.

Jack shook his head, dismissing the idea. "But it's not going to happen," he said softly.

"It's already happening, Jack," Del Rio said. "It's been set in motion. And it's too fucking late for you to do anything about it."

Del Rio's face was now flushed with anger. He was furious that Devlin had put himself in this position.

"When the papers get ahold of this, it'll be the biggest fuckin' story in Boston in years. And it will lance the boil like nothing else ever could. The father and son. And the brass'll lament it till the fucking cows come home, and you'll go away and be disgraced and they'll go on their merry fucking way and nobody will worry about corruption again on the BPD until all these guys are long retired.

"You went toe-to-toe with them, Jack, and they fucking beat you."

Abruptly, Del Rio sat down on the bench, crouched over, his head in his hands. Then he got up and turned his back to Jack.

"So all along, you've been assigned to cover me," Jack said, though it was a question.

"It's like in those games where Gretzky comes to town," Del Rio said. "When he was in his prime. You know, they'd shadow him. One guy assigned to do nothing but get inside his jersey."

Del Rio turned and looked closely at Jack.

"You're Gretzky and I'm the shadow," Del Rio said. He stared at Jack for a long moment, then shook his head, ashamed.

"They set him up," Jack said. "They set him up. Not a perfect man, but a very good man. He was a good man. And look what they did to him."

He shook his head in disbelief.

"I'll have to hand it to them," Jack said. "Very clever. Get the feds to believe that the guy who's supposed to be cleaning up the place is in a perfect position to steal. So what's the plan, bring me down, set me up, frame me? Then the papers are happy and the politicians and everybody go on their merry way. Right?"

He leaned closer to Del Rio. His jaw was clenched, though his fury was well-controlled. "Am I right?"

Del Rio nodded and looked away. He walked a few steps, and Jack thought he was about to leave, but Del Rio stopped, pausing, then walked back. Still, he didn't look Jack in the eye, but rather looked out at Arlington Street, over toward the Ritz. A light snow began to fall.

"How long have you known?" Del Rio asked.

"Known?"

"About me."

Jack shook his head. "Last night," he said. "New England Medical Center."

Del Rio shut his eyes again.

"So who killed Murphy?" Jack asked.

Del Rio shook his head. "I could guess," he said, sounding genuinely sorrowful. He turned and looked toward Beacon Street for a long moment. The traffic was jammed, backed all the way up past Charles Street.

"They're bad people, Jack," Del Rio said. "Very bad. No conscience there. None. They're capable of anything. Absolutely anything. If they think you've become more of a threat than an opportunity, then watch out."

"Meaning?"

"Meaning right now they've got you," Del Rio said. "You may not think it or believe it, but they do. But if they think the tables are turned, they won't hesitate to blow your fucking brains all over the sidewalk."

Del Rio stood still for a long moment, staring down at the pavement. Then he shut his eyes hard and shook his head as though he had just seen the execution of Jack Devlin in his own mind.

Del Rio looked up, a ghostlike pallor on his face. His expression was one of pain, agitation. He looked Jack in the eye for only the briefest moment, then quickly shifted his gaze back to the ground, his chin pressed into his chest.

"I gotta go," he mumbled. He turned and started to walk away.

Jack wanted to stop him but didn't know how. And as Del Rio walked away, Jack was not certain, but thought he heard him mutter the words "I'm sorry."

CHAPTER 25

COAKLEY DRANK PEPTO-BISMOL from the bottle. He'd been up throughout most of the night drinking coffee, and now his stomach was on fire. He waited until six o'clock, then picked up the phone. Emily Lawrence had said she wanted the call placed at six, precisely, so that's when Coakley dialed Jack Devlin's home.

Jack, wide-awake, answered on the first ring.

"We have to meet," Coakley said.

"What's happening?" Jack asked.

"We have to talk," Coakley said.

"When?"

"Now."

"Take the trolley to Cleveland Circle," Jack said. "The rink."

Coakley hung up. He opened a fresh pack of Rolaids and started chewing on four of them. Leaving his home, Coakley walked through the darkened streets and saw the maroon van following at a respectful distance. It had been outside his house, half a block down, all night. The indignity of it all. They had required him to wear a bracelet, the kind they placed on white-collar criminals to ensure that they remained within their houses. His phone had been tapped.

He walked along the street and pulled his overcoat tighter around the neck. He wondered who, exactly, was inside the van. Was she there so early in the morning? Or were there FBI men? Technicians only? Young men or women who understood how to make the wire he wore relay whatever sounds it picked up back to the recording machinery inside the van.

The walk to the MBTA stop was a short one. Once there, he dropped coins into a yellow newspaper box and withdrew a *Boston Herald* from atop the stack. Soon, a trolley came, headed outbound, and Coakley got aboard. He rode out toward Cleveland Circle, and as the car swayed from side to side he felt worse and worse.

He folded the paper open to the crossword puzzle and began slowly printing letters in the boxes. He turned the newspaper over to the back page. Above a headline that lamented yet another loss by the Bruins, Coakley printed two words. He tucked the paper under his arm and waited until the trolley arrived at Cleveland Circle. Once there, he went to Dunkin' Donuts next to the station, where he bought two black coffees. He walked across Beacon Street toward the skating rink. As he approached, he saw the maroon van a half block down.

INSIDE, JACK STOOD by the boards and watched the Brookline High School girls' team practicing. The sounds of sticks banging the ice echoed off the cavernous walls of the place. It was freezing and the lighting was terrible. But Jack felt comfortable. He always had inside rinks, and he felt an odd sense of comfort now in the early morning that he was somehow connected to this fraternity. He was amazed by how fast and skilled these girls were. When he'd been growing up, it was rare for a girl to play. Now there were girls' leagues and even a women's Olympic team.

Coakley entered the rink appearing pale and ill. He looked through the glass from the warming area out toward where Jack stood. Seeing Coakley, Jack went inside.

"You probably like it here," Coakley said.

Jack smiled. "I do, as a matter of fact."

"What's the earliest you were ever in a rink?"

Jack thought a moment. "Maybe five," he said. "No, probably five-thirty. I remember as a Mite having a game in Worcester at six on a Saturday morning. My dad drove me. We left the house at four."

They walked across the waiting area and sat down opposite each other on benches where players sat to tie their skates.

Coakley placed the *Boston Herald* down on the bench next to Jack with the sports section facing up.

"Bruins got beat again last night," Coakley said, his eyes drawing Jack's gaze to the top of the sports page: WIRED—FEDS.

Jack stared down at the block letters Coakley had written. Then he looked up at Coakley, who nodded, ever so slightly.

Jack looked around the rink. There were no other adults.

"See any of the game?" Coakley asked.

"Some of the third period," Jack replied. "I saw the Flyers tie it up."

"The LeClair goal," Coakley said. "Kid's amazing."

"So much power."

"Imagine him and Lindros on the same line."

"Thanks for the coffee," Jack said, sipping it.

"So when do we move?" Coakley asked.

Jack hesitated. "The stuff's in. We'll go tomorrow night."

Coakley nodded. "Tomorrow night," he repeated. He fished a pack of Rolaids out of his coat pocket and popped four more in his mouth. He took a mouthful of coffee.

Jack studied Coakley closely for a long moment. The lawyer was overweight and looked unwell. There was a sharp contrast between his pasty countenance and the broken blood vessels around his nose.

The two men rose from the benches as a dozen high school girls came streaming through the doors, walking on skates across the rubber mats. They were sweating and gasping for breath, having ended practice with a series of wind sprints.

Jack and Coakley stopped at the door to the rink.

"So where?" Coakley asked.

"Here," Jack said. "Right here. Eleven o'clock."

Ninety minutes later an agent of the FBI handed the tape to Emily Lawrence. She played it. She sat stock-still, her heart pounding. The conversation stunned her. When it was done, she shut her eyes and said softly, "Oh, my God."

"YES, HELLO, I'M trying to reach a Dr. Robinson, please," Jack said into the telephone. "Have I called the correct number?" He was calling a residence in a suburb of Phoenix.

"Oh, well, he's in the garden right now," an elderly woman replied. "May I have him return the call?"

"Actually, ma'am, it's quite important and I was wondering whether it would be possible to speak with him now. I'm calling from the Boston Police Department."

"Is something the matter?" the woman asked. "Is Lawrence all right?"

"I'm sorry?"

"Our grandson Lawrence goes to college in Boston," the woman said. "It's not about Lawrence, is it? Has something happened?"

"Oh, no, Mrs. Robinson," Jack said. "Please, let me assure you this has absolutely nothing whatsoever to do with your grandson. I'm calling about an old police matter, and, it seems silly, I know, but we're trying to set our records straight. That's really all it is, but the problem is, I'm supposed to have it done today, so speaking with Dr. Robinson now would be a huge help. And it will take no more than five minutes."

"All right, then," she said. "Hold on."

She set the phone down and was gone for four to five minutes. Finally, Dr. Robinson picked up the receiver.

"Hello?"

"Sir, this is Detective Jones from the Boston Police Department calling," Jack said, "and I wanted to reach Dr. Robinson. Dr. Francis D. Robinson."

"Speaking."

"Sir, you are the Francis D. Robinson who for a period of time in the early 1970s was an assistant medical examiner in Suffolk County, is that correct, Doctor?"

"Oh, yes, that was quite a while ago, wasn't it," the old man said. "Yes, I was in the Pathology Department at New England Medical Center, and the state, and the county, I guess, too, were having all sorts of budget problems and they were short of people. And so a number of us were asked to pitch in on an interim basis and that's what we did. We each did a week or so every other month. You're calling about a particular case?"

"Actually, I am, Doctor," Jack said. "I'm interested in a case from 1972. We're actually doing a retrospective study here in the department, Doctor, concerning the decision to perform an autopsy. It's a topic of some debate now, as you surely know. And so what we are trying to do is analyze what we have done in the past and perhaps use that as a guide to help us determine future policies."

"I see," the old man said. "So how may I help?"

"We've selected several hundred cases—deaths of various kinds—and pulled the files. Randomly chosen. And we're going back and looking into the decision in some cases to perform an autopsy and in other cases not to do so."

Robinson chuckled. "Well, I'll help if I'm able, but I must tell you my memory isn't the best."

"This is a case from 1972," Jack said. "It's—"

"Pardon me, but what did you say your name was, again?" the doctor asked.

"Detective Jones," Jack said.

"Detective Jones, fine," Robinson said.

"It's a case involving the death of a Boston officer," Jack continued, working to keep his voice steady and calm. "There was a suicide. A man named Devlin . . ."

"Oh, my God, I remember it well," Robinson said. "How could I forget that one. That was such a terrible thing, I remember."

"So you do recall?" Jack asked.

"Of course," the doctor said. "He shot himself at some fraternal organization of some kind, I don't recall exactly where, but he killed himself because he didn't want to face trial. He'd been charged with some horrendous corruption charge of some kind. Stealing from nightclubs, I think. Something like that.

"I remember going out there that night and one of the men was quite drunk and he was shouting and swearing and everyone was just shocked by it. He had been disgraced in the newspapers and evidently he couldn't face the trial, so that was it."

"And you, sir, pronounced him dead," Jack said, his cadence slower, his voice softer.

"Yes," Robinson said.

"And then the decision was made to forgo an autopsy, is that correct, Doctor?"

"It was somewhat unusual," Robinson said. "Typically, with a suicide, we would do an autopsy to confirm. But in this case the circumstances were such that, I don't know, I guess you'd say based on humanitarian grounds, we decided not to."

"Humanitarian grounds?"

"Well, in the sense that here was the department under siege in a way, everyone suffering enough from the corruption charges. It was quite humiliating and I take it quite bad for morale. And then on top of it this man takes his own life. It was almost too much. And you know, these decisions are subjective. They aren't made in a vacuum. There are various considerations.

"And in this matter, naturally, I discussed it with the police. A couple of detectives came to meet with me that day, you know, within hours after the death. Two good men. And they said basically, 'Look, the department is in turmoil, there is terrible grief, and let's just put this to rest as quickly as we can. For the sake of the city and the department and the family.'

"I remember one of the men, in particular, was close to tears talking about the officer's family. Evidently he was a widower and had a small son. And the leaders of the detectives' association came to me and said, essentially, 'Look, the department has suffered enough trauma. Let's put it behind us and ease the pain. And an autopsy will only prolong it.' So on the basis of that, you know, the appeal from the two officers and considerations for the family, we decided to forgo the autopsy. I know today that they do this at the drop of a hat, but I think that presented with the same set of circumstances today I would make the identical decision. I really do."

Jack Devlin's breathing was rhythmic, intense. His heart was beating hard, his hands shaking.

There was a prolonged silence.

"You there?" the doctor finally asked.

"Yes," Jack said. "I'm here, I'm sorry, I was distracted for the moment."

"So was there anything else?" the doctor asked.

"The two officers who came to see you to talk about the autopsy, would you happen to recall who they were?"

"Oh, Jeez," the doctor said. "They were a couple of tall fellows, one quite tall. I'm six-two and he was a good three or four inches taller than me. Basketball tall, I call it. And the other fellow was tall, as well, but, no, I don't think I do recall . . . though the very tall one had a name like . . . let me think. Jeez, I just don't remember."

Jack waited.

"Mahoney, maybe was the other one," the doctor said. "The quieter one."

"Might it have been Moloney?" Jack asked.

"It could well have been," the doctor said. "Big beefy fellow. Tough-looking customer."

"Are you sure that—"

"I know," Dr. Robinson said all of a sudden. "When he introduced himself he said like the senator. I remember that. Kennedy, like the senator. Tom Kennedy, maybe? He was a very close friend of the family."

Jack closed his eyes and buried his face in his left hand while he grasped the receiver with his right. He felt a confused mix of emotions, but more than anything else, he felt a sense of relief. Of triumph. He knew now. He knew what he'd longed for so many years to know.

"Did he say anything to you about discussing the decision or not discussing the decision?" Jack asked.

"Well, I remember he was very concerned that the family be protected. That was his overriding concern. And he said to me that undoubtedly reporters would come to me and badger me about the decision and why and how it was made and that sort of thing. And he advised me strongly to avoid talking with any of them. He said that they would twist what I said out of context and who knew how it would appear. And I thought that was sensible advice, so I said nothing to anyone."

"Doctor, I want to thank you for your help," Jack said.

"Certainly, any time," Robinson said. "You know, there was something about that case. It got to everyone involved. You know that cop, the crooked cop, he was a widower, and when that was all said and done, my wife told me she felt so sorry for that man's son. She harped on it for a week. She said to me: 'What do you think will become of that poor child?' "

IT HAD GONE too far.

Devlin had to be stopped.

When he was dead, there would be indications of some vague connection between him and organized crime figures. Fabricated, but believable enough to the feds, or anyone else who cared to examine it. There would be allusions to narcotics, perhaps weapons. There would be nothing definitive, but there would be indications. From sources. Confidential, for the most part. And Devlin would be dead and it would all be over. And they could get on with life.

Two men were sent.

Late, close to midnight, they met at the Rathskeller, a Kenmore Square bar more commonly known as the Rat. They sat together at the far end of the bar, one drinking Coke, the other coffee. They would drink no alcohol this night, for they needed to be sharp. They would need their wits about them. Anything that slowed or in any way impaired their reflexes or reaction times could not be tolerated.

One man was of average height with short black hair combed straight back. His was the physique of a bodybuilder, bulging shoulders, arms, and chest. His neck was so thick it seemed more square than round. He wore gray slacks, a light blue shirt open at the collar, and a ribbed down parka. The other man was thin, wiry. He was an inch over six feet tall with a chiseled face and very long black frizzy hair pulled back into a ponytail. He wore black jeans, a black turtleneck, and a black Planet Hollywood jacket.

These were men of experience, men who had performed such tasks before. This was how they earned their living: by taking action where other men were cowed; action that left lesser men shaken. And then by saying nothing to anyone ever. Anyone could kill. Only a true professional could kill and remain silent.

They reviewed the plan. They would remain at the Rat until one-thirty. Then they would drive out to West Roxbury and park a block away, up on Dwinell Street. They would approach the house from the rear. At the back entrance, they would disable the alarm system. That would take fifteen seconds. They would use a master key to open the back door. Because they had studied the layout of the house, they knew they would then walk through the kitchen into the hallway, up the stairs, and right into Devlin's bedroom. One man would enter, his silencer fixed in place, and immediately begin firing into the body on the bed. While the first man entered Devlin's bedroom, the second would hang back on the chance that Devlin was ready and fired first. In that case, it would be the job of the second man to take Devlin out.

Their plan was to enter Devlin's home at two A.M. If all went according to plan, by 2:01 A.M., Jack Devlin would be dead.

CHAPTER 26

JACK DEVLIN SAT in the living room of his home shortly after eleven o'clock at night. The streets of West Roxbury were quiet and most houses were dark.

Jack spread the letter out and began to read. He had taken to sitting back in a quiet moment every few days and reading the letter slowly, carefully, savoring the sense of connection to his father that it brought.

It is my hope, and I certainly expect, that you will never read this letter, because I expect to live a nice long life.

The greatest reassurance Jack had was the tone of the letter, a tone that gave no indication at all that his father might be a desperate man, a man on the verge of taking his own life. There was not a hint of it.

. . . I am gathering my thoughts as best as I can so that you will know the truth, because to me at this point that is more important than anything . . .

Jack paused as he read this line, and he drew a deep breath, for he believed that the truth was at hand. He believed the time had come when the truth would be revealed to him. He was not yet sure how, precisely, the final pieces would be snapped into place. But he would read the letter and then sit up through the night, if necessary, to complete his plan.

If you had gone up and down Corinth or Wash or Centre or Belgrade, whatever, to Boschetto's, anyplace, and asked, they would have told you the same thing: Jock plays it straight. Jock watches out for you whether you're a Jew or colored or Italian or whatever you are or may be. Jock watches out, keeps an eye out. And it's true.

And Jack believed it; believed it was true, and the thought of it, of his father being the benevolent, fair-minded protector, brought a smile to his face.

His expression became more serious as he read on, read through the progression of corruption in which his father had engaged. And his heart yearned for the line he knew was coming, and as he read it, he felt great pride in his father.

But then one day I woke up and wanted out. I just decided one day that it wasn't right and I couldn't do it anymore. And I went to a couple of guys and told them, "Cut me out . . ."

Cut me out, Jack thought. To do the right thing in normal circumstances required little in the way of courage, he knew, but to try and do the right thing when it meant a change of course, when it meant going against the grain—that required real fortitude.

All that matters now to me is you and your future. My lawyer figures I'll get three years and have to serve one. Being a cop in prison, a nasty federal place, will not be pleasant. But I can handle it. I can handle anything because I know that my ultimate responsibility is to be there for you, and I will. I will serve my time and then that will be that and I'll get some kind of job and we'll have a grand life together.

The worst thing about this to me is that you will now grow up known by some as not just Jackie Devlin, but as Jackie Devlin son of Jock Devlin, the crooked cop, the cop who went to prison. I am sorry for that. But I will make it up to you.

If you are reading this, then that means I am gone. How strange it is to write this. If you ever read this I want you to know that your father is out there somewhere and that he loves you with all his heart.

Jack shut his eyes tightly against the sting. He shut them so tight, he fought back the tears, for he did not wish to cry. He wanted, instead, to stay focused on the task at hand. He folded the letter carefully and held it in his hands.

Yes, he thought, I know you're out there, Dad. I know that you are, and what's more, I know that you do love me, for I can feel it. I can feel it at this very moment, and it gives me strength.

HE MUST HAVE dozed off, for he was jarred awake and saw by his wristwatch that it was nearly one A.M. Jack set the letter down on the coffee table and yawned. Then he heard it again: a noise from the back of the house. It had been the sound that awakened him. A tapping sound.

Jack went quickly into the darkened hallway and got his service revolver. He turned off the kitchen lights and went toward the back of the house. Through the rear window he could see the shape of a man dressed in black on his porch, huddled by the door. Jack's heart raced. Had they come for him as they had Murphy? Would he be killed here and now, this very night? Would they take the letter, his precious words from the grave, and destroy them?

Jack moved silently, slowly, toward the back door, his gun in position. Then he was startled by the sound again and realized that the person was knocking quietly on the glass. Jack moved to the door and looked out.

Del Rio.

Jack unlocked and opened the door.

"They're coming for you," Del Rio said as he entered the kitchen. "Tonight."

The two men stood silently, facing each other across the kitchen table.

Del Rio frowned. "I wanted to warn you," he said.

"Who?" Jack asked.

Del Rio shrugged. "Some guys," he said, a look of distaste crossing his face. "Wiseguys. What difference does it make? Some guys they got who'll do what they want and get protection in return."

"How do you know this?" Jack asked.

Del Rio glowered at him, then looked away. "What the fuck," he muttered. "How do I know . . ." He shook his head, then looked back. "I know," he said.

Jack regarded Del Rio and wondered whether he could trust this man, this man for whom he had developed a genuine affection. Or was this part of the scheme—Del Rio comes in the night posing as his savior, then leads him into a trap; leads him to his ruin, destroys him and shatters his dream of getting to the bottom of it all, of solving the mystery, of understanding. Worst of all, depriving Jack of the chance to claim redemption for his father.

"So you come here to warn me," Jack said.

Del Rio looked back at him and said nothing.

Jack shrugged as though to say, I don't get it. "So help me with that," he said.

Del Rio frowned and looked away again. He was deeply ashamed in Jack's presence. Then he looked back, and into Jack's eyes. "I owe you," he said.

Jack was surprised. "How so?"

"You trusted me," Del Rio said. "I betrayed your trust. I want it back."

Jack did not know what to say.

Del Rio took a breath, exhaling in a deep sigh. "I always thought of myself as intelligent, as able to use the God-given intelligence I have. I always thought of myself as determined and having balls. Real balls, you know? And I always thought of myself as the one who persevered, who hung in for as long as it took."

Del Rio squinted, his brow furrowed, a pained expression overtaking his face.

"But I've found something out about myself," Del Rio said, his voice quieter. "I've found out I'm a pretender. I'm not who I thought I was. I'm not the image I've had of myself."

He hesitated, then looked at Jack in a searching way.

"You're more who I thought I was than I am," he said. "You're the one with balls. Perseverance." Del Rio's eyes widened and he nodded in affirmation.

Suddenly, Del Rio seemed very tired, and he sat down, propping his elbow on the kitchen table and leaning the side of his head against his fist.

"I thought about getting out," he said. "Twice I was close. Lisa convinced me—just about."

His voice trailed off and he shook his head slowly. "You can't," he said. "It's not part of the deal." He stared at Jack. "You know that better than anybody. But I want you to know that I tried. In my own way I did try. I wasn't strong enough."

Jack had to fight an impulse that said he was being set up. And he did fight it, and fight it successfully, for he believed that what Del Rio was telling him was the truth. He believed he was seeing Del Rio unvarnished, without the bluster and the facade. Within Del Rio, Jack believed, there was decency. And as he thought this, Jack had a strong sense of feeling sorry for Del Rio, sorry for the choices Del Rio had made, choices that had diminished him.

Del Rio looked up at him. He rubbed his eyes with the fingers of his left hand and checked his watch. "We should go," he said. "This is not a safe place to be."

"Where will we go?" Jack asked.

"I'd suggest Lisa's, but I'll take you wherever you want."

Jack wasn't sure he was comfortable with the idea of simply showing up at Del Rio's girlfriend's house in the middle of the night.

"She'd be fine with it, if that's what you're worried about," Del Rio said.

"You sure?" Jack asked.

"Definitely," Del Rio said.

"Okay," Jack said. "Let me get some things."

Jack went to his bedroom and quickly packed a bag. Then he went to the living room and retrieved the letter, which lay on the sofa where he'd been reading. He folded it and put it into his pocket. He then slipped into his shoulder holster, put on a jacket, set the alarm system, and followed Del Rio out the back door.

Del Rio hung back in the doorway scanning the yard, the driveway, and the street. He nodded to Jack to follow, and they turned back through the yard and hopped a fence, cutting through a neighbor's yard. Del Rio led the way down an adjoining street to where his Crown Vic was parked.

They climbed into Del Rio's car and quickly, quietly, pulled away and drove off into the night.

JACK SAID NOTHING as they rode out the VFW Parkway and then cut over through Newton out Commonwealth, across Route 128. They followed a series of twists and turns into the town of Weston, then rode down a long country road where the houses were set back hundreds of feet. After a few miles they turned right and went down a dark road through the woods. At the end of the driveway was a house of modern design set on a plot of land overlooking a pond. They pulled into the garage and entered the house. Few words were exchanged.

"She's asleep, I'm sure," Del Rio said. He removed his jacket and took off his shoulder holster. He placed his gun on a kitchen counter. "There's a guest room down that hall. You hit the hay. I'll stay up."

Jack shook his head. "I can't sleep."

Del Rio went into the kitchen and Jack followed. Del Rio was scooping coffee into a cone-shaped filter. Once he had the coffee machine in place, he sat down in a kitchen chair and sighed heavily.

"I know how he must have felt," Del Rio said. "I know." His eyes were narrow and he was clearly pained. "He couldn't stand it anymore. He must have wanted redemption. He was legit. That's why he scared them so much, 'cause he was legit. He'd gotten religion. Road to Damascus."

Then suddenly, inexplicably, Del Rio smiled. "He must have been one tough bastard to get out," he said. "That's real balls." He nodded admiringly.

Jack, acting purely on impulse, walked back to the hallway where his jacket hung and retrieved his most precious possession. He returned to the kitchen and placed it in Del Rio's hands.

Del Rio unfolded the pages and began reading. "Jesus Christ," he said softly as he realized what it was. He read it through without stopping, without comment, and when Del Rio, the toughest of tough men, was finished reading, he started to cry.

It was then that he and Jack made the plan.

CHAPTER 27

"I CAN'T EXPLAIN it in any more detail, all I can say is that you should not go home," Jack said. "You should go to a safe house under the protection of federal marshals."

Emily had difficulty believing what she was hearing. "This is madness, Jack," she said, her voice marked by incredulity.

"I'm sorry, Em," he said. "I'm sorry to be the cause of this."

"But what happened that makes you believe I may be in danger?" she asked.

"I can't go into it, Em, other than to say I am in danger and the people after me might very well look for me at your house. You have to be careful."

"You can't go into it!" she said angrily. "You have me beeped, pulled out of a sensitive deposition, and you tell me that I should not go to my home but instead go to a safe house and place myself under the guard of the U.S. Marshal Service. You suggest someone might try to kill me—that someone has already tried to kill you and you can't go into it! Well, you goddamn well better go into it, Jack."

He had no choice. He could not explain any more at the moment. The explanations would have to wait. And as angry as she was at him now, he knew it was about to get worse.

"Please, Em," he implored. "I beg you. Do not go home. Let the marshals protect you. I love you."

And he hung up the phone.

JACK PARKED HIS Jeep by the back of the school early in the evening, leaving it there. He went to the church and worked his way down into the subbasement, a catacomblike series of dank, narrow hallways. At the farthest end of one of the ancillary hallways, he pushed back a huge stone, loose in the wall, revealing a large open space of two feet by two feet. In the space was an airtight canister he'd put there weeks earlier. The time was finally right, and he withdrew the canister and unscrewed the heavy top. He trained his flashlight on the contents and found the white crystalline powder within.

He breathed a sigh of relief. Not that he had ever doubted it would be there. But he was relieved that the time had come, that the waiting was about to end. He felt alert, though there was anxiety mounting within.

He pushed the stone back into place and carried the canister to a section of the subbasement leading to a tunnel. There, he checked his watch with his flashlight and saw that it was still early. He sat down to wait. There was a musty smell in the air, and in the darkness he heard creaks and groans within the massive stone structure. But he heard no signs of humans. For that, for the silence and the tranquility of the moment, he was grateful. For he knew that in the hours ahead all would be determined. The plan would either succeed or fail. There was no middle ground.

Jack sat back, leaning his head against the cool stone wall. He closed his eyes and tried to clear his head. He felt very calm. He felt certain that he was doing what he had to do, what he'd been destined to do for so many years.

Soon, the time had come. He rose and brushed the dust off his pants. He carried the canister under his right arm and worked his way through the tunnel, traveling under the West Roxbury Parkway to the Holy Name school. He came up from the ground into the school's boiler room and out a heavy metal door that shut loudly behind him. It was very dark as he took the stairs up to the rear parking lot. The lot was enclosed on three sides by the three-story school building. It was a horseshoe-shaped structure and he was within the U. There were no houses or stores for a thousand yards.

As Jack started across the lot toward the Jeep, Del Rio stepped out of the shadows directly behind him. From a distance, a danger-ous, violent man named George Tran, sitting in the driver's seat of a black Chevy Blazer, watched the scene unfold. He saw Devlin stop, watched as Del Rio held his gun to the back of Devlin's head. George Tran saw Devlin bend very slowly and place the package on the ground. He saw Del Rio kneel down and place handcuffs on Devlin's wrists. Because of the distance, George Tran could not hear what was being said.

"Follow the script," Del Rio had said, pointing his pistol at the back of Jack's head.

"Following the script," Jack had replied, bending slowly and placing the package on the ground. He then lay facedown on the pavement and placed his hands behind his back. Del Rio placed the cuffs on but did not lock them. He wrapped a scarf around Jack's eyes as a blindfold.

"Okay?" Del Rio asked.

"Fine," Jack said.

"See you in the morning," Del Rio said.

"Good luck," Jack replied.

George Tran watched as Del Rio scooped up the package and raced across the parking lot to the Blazer.

"Let's roll," Del Rio said, out of breath, as he jumped into the passenger seat.

Tran pulled out of the lot and headed south on the West Rox-bury Parkway, headed for the first of three delivery points. Within a couple of hours the drugs would be passed along to distributors who would, in turn, pass them out into channels that would carry the morphine to thousands of customers throughout eastern Massachusetts. The drug that Emily Lawrence had so desperately wanted to head off had officially made its way into circulation.

JACK TUGGED OFF the cuffs and removed the blindfold. He climbed into his Cherokee and eased out of the lot, heading north on the parkway. He felt a tinge of guilt about the distribution of morphine, but that was not his concern at the moment. He knew the deal had to be real, had to be done in order to get them with their guard down.

From Holy Name Circle, Jack drove out the parkway to Brookline and followed Chestnut Hill Avenue to Cleveland Circle. He parked down Beacon Street and walked to Dunkin' Donuts, where he bought coffee and a honey-dipped cruller. He ate the doughnut and sipped the coffee as he crossed Beacon and stood outside a bar where he had a view of the rink. While he waited in the cold, he spotted FBI units getting into position—one on Chestnut Hill Avenue, two on Beacon Street. He saw two agents get out of a Chevy Suburban and enter a wooded lot behind the rink.

Jesus, he thought, why not just put up a neon sign out front saying "This property under federal surveillance"?

He watched for over an hour, until he was thoroughly chilled, and went inside the bar. He took a seat down at the far end and watched the third period of the Bruins game against the Colorado Avalanche. The Bruins played well and the game was tied at two at the end of regulation. Throughout most of the overtime period the two teams were scoreless. Then, suddenly, with three seconds left in the overtime period, the Bruins suffered a momentary defensive breakdown and Claude Lemieux of the Avalanche scored the winning goal.

When the game was over, Jack thought about Emily. She was out there, he knew, somewhere nearby, waiting for the deal to go down.

He looked at his watch and calculated that Del Rio and Tran would have made their deliveries by now. He took out his cell phone and called Emily's beeper number. One minute later the phone rang.

"Jack?"

"Hi," he said.

"Jack, where are you?" she asked.

"I'm at a bar across the street from the rink," he said. "You can send your troops home, Emily. The deal's been done already."

There was a stunned silence. "But you told Coakley—"

"The deal's done," he said. "The stuff is in the hands of secondary distributors already. It's done. Gone. It's too late, Emily."

"I don't understand," she said.

"I know," he said. "I'll explain it to you. I'll explain it all. Why don't you send everybody home and then come over here. Christo's across the street. We'll talk."

She hesitated. "But Jack . . ." She was thoroughly confused.

"If you don't believe me, then keep them there, continue the stakeout," he said. "They can do it without you. Come talk to me. Please, Em."

He sat at the bar, waiting. He was about to go outside to see whether the FBI agents were sent home, but he did not want to see. He did not want to know that she mistrusted him.

A few minutes later she entered the bar. Her face was set in a grim expression. A scary expression, for it was chilly, removed. He hadn't seen this before, and it frightened him.

"Let me ask a question," she said.

He nodded.

"Was I set up?"

He looked down at the floor, at the sawdust that had gathered under the stool where he was seated.

He looked up and into her eyes.

"Yes," he said.

She shut her eyes and drew a breath, her mouth open. She spoke in a whisper. "How could you," she said, shaking her head slowly back and forth, her eyes still shut. "How *could* you."

She turned and started out of the bar. He scrambled quickly to his feet and went after her, grasping her elbow in his right hand.

She shook free, yanking herself away from him. And as she did so she wheeled and with fury in her eyes hissed: "Don't you dare touch me!"

And she charged out into the cold night air and was gone.

CHAPTER 28

SHE WOULD NOT take his calls.

So deep was her anger and hurt that she could not bring herself to speak with him. He called and called and called, but the answering machine was her screen. Late in the night he got into his Jeep and drove to her house. She told him to go away, that she did not wish to talk.

He did not leave. He could not. He sat down on the back steps to her house, tugged his jacket tight at the neck, and waited. She looked through the window and saw him there and grew angrier.

Let him freeze, she thought, and went up to her bedroom. For a while she read. Or tried to. But concentration was difficult and sleep impossible. She channel-surfed for a while, thumbed through a stack of architectural magazines.

She listened for the sound of the Jeep's engine starting but did not hear it, thought perhaps he had gone without her knowing it. She kept herself away from the kitchen, away from the back door. She did not want to look out, as the hours passed, to see whether he was still there. Rather, she wanted to, but fought the urge.

At four-thirty A.M. she showered, washed her hair, and changed into clean clothes—snug-fitting brown corduroys and a black cashmere sweater. Her hair still shiny and wet, she went downstairs at ten minutes before five to make a pot of coffee. The light in the kitchen was still on.

She did not go to the back door to look out to see whether he was there, on the steps. She did not go to the window to see whether the Jeep was still there.

She went instead to the counter and the Krups coffee-maker. When she was alone, she made four cups, but now she ran tap water and filled the container to the eight-cup line. She carefully scooped the coffee into the gold cone and flicked the machine on. Soon it was percolating. She went to the cabinet and got out two mugs, setting them on the kitchen table. She got milk and half-and-half from the refrigerator and set them down on the table next to sugar and packets of Equal. She set spoons out next to the mugs.

The Krups container was filling. She took a deep breath, pushed her hair back, and walked to the back door. Her heart was pounding. She looked out into the darkness of the early morning and could see his jacket pulled up around his face, covering everything from his nose down. She saw him blink.

She opened the door and looked down at him. "Coffee?" she asked.

"Love some," he said. He got up very slowly, and she could see he was trembling with cold, his teeth chattering. She held the door open while he came inside. She went into the TV room and retrieved a thick wool blanket, which she handed to him. He removed his parka and wrapped the blanket around his shoulders. She said nothing as she went about pouring the coffee and taking her seat at the table.

He sipped the coffee, and it tasted delicious and warmed him as well. He put the mug down and looked across at her for a long moment. She sat impassively, waiting for his explanation.

"I want you to know that I had to do what I did," he said. "I feel I had no choice. I also want you to know that I love you very much and I want us to be together."

She shut her eyes and sat quite still. His words had a calming, soothing effect on her.

He told her everything. He told her his entire story from the start. He explained that he made a fundamental decision at the beginning that in order to coax them out into the open he would have to put together a deal that was real; not a sting that looked real, but an authentic deal; a deal from which they would make money; a deal that would result in the distribution of narcotics. He explained that he had considered a sting operation, one where he would work in concert with the D.A.'s office or the Justice Department. And he had rejected those thoughts for fear that the operation would be leaked and thus compromised. He explained how he had worked with Coakley, how Coakley had in turn recruited Young; how Coakley had fed information through his client, Mr. Jones; how he himself had made contact with a man who stole a morphine shipment.

She listened carefully all the way through. And then, at the end, he asked for her understanding and her forgiveness and her love, and she did not hesitate to give him all three.

THOMAS KENNEDY'S HOME in West Roxbury—a basic Cape Cod–style structure that had been added on to twice through the years—was set back up on the hill near St. Theresa's School. It was not an ostentatious home, but it was comfortable and certainly the most attractive house in an area of attractive homes. The work, through the years, had been done gradually, so that at no time would anyone have wondered how a police department official could afford such a home. In fact, the reality was that Kennedy was among the highest paid city officials and had been for some time. Kennedy's yard was ringed with a five-foot cedar fence. On this sunny December morning, Kennedy sat in his family room looking out over the yard. He watched as two squirrels scampered down a maple tree, searching the frozen ground for food.

Kennedy was dressed in police uniform pants and a white uniform shirt open at the collar. His hair was combed straight back, he was freshly shaved, and when he stood at his full height he looked like the consummate police commander. He looked out over the frozen grass and sighed. He was tired. He was tired of Boston and of the department; tired of always having to be so very careful, tired of having to cover his tracks at every turn; tired of appearing to be one thing and in reality being something quite different. Deceit was an arduous business.

But Kennedy knew he could not slack off now, for there was still work to be done. He thought of the three distributors waiting in three different locations. He was insulated from them. None of the three knew him, could in any way connect him to the arrangement. They sat within two miles of each other, each prepared to receive his share of morphine. Each was required to make a deposit—a wire transfer of funds—into a specified account at the Bank of Boston.

The first deposit went into the Law Enforcement Education Association account, the second to the Law Enforcement Education Foundation, and the third to the Law Enforcement Strategies Council.

These deposits—for $315,000, for $366,000 and for $317,000—were substantial, though hardly amounts that would attract unwarranted attention. The accounts, after all, had been in existence for some years, and millions had passed through each.

The phone in Kennedy's kitchen rang loudly, startling him. He picked it up.

"Hello?"

"Mr. Kennedy, Helen Spellman calling. You had asked for confirmation on deposits expected this morning. I can confirm the three deposits expected for a total of $998,000. Will there be anything else?"

"Thank you," he said. "That's all at the moment."

And he hung up.

THEY PULLED INTO the garage of the State Street Bank building and parked, rode the elevator to the twelfth floor, and walked to Felix Dexter's office.

"Morning," Dexter said, getting up from his desk and coming forward to shake Jack's hand. Jack introduced Emily.

Dexter was clearly excited by the challenge that lay ahead; he turned and indicated the three computer screens on his desk and an extension. "We're ready," he said. "As soon as the funds are deposited, we'll know it. Then strap yourself in. We'll see where it all goes."

One of Dexter's assistants said that coffee was available in the conference room down the hall. Jack and Emily went in, and stood by a window that offered a view of the Southeast Expressway, Harbor Towers, a portion of Boston Harbor, and the airport. Jack stood in silence sipping coffee and looking outside. Emily turned away from the window and paced around the room, circling the long mahogany table with a dozen padded chairs. Along one long wall were nautical prints. The other wall consisted of large windows offering a view of Harbor Towers and the water.

Emily walked to the window and looked out over the airport, where a British Airways 747 was gliding slowly in for a landing. "So by the end of the day, you'll either have him or you won't," she said.

She walked back to the window and stood by him. "I mean, if this works, then, glorious. But if it doesn't, then what have you got? Nothing. Worse than nothing, really, because you've actually gone out and without notification or authorization conducted a narcotics deal. Initiated, orchestrated, and completed a narcotics deal, and there are plenty of federal prosecutors who would haul you into court and on the basis of what you did convict you of trafficking. It could be portrayed as an outlaw scheme, Jack, you understand that?"

"I do," he said. "Yes."

But even as he said it he appeared calm and self-possessed. She was taken by this.

"Are you afraid?" she asked.

He squinted, considering this. "I'm very afraid," he replied. "I am very afraid that I might not know the truth." And that was true. That was the only thing he feared—failing to find the truth.

She took his hand in both of hers and squeezed it. Then she slipped her arm under his and around his waist and pulled herself close to him as they looked out the window together.

"Don't be afraid," she said.

THEN DEXTER'S ASSISTANT was at the door. "You'd better come," she said, and they hurried down the hallway to Dexter's office.

He was seated behind his desk, glancing from one screen to the next, smiling. "We have ignition," he said. "It's moving."

"All of it?" Jack asked, stepping in behind Dexter so he could see the screens.

"Every dime. Every penny." Dexter hit several keys on one machine, then slid over to the keyboard beside it.

"Okay," he said, his eyes riveted to the screen. "Everything has moved out to other accounts—mostly, it appears here, money market accounts. Looks like it's been broken into nine lots of about a hundred grand each and shipped off to seven different banks including Chase, Citibank, B of A, First Chicago, Nations, Banc One, and Rocky Mountain. And all of these accounts, hold on . . . are some form of this Law Enforcement Education thing. All are named that way or something close to it. We can print out all the names . . . in fact, let me do that now while I have them here."

Dexter hit print and a list of banks, account numbers, and amounts and times of deposits was printed.

"So what happens if this is it?" Dexter asked. "If this is the destination?"

"Not good," Jack said.

Dexter sat back in his seat and watched the screen. "You see that number there?" he asked, pointing to the screen displaying the number $107,000. "That's how much has been added to the Chase account at the moment. See below? Each account contains two hundred dollars over that. So these accounts are shells. They exist purely to hold something for some short term. Somebody spent real money to open these accounts for some odd purpose."

"So how can you tell if any of the money moves again?" Emily asked.

"We're looking at live, real-time information here," Dexter replied. "If someone deposits or withdraws a dollar into or out of any of these accounts it will show instantly on the screen."

"So we watch to see whether the numbers change?" Jack asked.

"Exactly."

But as they sat there, drinking coffee and fidgeting, the numbers did not change.

They sat for an hour as the level of tension in the room increased.

"Jesus, I don't know if—" Dexter began, but Emily interrupted.

"There!" she said. "The last number changed."

"Back to two hundred bucks," Dexter said. "Everything's been moved out of that account."

"And the one above," Jack said.

"And the one above that," Emily said.

They watched as the numbers on the screen all reverted to two-hundred-dollar balances for the nine accounts.

"It takes a minute to track," Dexter said. "We're locked on to their system. It takes our system a minute to adjust. It's like flying an F-18 and following someone else in an F-18. You're going seventeen hundred miles an hour and you can easily stay with him, but when he changes course it takes you a second to react. That's all the delay is."

"And there's no way the other system can detect that it's being followed?" Jack asked.

"There is," Dexter said. "But I have a shield on my system, a kind of radar that would tell me whether they have the software needed to do that. And they don't. So we're watching everything and nobody knows."

The movement of the money fell into a pattern that lasted throughout the morning and into the afternoon. The funds would move to an account, stay there for up to an hour, then be moved again. And as the money moved, Dexter noticed that the accounts became increasingly restrictive. Early on, all the accounts were strictly philanthropic—he was able to judge that by the tax codes within the system. But during the course of the afternoon, though the money still mainly moved into philanthropic accounts, there were fewer signatories.

And there was another pattern. The funds were moved into institutions with international reach.

When an instruction flashed on the screen—a numeric code incomprehensible to Jack and Emily—Dexter said, "Ouch. Swiss. It's headed for no-man's-land, I'm afraid. At least a chunk of it.

"Technically," Dexter explained, "it's not possible to penetrate the Swiss banks. I mean you literally cannot get in there. You watch here when the money moves there—what is it, about 375 grand— watch. It'll move and we'll get an Access Denied signal."

They watched as the amount blinked and then disappeared, replaced by the words ACCESS DENIED.

"Impenetrable," Dexter said. "It's gone."

Jack was shaken. "No way of finding it?" he asked.

"It's impossible without someone on the other end pitching in, and they don't do that," Dexter said. "They do not do that. I mean, these are people who'll hide hundreds of millions for the Nazis. Tucking away a few hundred grand for a crooked cop is like a joke for them."

Emily sat forward. "So what about the rest?" she asked.

"I'll bet you anything it's going offshore," Dexter said. "Bahamas, maybe."

With $375,000 having gone into a Swiss account, that left $623,000. Suddenly, $375,000 of that moved as well.

"Bahamas," Dexter said. "Gone from our view."

"That leaves $248,000," Emily said.

"Look," Dexter said. "The 248 is moving." A series of numbers appeared on the screen. "A bank code." He shouted for his assistant. "Wendy, where's that receiver directory, please?"

She came through the door with a thick spiral notebook and handed it to him.

"Thanks," he said.

"What are you looking up?" she asked.

"That code," he said, motioning toward the screen.

Wendy glanced at it. "Oh, that's the China Fund," she said. "Hong Kong based. I just did a big transfer with them a week ago."

"You sure?" he asked.

"Positive," she said.

Dexter found the correct listing in the book and nodded. "Good, yeah, you're right," he said.

He looked at Jack and Emily. "It's a Hong Kong–based mutual fund," he said. "All the rage now, these country funds. You want to diversify your portfolio, spread your risk, you diversify not only over asset classes—equities, bonds, cash, et cetera—you also diversify across economic borders. The China Fund is run out of a big Hong Kong bank."

They all sat looking over Dexter's shoulder as confirmation appeared that $248,000 had been transferred to the China Fund.

"What are the chances that with all this activity someone notices or gets suspicious?" Jack asked.

Dexter shook his head dismissively. "Do you know how much financial traffic there is in the world each day? Try trillions of dollars. Trillions, literally, being moved from one country to another into stocks, mutual funds, money from individuals, corporations, pension funds. Nobody notices what anyone else is doing because everybody's busy watching their own assets. Plus, with all due respect, compared with the numbers major financial institutions deal with on a day-to-day basis, you're talking a piddling sum here. Less than a million bucks. I mean it's nothing."

"What's that," Jack said, watching the screen.

"Another transfer coming," Dexter said.

The code for the bank into which the money was to be deposited began feeding onto the screen.

"Domestic," Dexter said. "It's coming back into the U.S. federally chartered," he said as additional codes appeared. "Bank of Miami, if I'm not mistaken." Then the words appeared confirming his guess.

"You know what?" he said. "I think whoever's doing this thinks that once you get overseas you get a clean slate. That coming back in is like flying under radar at night from Mexico. But it just ain't so . . ."

"Jesus," Emily said, "is that—"

It happened so fast that it stunned everyone in the room. Suddenly, there on the screen, all $248,000 was transferred into an account at the Bank of Miami that already contained $204,000, bringing the total to $452,000. And there on the screen, as clear as could be, was the name of the account—Law Enforcement Education Association of South Florida—with a single signatory listed. One person who could move money into or out of the account. And one person alone.

The name on the screen was Thomas F. Kennedy.

CHAPTER 29

WHEN DEL RIO arrived at eight o'clock on a clear, frigid night, Thomas Kennedy was sitting alone in the den of his West Roxbury home, sipping from a tumbler of Glenlivet. Kennedy rose unsteadily when Del Rio arrived. He poured a glass and handed it to Del Rio, then raised his glass toward Del Rio and smiled. "Success," he said, the word slightly slurred.

Del Rio held the glass, hesitating. He nodded slightly, said, "Success," and sipped the drink.

"It feels good," Kennedy said. "But it should feel better."

Del Rio reacted with a surprised expression.

"I mean, hey, let's face it," Kennedy said, "you never want to screw a fellow cop. In all honesty. A member of the fraternity is a member of the fraternity." He shook his head then, as though remembering what he believed he'd gotten away with, and smiled. Kennedy's face was flushed, his eyes bloodshot. Del Rio could see he'd been enjoying a few cocktails.

Jack Devlin and Emily Lawrence sat in the Jeep two blocks away from Kennedy's house and listened to the conversation.

"So you've come . . ." Kennedy said, then hesitated, not certain how to phrase it. "Come for your treasure," he finally said.

Del Rio shut his eyes for the briefest moment. Unable to bring himself to say yes out loud, he nodded. He was pained by this; by the fact of what he'd done with his life; by the fact that he'd been exposed before Jack Devlin. Suddenly, Del Rio thought about Jock

Devlin. Del Rio had joined the force after Jock was dead, but through the years, he had heard bits and pieces of the story. He knew the essence of it, of course, and it was only now, after years on the job, that Del Rio could fully appreciate what Jock had done. The idea that someone in the tank would be hectored by an insistent conscience was not a revelation. That someone would act upon that impulse—that was unusual. It would have been something that astonished others within the department, that angered them and left them suspicious. It must have been something about which they were deeply mistrustful.

Del Rio had thought quite a lot of late about Jock Devlin, and he had come to admire him. There was a certain nobility about what he'd done. Changing habits was a hard thing, Del Rio knew. Being strong enough to do what was right was harder still. Jock must have been a very strong man. But not, Del Rio knew, as strong as his son.

"For my treasure," Del Rio said.

Kennedy got up from his chair, somewhat unsteady, and went over to a bookcase. He removed a dictionary and opened it to the middle. He removed an envelope, thick with cash, and handed it to Del Rio, who accepted it and laid it on the coffee table in front of him.

There was a protracted silence. Del Rio thought Kennedy looked as though there was something he wanted to say. Finally, he did speak.

"I'm getting out," Kennedy blurted, watching Del Rio for a reaction.

Del Rio was taken utterly by surprise.

"I'm putting in a paper with the retirement board tomorrow," Kennedy said. He smiled and raised his glass. "I'm getting the fuck out."

"What prompted this?" Del Rio asked.

Kennedy waved a hand dismissively. "Enough," he said emphatically. "I'm sick of it. What do I need it for? I've had my time."

Sick of it, Del Rio thought. Of course. That was how he felt as well. Sick of the deceit and the lies. Sick of pretending to be one thing but in reality being something else. It was the ultimate violation, in a way, he thought. Pretending to be an enforcer of the law while willfully being a violator.

"I'm renting a condo in Naples for February, March, and April," Kennedy said. "Then I'll buy. House on a nice course somewhere."

"Yeah," Del Rio said. "That sounds nice. I'd like to . . ."

But Del Rio did not finish the sentence. He thought that would be very pleasant, he and Lisa down in Florida, Naples or maybe Boca, or up around Jacksonville even. He liked it up there. Lisa would like that, too. Start over somewhere new, somewhere he had no identity, no baggage, no debts, no entanglements. I could do that, he thought.

"I'm sick of this," Kennedy said. "Too long in one place, and, let's be honest, the stresses and strains of what we do . . ."

Of what we do, Del Rio thought. Of what we do. Not police work, though partly that. What we do was the combination, Del Rio realized, of police work—stressful, difficult, trying work—and living a lie; being a thief, someone who had convinced himself that doing wrong is justified, that you're owed something because you have permitted your life to be taken over by this absurd business.

"Have you told anyone?" Del Rio asked.

Kennedy shook his head no. "I'm telling them tomorrow," he said. "But the feeling of relief I feel . . ." He shook his head. "Un-fucking-real."

Kennedy watched Del Rio carefully. "You're not yourself," he said. "You don't seem it. What?"

Del Rio squinted, peering at Kennedy as though trying to read tiny writing on Kennedy's forehead. "It's all fucked up," he said. "You're doing the right thing." Del Rio paused. "I'm out, too," he suddenly said.

Kennedy was taken aback. "Yeah? For real?"

Del Rio nodded.

Kennedy sipped the Glenlivet. "Great minds think alike," he said as he rose from his chair and held out his glass, clinking it against Del Rio's. "This is a momentous occasion. A time to celebrate."

Kennedy opened a humidor on the bookcase. "How about it?" he asked, holding up a thin cigar.

"No, thanks," Del Rio said.

"Royal Jamaican," Kennedy said. "Sure?"

"I'm all set," Del Rio said.

"Hey," Kennedy said, shrugging, "it's a good time to get out. The heat's intense. It's only a matter of . . ." But he did not finish the sentence. He did not need to.

Suddenly, Kennedy said: "He's your fuckin' pal."

Del Rio stared at Kennedy, resisting the impulse to get up and drive his fist into Kennedy's smug, motherfucking countenance.

"My pal," Del Rio repeated.

"He's a troublemaker," Kennedy said. "He thinks he's better than us, better than the rest. The old man the same. The rules are the rules. You support your own people. And you don't forget who you are or where you came from."

Kennedy looked away, a deep frown creasing his forehead. He put the Glenlivet to his lips and took a long drink. "The father should have minded his own business," he said, his voice carrying a trace of lament.

Del Rio was surprised by this comment. "I thought he had," he said.

Kennedy shrugged. "He wanted out. It was a bad situation. Bad for too many people. Good men."

"So he was talking to the feds?" Del Rio asked.

Kennedy was lighting his cigar, two wooden matches creating a tall flame as he puffed, rolling the cigar between his fingers to get an even burn. "He wasn't," Kennedy said.

"No?" Del Rio tried to muster surprise in his tone.

"But it was inevitable," Kennedy said. "We got together, several of us, and discussed it. Was it inevitable or not? Could he make it through the preliminaries and the trial and the sentencing? You know, without opening his mouth."

Kennedy drew on the cigar and exhaled slowly. Then he sighed, a heavy, regretful sigh. "We thought no," he said, his voice much quieter now. "We thought there was no real possibility. You understand?"

Kennedy looked through the haze of alcohol and smoke at Del Rio, as though beseeching him for support, for affirmation.

Del Rio was motionless.

"We asked ourselves what we would do in his shoes. And what we would do is rat like fucking crazy. Anything to stay out of prison. I think that's only natural, don't you?"

Del Rio did not answer right away. After a moment he said, "I do." Then: "So you had Moloney deal with him. At the Knights hall."

Kennedy shifted uncomfortably in his seat. "You're a little close to the bone there," he said.

Del Rio shrugged. "Hey, it's a long time ago. I'm interested. What does it matter now?"

Kennedy drank deeply of the scotch. He appeared quite agitated. "All he talked about was the fucking kid, as though the kid was the only human being on the planet who mattered." Kennedy's face and neck were reddening. "I pointed out to him that there were men with families, men with kids, with boys, little sons, just like his, little kids just as important to them as his kid was to him. And they couldn't handle a defector. Too much. Too destructive. The potential was there to destroy so many lives." He shook his head at the thought of such a tragedy. "So many lives, my God. And he cared only about his own and his fucking kid's, as though none of the rest of us mattered."

Del Rio was going to ask again, but instinctively he remained silent. Kennedy stared into the distance for a moment, then another, as though fixated on some memory.

"No," he finally said, slowly, deliberately. "It wasn't Moloney. Though he volunteered. It was me. I was the one. I had to be the one. I was the only one he trusted."

LISTENING IN, EMILY leaned forward and put her face in her hands. "Dear God," she whispered.

In the driver's seat of the Jeep, Jack's hands were folded in prayer, pressed hard against his mouth. His eyes were closed. He sat perfectly still. He had wanted for so very long to hear the truth, to know it for certain, and now, at long last, he'd heard the truth, he knew the truth.

"And Ray Murphy?" Del Rio asked.

Kennedy shook his head dismissively. "He had a big mouth," Kennedy said. "He could have hurt us very badly. I had Moloney deal with him."

Emily turned to Jack. He remained frozen in his seat, fingertips just touching his nose, hands clasped together in prayer.

Emily reached over and placed her hand on his shoulder. "Heard enough?" she asked.

He nodded that he had.

She took up a walkie-talkie and clicked the side. "Unit one, you may proceed," she said. "Please acknowledge."

"Unit one proceeding," said one of the two FBI agents in the first car.

"Unit two, you may proceed," she said.

"Unit two proceeding," said one of the agents in the second car.

Jack shifted into gear and drove two blocks to the front of Kennedy's house. The FBI agents pulled up as he did, at a respectful distance, but two of the agents moved swiftly across Kennedy's front lawn and stationed themselves by the front of the house. Two others moved around back and concealed themselves.

Emily stood by the car as Jack went to the front door and rapped three times in succession. In a moment Del Rio answered the door.

He looked into Jack's eyes but said nothing.

"Thank you," Jack said.

Del Rio nodded and went back inside.

"You have a visitor," Del Rio said as Jack moved swiftly across the room, his service revolver drawn and aimed at Kennedy's heart.

"Stand up!" Jack ordered.

"What the—" a flabbergasted Kennedy said.

"Stand up!" Jack said, and Kennedy did so.

Del Rio guided Kennedy against the wall, face first, and frisked him. "Okay," he said.

"Thomas Kennedy," Jack said, placing handcuffs on Kennedy's wrists, "I am placing you under arrest for the murder of John Devlin."

CHAPTER 30

SNOW CAME IN wispy flakes, riding the frigid winds out of the northeast. The sky was heavy and gray, the temperature in single digits. Jack pulled his Jeep into the parking lot at the Holy Name Church. It was just quarter of five in the afternoon, but already darkness had fallen. Jack was surprised at how many cars were already in the parking lot. Normally, this Mass attracted sparse attendance, but on this night the lot was three-quarters full. Older men, mostly, climbed out of their vehicles and walked slowly toward the church.

Jack sat in the car a moment, looking around.

Emily reached over and put her hand on his. "You okay?" she asked.

He took a deep breath and nodded. "I'm okay," he replied.

She smiled at him. "You look very handsome in your new coat," she said. "Very distinguished."

He looked down at the navy-blue overcoat he'd bought the day before. He had not owned a good coat, and he wanted to dress well for this occasion. He wanted to feel an appropriate level of formality, for it was, after all, the moment toward which he'd been working . . . for how long? For most of his life, it seemed. They had gone out together the day before, Jack and Emily, and shopped for the coat. Jack had been nervous about it, for he wanted the new garment to be right. They had gone along Newbury Street first, but the coats there were too stylized, too European for his taste. He wanted something very basic, straightforward, but well-made. At Filene's, the big department store downtown, Jack tried on a dozen coats in the price range he had stipulated, but none of them quite did the trick. Then, on a nearby rack, he spotted the coat. The salesman, a patient and helpful older gent, said it cost substantially more than the amount Jack had said he wished to pay.

"Let's just try it on," Jack said. The older man nodded and re-moved the coat from its hanger. He held it behind Jack, and when Jack put each arm through and stood up straight, gazing into the mirror, he knew this was right.

The coat sat well on his broad shoulders and hung nicely from his body. The material felt smoother to him than the others, and there was about this coat an altogether more elegant feel than any-thing else he'd tried on. That was explained in part, said the sales-man, by the fact that the garment was eighty percent wool, twenty percent cashmere.

Jack buttoned it and stood looking into the mirror. He turned sideways and looked back over his shoulder to see how it fit from the side. It was as though the coat had been made for him.

"What do you think?" he'd asked Emily.

She smiled widely. "Perfect," she said.

And so he bought it, paying more for it than he ever had for any article of clothing in his life. And he was glad. That night, at his house, he and Emily had eaten take-out Chinese food and sat around the fireplace talking about Jack's dad.

Late in the evening Jack had gone into his bedroom and opened up his closet. He took out a charcoal-gray suit that he'd worn to his law school graduation. He chose a blue and white striped dress shirt with spread collar and a simple print tie with green and blue. He had brought Emily in to review his selections, and she nodded her approval. All the garments were arranged carefully together in the center of the closet.

Jack got his black dress shoes out of the closet and brought them to the living room, where he carefully dusted them off, then applied a thorough coat of shoe polish and buffed them to a high shine.

Now the moment had arrived, and Jack's palms were sweaty, his heart beating fast. He felt good, though. Ready.

She gripped his hand and smiled at him again. He took another deep breath and got out of the car. Standing in the cold parking lot, Emily slid her hand under his arm and walked close to him, her head down against the wind. She wore a black evening dress with a chocolate-brown shearling coat. Her hair was pushed back on one side, held in place by an elegant silver and pearl clip. They were a handsome couple.

"Jackie," called a voice, and Jack turned to see Eammon O'Brien, the retired cop who had been on the job with his father. Eammon was old and stooped, but he moved swiftly across the lot, vapor coming from his mouth as he breathed. He patted Jack on the shoulder, a broad, warm smile across his reddened face.

"It's a good thing you done, Jackie," Eammon said. "It's a good thing, Jackie. Your father, Jesus, Jackie, he'd be so damn proud of you."

Eammon shook his head, squeezed Jack's hand, and moved off toward the church.

"Thank you . . ." Jack said, his voice a whisper. "Thank you, Eammon."

Emily held tightly to his arm and studied Jack's face to see if he was all right. He seemed to her suddenly very far away.

Inside, the church was warm and inviting. The altar candles were lit, shimmering in the draft near the stained glass. There were dozens of people already in seats, men mostly, retired cops, a few with their wives.

Jack walked with Emily slowly down the center aisle. As they moved, Jack saw many familiar faces and nodded to each, smiling, saying a soft hello. They reached the second row and Jack genuflected, then entered the pew after Emily. He knelt and shut his eyes as he prayed. After a minute he sat down on the wooden bench.

In the minutes before Mass began, ushers from the Patrolman's Benevolent Association appeared and distributed the plain white booklets listing police officers through the years "who had served honorably."

An usher placed the booklets at the end of the pew and then, hesitating, handed one to Jack. He took it and froze. As he stood with the booklet in hand, the priest swept onto the altar and Mass began. Jack stood with the booklet in his hand, clutching it.

The Mass was a blur until it came time for the priest's sermon. Father Reilly, the chaplain of the Boston Police Department, stepped to the front of the altar and began speaking.

"We gather here this afternoon as we do every month at this time to pause for just a moment from our daily lives to recall the good works of so many of our brothers and fathers and grandfathers and beyond who served as police officers in our city," he said. "This month, as we do each and every month of the year, we add to our roll of honor."

Here, Father Reilly paused and glanced down at Jack. The church was hushed.

"We add one name this month," the priest said. "A name that deserved to be here many years ago, but God is patient as so must we be. And through the nobility and the courage and the perseverance of his son, the name added this month is that of deceased detective John Devlin."

Jack bowed his head in a brief prayer of thanks, and as he did, he opened the booklet, and there, on the first page, was his father's name—a place of honor for a new name on the list. Having heard the priest say his father's name and having read it on the page, Jack Devlin was overwhelmed. The tears came streaming down his face and he found himself being embraced by Emily and he felt safe and protected and he thought of his father and he felt a great surge of love in his heart. He thought of that good man whose crime had been that he was human, that he had been flawed, a sinner. But he had sought to better himself, not only as a man, but as a child of God; he had sought to do the right thing, to redeem himself, and Jack believed he had sought this for him, as much as for anything else. For Jock Devlin had been the greatest of fathers, and he'd wanted nothing more than the chance to raise his son, to be with him and watch him grow, to help him become a man of strength and goodness. All he had wanted was to be a good father and to love and protect his son.

But that chance had been taken away from him. Now Jack had given him something back.

"And so today we pay special tribute to John Devlin, Sr., and we ask God to place him in a special place near Him in Heaven for all of eternity. And we pray for all of the others listed in your booklets, available to you in the pews or in the back of the chapel, all of those who have served with honor on the police department. Let us pray . . ."

When the Mass was ended, Jack moved out of the pew and began, very slowly, to walk back down the center aisle. No one else in the church moved. Only Jack and Emily walked toward the back, and as they did so, Eammon O'Brien stood in the middle of the church and began to clap his hands, slowly, rhythmically. Jack looked at him, standing alone, clapping, smiling broadly. And as he clapped, a few others joined in, and then others, and more and more, until all of the men in the church were on their feet clapping and the sound was thunderous within the nave of the church. Jack glanced back and saw that Father Reilly was clapping as well, and the men cheered and shouted their approval, and Jack put his head down and the tears came again. But this time he smiled, too, and he clutched Emily's hand, nodded, and whispered, "Thank you, thank you, God, for allowing this redemption."

ABOUT THE AUTHOR

CHARLES KENNEY was a reporter and editor at *The Boston Globe* for fifteen years. He is also the author of *Code of Vengeance*. He lives in Boston with his wife and two children.